GW00715916

THE PRINCESS ROYAL

THE PRINCESS
ROYAL

Virginia Coffman

This first world edition published in Great Britain 1994 by
SEVERN HOUSE PUBLISHERS LTD of
9–15 High Street, Sutton, Surrey SM1 1DF.
First published in the USA 1994 by
SEVERN HOUSE PUBLISHERS INC., of
425 Park Avenue, New York, NY 10022.

British Library Cataloguing in Publication Data
Coffman, Virginia
    Princess Royal. – (Royles Series; No. 3)
    I. Title II. Series
    813.54 [F]

    ISBN 0-7278-4608-6

Typeset by Hewer Text Composition Services, Edinburgh.
Printed and bound in Great Britain by
Redwood Books, Trowbridge, Wiltshire.

To Donnie Coffman Micciche
with love always

PART ONE

Miravel

CHAPTER ONE

The All Clear sounded and the midday crowd began to pour out of the Underground shelter. It was not until then that the dark lean man calling himself Count Andross caught sight of the girl again.

She must have moved closer to the steps during the bombing in spite of the earth-shattering noise overhead. He slowed his own stride. He didn't want to call attention to himself yet. It would be far too obvious a ploy.

Still, a girl with her background didn't often travel unattended, especially in London, where her family was not in good favour at the moment. What was she doing here alone, with the Luftwaffe dropping its little calling cards around her? Did she think they would avoid her because of her family? Unlikely, to say the least.

He followed her in a leisurely way, noticing qualities about her that would make his purpose much more pleasant. He had never thought she would turn out so well. She had become a real beauty, far from the plain, sharp-eyed teenager he had noticed years ago in 1934. That would be at the Silver Anniversary Commemoration of Kuragin rule in tiny Lichtenbourg. He wasn't likely to forget that. Also, Lichtenbourg's neighbour, the Third Reich, had honoured the girl's parents with the presence of Chancellor Hitler, the Fuhrer himself, but the girl hadn't looked as impressed as she should. Her reaction had secretly amused Andross.

3

Considering that the bombing of Central Europe might occur very shortly, as an answer to the horrors of the Luftwaffe in Britain, what the devil was the Kuragin princess doing here in virtually enemy territory? She appeared to be heading toward the battered railway station whose cars, with any luck, would carry their passengers to Shrewsbury and the Welsh border. Hardly an enticement for the Lichtenbourg princess.

Then he remembered the connection. The train would pass a village called Miravel on the way to Shrewsbury. Only a few days ago Oscar Fulke of the Swedish Embassy had mentioned to Andross that the small village was presently treating a few service convalescents. The village had been named after the vast Miravel properties.

Princess Alexia, as the popular press called her, was going to visit her English grandfather, Lord David Miravel, a recluse in his beloved Miravel Hall. It was common knowledge in London circles that Lord David hardly knew there was a war on.

The young princess disappeared into a station that had recently suffered from a "near miss" but was still operating. She motioned to a porter who seemed to have taken good care of her two worn Vuitton bags during the raid. He showed up now, calm as if he had spent his life dodging the Luftwaffe. He led the young woman around some overturned tissue-thin newspapers toward the train. She must have her tickets already. Damn!

Andross went over to get his own ticket, motioned to a porter and pointed out the young woman. "My niece is headed towards the wrong car I believe. Will you see if that young lady in the gold suit is in the Miravel car?"

The porter brushed his heavy white moustache, pocketed the coin, said, "Ay, Sir," and loped off.

By the time Andross had his ticket and was starting toward the tracks the porter ambled back in no particular hurry. He assured Andross, "Young Lady is in the last car. That's for Miravel and Shrewsbury. A lovely young lady she is, Sir, if I may say so."

"Thank you. I think so." Andross began to pick up speed as he heard a good deal of puffing and blowing of steam ahead of him. Somewhere in the nether regions of the station an anonymous, asexual voice began to announce the stations to the Welsh Border.

He reached the car and swung in just as a station attendant called out a warning to him and the train moved off. "That was a close one," he murmured, more to himself than to anyone else.

She was not alone in the carriage. Two young men, Yankees from their careless look and easy familiarity, answered Andross.

"You can say that again, Brother."

The other one put in, "At least back in the States they give us a little breathing space. But anyway, we're off."

"Nice company," the first one muttered under his breath, looking sideways at the young lady.

Andross glanced at her, wondering when he would have a chance to speak to her. He hoped the two Yankees were not going to share the carriage all the way to Miravel. They had left her little room on the seat across from Andross and she was crowded against the corridor wall. Andross stirred. She glanced at him, then blinked and looked away quickly.

Good God! Did she remember him after all these years? He hadn't allowed for that. She was so changed, he had assumed that his own twenty-eight-year-old self was vastly different from the twenty-one-year-old youth he had been in 1934, jealous, resentful, and ambitious. Maturity and experience had taught him that there were more practical ways of righting a great political wrong.

And how different the girl was these days! Her once

5

nondescript hair. was now a lustrous light golden brown that showed off her fascinating hazel eyes. They might still see a great deal, as they had when he watched her with interest seven years ago, but they masked their observant quality now. Her mouth which had seemed so uncompromising was now subtly made up to look generous, even sensuous. Great were the wonders of cosmetology!

And where were her attendants, maids, guards, escorts? What were her family thinking of to let her run about alone in wartime London? When he had first discovered her presence in London this morning, and entirely alone, it had seemed too good a chance to miss considering the plans discussed so often at his mother's home. He could appear to Princess Alexia as a stranger, without any stigma. At least it would be a beginning.

All the same, it hadn't been very intelligent of her parents to let her wander about, prey to all sorts of unpleasant adventurers. Including me? he asked himself wryly. He didn't like the sound of that and tried to change the direction of his thoughts.

The two Yankees stared at the girl, nudged each other, but neither spoke. Andross suspected they might have recognized her, in which case they could be useful to him if they got a little brash or aggressive.

Presently the attendant stuck his head into their car and spoke directly to the young lady: "Luncheon, Miss Alexia. They'll be pleased to arrange it privately."

He must be well acquainted with her. Andross saw with interest that she smiled at the attendant and said, "I've had my luncheon in the City, thank you. You remember me, then? It's been several years now."

"Indeed, yes, Ma'am. We don't forget the Miravels around here, Ma'am. They're as much a part of us as those little hills and valleys and canals we're heading into."

Andross thought it was interesting that the sole interest in her was as the daughter and granddaughter of the Miravels of Shropshire and not as the Princess Royal of Lichtenbourg, heiress to a throne; a small throne but unquestionably royal. No, make that, "Heiress *Presumptive*". Then he smiled inwardly at his own presumption.

The two Yankees were whispering to each other again, the younger one, much thinner and rather naive-looking, kept nudging his older, heavier buddy who scowled and muttered, "Why, for Chris' sake?"

"It is," the younger one insisted, *sotto voce*. "I tell ya, it's her."

The disencouraging answer to that was, "So what?"

It wasn't hard for Andross to guess the subject of that conversation. Probably the princess was aware of it, too. She changed her position as if uncomfortable and kept her attention strictly on the corridor beyond the door.

The young Yankee leaned toward the princess holding out a stick of gum. "Would you like one, Ma'am? You just chew 'em. Don't swallow it. This 'un's grape. Real taste to it."

Andross had expected she would greet this with the haughtiness of all those Kuragin ancestors and was surprised and oddly pleased when she laughed as she refused. "I've lived in the States. I really have chewed gum. But I'd rather not now, if you don't mind."

He shrugged. "No skin off my back. I just didn't know princesses chewed gum. You are Princess Ava Alexandra, aren't you? I saw a picture of you in *Life* magazine."

She did not reply and the boy's heavy-set comrade said, "Lay off, you twit. Lady don't want to talk about it. Not that I blame her. I wouldn't either. All that Nazi crud." He turned to his buddy. "Could you believe it? This nice lady was named after Hitler's girlfriend."

The princess stiffened and turned her attention to the

7

corridor where a man in RAF uniform and a girl of the ATS were walking back from whatever the dining car had been able to scrounge in these tightly rationed times.

Andross thought of laying down a few well-chosen phrases to these fellows but decided the girl would only feel more upset by a scene. Instead he got up, nodded slightly to the princess, and went out into the corridor. At the same time the train slowed down for a stop and Andross found the attendant helping a sailor out the platform door of the next carriage. From the platform the sailor looked back and with his left hand, waved his thanks to the attendant. The right side of his face, including his eye, was heavily wrapped and finished off with gauze and adhesive like his right hand. But he was able to grin.

The attendant closed the door and turned around. He looked startled to see this dark, tall stranger, obviously a foreigner, close behind him, but he asked politely, "Help you, Sir?"

"You might ask the young lady in the next carriage if she would like more privacy. For example, she may now have this carriage to herself."

His low-pitched voice, though seldom loud, had its usual effect. The attendant was more puzzled by Andross's cool authority than by the suggestion. But after a moment or two he agreed willingly.

"Yes, Sir. Of course, Sir. Has somebody been giving Miss Alexandra trouble? Those Yanks did seem good natured."

"I'm sure they are. But they've begun to ask questions about her family."

"Ah! Sure now, that won't do at all. Not but what her Miravel kin are a credit to any race. But the others, over the way," he indicated anything east of the English Channel. "Well, then!"

8

"Thank you." Andross stood aside for him to pass and then strolled out into the corridor to watch the deceptively peaceful countryside move slowly past as the train took up speed again.

Behind him he heard the slight commotion of the attendant opening the corridor door for the princess, ushering her in, and tossing her two bags up.

"Anything you'll be needing, you've only to let us know, Ma'am."

"Thank you. This is very kind of you."

"Well, now, Ma'am, it wasn't my own but that gentleman's notion. Have a pleasant trip."

The stoutish attendant went off down the corridor after a nod to Andross as he passed. The latter began a leisurely saunter along the corridor, away from the princess. Just as he was beginning to think his little plot had failed he heard her voice in the doorway of her new carriage.

"Sir? It was thoughtful of you. I really appreciate it."

He hesitated, then looked around, frowning as if uncertain that she had spoken to him. Then he pretended to see her and smiled.

"Those boys really didn't mean to be rude. But there are moments when I imagine Your Highness would much prefer your privacy."

She laughed. He was a little disconcerted inwardly at just how charming she could be.

"I have American relations. Believe me, no one likes them better. My great-grandfather is Tiger Royle. In my opinion, Tige is the greatest man living today. And he's nothing if not a Yankee."

He knew the relationship very well but looked surprised and agreed as to Tige Royle's place in the world's hierarchy of great men. "I suppose it might disturb FDR and Prime Minister Churchill – not to mention the Fuhrer – but I am inclined to agree with you about your great-grandfather. Still as strong and tough as ever, I imagine."

"He's a very young seventy-five and acts like a boy of twenty, but – "

"He'll do. I agree." He inclined his head and turned away, not wanting to push things. He had gone several steps before she moved towards him.

"Excuse me, Sir, but I don't suppose you will want to return to your carriage. Would you care to share mine? Until I reach Miravel, that is. I get off there."

It was almost too easy. He had to be careful. He didn't want it to sound planned. "That is a coincidence. I am bound for Shrewsbury. I believe that is a trifle beyond Miravel."

Her gracious acceptance of his spur of the moment explanation made him ashamed. She said, "Do sit down. You have a long ride ahead of you."

She stepped back into the carriage and took her own seat, looking up expectantly as he bowed again and followed her. It was too good to be true. And Ava Alexandra Kuragin was definitely far more charming than he deserved. In many respects her loveliness made things harder for him. He couldn't get over the way that plain frowning little girl had changed in the past half-dozen years.

CHAPTER TWO

In spite of her smile Alexia's thoughts had never been busier. Where had she seem him before? It was a long time ago, on an occasion that held a note of revulsion. Chancellor Hitler was there calling her "Ava" after his friend Eva Braun, as if she had been named for her, like a political possession.

This man was attractive in his dark, unreadable way, but his attraction didn't hide the fact that she knew he had been trailing her ever since they left the Underground shelter. And then to be going so close to Miravel, he must take her for an idiot.

If he hadn't been so dark and ever so slightly foreign, it would have seemed obvious that he was sent by British Intelligence to check on her doings in Britain, considering her country's unhappy ties with the Third Reich. But why not keep her out of the country in the first place? Perhaps because she had come from the neutral United States and in a military plane arranged by Tige Royle. Well, let this fellow do his damndest. She was on to him, whoever he turned out to be.

Her companion produced his card for her before he sat down. He didn't use the opportunity presented to him of sitting beside her and she appreciated the delicacy of this, although it tantalized her. She couldn't help wondering why he hadn't done so. In any case, this gave her a much better chance to study him as he sat across from her, leaning forward, ready to take back his card when she had read it.

Stefan Miklos Berndt, Count Andross, she read. Placing the card in his palm she found herself staring into his eyes, their hard penetrating depth suggested an inflexible quality. Ruthless, in fact. He had to be someone official, in spite of his card.

"How nice!" she murmured. "It sounds a little Hungarian, except, of course, the 'Berndt'. That's German, I suppose."

"I'm a little of everything. A League of Nations all to myself, you might say. I am with the Swedish Consulate. Matters concerning neutral citizens, especially those with our passports who are, in fact – " He hesitated. "But you must have met them. Those who claim our citizenship and are actually citizens of the Third Reich."

She couldn't imagine how he could be with the Swedish Consulate and still have all those Slavic or Hungarian names. But considering her suspicions of him he might be anything. His name did not reassure her. And he certainly didn't look like a Swede. She made an effort to uncover whatever he was up to.

"It's the oddest thing, but I keep imagining I've seen you before. I wonder . . ."

She was pleased to see she had caught him off-guard. For a couple of seconds his face looked quite blank as if the expression had been wiped off. Then he smiled. She tried not to be influenced by his lips which were more sensuous than his eyes.

"I often have that commonplace effect on people. I'm a very ordinary fellow. You may see me, or someone like me, everywhere."

This was totally untrue. She wondered if he knew how untrue it was. He would make a terrible spy. He was so distinctive. If he wasn't a British spy checking on the

12

Princess Royal of Lichtenbourg, what was his object in pursuing her?

Maybe he was just on the make for her. He wouldn't be the first man who thought he would have his fortune laid in his lap if he could marry the heir to a throne, even little Lichtenbourg's throne. She almost giggled at the notion but refrained in time. It was the least likely of all her ideas about him. Possibly he just wanted to worm his way into Miravel and steal some of the old family heirlooms.

She went on making conversation. He seemed to find her genuinely interesting. Had she been saying too much, something he was waiting to hear? She began to be more careful. But no matter what subject she brought up he was obliging, answered with casual evasion and revealed nothing about himself.

She wished Dan Royle were here. He would pry the truth out of this man. Dan was Tige Royle's adopted son and Alexia's closest friend in all the world. Perhaps more. There were times when she wondered if he would be the great love of her life. He had all the qualities she most cared about in a man and he had been reared in California by Tige Royle. How could he be other than dear to her?

She ventured onto the subject of Tige, remembering that Count Andross knew all about him. Maybe he would forget himself and accidentally let out some interesting truth about the real Andross, if that was indeed his name. These were war times. You never could be sure.

"How nice that you know my great-grandfather! Of course, I never think of him as that old. Not like my maternal grandfather, Lord Miravel."

"Miravel. I was sorry to read of his illness. His heart, I believe. I am acquainted with several of his books. An excellent historian."

"I think so. I did a thesis on one of his books for my sophomore to junior finals."

He returned to what seemed to interest him more. "But in my business we are more likely to deal with international figures like your Tige Royle. He has an adopted son, I understand. Boy named Daniel."

There seemed to be no harm in building up Dan. It might even help with a Churchill interview. She said, "Dan Royle is a reporter on a San Francisco paper. Very clever, too. Next month he is flying to Manila on the China Clipper to interview General MacArthur. About a possible Pacific war in the spring."

"Enterprising young man."

"Takes after Tige, we say. Right now he's been in Berlin trying to get an interview with Hitler. He's already made it with Goebbels. I imagine the British Government will be interested in what he learns."

If Count Andross had been sent to spy on her by the British Government this ought to help Dan with a Churchill interview.

But he refused to take the bait. "I admire his efforts. Goebbels should be an interesting interview, even if Hitler isn't available."

She pursued her build-up of Dan. "Dan is returning to London tomorrow. Then he's off to the Pacific."

"And you too, Your Highness?"

She laughed. "Just the opposite direction. Dan hopes to contact names in London that Tige gave him. By hook or by crook, they will get me home to Lichtenbourg."

"Perhaps through Sweden," he suggested. "I might be of some help there." He offered her his card again. He was certainly persistent. "If all else fails," he added. After a moment's hesitation she took the card and slipped it into her handbag.

Andross remarked a bit drily, "So Tige Royle's adopted son lives in peaceful, neutral California. A fortunate young man."

14

"I think so. I've just returned from Cal-Berkeley. I was studying World Governments. It was Tige Royle's idea." She still regretted what she had lost when her Miravel grandfather sent that peremptory cable telling her she "owed" a visit to a dying man. She had been within two months of taking her Finals and graduating in February of 1942.

Andross surprised her by asking, "Does your father enjoy governing Lichtenbourg?"

What an idiotic question! "Of course he does." The second after she said it, she wondered. She knew her father had wanted to be His Serene Highness, the Prince Royal of Lichtenbourg. But once he came into the position people kept saying how different he was from the charming and not too brilliant prince he had been before he connived to take over the throne.

Andross said, "I see," and looked out the window as if he had lost interest in the conversation. A bit miffed she told herself with a pretence of satisfaction, at least I've finally gotten the best of this odd character. He's run out of small talk, or whatever it is he has been trying to get out of me.

Feeling unsure of herself with him, having found out nothing whatever in the last hour, she made up her mind not to initiate any more small talk. As the day wore on she was consumed with curiosity over what was at the root of his presence on this train and, especially, why he had followed her in London.

She unfolded the American movie magazine she had found in the air raid shelter that day. She read every subject she cared about in the magazine, but didn't like to put it down, as if she no longer had anything to occupy her. She would like to have been caught with a biography of Queen Elizabeth, or Catherine the Great, or better yet, a peculiar college favourite of hers, *The Usage Of*

15

Negative Councillor Advice. She had heard plenty of the latter when eavesdropping on some of the State Council Meetings presided over by her father and she felt that such a book might be useful to her when, in future, she sat in her father's rigid and uncomfortable chair.

Meanwhile, they were approaching what she thought of as Miravel country, full of canals and locks between gentle rolling hills, with the late November countryside still dappled by green stretches.

Surreptitiously, beneath her lashes, she looked at the man in the seat across from her and then was startled to note that he was observing her. Even allowing for her suspicions she couldn't fault him for his thoughtful, almost gentle, look.

What on earth had made him follow her with such determination and now look almost as if he were sorry for her? It annoyed her more than his flippancy. She did not regard herself as someone to be pitied.

She left the magazine on the worn, cushioned seat, eased on her soft leather gloves, and got ready for the Miravel stop just beyond a low ridge of hills on their left.

Count Andross looked up at her two bags and as he rose he said pleasantly, "May I get those for you?"

"The attendant will do that." Less rudely she added, "Thank you."

She might as well not have wasted her breath. He was already lifting her bags down.

She was about to ruin his little effort by asking the attendant to oblige her but the train came to a jolting halt, blowing off steam. A station attendant opened the carriage door and Count Andross set her two cases on the platform.

"Will Your Highness be met?"

"Yes, thank you. That American car, the Packard south

of the platform. It's old but still running." She added, "When the gasoline – I mean petrol – is still available."

He took her arm, helping her off the train. For a minute she was very close and staring directly into his eyes. Shaken by the unblinking intensity of his look she lowered her gaze. Her body felt warm, prickling with a fiery awareness of him. Then there was a plaintive whistle. The Count freed her hand, stepped back into the carriage, and in seconds the train was on its way. She looked back, almost without intending to. He was still watching her. She did not know whether to feel uneasy or to remember that last, unexpected thrill of contact with him.

CHAPTER THREE

In the small salon of Miravel Hall Alexia waited anxiously for more than two hours. It was approaching sunset when she was told by her grandfather's nurse that there would be another hour's wait.

"I'm afraid Lord Miravel hasn't asked for you yet, Miss Alexia. Mr Nick Chance is reading His Lordship's latest book aloud. Proofing, I believe they call it. Mr Nick always checks His Lordship's work. I'm afraid His Lordship never lets anything interfere with that. Even death, if I may say so."

It took an effort to remain patient. After all, Alexia had been abruptly summoned across a continent and an ocean to pay her last respects. But this was typical of Lord David Miravel.

In her childhood prayers Alexia had been taught to include her grandfather, David, but on the rare occasions when the recluse agreed to see her she had been disappointed by his vague indifference. Now he was dying, quite painlessly according to Nick Chance's cable to her in California, and she couldn't even feel the deep sadness that the death of one's grandfather ought to bring.

She accepted her temporary dismissal now, ashamed of a relief that she needn't face him yet after all; since it was plain he had changed his mind after sending for her. She had always known it had nothing to do with his will. Alexia's family understood that he was leaving Miravel to his estate manager and secretary, Nick Chance, who had devoted his life, sometimes reluctantly, to the service of Lord David Miravel. Nick had earned the estate. Nothing else had occupied his mind since he was a child of eight.

Alexia did not want to waste any more time with the officious nurse. "Very well. My grandfather did send for me, as you probably know. But I will be out in the grounds looking at the changes. The war has brought about so many food shortages."

"Not quite the changes you must have seen in London as you came through, Ma'am," the woman said. "The Blitz has devastated most of the old landmarks. You were fortunate to have spent the last years in the States. You won't find the Luftwaffe dropping their calling cards on California."

"I am aware of that."

She swung around and walked out the side door that used to lead to the stables but now was handy to the big garage. She had heard nothing about bombs dropping on Lichtenbourg but the possibility was always nerve-wracking. Her mother and father were so vulnerable there, and the New Palace such an obvious target.

Lichtenbourg! There was the connection . . . She had seen Count Andross in Lichtenbourg City at some celebration a long time ago. Probably a casual visitor, come to see the festivities. She looked down at her hand remembering the hot excitement of that hand clasp between her and Count Andross. Ridiculous that a mere touch could arouse her like that.

Who was he, really?

There was something about the memory of him that was sinister. What had he done? What could he do to her or her mother and father in Lichtenbourg? It must have been the Hitler presence. Probably she would never know. He was gone from her life. When she left the train he made no effort to follow her. Surely, that was a relief.

She studied her hand, imagining she felt again that tingle of sexual excitement. How silly could she get over a sinister stranger's touch? But was he a stranger?

She took a breath of the late fall air. She felt better after she walked past the west front of elegant Miravel Hall. She had been afraid much of the five-hundred-year-old estate had been sold off for housing developments. There had been wild rumours through the family about how the estate manager, Nick Chance, had managed to turn the land into a series of cheap, badly rundown housing areas that had been left half-empty and now gone to rack-and-ruin during the war.

But Miravel still remained intact. Alexia did notice some minor problems that were to be expected. Part of the vast water-gardens had been drained off and turned into wartime vegetable patches. The rest were badly tended or, to be exact, untended.

Recuperating servicemen from the village hospital earned extra money from Miravel as gardeners, volunteering with great enthusiasm. But nobody seemed to want to trim hedges and the Azalea bushes lining the path. Certainly no one thought of picking up gum wrappers or crumpled cigarette packages.

Still, so many beauties remained, like the carpet of bluebells, dormant now, under the trees that lined the estate road, and above all, the woods themselves, their crisp leaves fluttering down in the afternoon breeze. Would they all disappear as soon as Nick Chance inherited the Miravel Estate?

Very likely. After all, though he wasn't a Miravel, he had been responsible for the sale of the properties over the ridge and down along the Miravel Canal. Nick had been estate manager since the end of the Great War in

1918. Without him the estate would have gone to rack and ruin long ago. Alexia might regret the changes he would make when her grandfather died, but she was fair enough to know Nick had earned the estate.

Speak of the devil. Nick's voice, edged with sarcasm, called out, "Her Serene Highness is out surveying the ancestral property, I see."

He knew perfectly well that when Alexia was visiting Miravel none of the villagers and very few of the neighbouring estate owners referred to her by title. Here, at what the Royles and Miravels called "home", she was universally known as "Miss Alexia". Princess Ava Alexandra Kuragin was too much of a mouthful.

She ignored his effort to annoy her. "There don't seem to be many gardeners among those servicemen who volunteered. But it should do them good anyway, if they like our cool summers."

"'Our summers.' How possessive we are, We Miravels," he murmured and pretended to soften the comment by a tight smile that did not lighten his cold grey eyes. He was a strange man, not unattractive in his chilly way. He hardly looked his age, which must be a little over forty, but then he had never looked young to Alexia. She had never seen him show genuine liking for anyone with the possible exception of Alexia's mother, Princess Garnett, who was Lord David's only acknowledged child.

Nick Chance was of middle height but looked taller because of his lean frame. He never seemed to enjoy himself or to waste time. He was a widower whose wife had died some ten years ago, not surprisingly, of cirrhosis of the liver. She did not leave him the nest-egg everyone said he was waiting for, but she left him an unwanted stepson. Luckily, the boy, Dan, was taken in hand by that world-renowned patriarch of the Miravels and the Royles, Tiger Royle, Alexia's forever vigorous great-grandfather.

Alexia was very fond of Dan Royle, but she could never decide whether the grown-up, good-looking Dan would make a better brother or lover. Meanwhile, they remained the best of friends, confiding in each other every time she returned to the States to visit Tige in San Francisco or her godparents, Laura and Chris Royle, in Hollywood.

She had hoped to spend Christmas of 1941 with Tige and Dan in San Francisco but since it was now mid-November, it appeared that Christmas of 1941 would be a grim one, perhaps here at the bedside of her grandfather. It was a selfish thought, and she knew it, but she missed the youthful enthusiasms she found at her university and in San Francisco.

War or no war, she infinitely preferred the States to her Lichtenbourg birthplace, where Nazi uniforms were in and out of the palace and the Royal Hall of Justice at all hours, paying their respects to Prince Max, her father, and the "absurdly named Princess Garnett" to quote Hitler's *Voelkischer Beobachter* in an earlier, less friendly day.

"How long are you staying?" Nick asked. "We had a cable from Prince Max yesterday afternoon asking that his wandering daughter rustle herself home to Lichtenbourg as soon as she leaves here. I sent him my promise," he added lightly. "I'll be curious to see how you cross Europe with everyone at war. How did you intend to reach your little dot in Hitler's backyard?"

"Front yard," she reminded him, pretending to take all this with humour. "Lichtenbourg is still reasonably neutral."

"If you can call it neutral to be jammed between the Third Reich and Hitler's Austria, not to mention Hungary. All of them at war with us. Clever little Lichtenbourg. Everybody's friend."

He had hit her in a vulnerable spot, knowing quite well

that she and her father did not see eye to eye on the subject of his Nazi neighbours.

"How is my grandfather?" she asked, hoping to change the subject.

"Dying."

There was no emotion in his voice, but perhaps he had no reason to show any feeling toward his employer, the companion Nick Chance had known for most of his lifetime with little love lost on either side. None of the present generation ever understood what had held them together so long.

"I mean – " She began patiently, "is he feeling well enough to see me yet? I understand dropsy is not so very painful a disease."

He laughed. "You and I are alike, after all. The vultures circle when they smell blood . . . And last testaments."

She turned away from the fountain and looked directly at him. "Everyone in the family knows the estate should go to you. You've worked hard enough for it, God knows!"

His eyes narrowed as if he might have found a barb in her words but he admitted without hesitation, "Very true."

This cat-and-mouse business was beginning to tire her. "When can I see my grandfather?"

"Oh?" He made a pretence of surprise. "But of course. That is why I came out to find you. He wants to see you. He expected you some minutes ago."

What a bastard Nick was! No matter. She did want to see Lord David. She had been touched to think this lonely man would actually enjoy her company. She wanted to let him know her mother cared for him and had never forgotten their devotion to each other in her childhood. If Lord David tried to explain his will, as Alexia suspected he might, she wanted to tell him that her mother understood why he must leave the estate to Nick Chance.

23

Aware that he was still watching her every move, Alexia hurried up the path to the impressive southwest entrance of Miravel Hall. At this hour in the afternoon all the bricks of the lovely three-storey southwest facade glowed with a soft, pink warmth. The original house was centuries old, but it had been restored with considerable artistry less than a hundred years ago.

With the present shortage of help due to the war's priorities Alexia knew what to expect, but it was surprising to see the stout butler, Horwich, back at his old station, guarding the sacred portals of Miravel. He must be past eighty now but as officious as ever.

He had retired in the mid-thirties but here he was, back at Miravel and, if she was any judge, still drinking on the sly. She couldn't blame him. The Miravel village pub, besides being a stiff, five-mile walk, must be lonely after his life with his daughter in London during the horrors and excitement of the 1940 Blitz.

He bowed to her in a stately fashion, his eyes looking a little more glazed than they had appeared when he greeted her arrival and that of the ancient chauffeur upwards of three hours ago.

"Your Serene Highness is expected. You will find His Lordship in his study. He refuses to remain in bed."

She couldn't resist the reminder, "I'm sorry I was not told. But thank you."

Hurrying along the Regency reception hall, she was not fast enough to miss his reproof. "His Lordship's time is carefully allocated, being so short, I regret to say."

There used to be a footman or two lurking about, waiting to escort her up the great staircase to the gallery floor. There were none at hand now. Above the gallery floor a narrow pair of twin staircases took a precipitous rise to the top floor where that secretive loner, David Miravel, spent his life in the little study he had inherited from his dead brother during the Boer War.

Alexia reached the great staircase seeing no one but her grandfather's nurse who was headed for the housekeeper's dining room. The woman bent her head stiffly to Alexia without stopping.

The ubiquitous Horwich trotted after Alexia. "Can you find your way, Ma'am?"

"Oh, yes. I've visited Lord Miravel's study before, you know," she reminded him.

"Just so. It's been difficult, obtaining household staff in these times. But I don't suppose Your Highness would have this experience. We were all relieved, Ma'am, that you wisely chose to take your university studies in California, such a calming, neutral area, with the rest of the world in flames."

"Fortunate, indeed," she said, ignoring his sarcasm as she had ignored Nick's. They probably had their reasons, in which envy might play a part. They had been through hell and were not done yet. Neutral countries must seem just one step above the Axis powers.

She went up the staircase under the great crystal chandelier that dangled from the glass dome high overhead. Sunset had caught the glass dome and cast a lovely light over the crystal prisms. She tried to concentrate on that, not letting herself be upset by some home truths thrown at her by Nick and Horwich.

Her father, Prince Max, had reminded her so often, "Children born to royalty must never permit themselves to be cross or irritable in public. I mean, my dear, *never*. No matter what the provocation."

No use in reminding him that his beloved Garnett said and did what she pleased, got angry or laughed, kissed some visitors presented to her, ignored others, joked and flirted outrageously in spite of the references to her, both glamorous and politely snide, that appeared in the press of Berlin, the United States and, occasionally, London.

Not that any of Garnett's bad press mattered. She was an enchantress and always would be. She was also the only one who had ever been able to wean her father away from his books.

Sometimes it had seemed to Alexia that there was no use in trying to acquire whatever it was that Garnett Miravel Kuragin had been born with. But now, with the problems she faced as Max's wife, even Garnett must be uneasy about the future. If the Allies won the war, and if the United States came in, the Kuragins would be considered a part of the Hitler plague that spread itself over Europe.

Alexia pulled herself together, tried to think good optimistic thoughts when she faced her grandfather in his dreadful little cubbyhole of an office that he loved so well.

She knocked, heard his querulous voice that had once been very pleasant: "Who is it?"

"It's me, Grandfather. It's Alexandra." She could never bring herself to say "Ava" since her childhood when Adolf Hitler boasted of their connection through the care her parents had taken in naming her to please him.

She suspected now that her father's chancellor, Janos Becque, a lascivious little man who liked to fondle her, was lying to Prince Max over hidden terrors in the Third Reich. How many people had been sent to labour camps – whatever they were? – in the Reich and not returned to Lichtenbourg?

"They must work like honest people," Becque had insisted at her father's Council Meetings. Did they like their work so well they did not want to return?

Janos Becque's mother was no better. Alexia's mother had as little to do with Frau Becque, royal housekeeper at the New Palace, as she could help.

There had been many Slavs in Lichtenbourg before the war. Their sympathies had probably been with the Russian Colossus fighting for its life on the Eastern Front against the Nazi invaders. Like the royal Kuragins, they never quite got used to having a third of Lichtenbourg pro-German, with the German and Austrian Reichs just across the border.

Alexia hoped her grandfather would be cheered by her arrival, but his hesitation was uncomfortably long. Then he called in a shaken voice, "Come in, my dear. The door is unlocked."

She hurried across the well-worn carpet and would have kissed David Miravel on the cheek, but he drew back murmuring, "Take care. This dropsy business may be catching. It runs in the family . . . My mother died of it. Take that chair before me. I can see you better in the lamplight."

How could he bear to be cooped up in this awful little cell like a criminal or a state prisoner?

Two weeks ago, before Dan left for his German interviews for a San Francisco paper, he had invited Alexia and a couple of their mutual college friends to what had once been the Barbary Coast in San Francisco, where they shared a midnight speciality from Gold Rush Days called "Hangtown Fry". It was then, after several glasses of hearty red wine, that he had told the girls that the rumours and whispers about mass disappearances in the Reich-controlled countries were true. Jews, gypsies, Protestants of masonic orders, the ill and mentally incompetent, were being sent to work camps where conditions, according to Dan's sources, were barbaric. "Those of us who aren't Jews or gypsies," he had told the girls, "are just as likely to disappear. I think we'd better stop considering it as a 'Jewish matter' and I mean to look into it if I can interview some of the bigshots."

27

With half the world in bondage David Miravel had imprisoned himself in his own lovely home, unaware of the world outside, slowly dying without ever having lived, so far as Alexia could tell. She hoped this deliberate choice of loneliness could not be inherited. It was far more frightening to her than dropsy.

The metallic green desk lamp shed a little puddle of light on the desk and upon the sheaf of papers, obviously his latest manuscript, but the drapes were kept drawn all day, not just at sunset. She knelt before her grandfather, hugging him, hoping to instill in that handsome frame some feeling for life, for sunlight. He patted her shoulder gently, then studied her face.

"A pity you don't take after your mother. Did I ever tell you Garnett was the prettiest child I ever saw?" He took a tired breath. "According to the press, she is still the most beautiful woman on the Continent."

She said obediently, "She took after you, Grandfather."

He patted her shoulder again. "Yes. Many have thought so."

He looked frail but no more so than he had when she visited him as a child. His features had a certain haggard beauty, but they lacked animation. Alexia used to think he needed more blood, maybe tonics, exercise. Above all, he needed some common touch that made him human. In spite of his heart problem he hadn't changed much physically. His ankles were probably swollen with the disease, but no one would see that. He might appear a little weaker but she always remembered his pale lashes drooping over tired, watery eyes where the marks of his heavily lensed eye-glasses remained at either side of his nose.

She brought up a subject that usually animated him. "I hear your book about pre-Roman Britain is going to be required reading. That's wonderful. We are all so proud of you."

Self-satisfaction and pride did something for his features. "Yes. I was very pleased. I imagine that impressed my worthy father-in-law." A little flash of dislike lighted his eyes. She knew the feeling was mutual with Tige Royle.

She put all her enthusiasm into her agreement. "Tige has told everyone about it."

She knew from her mother that Tige Royle had settled over a million pounds on David Miravel in 1900 when David married Tige's dearly loved daughter, Alix, for whom Alexia had re-named herself. It was Tige, the financial tycoon and international trouble-shooter, who had kept the Miravel Estate financially afloat ever since, along with the physical labour of Nick Chance.

Alexia looked at her grandfather's frail, elegant fingers. If he had been Tige Royle she wouldn't hesitate to caress his hand. Tige was an expressive personality who welcomed affection, but David, seeing her gaze, slowly withdrew his fingers. Perhaps he felt her pity.

"Well, my dear," he said as he removed his glasses and wiped them on his immaculately folded handkerchief. "I imagine you are wondering why I asked Nick to send for you. I tried to persuade your mother to come, but this idiotic war and that vile fellow with his Chaplin moustache seem to have made it impossible. I told her she might come by Sweden or Portugal. But it seems to have been too complicated."

"I'm sure she tried," Alexia murmured. "I suppose the technical problems are enormous. I only hope Dan can help me. He should be in London soon."

He changed the subject suddenly, his fingers nipping at the back of her hand. "Has anyone mentioned my will, the uncertainty?"

She stiffened. "Of course not. You told Mother some time ago that she must understand you owed a great deal to Nick. We all understood from that . . ."

"We will say no more about it at this time. I'm feeling a little tired now. All this babble of voices . . ."

I take it the babble is mine, she thought. "Shall I send for your valet, Sir?"

"Cornbury?" He snorted the name. "Fellow is ready for the rag-bag. But in spite of his age he had to volunteer. He's some sort of fire-watcher, hanging about on rooftops in London. Would you send up my infernal doctor's child? Shy little thing named Rose. Very helpful. Knows how to massage my forehead. I don't know how I would get on without her. These terrible eyestrain headaches bother me more than the dropsy business."

"Yes, Grandfather."

Feeling hopeless about their relationship she kissed his temple and left him. She crossed the book-lined little room which was still gloomy with that single desk light. As she opened the door Lord Miravel heaved a long sigh of relief. She tried not to take this personally, although it was obvious she had tired him.

She found the girl, Rose Tredegar, in the kitchen helping Mrs Skinner, the cook-housekeeper, lift a lamb roast pan into the oven. Although Mrs Skinner was well along in years, she appeared far stronger than Rose Tredegar.

The girl was small with a shy smile and seemed well suited to Lord Miravel's tastes, probably because she would speak softly when spoken to and in no way disturb him.

When told of Lord Miravel's summons the girl took off at a run, shedding her apron as she ran. She slipped out into the hall. Alexia could hear her flat-heeled, childish pumps pattering up the staircase.

"Grandfather says she is a great help to him," Alexia

30

remarked to the cook. "She must be helpful to you in the kitchen, what with the shortage of staff."

Mrs Skinner shrugged and slammed the oven door shut. "I'll allow her that. She's a good lass. Not above herself, either. But not too bright. I daresay, His Lordship prefers them that way. Not like his wife was. Ah! Your grandmother, Lady Alix. There was a female for you." She sighed. "Gone now. And where's another, I'd like to know."

Alexia went away reflecting that this was not her own day for self-esteem.

CHAPTER FOUR

Lord Miravel had sent down his apologies with Horwich. His day had been tiring and he would not be able to join his granddaughter for dinner, but he would appreciate seeing her before he retired.

She found herself alone at the long table with Nick Chance who did not take her grandfather's chair at the head of the table as Alexia expected. He motioned for the untrained young footman to seat her in the hostess's place at the foot of the table and himself sat at her right hand, making conversation easier.

He looked her over as if surprised that she wasn't in evening dress. This was essential before the war. Lord Miravel would have insisted on it. But tonight she wore her raw silk, gold suit, changing only her blouse to a lime green chiffon that flattered her hazel eyes and her hair which she wore up tonight in a more formal style. She hadn't the faintest idea whether Nick's expression was approving or not. It didn't matter, in any case.

Meanwhile, Mrs Skinner had certainly done her part with the meal. The roast lamb from the neighbouring flocks was succulent and savoury, with vegetables from the Miravel gardens. The mint sauce was Mrs Skinner's pride and, when Alexia mentioned it, Nick pointed out that the mint had come from Mrs Skinner's special herb garden.

"Matter of fact, she makes a tidy little sum by selling

bouquets of her herbs and spices. Amazing how spices can disguise the wartime diet."

"You don't mind her sales, surely?"

He shrugged. "I simply like to have an accounting of all profits taken from the Miravel land." He evidently expected her to say something. When she didn't he looked at her a long minute before adding blandly, "For His Lordship's accounting, of course."

"Of course." Then she broached the subject that had occupied her thoughts since meeting Rose Tredegar in the kitchen.

"Miss Tredegar doesn't share the family dinner?"

She half-expected he would resent Miss Tredegar who might be usurping his place as her grandfather's aide, servant and palace favourite. To her surprise he was a bit smug.

"Little Rosebud? She and my – His Lordship seem to be getting on quite well, don't they?"

It wasn't the first time she had noticed his slip of the tongue when speaking of his employer. *My* what? *My Lord*? Maybe. And why had Nick Chance never left Miravel for greener pastures? Surely with his talents – he had been a brilliant cryptographer in the Great War – he could find more financial security elsewhere. Waiting around in the hope of being a beneficiary in David Miravel's will might be satisfactory if Lord Miravel was a man of his word, but suppose, like others in her grandfather's condition, he fell in love with his nurse? In Rose Tredegar's case she seemed to be a reasonable facsimile of a nurse.

She said, "Miss Tredegar may be overdoing the attentions, interfering with you."

"Oh? How so?"

"Well, Mrs Skinner doesn't seem as grateful for her help as one would expect."

He laughed away the cook-housekeeper. "That old hag? You can ignore anything from that source. Lay it to jealousy. Is our little Rosebud responsible for that wistful look you have?"

The question came so suddenly it sounded like a challenge. She tried to take it coolly. "Not at all. To tell the truth, I don't know why I was sent for all this distance at a time like this when – "

"Well?"

"When he seems to be too ill to see me at all."

He played with the well-polished old Miravel silver, running his fingers over his butter knife. "You thought it was about his will, of course."

"No." She might as well be frank. "As I told you, that is all settled. He explained to Mother months ago. Besides, she has always thought it would be yours, even if – " She bit her lip. "I mean, you've done so much."

He looked up from the knife with his malign smile. Sometimes she thought he was having amusement at her expense, and occasionally at the world, but she suddenly had a weird notion he was laughing at himself.

"You were about to say – what? Even if I am not a Miravel?"

She was disgusted at her blunder. How could she have been so stupid and unthinking? "The estate isn't entailed. Grandfather named you. That should settle it. The only thing that won't go with Miravel is the Miravel title."

"No Lord Nick Chance? Beastly shame. It would really shake up the House of Lords. Unless, of course, I were legitimized."

That startled her. "Legitim – Does that mean what I think it does? But that could only happen to someone of Grandfather's blood."

"A bastard, in fact."

Could this be why her mother felt that he was entitled

to the estate? One blazing, shocking result would certainly shake the world if David Miravel went through some mumbo-jumbo, pretending he had secretly married Nick's mother. It could have a disastrous effect on Lord Miravel's daughter. Scandal would be sure to claim that Garnett Miravel Kuragin, Princess Royal of Lichtenbourg, was a bastard. Even the Lichtenbourg throne could be in danger. There was always a chance that the von Elsbach House would win a free election and return to power. For centuries the tiny principality had been quarrelled and fought over by the slavic Kuragins and the germanic Elsbachs.

Alexia wondered if this was why her mother made no protest over the inheritance from her father. She didn't want to provoke Lord Miravel into legitimizing Nick Chance. If, of course, there was any truth in the story.

But it did explain the odd reticence of the family when the name of Nick Chance came up in the conversation. If the story was true it was a terrible injustice to the boy who had always been known as Nick Chance.

She looked up uncomfortably, discovering that Nick had never stopped watching her. There was very little to say. She tried to return to the original subject, playing it lightly. "But aren't you afraid my grandfather might fall under Miss Tredegar's spell and leave her part of the estate? For her kindness to him, you know."

He looked awfully confident. "Not my little Rosebud." He startled her by dropping the bread knife. It made a ringing noise on the dessert plate under his soufflé. "Your grandfather found his nurse – his previous nurse, I should say – quite indispensable. She was constantly at his beck and call. Began to read aloud to him. My job, in fact," he reminded her. He waited for her to ask the obvious question. Clearly he was proud of his cleverness.

"All right. What did you do, strangle her?"

He blinked. Evidently she had surprised him. After a minute of what Alexia thought of as pregnant silence he explained.

"Not quite. There are so many easier ways. The poor girl – sleeping on the job. The rest, as they say, is history. Miss Tredegar won't make those mistakes."

"I'll bet!" she muttered sounding like Tige Royle.

He didn't seem the least upset over her suspicious attitude. He seemed pleased. "Then we understand each other."

She wanted to ask on a note of irony, "What arrangement did you make with the Tredegars?" But she didn't. She wanted to get away. She wished she had ignored her grandfather's cable. You can't give affection and concern when the recipient remains like a statue, cold, beautiful and unfeeling. And then to find out he may have spawned a child and refused to claim him. Now he was apparently repaying the man who was, very possibly, his son by giving him the estate, but not his recognition.

Or had Nick achieved that, too? And with it perhaps the destruction of her mother's life and that of the Kuragins?

The big dining room had always been draughty but never more so than now.

"Are you feeling quite well?" Nick was all concern. "I hope it wasn't the soufflé. The old lady does it with a surprisingly light hand. And in these times I've learned to appreciate such luxuries."

She wished she could get even with him. She knew he was playing her like a fisherman with his catch. She would not give him the satisfaction of knowing his darts had all found their mark. "It's excellent. But I'm so troubled."

"I hope I didn't say anything to upset you."

This was the last straw. "No, indeed," she assured him. "But it was sad to see Grandfather frail and weak like that.

Poor man. What an unhappy life he has led . . . after my grandmother died."

The smooth unlined skin of his face seemed frozen into faint surprise. "Did he tell you that?"

Two could play at his game of innocence. "Yes. I've never forgotten it. He spoke of her with longing and affection. You'll think I'm dreadfully romantic but I couldn't help it. I've always carried that letter with me."

"Oh?"

"It was some months ago. I had written some nonsense about a boy at Berkeley. I said I thought it was true love but I wasn't sure." She sighed. "Dear Grandpapa! He wrote to me that when I met the great love of my life I would know it – I think he said – once and forever more. Others were mere encounters, casual and soon forgotten. When his wife died the lights of the world went out."

"It doesn't sound like him."

"I know. He only revealed his true feelings to the family, to my mother and me. Dear Grandfather!" She pretended to wake from her revery. "Would you like to see the letter? I can get it from my handbag."

Thank God he said, "That won't be necessary." The silence that followed was broken by his puzzled remark, "I thought I took all his mail to the post. I don't recall his writing to you for the last year."

She smiled. "What a sly one he is! He was probably ashamed of this sentimental side of him. He said his nurse was going to the village and would mail this. Oh! Of course. It must have been the young lady you discharged."

"Probably." He busied himself buttering and swallowing a piece of the coarse wartime bread on his plate.

She had never been so glad to leave the dining room as she was that night. At home in Lichtenbourg the banquets might go on forever but she spent most of her time closing her mind to her surroundings. Here at Miravel it was impossible to ignore Nick Chance. Tonight his sardonic and frightening humour had made him a man whose conversation, perhaps half humorous, no doubt deliberate, was enough to worry her for the rest of the evening.

She was more than relieved when he excused himself to go for a stroll in the grounds, as he put it.

A few minutes later in the reception hall Rose Tredegar almost ran into Alexia. She was in a panic. "Miss, Your Highness, he's that ill, Ma'am. Coughing like. It's water on the lungs or some place. Could you sit by him? I must ring down to Papa and go and collect him. I do hope he's still at Lacey's Pub."

Everything seemed to change at the thought of one of the family actually in pain. He might lack feeling for others but he was human enough to suffer pain just like anyone else. Besides, the same blood ran in her veins as in those thin, parched veins of her grandfather. Alexia hurried up the great staircase.

On reaching the door of Lord Miravel's old-fashioned bedchamber on the gallery floor Alexia could hear the dreadful choking cough of the sick man. She had no experience with the edema aspects of this disease, but could only hope that her commonsense might save him until Dr Tredegar came.

She found one of the two housemaids sitting by the canopied bed with her hands folded. Perkins was an elderly woman, large-boned and heavy without being fat. She got up quickly, relieved at Alexia's arrival.

"Well then, Ma'am, it's glad I am to see you. I did what I could, which I'm bound to say isn't much, not being any hand with sick folk."

"I know. I'm the same way," Alexia assured her. "But at least you have him sitting up, leaning forward. That might stop him from choking."

She reached around behind the exhausted invalid, punched the pillows up to keep him erect, and did the best she could to calm him. After a few minutes she sent Perkins for cloths to relieve the sweat on his face.

It might not be prescribed but it seemed to work. Her grandfather's paroxysm slowed and he began to gasp, catching his breath. One of his wasted hands felt for hers blindly.

"Don't leave . . . thought I was gone . . . hurts to breathe – "

"Just be easy. You'll be all right in no time." While waiting for Perkins and the doctor Alexia found his clean folded handkerchief behind his pillows and wiped his forehead. He caught her hand, held it on his moist forehead.

"Feels better. You were always – " He took a cutting breath. "Always like a tonic, little Garnett."

She felt it was pointless to correct him. Maybe it helped him to feel his daughter was with him. In spite of the deliberate lie she had told Nick she suspected David Miravel had only loved one person in his life, his daughter Garnett.

Alexia loved her mother but also recognized her faults and while Garnett certainly cared for His Lordship, she was not one to put herself out for anyone. In fact, she was a true daughter of David Miravel.

Alexia realized suddenly, with the dinner conversation burned into her memory, that Nick Chance showed those same qualities of self-concern characteristic of David Miravel and his daughter. Nick Chance might easily be her grandfather's bastard son.

"Garnett? Are you still with me?"

"Yes, Father," she said quietly. "I won't leave you."

By the time Dr Tredegar, a stocky, jolly kind of man, arrived to care for the invalid murmuring all sorts of cheerful platitudes, Lord Miravel was more calm, though Alexia still thought his heartbeat was too heavy and uneven. But she was no doctor and knew nothing about medical facts.

When Lord Miravel addressed Alexia by her mother's name the doctor looked at her, puzzled. She shook her head. He made no effort to correct the sick man but asked her to hold her grandfather's head while he coaxed him to drink the powders he had mixed in a glass of water.

"Down the hatch, Sir, as we old seadogs used to say. Did I ever tell Your Lordship about the time they gave me Epsom Salts instead of powders for a fever? If that didn't cure me, nothing would."

He chuckled in his jolly way. Alexia doubted if her grandfather even heard him. After a half-hour of more or less light-hearted attendance on his patient, Dr Tredegar yawned, explaining to Alexia in a conspiratorial voice, "Caught me at the little village pub, so she did. My daughter, I mean. I'd barely touched lips to glass. I was standing a pint for the boys from the Elder Home. Against the rules, you know, but they're only young once. The Elder Home's been adapted to a hospital for the duration, you know. Thrown out the old ladies. Not that they mind. Always fussing over our lads."

He's had more than one sip at the pub to judge by his breath, but this was no time to look a gift horse in the mouth. Miravel needed him.

"But then you've had nothing to eat, Doctor. You must tell Mrs Skinner to heat up some dinner. It was excellent tonight. I'll stay with His Lordship."

He brightened. "I just might at that. Can you spare me for say, half an hour?"

"Of course. If His Lordship becomes restless again I'll call you at once."

He started out of the room, sticking his woolly head in

to command, "Mind you, let me know the instant there is trouble. Just press the little button behind the right hand bedpost. That'll fetch me."

The room was very silent when he had gone and she jumped at the crackling, snapping noise of the fireplace. The sound half-aroused her grandfather. His head turned back and forth as if he were troubled by some dream or sudden thought. He opened his eyes, staring at her.

"Is he really dead?"

The question at this particular moment puzzled her. "Who?"

"Bayard of course." His older brother. The dashing idol who was going to bring back glory to the family.

She said gently, "He died in Africa. The Boer War, a long time ago."

He waved his hand impatiently. "But not to Mother."

She had never known Lady Phoebe Miravel. The only one who ever got along with her, Garnett said, was Tige Royle. Lady Phoebe had had a crush on him and he was always good with the ladies, making them feel desirable and popular.

"Lady Phoebe is gone, too. I'm sorry. Try not to think about it."

He roused himself. He must be fully awake now. "I never stop thinking about it. She ruined my life. She let them get me drunk at the Midsummer Fair and that creature, that girl, I don't remember. I can't believe I did that. But everyone thinks I did. I hear their gossip. As if I would – copulate with some village whore!"

"Grandfather!"

He waved away her protest. "Do you know what she said?"

Not the village whore, surely. Confused she asked, "Who?"

"How dense you are! My mother. When they told her

41

Bayard was dead she looked at me and said, 'Why wasn't it you?'"

She winced at the cruelty of that. "I'm sure she didn't mean it. People say things when they are in great pain."

He began to cough and she wiped his mouth. "But Grandfather, think how great you've become. You showed her. Showed the whole world. You are a famous historian."

He sat up and leaned forward, trying to find a position in which to rest. She heard him mutter something and put her head nearer. The words were faint but still audible. "Why wasn't it you? That's what she said."

She held one of his hands between hers. She hadn't really thought she would cry for him but here their hands were locked together and though she tried to blink back the tears, she felt them on the locked hands. It must be dreadful to die so alone and unloved.

Alexia heard no sounds except the now low-burning fire, but she sensed that she and the sick man were no longer alone. She pushed the bed curtain aside with her free hand and saw a motionless figure. For an instant the pale eyes glared at her but this must have been a trick of the small distant lamp on the stand beside His Lordship's big easy chair.

In a quiet voice, without emotion, Nick Chance asked, "Is he dead? Or only unconscious?"

Wondering how long he had been in the room she hoped he hadn't heard the sick man's reference to "that village whore" who must have been Nick's mother.

"He isn't dead."

"What a pity!"

CHAPTER FIVE

"Nick, for God's sake, he may hear you!" She was conventionally shocked, but only conventionally. She could hardly blame him.

"I didn't know you were so . . . compassionate." This time the old smile was back. She took little note of that. He looked over her shoulder at the sick man. "He is still breathing, but I doubt if he hears us, or even knows who we are. His memories are back at the turn of the century when his so-called tragedies began. Poor fellow, so misunderstood, so mistreated. It must be hell to be a peer without trying, a success on work that is half another's and all the time earning the tears of his sentimental granddaughter."

She looked up into his face and surprised herself by the firmness of her reminder. "You can't blame him for taking advantage of what you offered. Why did you do it? Tige once said you were brilliant when you worked in his New York office two summers. And I know you did a great deal of intellectual work during the Great War."

"Well?" He didn't deny it.

"Why did you come home to this backwater and become my grandfather's slave? For the estate? Tige has put up most of the money to keep it going. It really is your fault."

He was still speaking in a low tone, barely above a murmur, but his anger had been diverted to something else, a thoughtful appraisal of her words. He turned and shrugged. "Do you think it was the estate? I'm sure you do. It never was. It was the name, you fool. The Miravel name. I wanted his recognition. I wanted those filthy gossiping villagers to take their hats off to me, Nick Chance Miravel. Now – "

She thought of what this would do to her mother but honesty made her say, "Maybe it will be yours anyway. I'm sure that is what Grandfather meant when he wrote to my mother and told her you would be his heir."

He walked silently around the room, stopping by the fire and then returning to her. "You've been cooped up here all evening. I'll take over the job for a while. Why don't you get a little sleep?"

She would have liked to get up. Every muscle in her body ached from the stiffness of her position. She hesitated, started to move, then stopped. "It's all right. I'm really not tired."

He studied her while she tried to rouse herself to some kind of brightness. "You actually think I would murder the old bastard! Pardon," he caught himself, "an odd choice of nouns. I am the bastard, of course. Sometimes I forget that." He looked down into her eyes. "I can see the thought processes now, churning and grinding in that empty head of yours. You are wondering if you can trust me not to strangle him. Or – what? Smother him with one of those pillows. Why not give me the benefit of the doubt? Just once. I don't recall that anyone else ever has. Why don't you try to be different?"

Challenged she got up. "Why not? You are many things but I don't think you were ever a fool. Hanging at wherever they hang people now in London isn't going to get you anything. Yes, Nick, I trust you. Take over."

She released her fingers from the sleeping man's hand

and left the room before she could get scared and change her mind.

She was not too reassured when she found Rose Tredegar standing at the foot of the great staircase looking up, waiting for – what? It was hard to say. She looked tense. Or maybe she merely look frightened. Her father came out of the small dining salon where the best liquor was kept. He waved a big beer mug at Alexia asking her in a jolly but reasonably sober voice,

"Won't you have one now, Ma'am? You've earned it. Puts hair on – "

"Papa!" his daughter cried, cutting him off. "You don't talk to a princess like that!"

Tired and worried as she was Alexia had to laugh. "Oh, but they do. At least at my university. And I could use a mug of something," she said on an impulse.

No sooner said than done, Dr Tredegar made a sweeping turn, spilled what foam wasn't on his lips, and returned to the small salon where so much of her family's early life had been spent, quarrelling, entertaining, and sometimes changing lives.

She was glad to get the beer even if the good doctor had no regard for "suds" and poured it so that half the mug was foam. She tried to relax in the room opening off the small salon. It had once been called the "Ladies' Withdrawing Parlour" and she couldn't understand how Victorian and Edwardian women ever found room for their voluminous skirts and endless petticoats. Since everything in the old crimson and gold room was badly worn, she could only assume the ladies managed somehow. She was just beginning to unwind, like a clock too tightly wound, when the phone rang.

It was one of the peculiarities of Miravel that the big house had a scarcity of telephones. There were only two among the public rooms on the ground floor and only two in the bedrooms on the gallery floor. Worse yet, Lord Miravel's study on the upper floor was the only one above the gallery to have a telephone of its own. The nearest one to Alexia was in the back hall outside the doors of the small salon. The hall itself was usually dark and ran from the kitchen, pantry and housekeeper's area across the width of the house, past the foot of the great staircase to the far westerly side door. This opened onto the steep, descending approach of the Estate Road.

Alexia started out into the hall where she was summoned by the nervous Rose Tredegar.

"It's a gentleman, Ma'am. Says he wants Miss Alexia. Must be you."

Good Lord! Had Dan Royle arrived in London already? Alexia raced to the phone, calling to the girl, "Thank you, Miss Tredegar. Be sure and tell me if I am wanted in my grandfather's room."

"Yes, Ma'am. But very likely Papa and Mr Nick will take care of things." She seemed to become aware that Alexia was looking at her rather fixedly and added, "They will call you if you're needed."

"Thank you. I'll join them shortly," she warned the girl, hoping she had made it clear that she was monitoring what went on in Lord Miravel's room.

Rose didn't look frightened. "If you would, Ma'am. Papa and Mr Nick have been with His Lordship steady, whenever the nurse is being relieved. I sit with His Lordship too, of course, when he asks for me. Nurse will be back on duty at midnight."

Alexia took up the phone, eager to have a real friend, someone she could trust, nearby.

"Dan? You made it in record time."

"Good evening, Your Highness. I hope you found your grandfather feeling better."

She was startled by the deep voice that answered her

46

with its faint accent. Continental, she thought, mid-European. The so-called Count Andross who said he was connected with the Swedish Embassy, though he certainly didn't sound like it. Evidently, not content with tracking her through the ghastly rubble of London and pushing his acquaintance on the train, he made himself a further nuisance calling her at home.

She answered him coldly, angry at herself because his voice excited her. "He is doing reasonably well, thank you. I will tell him you called."

"No. Sorry. It was another matter."

"I rather thought it would be."

Her clipped voice did not disturb him. "I have been trying to get Dan Royle at the Savoy in London but he seems to be out on business, probably those London interviews you mentioned."

Why would the mysterious Count Andross want to contact Dan? Maybe he really was legitimate, but if so, he was damned secretive.

Miravel Hall would certainly be brightened with his presence, whatever his motives. He was lively, interesting, and his air of mystery beneath the surface was challenging. On the other hand she certainly didn't want to give him free reign to visit here as if he were a member of the family, especially while the owner was so ill. No, it was out of the question.

Her brittle tone softened a little. Even if he was up to something, there was no need to scare him away for good. Then she would never find out what his game was.

"I didn't know he had arrived in this country yet. I imagine he will call Miravel when he returns from his meetings in London. He will want to know how my grandfather is. He lived here with the estate manager before his mother died."

"So they tell me here in Shrewsbury. If you could give

Mr Royle my hotel number here . . . Tell him, if you would be so kind, that I have just returned from Manila on a military matter between the United States and Sweden, as I told you, and I may be able to help him with the MacArthur interview."

She was sure he hadn't told her about his visit to Manila, but maybe he really did have business with Dan. She wondered why he hadn't told her on the train. It would have made their casual meeting much more legitimate.

"I'll give him your message, Count. What is the number?" She wrote it down and folded it into the little looseleaf notebook beside the phone.

"Thank you," he went on. "You are very kind."

"Not at all. And I should hear from him soon."

She was sorry when the phone went dead. Even his voice reminded her of the excitement she had known while in his company.

Maybe Dan could explain why Count Andross hadn't mentioned the Manila business when she told him about Dan's proposed trip. Or was this business with Dan contrived after she mentioned Dan's upcoming flight to Manila?

She set the phone back, almost as puzzled as ever. There was one thing that Dan would know, whether there was any truth to the count's supposed government dealings in Manila. It seemed highly unlikely: Sweden and the States with business together in the Philippines, of all places? Pretty far-fetched.

It was after eleven and the events of the day were catching up with her. First there had been the long tense minutes in the Underground shelter. Then the uncomfortable knowledge that she was being followed, probably by British agents who didn't trust the assurances provided by Tige Royle's friends in the State Department. After that the long train ride had tired her physically, even with her intriguing and mysterious company. At Miravel there was the tedious wait while Grandfather and Nick edited his precious manuscript, followed by the first painful visit with the sick man, and last this evening's events. There was the tension and sometimes secret fear with Nick Chance, and afterward an unexpected sympathy with both her grandfather and Nick. It looked as though the possibility of a good night's sleep had drifted further and further away.

She had hoped that since Lord Miravel was so insistent about her coming he would express some affection for her. Alexia had lived her life of eighteen years perfectly aware that she was not first in anyone's affections. She had never been close to her parents and very early had learned to be self-sufficient. It was a trait much admired by her great-grandfather, Tige, and highly useful, but it was essentially cold. It didn't take the place of the warm passion others in her family had known.

She had just started up to her grandfather's bedchamber suite when the aged knocker in the shape of a fox vixen clanged against the double doors at the far end of the reception hall. She turned and started along the hall. A sleepy yawning Horwich came out of the library behind the long gold salon.

"Never mind, Horwich," she called. "I'll see to it. Probably medicine Dr Tredegar has sent for."

Relieved at his dismissal Horwich pulled himself together, bowed stiffly and returned to his port and his easy chair. She envied him.

The southwest doors were locked and bolted. The war had brought an occasional odd and unsavoury character to these parts, drawn by the chance to prey on the invalided servicemen stationed in Miravel. Before Alexia opened the door she looked out of the long, left window and was delighted when a windblown, auburn-haired Dan Royle grinned back at her with only the cool glass between them. She unlocked, unbolted and threw the door open.

Dan pulled her into his arms, hugging her but assuring her at the same time, "I'm doing this just to keep warm. Damned if it isn't more like the Klondike every day. Well, can I come in?"

"Of course you can. And you are so welcome!" She stepped aside feeling that Dan's bright, fiery disposition, quick to anger, quick to laugh, quick to tease away anyone's depression, was exactly what was needed at Miravel. Maybe he could bring some of his cheerful spirit to her grandfather who lived in his eternal solitary gloom. Dan might even prolong the sick man's life.

He was moderately tall and well built. He had been an all-state halfback at Cal, his Senior year. Alexia always felt safe with him. When she mentioned this once or twice he was not thrilled.

"That's a hell of a thing to say. Nobody wants a girl to feel safe with him. Thrilled, maybe, or excited, but *safe*?"

She thought of this now and laughed in sheer pleasure as he set down the dated old snap-top overnight case and shrugged off the worn trenchcoat that made him look like a movie reporter. Yes, she felt safe with him.

"I'll have Horwich take your things up to the bedroom. The one Tige uses when he makes a rush visit?"

He scowled heavily, pretending disgust. "You're not dealing with Kuragin bigshots now. It's just Old Dan, remember? I can carry this stuff. I'm not crippled. Come along."

He took her arm, hustling her over the exquisite carpet that had become shabby and threadbare in less than three years under the shoes and boots of military visitors. He looked around at everything that reminded him of his childhood when the transplanted Yankee boy

50

had lived here with his buxom mother as Nick Chance's stepson. No love lost there. He had blamed Nick for his mother's drinking and her infidelity, but observing the family during childhood visits Alexia thought the original blame lay with Dan's mother who had her own reasons for marrying Nick.

Mufalda Chance had seen at once how Nick was making himself indispensable to Lord Miravel. If Nick had married her selfishly, hoping she would share her previous divorce settlement with him, Mufalda had seen herself as the future mistress of Miravel.

Alexia was anxious to ask Dan about Count Andross, whether he was known to Dan and could help Dan's Manila business but she approached it obliquely as they walked arm in arm to the great staircase.

"Did you ever get to see Hitler?"

"What? With his fancy new war going full blast? They said he was off telling the Wehrmacht what to do on the Russian Front. Goebbels was an interesting little creep, though. And he's no fool. He uses everything to push the glory of the Third Reich, the newspapers, the radio, and man-on-the-street opinions by characters who just happen to be living on every block in every city. Far as I can see he hasn't missed a trick."

The delicate bracket lights had been turned off and the big, high-ceilinged ground floor was full of elongated shadows beyond the light cast by the two lamps at the foot of the staircase. Dan stood a minute looking back along the straight vista of cool Regency splendour to the far southeastern door.

"You know, Lexy, you can't imagine how good this looks after where I've been."

"Badly bombed?"

"No. But it's going to be, God willing. And the thing is, they really want it."

51

"I doubt that." She thought she knew Lichtenbourg's neighbours better than an American visitor could.

He pulled her hair as he had when they were children. "This whole European War is damn bad, Honey. I get this creepy feeling that the minds of all the decent people have been trapped in one of those – what do they call them? – glass things that slip down over – "

"A bell jar?"

"I guess so. And they just stand there, not seeing anything beyond the glass. I had a feeling something was going on all the time I was there, just at the edge of my vision. And I didn't know what it was. Damndest thing! One of the CBS men felt the same way on the plane back to London."

He hoisted the case and his coat in his other hand and they went up to the gallery floor. She took a breath and asked, "Will you have any difficulty getting your interviews and whatnot in Manila? There's a hot war going on in China and the Orient. Or have you forgotten?"

He shrugged. "Makes it a better story. We've felt out the lay of the land. But I'm going to be dogged about it. I'll chew his slippers 'til he gives in and sees me."

"By the way, do you know a man who calls himself Count Stefan Andross?"

He pushed open the door of the room that had belonged long ago to Lord Miravel's mother, Lady Phoebe, and was now kept in order for Tige's unexpected visits. It looked out on the southwesterly view of the water gardens and the neat, carefully planted, vegetable garden, somewhat the worse for wear by this time of the year.

Recalled to her question by the silence he said, "Andross? Not that I know of. You meet a lot of people in this business but not too many counts, unless he's German. God knows I met a slew of them there. They call themselves something else high-and-mighty. A Nazi?"

"I certainly hope not." He could be, of course, she thought.

Stefan Andross was no longer on Dan's mind. "Will you look at that view!"

CHAPTER SIX

Obviously Dan had paid little attention to her question, impressed as everyone always was by the sight of the rich, spreading jungle of vegetation lying silent in the moonlight. He looked out, leaving the drapes open wide. "No wonder Nick has thrown his life away for it. It's almost worth a lifetime."

She started to turn down the big, oaken bed which lacked a footboard and looked strong enough for the muscular Royles. He stopped her.

"Honey, I'll get the bed ready. You're not cut out for those delicate chores." He pushed her away and began to fluff up his pillows after he removed the bolster. Meanwhile, he gave some thought to Nick Chance.

"He's a funny duck. I tried my damndest to do everything he asked. I needed a real parent, a man I could look up to. Somebody with authority and understanding. But nothing worked. Sometimes I think he hates the world."

She tried to explain what she had discovered tonight. "I don't think Miravel is Nick's first priority. It's the name of Miravel, and the title. He wants to be acknowledged as Grandfather's legitimate son. Then he won't need to have anything to do with any of us. He can say goodbye and be his own master. Even when he inherits the estate, if it's without the title, he certainly will wash his hands of us."

The idea of Nick being related to the family by blood was a shock to Dan as it must have been to her mother if she thought about its consequences to her. "I've heard the rumours, of course, in the village. What gossips they are! But I thought it was just the usual dirt, people trying to throw mud at your family."

Having tousled the bed up into a mess he turned to her again, taking her by the shoulders and then walking halfway around her, surveying what he saw. She was amused. He always made her laugh with his antics. He praised her in a businesslike way.

"I know princesses are always called beautiful, but you seem to be overdoing it. What's your mother going to say when she sees you've outdone her."

"Don't be silly. I've just read an article in *Life* magazine about the decline of royalty, and guess who was the 'fairest of them all' on the cover?"

"Don't tell me. She may be Garnett to the world but my pal here is all emeralds and amethysts."

"Not emeralds. Semi-precious stones, amethysts, that's me."

When he hugged her, with his cheek beaten by the wind cool against hers, she felt the depression of the last few hours wash away.

He must want to put away the few articles of his travels she thought but when she said she would go and find something for him to eat he kicked his grip under the luggage rack and, claiming he was "starved", followed her down through dimly lit rooms to Mrs Skinner's kitchen. It was useless to think she could hide anything from that gruff, good lady who came out into the large, old-fashioned room wearing a heavy robe fastened to her neck while wisps of her steel-grey hair peeked out here and there beneath her frilled cotton bonnet.

She threw up her hands in pretended outrage. "I might've known, Mr Royle. You're rummaging around in my kitchen like you was ten again. Thievin' rogue that you are. And hungry as usual, I'll be bound."

"If it isn't the queen of the kitchen! I swear you're handsomer than ever." He squeezed her ample shape hard, which didn't do him any disservice in her eyes.

Alexia watched them fondly, wondering if anything in the world could ever take away his exuberance about life and his affection for people. While Mrs Skinner and Dan argued over how long ago he had last visited Miravel Alexia set the big kitchen work table for him. The two of them were so busy arguing, the cook punctuating her arguments with a soup ladle against his backside, that Alexia was the only one who heard footsteps in the hall. She went over to the door and pushed it open almost in Nick Chance's face. He looked a trifle surprised but didn't seem upset, thank heaven! Evidently, he wasn't bringing bad news.

Before he could make one of his typically sarcastic remarks Alexia pointed out, "Here is your stepson, come all the way up here after that long flight from Germany. Say hello and stop flirting with Mrs Skinner, Dan."

Nick and Dan looked at each other over Mrs Skinner's head. Alexia, watching them, reflected that Nick was one person who never seemed to be hypnotized by Dan's cheerfulness. Too bad, he could use a little liveliness.

Dan offered his hand. "Good to see you, Nick. I wish it was under happier circumstances."

"Well, we all have to go sometime."

"Really, Mr Nick!" Shocked, Mrs Skinner dropped her soup ladle and picked it up, swiping it briskly across her bathrobe.

Nick took the hand Dan offered and, having covered the pleasantries, let it go. He turned his attention to the cook. "Lord Miravel's water carafe is broken. We need another. Is there one handy in this benighted house?"

This was still Mrs Skinner's domain, including the houseware and the beautifully monogrammed crystal objects. She went into the century-old china cabinet with its cleaned and polished Waterford crystal. Her ruddy face was tight with anger. She had a strong proprietary sense. While she hustled around she demanded, "And who's responsible for the breakage, if I may make so bold?"

Dan watched with interest, probably wondering, as Alexia did, whether Nick's indifference to the loss was due to the fact that the carafe could be easily replaced.

Nick shrugged. "An accident. The doctor's hand must have been a trifle unsteady. Either that or it slipped through his daughter's hand as he passed it to her."

Mrs Skinner muttered to Dan, "Most likely soused the Doc, anyway," as he helped her get the new carafe down.

Alexia cut into the beginnings of a very pretty quarrel, "My grandfather hasn't had any more coughing spells, I hope."

Accepting the carafe that was ungraciously offered, Nick reassured Alexia with his cool manner. "No. Quite himself again. Asked me to come in early tomorrow morning and go over the new outline with him. A geological history of the Pennine Hills."

"Thank heaven for that."

"Thanks be to God," Mrs Skinner echoed fervently. When Nick had left the kitchen she set the warmed-over lamb and potatoes on the table for Dan, explaining to Alexia, "Such a kind man is the master. I never saw such manners. Always a gracious little nod, sometimes a smile. He was never much for the long gab, but you had to know he was a true gentleman." She caught herself. "What am I saying? He's still a true gentleman."

Dan had begun to eat, obviously enjoying every mouthful, but he looked up in time to catch Alexia stifling a yawn. "Here, what's this? I'm keeping everybody in the place up. All I came up for was to collect Lexy here and get her safely on her way home." He punctuated his remarks with his fork as Tige often did. "Go to bed, Lexy. Those are orders."

She protested. She felt infinitely better around Dan, but she was bone tired and gave in, seeing that Dan was already kneedeep in memories with Mrs Skinner.

"Remember when I stole those cherry tarts and skedaddled out to eat them on that bluebell carpet under the trees?"

"I remember, I whacked you hard with a kettle."

"Yes, but when I pretended to cry you – "

Alexia was still laughing as she closed the kitchen door quietly and went through the darkened house to the bedroom that once belonged to her grandmother, Tige's daughter.

As a child, Alexia had been aware that her grandmother was much loved by some man, but apparently not by her indifferent husband, David Miravel, and certainly not by her daughter, Garnett.

Clearly Garnett was used to being the star of any gathering and resented her mother's popularity, as well as the universal mourning when Alix Royle Miravel died in an accident back in 1918.

Alexia wondered if she would be called in the night and took off only her outer clothes, skirt, jacket and blouse. She wrapped herself in a satin travel robe and lay down. She looked around the room tiredly and thought it strange – maybe the feeling ran in the family – that she would have loved the woman who once slept in this charming bedchamber that was feminine without being frilly.

On the other hand her feelings for Garnett, her own mother, were ambivalent. She liked Garnett, but disliked her shallow, self-centered ways. However, she didn't feel

58

the deep resentment she felt against Prince Max, her father. But that went back to a terrible day in her childhood when he behaved with contemptible cowardice about the assassination of the most wonderful man Alexia had ever known.

This was no way to get to sleep. She punched her pillow and tried to banish painful thoughts. She wondered what Count Andross was doing at this minute. Probably asleep if he had any sense. Strange that she should think of him when she was remembering the hero of her childhood, the hero who died.

Suddenly, she remembered that she hadn't given Dan the phone number of Stefan Andross. Surely Andross wouldn't give her a telephone number for Dan if he had no connection with him. Maybe Dan didn't know him, but his acquaintance with General MacArthur, if it was genuine, ought to help Dan in Manila.

She snapped the bedside lamp off, but her brain was so crowded with ideas, fears and dread that she wondered if she would ever get to sleep.

She was still wondering when she woke up with the high bright light of early winter illuminating the room. It was a cheerful sign. Perhaps everything was all right in spite of her fears.

Somewhat belatedly, in the late thirties, the bedroom next to hers had been modified to a large bathroom, shared by a currently empty suite beyond. She glanced at the elegantly simple gold and glass clock on the fireplace mantel. It was just like home in Lichtenbourg, to enjoy a roaring fire while taking a bath in one of Lichtenbourg New Palace's gigantic bathtubs.

Long ago the clock, though not the bathroom, had belonged to Lord David's wife, the girl who had the secret lover. Everything about Alix Royle Miravel was romantic to her granddaughter. She ran her fingers over the rectangular gold frame of the clock, thinking of that far-off lady who looked at this clock and no doubt counted the minutes until she ran out to meet the real love of her life. A sin, of course. And a cruelty to her husband.

Alexia turned away, bathed quickly and dressed, remembering her grandfather's condition. Poor Grandfather. Had he known? No wonder he was a bitter man. No wonder he got drunk and made love to the village girl who was Nick's mother.

Alexia stopped with her hairbrush in mid-air. Impossible! Nick Chance was in his late forties now. David Miravel and Alix Royle had been married in 1900. So Nick had been several years before the Miravel-Royle marriage.

Alexia was enormously relieved. It seemed to matter a great deal that there was an excuse for Grandmother Alix's adultery. She set the brush down and finished dressing.

A little click in the bathroom puzzled her. She looked in from the dressing room and saw everything in order. No, the brush had slipped off the mantelpiece and had fallen on the edge of the floor mat. In fact, the lovely clock was also fairly close to the marble edge of the mantel. She returned to the bathroom, picked up the silver-backed brush with its Kuragin Royal Crest and set it on the mantel, carefully lifting the clock by its base.

Most housemaids would have lifted the clock by its glass sides she thought and wondered why she had not done so. As it was, the tips of her fingers came upon an odd, rough surface on the bottom of the clock, perhaps a price tag, but surely not because it was several inches square.

She tilted the clock gently. The inner workings, seen through the glass sides, were still in order, but on the base of the clock someone had used adhesive tape to attach a piece of thick paper. Probably a photograph.

The dust-stained tape must have been stuck on years ago. She couldn't pry it off until she used her nail file. An old camera snapshot had been concealed, pressed against the base of the clock. The picture was of a man in uniform. Even if the black and white snapshot had been a coloured portrait it could not have been more clearly the idol of her childhood, Prince Franz Kuragin. No one in her life since, even Tige Royle, had been the hero in her eyes that Prince Kuragin was. A martyr and a hero, murdered long ago by Nazi snipers outside the great Lichtenbourg Cathedral. Here were the glowing dark eyes gazing straight at her, barely shaded by his peaked uniform cap. His lips, sensuous without being sensual, were smiling at her.

No, not at her. At the person who snapped the picture. Surely it must be the woman who originally occupied this suite, Lady Alix Royle Miravel.

Alexia studied the snapshot a long time, telling herself, "All those years are gone. They are both dead. He is smiling at me now."

Softly, the ball of her finger caressed his face, the high cheekbones, the eyes . . . She remembered how he used to swing her up over his dark head and then down, how he had taught her to dance. He had even taught her the Hungarian Csardas. She recalled Garnett saying with amusement, "He doesn't teach that to just anyone."

Strange that her own mother never felt Prince Kuragin's attractions, probably because her own husband, the prince's son, had always resented his father and Garnett was loyal to her beloved Max. Max, who never punished the Nazi snipers for their crime. It was easier to charge a half-witted communist who was nothing but a Nazi decoy.

Alexia had seen the Lichtenbourg tragedy. It was seared on her memory.

She heard her name called, rather impatiently, and

guessed Nick Chance was annoyed that she hadn't heard his knock. She called, "Yes. I heard you. I'm coming."

She took the snapshot into the bedroom and carefully slipped it into a compartment of her handbag. Then she joined Nick.

"Is Grandfather ill again?"

"Not that I know of, but he wants to see us. Both."

At least, her grandfather was aware of her presence.

As she walked along the hall, past what Garnett had always called the "Miravel Rogues' Gallery", she stopped suddenly, shocked by an idea that came to her from nowhere.

Nick looked at her. "What now?"

She shook her head. "I just realized who Count Andross reminds me of a little, not as handsome, of course, and maybe harder features. But there really is a slight – "

"Well, who is this paragon?"

"Nobody you know," she said quickly.

He rapped on Lord Miravel's door. When there was no answer he knocked again and called out, "It's Nick, Your Lordship. With your granddaughter."

Evidently, he had not been heard. Nick opened the door. The room was too hot, a querulous sick person's room. Alexia followed Nick to the bedside. He reached out, taking the sick man's wrist.

Nervously trying to make her voice sound quiet and reassuring, she called, "We came, Sir. You wanted to see us?"

There was no response from the bed. The firelight barely touched on her grandfather's profile. It looked like marble as did those effigies she had seen in the Lichtenbourg Royal Chapel and just as cold. She tried again. "Grandfather?"

Nick laid Lord Miravel's hand on the counterpane. "Don't bother. He is gone."

62

CHAPTER SEVEN

There were people coming and going all day, mostly villagers who still felt an obligation to the Miravels who had been at the heart of the area since the fifteenth century and in a less exalted position even before.

Both Alexia and Dan Royle handled most of the visitors, depending upon a bustling and important Mrs Skinner for the "funeral meats and drink" as she called them, to satisfy the visitors. It was Nick who issued orders, as succinct and emotionless as always. It was difficult for Alexia to discover what he felt, if anything, about the death of the man who was probably his father. At least, he was efficient. No one could have handled things better.

When Alexia mentioned that she had trouble reaching Lichtenbourg by telephone to tell her mother of Lord Miravel's heart attack, Nick took it from her.

"I'll do that. I still have a few strings I can pull in London."

She was grateful. She felt miserable enough, not entirely because of her grandfather's death, but also because the most terrible part of his death was how few people, if any, had loved him. She tried to tell herself she loved him, but the emotion was always pity.

Seeing Nick's cool behaviour she wondered if he realized that his own life might one day come to the same lonely end. Yet, there were infrequent occasions when he surprised her.

He did not motion her away from him when he finally got through to Lichtenbourg. As Alexia might have expected Her Serene Highness, Princess Garnett, was spending a long weekend at Royal House, an attractive little chateau in the mountains overlooking the Austrian Reich, Nazi Czechoslovakia and Hungary, an adjunct of the Rome-Berlin Axis.

The social secretary to Her Serene Highness announced that Nick's name would be recorded with other calls upon the Princess Garnett's valuable time, when she returned.

Showing no outward resentment Nick said, "You need not go so far. Simply leave a message for her to peruse at her leisure. This is Miravel, Shropshire, England calling. Lord David Miravel died this morning between six and six-thirty, British War Time. According to the report of his personal physician and a doctor from Miravel Elder Home, it was a massive heart attack. Funeral service will be conducted at Miravel Church in two days." Before the woman completed her gasp he cut off the connection.

All of Alexia's royal hackles were up. She had heard part of the conversation and was infuriated by the treatment Nick had received when announcing the death of her mother's own father.

Nick asked, "Do you have any of the telephone numbers at Royal House?"

"Certainly." Her eyes must have looked fiery to him. He backed away a step or two and held up his hands, palms out. "I'm innocent. Am I to have one of the numbers?"

"You may have them by all means if you promise not to use them today. If Mother is informed, and I am certain she will be by the Nazi Press if nothing else, let her call you. I don't want to talk to her. If she had cared about her own father she would have been here in my place."

Nick seemed to enjoy all this cut-throat family feeling. "Oh, she's not so bad. I knew her quite well for a year or two when I taught her how to write a letter to her beloved Max."

"Him! He's worse than she is." She would never forget his weak attempt to curry favour with Hitler's hatchet men when Prince Kuragin was assassinated.

She was overheard by Dan who had been in the village arranging the funeral with the new, shy young vicar.

"What's this? Who's Lexy mad at? I can always tell when the old family crest starts turning royal purple."

"It seems the Princess Royal is too busy to take callers," Nick explained.

Dan was shocked. "You mean she still doesn't know? That's going to be rough."

"Don't be silly. She's having too good a time to care." Alexia stalked away to lend Mrs Skinner and the maids a hand with the visitors clustered around the gilt-edged condolence book in the reception hall.

She was still brooding over the cold-blooded Miravels when the two extension phones rang. She went on talking to Viola Tenby, the vicar's wife. The woman looked uneasy. "It might be Buckingham Palace. Or 10 Downing Street. Mr Churchill said publicly that he read His Lordship's books."

"It might also be my mother," Alexia snapped to the dismay of the vicar's wife.

"Oh, but surely – "

Alexia saw Horwich coming to get Dan and wondered if it could be a call from Tige Royle who was currently on government business in North Africa. She excused herself and went to Dan at the phone.

His frank, square-jawed face, dominated by blue eyes that sometimes looked sea-deep, had tightened to a vague frown. "No, sorry. I don't believe I do recall the name. But if you've just returned from the Philippines . . . Yes, of course. I would like to discuss it with . . . Good Lord!

65

I remember the case now. Sheer stupidity on our part somewhere."

He winked at Alexia, putting his palm over the phone. "It's your friend on the train. Count What's-his-name."

Back on the phone he suggested, "Can you get here for the funeral? Lord Miravel, Princess Alexia's grandfather. Yes. It is too bad. But he's been a recluse for a long time . . . In two days. That'll be Thursday. I'm mighty grateful to you for giving me your time."

Stefan Andross would take some of the depression off the next few days. And he had told the truth about helping Dan with his Manila contacts. Alexia was also delighted for her own sake. She need no longer be suspicious of his motives in following her. It had been pure coincidence. He was on his way to Shrewsbury for personal reasons, was caught by the Blitz, and from the shelter to the station it was natural that they should both be going in the same direction.

Gloomy as the prospects of a funeral might be, her spirits were still raised by the tantalizing possibility of seeing Stefan Andross again, this time with her suspicions lulled. Surely, more than lulled. But her entire life and position had shown her that she couldn't take anyone's friendship at face value. Except Dan's and Tige's, of course.

Only one reaction to Count Andross's prospective arrival gave her a prick of doubt, perhaps less doubt than puzzlement, and that was the reaction of Nick Chance to the Count's name. When told that Dan and Alexia would appreciate it if Nick sent the gardener-chauffeur to meet the train from Shrewsbury, he looked thoughtful.

"Stefan Andross. I know that name from somewhere. Are you sure that is the full name?"

"He has a German middle name," Alexia volunteered. "It's Berndt."

66

Nick shook his head. "It will come to me. There is more."

Alexia wondered what that meant but did not pursue the matter. She suspected that Nick was up to his usual trouble-making tricks. He liked to see people worried, it gave him the upper hand.

At dinner that night with the vicar and Mrs Tenby as guests, Dan asked Nick if he remembered where he had run across Count Andross before.

From long acquaintance both Alexia and Dan knew when Nick smiled he was about to spring something unpleasant, but this time, in spite of the smile, Nick said only, "Something to do with the War Office. I'm sure he's well thought of. He is connected with one of the oldest houses in the Almanack de Gotha."

"Well, that settles that. Lexy here thought he was following her across London yesterday."

Nick looked over at Alexia. "So he was pursuing you. It would be interesting to know his motives in making your acquaintance, of all people."

"Of all people," Alexia echoed. What was he driving at?

Dan remarked to the politely interested vicar, "Nick always sounds like the Delphic Oracle, saying one thing, meaning something else."

"It comes from writing so many books," Nick explained.

Mrs Tenby was excited. "Oh, do you write books, Mr Chance? I simply hound the libraries. Would I find any of your books there?"

"Not under my name." Nick glanced at Alexia who was shocked, but it was clear that only she and Dan understood. Already he was stepping into Lord Miravel's boots, and even his mind. No doubt his first action after the will was read would be to insinuate, if not say clearly, that he had done most of the work on David Miravel's celebrated books. Well, why not, if it really was true? But it seemed underhand after Nick's longstanding obsequious behaviour to his patron and employer.

On the morning of the funeral, Miravel's little stone church, half engulfed by crisp red ivy, was crowded with locals as well as the servicemen and some of the staff from Elder Home Hospital.

Just before entering the Miravel family pew between Dan and Nick, Alexia heard one of the boys from the hospital say in perplexity, "You'd think he was Old Winnie, at least. I saw this Lordship once when we were digging up his lawn."

"He was a writer. He wrote about the olden days."

"Oh, one of them bloody bores."

Dan grinned at Alexia. She felt that she should be insulted for her grandfather's sake, but strictly speaking that was Nick's department if, as he hinted, he did much of the writing.

She was still upset over her mother's dismissal of His Lordship's death with a blanket of white hothouse flowers and a card that dripped sentiment: *My Dearest Darling Papa, you will never be gone from my heart.* It was signed, *HSH Princess Garnett Kuragin.*

Everybody was buzzing about the austere beauty of the flowers covering the coffin, but Alexia's resentment left her cold to the elaborate display.

By the candlelit altar the young vicar licked his lips, obviously nervous, and waited for the solemn music of the organ to end. The organ as well as the altar cloth and two stained glass windows were gifts of the Miravel family.

"Buying us a pew in heaven," Garnett had once remarked to Alexia who agreed in some ways.

"Sure cold in here," Dan whispered to Alexia who corrected him.

68

"I call it clammy."

Dan stifled a laugh but squeezed her hand with under-standing. He had always been sympathetic. He was a great one for sharing and sensing other people's problems. Did he feel now her pointless memories of every nice thing Grandfather Miravel had ever done for her? They were not big, important kindnesses but they proved he had been human.

She closed her eyes as the vicar spoke in his nervous way, little bunches of phrases at a time as if he feared he might forget them. Alexia did not think of the great gifts Lord Miravel had bestowed on the village, like the repairs to the railway station and platform, the rebuilt addition to the old Elder Home, his many charities, most of them given in his name by Nick Chance. She thought instead of something her mother had told her about her childhood. Young Garnett had been walking in the woods with her father when they almost fell into a fox's den. They saw the babies and the huge-eyed mother, wild with fear for them, waiting for the gunshot.

Garnett said she had asked her father not to harm them, to leave them and see that no one else harmed them. He had done so. Garnett never forgot it and now Alexia would never forget it. Such a little thing, but it illuminated some streak of kindness that did not involve his own self-centred concerns.

The organ roared out again, masking any noise from the entrance double doors but a shaft of light came and went. Alexia was nudged by Dan and looked around. She saw the tall figure of Count Andross slip into one of the pews in the back row. Several people eyed him curiously, especially the females. Alexia felt a bit proprietorial and resented them, asking herself a minute later, "Is it possible I am jealous? I scarcely know him."

She knew it was selfish and not very Christian of her to wish the ceremony would end when it was clear that the majority of the parishioners were enjoying the luxury of this solemn occasion.

When it all came to its equally sombre close, with prayers, music and testimony to David Miravel's goodness all completed, Dan muttered, "Amen to that," and took Alexia's arm.

On the steps of the church the Reverend Tenby received the thanks and praise of his parish with a pleasure that lighted his gaunt young face.

Nick told him the burial would take place in two hours. Except for the visitors from London who stood out in their elegantly tailored, pre-war black serge, the rest of the parish wandered into the village to kill time for two hours. They did not intend to pass up the usual alcohol and sweet cake pleasures of an important village burial, much of these being rationed.

Count Andross waited until the crowd around the Miravel party was drifting away before he came across the pebbled road to introduce himself. Ignoring Dr Tredegar and his daughter who had made themselves very much of the party, Dan shook the Count's hand in excellent humour, remarking, "I can certainly use any information you have about the Philippines and General MacArthur. Believe me, I'm most grateful."

Nick took the Count's hand on being introduced by Alexia. He was nothing if not friendly. "So this is the gentleman who is going to assist you, Dan. Count Stefan Andross, Your Highness said?" Alexia nodded, wondering what Nick was up to. He went on with the same friendly curiosity, "Andross . . . Now, why do I keep thinking there is more to your name, Sir? Have we met before? Perhaps in the War Office some years ago?"

Count Andross smiled. "I think not. I am accredited from Sweden. I was adopted when my mother remarried."

"Rather like my boy here," Nick said to Dan's surprise. "Fortunately, Dan preferred to become Tiger Royle's son. Can't say I blame him. I don't seem to have what his Yankee friends call 'the knack' with children."

Watching the Count, Alexia thought the muscles of his dark face tightened a little. He didn't like this talk about his name. She wondered why.

There were moments during the next two hours when Alexia felt more alive, more female than she had ever felt. It was impossible not to credit this marvellous, sexually tingling sensation to the presence of Stefan Andross in her life.

Knowing she would spend a long time in the wintry graveyard beside the church, Alexia had planned to wear a neat, maroon wool dress from Elizabeth Hawes. It was great for cool, dressy San Francisco, but it hadn't been quite suited to the saddle shoes and pleated skirt gang at Cal. Nor did it seem dressy enough to catch the eye of Stefan Andross. She reached into the ancient clothes press that had once belonged to her grandmother. Lady Alix would never have worn the maroon wool to meet Prince Kuragin.

But how about the black crepe Chanel with the grass-green top? She had worn it on several occasions, always happy times. It was her lucky dress. Not warm enough for the air of the ancient churchyard but the old mink jacket would serve, casually thrown over her shoulders. It had been a Christmas present from her father three years ago and the "gang" at Cal definitely looked down on it.

"You ever hear we're just coming out of a depression?" was the least of the cracks. So it was back to her cloth coats and ever-popular sweaters while she went to Cal. But she doubted if Count Andross was so conscious of the world's economy.

Evidently not. When she joined the four men, including the ubiquitous Dr Tredegar, who looked just a bit under the weather, she was received with flattering attention, but she especially noticed Stefan Andross. While Dan whistled Andross picked up her hand and saluted it with a kiss. During the time he looked into her eyes he said an odd thing: "How you have – " She could have sworn he was about to say "changed" but he seemed to cut off the word and corrected himself. "How you have grown!"

"From what?" she teased, enjoying the flirtation.

Nick repeated casually, "Grown from what, Count?"

Andross got out of this with no effort. "From the child I saw in *Life* magazine some time ago. You are now truly the Crown Princess of Lichtenbourg. Your country will be proud of you. By the way, how do you intend to return to Lichtenbourg?"

She confessed, "I don't actually know. If I can't get signed on an American plane Dan and I will have to pull some strings at a neutral legation. There aren't many neutrals left."

Count Andross examined her hand. He seemed to find it interesting but he let it go and she lost the warmth of his strong fingers. He looked at her blandly. "There is always Sweden. You have an acquaintance there."

Dan put in, "Sounds like the ideal solution. We'll talk about that after the funeral."

Mrs Skinner was busier than anyone else. There would be a good deal of standing around receiving the condolences of villagers who couldn't remember a time when there wasn't a Lord Miravel at the great hall. She persuaded the family and their guests to "take a bit of a luncheon".

Alexia, who dreaded the burial, had no appetite but

Dan, in his brotherly way, rustled her into the small salon where, surprisingly, delicious tea plus a mixture of watercress and cucumber sandwiches, obtained heaven knew where, took first honours from the atrocious coffee.

Dan asked, "Is it just the way they make it or is this actually ground up weeds?"

Count Andross, who had wisely stuck to the tea, overheard this and was amused. "No offence, my friend, but I have the same problem with American tea in some quarters." He was watching Alexia.

Dan backed away from the tea cart and nudged Alexia. "You've collected a new boyfriend since you left San Francisco. How are your language courses? Bet you never studied Swedish."

"I may start. Never too late, you know."

He took his sandwich over to the long windows that looked out on the still unpaved area between the hall and what had once been the stables but was now the garage. She followed him, wondering if he had something to say about Count Andross.

He had. "Would you believe it, Lexy? Old Stefan was sent over to the Philippines to straighten out some mess that the US and Sweden had got into, mostly my country. They got an order for planes from Sweden and had all navigational and directional stuff done in Swedish. Then, by mistake, I suppose, they sent them to the Far East."

She was very pleased with how this built up the count in international eyes. "Then, Count Andross is a hero. He went over and translated everything."

"Well, in a way. I guess you could say that. He's not a bad fellow. Sure likes you."

"That doesn't hurt my feelings."

"So it's like that, is it?" He glanced toward the tea cart. "What do you make of little Rosebud? I heard Nick call her that. Not bad looking, but I get the feeling that, well, none of my business."

There was no doubt of Rose Tredegar's interest in Nick. She was forever fawning over him which was understandable. He was an attractive man, ageless and still slender without showing any signs of weakness. He gave an impression of dominance without the height or aristocratic manner that impressed her with some others she had known, like Prince Kuragin.

That suggested Count Andross. He might have been a prince. It was almost surprising to discover he had no regal powers. If, of course, he was who he said he was.

Nick would never have that quality. Whatever he achieved would be silent and unsuspected. Years ago he had almost ruined the life of her godmother, Laura Royle, by leading her to suspect the worst of the man she loved. Nick had reasons. He always had reasons.

But now, with Miravel virtually in his hands, he could stop the sly little pranks, stop hiding secrets and playing one member of the family against the other. He certainly would see through the Tredegars' interest in him. His cool, unreadable face had its own charms for some women, not one as obvious as Rose Tredegar. Watching him, Alexia had one unpleasant thought: what was it about the Count's interest in Alexia that amused him? Was she the next person on whom he would play his tricks? She shivered and went back to the gold-rimmed glass tea cart where Horwich re-filled her cup. Where he got the lemon slice from she couldn't even imagine.

Sooner or later the summons had to come and it was sooner. Dan turned to help Alexia with her jacket but Count Andross got there first. She appreciated the unexpected gentleness in his eyes as his hands drew her jacket collar up around her neck. "It will be over, you know. These things can't go on for ever."

"I know. I don't miss him enough. That is the sad part."

"It often is. More often than we think." He looked beyond her toward the long window where the steel-grey signs of winter clouded the sky. Then he added, to her surprise, "It is the way with my mother. Her sole interest in life seemed to be dynastic. It still is. I might have been a better man without her use of the cattle prod of ambition on me."

She teased him, "I'm quite sure they don't talk about cattle prods in Sweden."

He smiled and played with her collar until it stood up around her throat and cheeks to suit him. "There. That ought to keep you warm . . . As for cattle prods, I assure you, we are very much a dairy country. Then, too, my mother is Swedish only by virtue of her second marriage. I think they are signalling to us."

They were. Dan started towards them, seeing the Tredegars about to leave with Nick. They appeared to be guarding him, one on each side. As for Nick, he hardly seemed aware of them. His pale eyes were fixed on something beyond, perhaps the great staircase and the bedchamber of the man who might be the next Lord Miravel if justice was served.

Just as Count Andross said of his mother and himself, Alexia thought, ambition consumed him. It seemed a strange and terrible life. Alexia had her own ambitions in life, but she hoped they were not as all-consuming. Since childhood she had resented her own father because he did not avenge Prince Kuragin. But surely he suffered every day for that and other weaknesses. He was miserable and apologetic with the family when he wasn't angry in self-defence. Life had punished the dashing young Prince Max for the ambition, the hope to reach something which was beyond his ability.

I'll be different, she thought. I'm not that ambitious. I only want to run the country as it should be run.

It sounded simple, but at least she knew her own conceit in even thinking such pompous thoughts.

Dan drove Alexia and Count Andross to the village in the car he had borrowed from a politician in London and was there minutes before Nick and the Tredegars. It seemed fairly obvious that the crowd waiting around the gates to the churchyard or a few more following the Reverend Tenby and his wife out of the church had their eyes on the approach of Nick Chance. Word had already spread that the man most of them disliked for his lack of camaraderie with the villagers would soon be the owner of Miravel and, in some magic way, also Lord Miravel.

"The news travels like radar," Dan remarked, not without humour.

Count Andross looked from Dan to Alexia. "Are you sorry? Will he be a bad landlord, so to speak?"

"He'll be very good, I'm sure," Alexia said firmly. She did not doubt it.

Some of the villagers seemed a little in awe of her, merely because of her position at Lichtenbourg. It went with guards, escorts and, when her visits were official, with newspapers and the Society pages.

During her semesters at the University of California at Berkeley, she had almost gotten used to being insulted for her clothes or slapped on the back, or drenched by a bucket of water in some fraternity fracas. Few people addressed her by her title except at some of Tige's parties in San Francisco. She learned rapidly to answer when someone called "Lexy".

She was still "Miss Alexia" in Miravel. She walked across the ground which was sunken in places, especially where the tombstones were very old, while Dan and the Count strolled behind her, more clever than she at avoiding three-hundred-year-old graves.

She mentally begged pardon of the quiet dead. Some of them were from the Great War of 1914 – 18, and a group of the Spanish Influenza victims of 1918 – 19, then others through the years to those of the present war, in fresh graves, since 1939.

Finally, she reached the big Miravel plot, shaded by overhanging branches of poplar trees that bordered the churchyard. Their leaves scattered in the chill air, forming a carpet for the grave beneath the headstone of one ALEXANDRA ROYLE MIRAVEL, LADY MIRAVEL, BELOVED WIFE, *LET ME SLEEP BESIDE YOU.* Remembering the legend of her grandmother's great love for Prince Kuragin, Alexia wondered how poor Grandmother Alix liked the idea of having someone, even her husband, lying beside her, his "beloved wife", when she would certainly have preferred to share a grave with Prince Franz Kuragin.

The prince's grave had none of the personal feeling that this one held for Alexia, guessing the secret story. The prince had been put to rest where Lichtenbourgers could come and leave flowers on his birthday, or the anniversary of his assassination. It was a great tomb in Lichtenbourg Cathedral, cold and dark, like most cathedrals, in Alexia's eyes. But his true grave was the big monument, a statue of Franz Feodor Kuragin in uniform from peaked cap to dusty boots, exactly on the spot where the bullet had reached him, only a few feet away from Alexia herself, a child of five.

Every month when she was in Lichtenbourg Alexia brought flowers to lay at his feet. There were always a few other flowers, even in winter, usually wild flowers, peasant gifts from the people who loved him and would never forget him. But she felt that he would have preferred to be buried here in Miravel beside his Alix, exactly where her husband, Lord David Miravel, was to be buried today. The grave yawned like a great mouth waiting for David Miravel. She felt Count Andross's hand on her shoulder and looked up.

"You are young. You must be happy," he told her, which seemed an odd thing to say at a funeral, but maybe he was right. Besides, she felt like a hypocrite, with people watching her and thinking the tears in her eyes were for her grandfather.

She started to deny, as if this were a small disgrace at the funeral of one's own grandfather. She said, "But I'm not – " then broke off. Unless he knew the whole story, which even Alexia did not know, she couldn't betray the family's secret scandals to a comparative stranger. Not even one on whom, she told herself, she had a gigantic crush.

The pallbearers were Nick, Dan, Sims, the muscular owner of Miller's Pub, and stout old General MacLiggan, the Miravel neighbour across the canal. Two other strong men had volunteered, having been acquainted with the Miravels since time out of mind. One was a merchant from over the Welsh Border, the other a local sheep farmer.

The vicar said a sympathetic word or two about how that great humanitarian, Lord David Miravel, had gone to his reward. He would now be reunited with Lady Alexandra.

An old lady, formerly living at Elder Home, stopped by Alexia to praise the dead Lady Miravel. She was one of the penniless widows and single ladies removed from Elder Home to the Miravel Woollen Mill during the present emergency.

"Her that lies there, Yer Highness, she was one angel."

Another ageless old lady in the rusty black of a former age put in, "That she was, Ma'am. Saw to it we was proper used for knitting collars and necklets and sweaters and such like, and her father, Mr Tiger Royle, he got 'em sold overseas."

The first lady boasted, "Give us a prideful feeling, so it did. We won't be asking for no financial assistance later, neither, Ma'am."

Alexia appreciated this and meant to speak to Nick about it. Perhaps if she appealed to his pride as a generous patron, admired by all the village, it would help.

She closed her ears to the hideous, thumping sound of dirt shovelled onto her grandfather's rich and heavy coffin, but the sight remained. Dan whispered, "You needn't stay. It will take time and you do look peaked."

She hesitated. She wanted to do what was right, but no doubt about it, she was deeply depressed by all these steps beyond death. She half-expected Count Andross to give some easy, meaningless denial and was surprised when he agreed.

"You are freezing, Your Highness. It is time you were getting away from this cold." He began to shed his heavily lined trenchcoat for her but she waved the gesture aside. She didn't like to make a scene. For one thing, everyone was looking at her.

She waited until several people on the outside of the crowd began to drift off into the vicar's neat lodgings beyond the church. She understood them perfectly. She, too, would enjoy something warm inside as well as outside.

She nodded to Dan and the three of them moved away from the coffin as unobtrusively as possible. Not unobtrusively enough to avoid Nick Chance's cynical grey eyes, however.

Inside the vicarage Mrs Tenby was already pouring tea to the ladies and what she called, "A Hot Rum Fustian for the gentlemen. Something my grandmother taught me. For emergencies, of course."

"Of course, Mrs Tenby," several of the ex-Elder Home ladies agreed, accepting not tea but Hot Rum Fustian. The hot mugs put the ladies in good spirits and they, along with a half-dozen other good church folk crowded around the heavy laden old buffet, its scratches covered by crocheted runners from the Elder ladies.

The Tenbys, perhaps subsidized by Nick Chance, had kindly provided sandwiches, cakes, puddings and the ever-present soup for the poor. There were those who had enjoyed a wee dram too much of the Rum Fustian and pronounced the burial service of David Miravel a great success.

Dan got in the spirit of the occasion at once. "Kind of sums up old David, I'd say. Anyway, it livens up the day."

"Good heavens!" Alexia reminded him trying, like Andross, to stifle her smile but not entirely successfully. "You get to sounding more like Tige every day."

"I hope that's meant as a compliment."

"Hush! They're coming."

Count Andross murmured in his low voice, "I should think your grandfather would have enjoyed being told his burial was a great success. I think I'll have that carved as my epitaph."

She laughed, accusing him of being as bad as Dan, but her laugh was cut off abruptly as Nick and the vicar entered the room.

The Reverend Tenby was in the midst of apologizing about something. "I'm most grateful that you understand, Mr Chance. I would never have rushed the matter but for the red tape in London. Why they must have a personal, word-of-mouth report, I cannot fathom."

"I understand perfectly, Sir. Say no more. This evening as soon as we reach home will be quite satisfactory."

Mrs Tenby put aside the tea and hurried to add her

explanation. "Jonathan is to drive to London with his parish records this very night. The interview is scheduled for tomorrow at ten."

"It is perplexing," the vicar added. "The young men at the hospital are usually on the way to recovery. Why London must know the details of our few burials, I cannot imagine. I should think my word and the evidence of my records sent to them should have been enough."

"Sounds exciting to me," Dan put in unasked. "Maybe they suspect some hanky-panky going on here. Somebody get Agatha Christie, quick."

While Alexia assured the distressed vicar that Dan was only joking, she stepped hard on Dan's toe. He winced but was silenced.

Dr Tredegar cleared his throat, volunteering to drive anyone to Miravel. His daughter chimed in. "Oh, yes. By all means. Mr Nick? Are you – "

Alexia turned to Nick. "If you and the vicar have an appointment the rest of us can go home in Dan's car."

Nick's eyebrows raised. "Ah. Home."

He did not stress it but Alexia knew he was insinuating that her possessiveness was out of order. After all, it was no longer her family's home. She reddened at his reminder and asked Dan, "Shall we leave? Whatever the business of the others, it is no concern of ours."

"Sure. That includes you, Count, doesn't it? We'll get in a little talk about the Philippines. I can sure use a first hand report. I don't trust some of those guys in San Francisco. Most of them have never been out beyond the Farallones."

They gave their thanks to the Tenbys and Alexia and Dan said goodbye to the villagers who had known them when Dan was a boy living at Miravel as a quasi-servant and stepson to Nick Chance.

As they were leaving Nick called after them, "The

81

Reverend Tenby is going to discuss the terms of Lord Miravel's will which is in his charge. I'm sure he would have no objection to your presence, Alexia, and yours, Dan. We will meet as soon as possible in the blue salon off the reception hall. If that is agreeable to the Reverend and Mrs Tenby."

The vicar rushed to agree. "Very much so, Sir. Thank you for your kindness in the matter."

"Perhaps my housekeeper will see that a substantial tea is laid on at the same time." Nick shook hands with the Tenbys, bowed to everyone else, and left the warm, comfortable old room.

"The Americans have an expression for my position," Count Andross said. "I will make myself scarce. I wonder if I might look over Lord Miravel's library. I am sure I would find it interesting."

"I wish I could join you." Alexia realized how that sounded and went on quickly. "I've seen too many movies about the reading of wills."

Dan clawed his hands and reached for her with a horrible leer. "It's midnight and the secret panel opens. The princess – "

"Heiress."

"I stand corrected. The heiress screams . . . But frankly, I'd rather join Stefan here than listen to Nick preening himself under that mumbo-jumbo. Why can't they just tell him it's his and let it go at that? I'm sure no one has tried harder to get it."

CHAPTER EIGHT

By the time Dan's borrowed London sedan jolted and roared into the Miravel garage Alexia felt that his driving needed a word or two of explanation, if not apology.

"I'm afraid he's been around Tige too long. It seems to have rubbed off on him."

Stefan Andross pretended surprise. "What? You mean Tige Royle actually dawdles along like that? I would have pictured him entering the Indianapolis races."

Dan was delighted. "Hear that, Lexy? That ought to put you in your place. Me, a bad driver? I'll have you know I was the safest driver in my senior class."

Alexia rolled her eyes but Stefan Andross was laughing. "You would be a novice, my boy, in Sweden. And God forbid that you should be turned loose upon a French highway. You would be a helpless infant."

"You're on, Stefan. I'll lay you a bet. Good Lord! It's beginning to rain. Poor Lexy is going to be soaked. I won't race you to the house. Your legs are too long."

Nevertheless, the three of them established a record of sorts getting over to the hall where they came in through the small salon and were welcomed by Horwich at his pompous best.

"Your Serene Highness is expected in the blue parlour at your earliest convenience and I believe Mr Royle is also awaited."

Touched to the quick Dan protested, "That Tredegar outfit couldn't have gotten here first. What did they do, fly?"

"I am not familiar with their mode of transportation, Sir, but I have been told to remind you that time is of the essence."

"Can't wait to get his hands on the property," Dan muttered and was rewarded by an understanding nod from Horwich.

A little later, having settled Count Andross in the late Lord Miravel's crowded, dusty library on the top floor next to his study, Alexia and Dan made themselves presentable and walked along the formal reception hall toward the blue parlour where voices reached them before they entered.

Miss Tredegar was saying, "It is the most thrilling thing, and absolutely fair. No one has worked harder than Mr Nick."

"Cute little thing," Dan whispered.

Alexia thought he was joking but it seemed from his expression that he wasn't. There must be some charms about Nick's innocent little Rosebud that escaped her. Am I jealous of this sweet little Rosebud? she wondered.

As Dan and Alexia entered the vicar cleared his throat and gave his wife a quick look. Alexia wondered what there was about Rose Tredegar's remark that disturbed him.

Nick was straddling the corner of a heavy Victorian credenza not far from the Reverend Tenby. The latter, probably at Nick's suggestion, had taken the straight-backed arm chair at the mahogany desk. Of the others present, the Tredegars sat on the edge of the divan and Mrs Tenby, equally anxious, leaned forward from a severe looking ladder-back chair.

Seeing Alexia as she came in with Dan, Nick swung off the corner of the credenza and came to meet her. Nick said, "May I borrow Her Highness?"

She and Dan were both surprised but she said, "Certainly." Dan, frowning and as puzzled as she was, went into the room alone.

Nick looked around. "What have you done with our princely Count?"

She was caught completely by surprise. "He is a count, not a prince, and he wanted to see my grandfather's books. There can't be any harm in that."

"No. Far from it. What do you know about him?"

So that was how the land lay. He was trying to put down Count Andross in some way. "I know he is accredited by the Swedish and American governments. He was sent to the Far East to mend a mistake in the sale of B-52s from America to Sweden. Isn't that enough?"

Someone coughed in the doorway of the blue parlour. Nick waved back Dr Tredegar. "In a minute."

"I think we had better postpone this interesting revelation – " She added, something shocking no doubt, "Until after this red tape is over."

He began to interrupt her but she ended firmly, "We all know what Grandfather intended. He told Mother. He wanted her to understand; so you needn't worry about your inheritance, or make up something nasty to upset the rest of us."

"I didn't intend to." He glanced towards the blue parlour. "I must talk to you later. It is important that you should know before you let yourself get more involved."

She said innocently, "Of course."

He was so obvious. She would make quite sure to avoid all this "secret knowledge", apparently concocted to ruin her friendship with Stefan Andross.

He returned to his rather precarious seat on the corner

of the credenza while Dan got up and moved a chair closer to his.

The Reverend Tenby, seeing them all eyeing him expectantly, cleared his throat, a sheaf of blue-backed papers rattling in his hands. "I deeply regret the necessity for this legal matter to be rushed on the unhappy day of Lord Miravel's last rites but – "

"Yes, yes," Dr Tredegar burst in, his fleshy face reddening with his impatience. "We understand. You may get on."

The vicar might have been shy but he was persistent. " – But I explained and Mr Chance very kindly gave me permission to attend to the matter at once. With his kind permission I proceed." Nick had been examining his fingernails intently. At this, he looked up and nodded.

The vicar, still rattling the papers nervously, began in a doom-laden voice:

I, Arthur David Guwaine, Lord Miravel of Miravel Hall, of this shire, do, on this first day of September, 1941, make this, my last will and testament, being fully possessed of my faculties and intending to right any wrongs I may have unintentionally committed:

Being the last of the males of my ancient family –

Without looking his way, Alexia felt Nick Chance's body stiffen. The vicar cleared his throat once more. It seemed to be a nervous gesture rather than a medical problem.

I do, therefore, bequeath the full estate and Hall of Miravel to my beloved daughter, Her Serene Highness, Garnett Phoebe Alexandra Miravel, Princess Kuragin.

Alexia heard a collective gasp at what she and the others

felt was an injustice, considering her grandfather's earlier insinuations that Nick would inherit the estate. Only Nick made no sound. The Reverend Tenby went on in a voice that shook slightly.

I had feared that the devotion of my only child and dearest relation might have drifted away, even that her love for me was based solely on an acquisitive desire to inherit Miravel. I therefore tested her in the cruellest way, telling her I was leaving my estate elsewhere. Her response was as loving as ever. I knew then that I was not mistaken in her devotion to me. It was as strong as ever. I can only reward this devotion as I have testified above.

I make one proviso: that she will give my faithful employee, known as Nick Chance, the position of estate manager for as long a period as he chooses, this to include the equal division of all profits made on the estate between mistress and servant.

Nick Chance is also to receive my entire library and, as a token of my appreciation for his long service and loyalty, my gold Masonic ring with the two-carat diamond.

As my dear child, Garnett, received her mother's and grandmother's jewels, especially the Miravel pearl and diamond parure, at her marriage, I leave my diamond cufflinks and tie-pin to my devoted granddaughter, Princess Ava Alexandra Kuragin with the full understanding that she will have the diamonds removed and made into a ring in memory of her loving grandfather. It is my understanding that the Miravel and Kuragin Jewels will descend to my granddaughter, HSH Ava Alexandra, upon the future demise of her mother, HSH Princess Garnett.

I feel confident, knowing my beloved daughter's

generosity, that Princess Garnett will see to it that out of the finances remaining in my estate in government securities and otherwise, at the time of my death, certain faithful friends and estate employees will each receive one thousand pounds sterling, according to the following list:

The vicar looked up. "At the top of the list is the name of Mr Nick Chance."

Everyone was looking at Nick, Alexia with shock and disgust at her grandfather's cruel manoeuvring, Dan muttering, "Good God, how typical!" and the Tredegars clearly horrified.

The vicar coughed again for their attention and continued. "Following Mr Chance, His Lordship bequeaths the sum of one thousand pounds to, and I quote: 'To a child who has been devotion itself to me in the past few months. I refer to Miss Rose Tredegar.'"

Alexia watched the Tredegars, cynically amused at their abrupt change from horror to self-satisfaction. The daughter glanced at her father, exchanging with him the merest hint of a smile.

Only Nick remained outwardly unshaken. He told the vicar gently, "It was a very generous will, and I am particularly grateful for my own thousand pounds, I assure you. There is so much to be done about the estate and the village once the war is over. The hospital, the Elder Home to be refurbished for those unfortunate widows and spinsters who have been without a permanent home during the war . . . Well, one can't do everything with one thousand pounds. But one can try."

The vicar bowed to him. "Most generous of *you*, if I may say so, to devote your inheritance to the betterment of Miravel. Very Christian, Sir."

Nick's pale features were perfectly composed. "I try

to be, Sir. Now, I do think all of us, but especially the Reverend Tenby, deserve one of Mrs Skinner's genuine high teas."

Alexia turned to Nick. "You won't lose by it. I'll see that my mother and I do our share." But she knew even as she spoke that he would despise her for what seemed like a sycophantic effort to soften his blow.

However, all the small movements and inane chatter attendant on a high tea involving virtual strangers would, at the very least, cloak the shock of the witnesses and the humiliation of Nick Chance. He completely ignored her remark to him. Nor could she blame him.

Mrs Skinner did herself and Miravel Hall proud with her delicious concoctions, not to mention several varieties of teas unknown to Alexia who had long been used to Californian coffees and that state's celebrated wines.

She could not again commiserate with Nick on the injustice her grandfather, perhaps his own father, had shown him, because she was sure he would think she was two-faced and secretly gloating over her family's windfall. She could only try and make her mother see that something more was due to Nick. It might be difficult.

Garnett Kuragin was famous for her generosity, but it was the generosity of a woman who gladly gave away what she herself no longer wanted. It would take some devious reasoning to persuade Garnett that she didn't need the Miravel estate, or at least its yearly income. She always needed money. Her personal budget was somehow always exceeded by her expenses.

When she believed she would not receive her father's estate because she was so well provided for at Lichtenbourg, she agreed she could get along without this added windfall. But the minute she heard about the will her budget would shoot ahead to eat up the windfall. She would point out with her piquant charm: "You don't understand, sweetheart. I simply must have the Miravel income. You wouldn't like to see your doddering old mama in a debtor's prison, now, would you?" It was the kind of question to which there was no answer, and it was Garnett at her most impossibly logical.

Dan had sent the young under-age footman to include Count Andross in their tea. Alexia wondered if Nick would have neglected the invitation entirely. Andross came down carrying a book on Lichtenbourg's pre-Christian era which he had found in Lord Miravel's library. It was one of those apparently written by David Miravel himself, based on notes taken during an early visit to the minuscule country presently ruled by the Kuragins.

The Count pronounced it, "Fascinating. The writing is vivid and alive, beautifully done. I wonder if I may borrow it for a few days. I should be finished before I leave Britain."

The Tredegars looked bored at this interruption, the Tenbys mildly curious. But Alexia saw the faint colour come into Nick's stony features and she guessed the truth.

"Count, I think you may congratulate the real author of that book, if you would like to."

"Very much." Andross looked down at the author's name in gold on the spine and then at Alexia. He was obviously puzzled. She nodded towards Nick. The Count followed the gesture to Nick who moistened his lips and managed a casual shrug. He was not about to be appeased by such a tiny gift from Alexia, one of the enemy.

"I edited here and there."

Alexia said, "It's been said in my presence, by witnesses who should know, that many of my grandfather's books were actually written, for the most part, by Nick Chance."

The Count held out his free hand. "Let me congratulate

you, Sir. I think it is time the scholastic community knew of your contribution."

Nick hesitated before taking the hand Andross offered. He took it finally. It was a curious reticence. What on earth did he have against Count Andross who had given him such a high compliment?

"Her Serene Highness exaggerates," he told the Count. "In the circumstances it would hardly do His Lordship's reputation or mine any good if I made such a claim against my own – " He paused just long enough for Alexia to guess the unspoken word was "father". He amended easily, "My employer."

The Tredegars exchanged startled glances. They must have heard the gossip. Maybe they hadn't believed it. The Tenbys seemed to have missed Nick's little slip entirely, if it was a slip. They busied themselves with helping Andross to the little sandwiches and some of Mrs Skinner's miniature vegetables, a small feast, considering the tight war rationing.

The vicar remarked to Andross, a bit obsequiously, "We have perused the late Lord Miravel's will and Mr Chance is very kindly remembered. We are all congratulating him."

Everyone looked at Nick whose tight, cold smile was very much present. "Yes. I am overwhelmed. It was totally unexpected. Such a fine man, so deeply conscious of what he owes to those of his blood. A true family man. But Her Serene Highness is not eating. Has our Mrs Skinner failed us at last? We will have to replace her with someone younger, more in tune with our world, like Rose Tredegar, here."

Alexia flexed her fingers to keep from showing that he had angered her. She laughed. "Oh, I think not. Mrs Skinner has been so very loyal, and always efficient."

"There!" Nick slapped the credenza so hard everyone

91

jumped. "I had forgotten already. The Kuragins now give orders at Miravel. I apologize with all my heart, Your Highness."

Not that title again. But she understood. It was his little needle prick of revenge against her family. She just happened to be the handiest "enemy". Her mother would never understand and never recognize the wrong that had been done to Nick Chance who was, very probably, Garnett's own half-brother.

Luckily, this volcanic seething beneath the surface was brought to an end by the Reverend and Mrs Tenby who got up with apologies to all present. "I do beg pardon, Your Highness, and yours, Count Andross, but as I explained to our good and generous patron, Mr Chance, we must be on our way." The Reverend Tenby hid an embarrassed laugh with a cough. "I am afraid His Majesty's Government, in its inscrutable way, has decreed that I report to them with local War Dead records tomorrow at ten in the morning."

The Tredegars awkwardly followed suit, shaking hands with Nick, the doctor adding a deep sigh.

Alexia was afraid now that no matter what she did she would offend Nick, so she merely stood up, shook hands with the Tenbys, and then went to the doorway to wave as they hurried out the front door at the end of the reception hall. The Tredegars went along after them, stopping momentarily to, "Wish Mr Chance well," as they put it.

Dan stood close behind Alexia, speaking softly. "What do you think of this will business?"

"I'm asking myself questions. Did Grandfather intend this rotten thing from the first? Imagine calling Mother and telling her he owed it to Nick who had thrown his life into Miravel."

"Probably what he says in the will. He was testing his darling little daughter."

"But he deliberately let Nick think he was the heir."

"Bribery."

She stared at him. "Good heavens, why? Was he afraid of Nick?"

"Not physically, and not for any secret Nick might be holding, like a typical blackmailer. In some ways, I think it was worse. When I lived with Nick and my mother it was plain to us that, besides managing the estate, Nick was doing most of the work on his damned books. If Nick left him, where would he be?"

"Then it was true, what I suspect?"

"Oh certainly. I don't doubt it for a minute. Don't forget, I used to see those hundreds of pages Nick turned out in his spare time."

"How rotten! Mother is going to have to make good on what her father did. She simply can't get away with this, nor can I. One of the things Father will remind me of is that I'm cutting off a part of my own inheritance if we reimburse Nick in some way."

Dan seemed amused at her words. "I like what you say, Honey, but it's young. You may change your mind as the years go by."

"Not if I push it through when I return home."

"And that will be my object," Count Andross said behind them. "Getting Her Highness safely home, I mean. But if Mr Chance wrote some of the work for which your grandfather received credit, I agree that the world should know about it. Though I don't imagine that would sit very well with Prince Maximilian and the Princess."

Dan gave him an odd look. Alexia wondered what suspicions were running through his mind. "Do you know Lichtenbourg's royal family?"

The Count relieved Alexia by his mild answer. "I only hope they are as generous as their daughter, but they are parents first, and I am sure no parent wants to deprive his child of an estate like Miravel. Or even its yearly income."

"Then you don't know the prince and princess?" Nick Chance put in. He had come upon them so silently in the doorway of the blue parlour that Alexia shivered at his unexpected nearness.

Count Andross seemed totally at ease. "I'm sorry to say I haven't had that pleasure. Perhaps one day in the future. But I am intruding. I wonder if one of your people could drive me in to the village. Tomorrow Mr Royle and Her Highness can discuss Her Highness's return to Lichtenbourg with me."

Before Dan or Alexia could suggest that he remain at Miravel Nick insisted, "It is all arranged, Sir. You must make your stay with us. Perhaps Dan can show you to the Wales suite. King Edward stayed there when he was still the Prince of Wales."

"You'll be impressed," Dan promised the Count who was shaking hands with Nick. "It's full of valuable junk."

While Alexia watched the Count kiss her hand she cried, "Dan, for heaven's sake!" But to the Count's amusement Dan refused to recant.

"Junk I said, and junk it is. All that Victorian bric-a-brac." He took the Count's arm and they went off to the great staircase, the Count assuring Dan:

"Whatever you call junk cannot compare with the Gripsholm Palace in my country. An accumulation of the ages, I call it."

Alexia started after them to her own room but stopped and looked back. Nick was still watching her. Then she remembered. "You said there was something very important you wanted to tell me. Something about Count Andross. Well, now is your chance."

He looked perplexed as if in deep thought. Finally he

94

shrugged. "It's gone right out of my head. Can't be very important, or I'd have remembered it."

She didn't argue the point, but she didn't believe him for a minute. Why wouldn't he tell her whatever his secret was about Stefan Andross? One reason occurred to her: whatever he knew was bad, and he had decided not to warn her.

What an absurdity! Was she seeing melodrama in everything?

PART TWO

Lichtenbourg

CHAPTER NINE

Less than a day after the funeral, much to almost everyone's relief, Dan and Alexia both received their marching
orders.

Dan got his news first, a telephone call from London
telling him in the best Oxonian mumble that, "The object
he had bid for at the auction would be his if he arrived this
afternoon at eighteen hundred hours in the Field Office."

Dan's eyes shone. "Field Office. Code stuff. We can just
make it to London, Honey, if we miss the damned Biltz.
There's a lot of fog. That's a blessing. You and old Stef
will high-tail it to Lichtenbourg as soon as Stef can make
it, with me off to the Philippines as soon as we can take
off. I hate to eat and run as the saying goes, but this must
be Tige's doing. He's back in Lisbon."

Much as she wanted to leave Miravel at this particular
time, Alexia felt bereft of her dearest companion. "Oh, but
you're going so far. Two oceans."

He clasped her shoulders, shaking her in a friendly way.
"Honey, don't look like it was the end of the world. I'll
be back from Manila before you know it. Maybe I can
get permission to interview old sacred Hirohito in Tokyo
before I come home. He ought to be glad of some good
publicity for a change."

"Just get back home before the first of the year. They are
all predicting war with Japan by the spring of '42. That's
painfully close."

99

"Don't be silly. I'm going to be celebrating Christmas in California. That's less than a month away. I only wish that hidebound family of yours would let you come over for New Year's Eve in San Francisco. Remember the time we all had last year with Tige and your godparents, Chris and Laura, up from Hollywood? That was fun!"

She thought, just now, New Year in San Francisco would be next to impossible. Once she was trapped in Lichtenbourg escape looked pretty bleak. She would be surrounded by Axis countries and people like Father's chancellor, Janos Becque, that smiling, evil little man who bowed and scraped and saluted when he mentioned that other chancellor, Adolf Hitler.

Alexia could never forget Janos Becque's suggestion three years ago at the banquet for Alexia's fifteenth birthday. "I will marry this little lady. That should keep her safe from the decadence of the West. And think how pleased our neighbour, the Fuhrer, would be."

"I'm thinking," Prince Max said drily. Alexia didn't know whether he would yield to such an idea or not. Lichtenbourg was in a much tighter spot now than it had been before the war started. How long would the Fuhrer feel that he got more out of this tiny country if it remained outwardly "neutral" than if he gobbled it up as he had gobbled up half of Europe, including more recently Romania and Bulgaria whose independence was in name only.

Alexia wondered if she couldn't persuade Count Andross to get lost with her on the way through the Greater German Reich and wind up in a neutral country.

What neutral country? Lichtenbourg was technically neutral. Sweden? That was going a bit fast, she told herself. Besides, no matter how much Count Andross fascinated her there was some mystery about him, something Nick Chance had been hinting at. There could be no doubt of it after Nick's recent performance.

100

Of course, Andross couldn't have a mystery in his past that equalled the mere presence of the repulsive little Janos Becque or his equally repulsive mother who had connived her way up the ladder to become royal housekeeper at both the New Palace in the city and the small mountain castle that looked like a French pavillon.

Alexia knew that her mother often spent weekends at the pavillon. Prince Max rarely accompanied her these days. He was far too busy trying to balance his government affairs with the least interference from the growing Nazi influence in his Royal Council. So heaven knew what Princess Garnett did at the pavillon. She liked walking now and then, Frau Becque often went up with her. There was no love lost between them but the princess seemed to depend on her in some way.

With the wartime staff so reduced at Miravel, Alexia was glad of the excuse to pack her own two travel cases. She was in the midst of this when the housemaid notified her with great ceremony, "Social Secretary to her Serene Highness calling from the New Palace at Lichtenbourg."

Alexia had a pretty fair idea that this was her summons, just as Dan had received his. The call need not detain her.

She started out of the bedroom suite that had been her grandmother's and was passing Lord Miravel's old-fashioned bedchamber with its heavy, dark furnishings, when she saw that the door was open. Nick Chance stood there, shoulders hunched over, his fingers tightly griping a bed post. He stared down at his "father's" bed. Was he wondering if it would ever be his legally?

He would certainly be surprised to know that her prime task with her mother would be to persuade that self-indulgent lady that her father's will was grossly unfair.

Nick straightened up and Alexia called to him, "We are leaving now, Nick." He gave her a look that was more contemptuous than indifferent or even hateful. She started to mention what she hoped to attempt, but decided it would serve no purpose. He wouldn't believe her. She went on to the staircase.

Beside the telephone below the stairs Count Andross took her two cases while Dan signalled madly to her from the door of the small salon.

"Cut 'em off!" he shouted. "No time to lose."

She spoke to the woman on the phone. "Yes, Baroness. You may tell my mother I am on my way now. Your call is delaying me."

The baroness turned away from the telephone to repeat her message. A minute later HSH Princess Garnett was on the line. "Darling, did the funeral go well? Oh, that sounds so crass. Poor Father. I mean, did the flowers arrive?"

"Very much so. You couldn't miss them. I've got to go now. We are driving to London if we can get through. And then – "

"But how are you coming? Heavens! We don't want you shot down by the British."

"About my coming, the truth is, I don't exactly know how." She glanced at Count Andross.

"By diplomatic pouch," he told her lightly.

She grinned at him before returning to her mother on the line. "I think I'm coming disguised as a sack of diplomatic mail to a neutral country."

"Now, don't joke. Oh, Darling. I felt awful not being able to get to Miravel. But of course, it was impossible, what with the bombings and all. You are about to start then? Your dear papa misses you so much, and so do I. But you know that."

"I thought you might call when you found out about the will."

"There seemed no need. Father explained very carefully a few months ago. He acted as though he might be feeling me out on the subject. I suppose he expected me to throw a fit. I hope brother Nick is divinely happy. It's what he always wanted."

"Brother?"

The princess did not mind her slip. "Oh well, the cat's out of the bag now, surely. It can't be a secret when the contents of that will are noised about and everyone realizes that Miravel belongs to Nick now. I have quite a few things that are mine at Miravel, but I doubt if he will try to keep them. He and I got on rather well, considering."

So she still didn't know that she was the sole heiress. There was a faint click and her voice faded. Alexia couldn't make out what she was saying and cut in loudly, "Someone is on the line, Mother. We had better cut this short."

Princess Garnett said just as loudly, "Oh, damn those British censors," and the line went dead.

Alexia set the phone back. Count Andross was watching her with a frown. "Someone on your line?"

"There certainly was, but I'm not at all sure it was from our end. The Lichtenbourg lines are too close to the Austrian border. We'd better go. Dan is getting anxious."

During all the fast, bumpy drive to London Alexia had to shake off depression. Dan was so excited about his great adventure which would lead to a brilliant future that he did not sense her mood. Count Andross did, however, and she appreciated that. He was sitting in the front seat of the car beside Dan, with Alexia enthroned in the back, very much alone and feeling rather sorry for herself.

"How does she feel about the Miravel will?" Dan asked finally when Alexia had added very little to the wit and humour of the occasion.

"She doesn't know about it yet."

Dan whistled and began to ask the Count questions

about the Philippines, General MacArthur and the possibility of hopping over to Japan to get an interview with
the Mikado.

Andross shook his head. "Not too likely. They think of
Hirohito as a god. Gods don't give interviews. I'd say the
smartest thing you can do – when do you reach Manila?"

"December the fourth or fifth depending on the Clipper
and a lot of connections. That's a little over a week from
now if I make all my Atlantic and US connections."

"Then take my advice." The Count's manner impressed
Alexia. She only hoped it did the same for Dan. "Take
my advice and get back to California as soon as you can
make it."

"But I keep telling you, the word is that if the Japs strike
– probably Allied bases on the mainland of Asia – it won't
be until spring. They simply aren't prepared, what with all
they're pouring out in Asia already."

"I've just come from Asia," the Count added quietly,
"They are prepared. They went to some pains to point
out to me that Sweden would do well to remain neutral.
We can hardly threaten them in the Pacific but they
made their point, all the same. They need not have
gone to quite such pains. I saw how easily they could
take Singapore."

Nervously, Alexia argued from the back seat. "That's
impossible. It's the biggest base in the whole Orient."

"By sea," the Count agreed. "But as far as I could find
out they have no protection at all against the Malayan jungles at their back. They keep insisting that it is impossible
to break through those jungles. I have never counted on
the power of impossibilities."

Alexia shivered. "Dan, I wish you'd never taken on this
idiotic job of yours."

But Dan was on the journey of a lifetime. Nothing he
had ever done was so interesting to him, and Alexia

suspected the likelihood of danger only added zest to the adventure.

"Anyway, I got Josef Goebbels and Winnie, so they won't do any harm on the ladder I'm climbing, say what you will."

Andross raised his hands. "I surrender. Surprisingly enough, I was young once myself. I do remember the feeling."

Alexia and Dan laughed politely. Alexia wondered why he seemed so much more mature than Dan. He was less than ten years older but he gave an impression of having seen a great deal more of the world, not only physically but psychologically. What was the mystery about him? What was his real interest in Dan and Alexia, if any?

They tore into London, then wended their way around the bomb damage and the surprisingly busy streets. Citizens and foreigners were alike in one thing. They went about their business calmly, numbed by the horrors of their daily lives.

Dan's car reached the Strand and the little street with its right-hand drive leading to the Savoy Hotel.

"We'll have to say goodbye here, folks," Dan announced after a glance at his wrist watch. "I've just got time to make it. Looks like you'll have to take care of my girl, Stef, old boy."

"Nothing would give me greater pleasure."

The Savoy's emperor of doormen was ready to signal for Dan's car to be removed but Dan waved him away. "I'm leaving in two shakes."

He got out anyway, shook hands with Count Andross, and pulled Alexia playfully into his arms. "Honey, be true to me while I'm away on crusade. Sorry I don't have a chastity belt." He squeezed her hard.

She was embarrassed by all this activity in front of Savoy employees, and worse before at least a dozen

105

Savoy patrons coming and going. "Dan, act your age." But the thought of his flight into what might soon be hostile waters reminded her again of his danger. "Don't do anything stupid now that would get you in trouble. I expect to meet you at Tige's penthouse on New Year's Eve . . . Or thereafter. Say, Valentine's Day."

She doubted if her family would let her leave so soon, which wouldn't be critical – she could handle her own affairs she reminded herself – but she hadn't the slightest idea how to evade submarines at sea and the air power of assorted countries. She objected, "I certainly didn't want to say goodbye like this in the middle of Times Square."

"Piccadilly Circus," Dan corrected her, giving her a big kiss and an extra squeeze.

She pushed him against the front door of the car and stepped back, almost on the Count's toes. She apologized without looking back. Her eyes were on Dan as he climbed into the car and then blew a kiss to her and was on his way.

Several witnesses, Savoy patrons, got into the spirit of things and, thinking he was going off to enlist somewhere, waved to him.

When he had vanished in the jumbled Strand traffic Andross took Alexia's arm asking gently, "Are you in love with that boy?"

"Certainly, I love him."

"Not quite the same thing."

She faced him. "If you want to know, he is my best friend, my favourite brother, and the closest person I have in all the world."

"I can appreciate that." He did not pursue the matter but escorted her towards the Savoy doors. "We'll see what luck we have here in wartime. It won't be for long. Our fight takes off at six a.m."

She groaned but agreed. "Good. The sooner this rotten trip is finished, the better."

He pretended to be insulted. "My company must be really distasteful."

That made her laugh. "It's not you. I just don't want to go home."

"I wish I might keep you in Sweden."

She looked up, surprised but not displeased at his bluntness. "Surely, we aren't saying goodbye for ever when we reach Lichtenbourg."

"Far from it. One day, I hope to spend the rest of my life there."

This sounded pleasant even if it was pure flattery. She took it as such without asking herself questions and went in, crossing the big lobby that looked like a gentlemen's club. They were welcomed by an assistant manager who recognized Alexia, addressing her as "Your Serene Highness," but slipped up with the Count's title, addressing him also as "Your Highness".

Andross corrected him, "Count Andross, Sverige, Malmö."

"Of course, Sir." The assistant manager nodded, but with what seemed to Alexia a kind of special courtesy. Obvously, the Count must represent some secret doings between Sweden and Great Britain.

There was no suite available, what with half the "Royals" of Europe having fled to London, but Alexia was very glad to get a single room and the promise of a fair dinner. The single for Count Andross was on a different floor but, with a punctilious air, he assured the young man that this would be quite correct.

"Her Serene Highness is travelling incognito. She has managed to lose her Lichtenbourg escort and her maid. She would appreciate it if nothing is said of her presence here."

The young assistant didn't point out that many people had already seen her and said instead that he understood perfectly. However, Alexia looked back as they headed for the lifts and saw him staring after them in a puzzled way until jogged to duty by a stout man with a middle-European accent.

She thought, My last night in England for God knows how long, and the last time I see Dan for even longer.

Still, he was so happy and excited at the adventures that lay ahead of him she hadn't the heart to wish he would turn around and come back.

"Well, here goes," she told Andross as they stepped into the lift followed by a reserved young man with keys. "Unless we are knocked out of the skies by one side of this war or the other, I'll find myself all too soon in Lichtenbourg."

He smiled, rather sadly, she thought, and surprised her by his reaction. "Lichtenbourg is a beautiful little country with endless possibilities, if only those possibilities were exploited in an exciting way. Not tasteless but worthwhile. Haven't you ever thought that your little country might eventually stand for something special?"

"Maybe, but my father isn't aggressive. He – never mind."

"Ah, yes. The Kuragins."

Her head snapped up at that. "There was a Kuragin once, before my father, who knew what to do. But he was betrayed by the Allies after the Great War. They kept secret the brave things he did for them. They had some political reasons."

He surprised her by agreeing. "Yes. I remember Prince Kuragin. How we hated him!"

"What!"

"He was so very successful, so much loved by the people. He did everything right. The family who were his predecessors did quite the reverse. But luckily for – for others, your father couldn't emulate that great prince."

108

Who were the others? What did he really mean when he said *we* hated him? It seemed more and more plain that Count Andross, if, of course, he was a real count, had always been her enemy, since the day he followed her to the train. It was a sickening thought. If this was so would he dare to accompany her all the way to Lichtenbourg? It would be a test, more of a test than his romantic air at the moment.

The young man opened the door for Alexia, bowing her in. He gave her the first key and started away. He still had the key to the Count's room and looked back, waiting for Andross to follow him.

Meanwhile, the Count took Alexia's gloved fingers and turned them over to expose the circle of her flesh where the glove was buttoned. He bent his head and she felt the warmth of his lips on her flesh. It was the now familiar sensuous touch that made her long for more. But she had sense enough to withdraw her hand. His talk the last few minutes had been troubling, if not downright sinister.

Her withdrawal made Andross look at her with some intensity. "Is my touch so unwelcome?"

She managed a light denial. "Certainly not, Count. But we have very little time."

"Of course." He was correct, formal as he bowed.

The clerk, meanwhile, watched from a distance, mildly interested. He had seen too much to be greatly impressed.

The Count said, "I will not intrude again until you are called at five in the morning. Is that satisfactory?"

It was not satisfactory at all. If she yielded to her natural desires she would have asked him to have dinner with her in her room and then let nature take its course. But he made it reasonably clear that all this laid-on charm had a devious purpose in which she, and probably her family, were the pawns.

CHAPTER TEN

Alexia's depression about returning to her native Lichtenbourg came and went during the flight. By the time the journey was over she could only be grateful that she need not stop at any of the cities where the plane touched down, or that she was forced to change planes. She saw nothing of Sweden but a tantalizingly small corner of an airport. Later, after a few minutes of half-sleep, the sight of Vienna with a banner flapping in the chill wind almost blinded her by its blood-red colour and the ubiquitous swastika. Gone were the Viennese memories of childhood visits. Vienna had always meant bright, romantic performances at the Theatre *An der Wien*, coffee shops with luscious whipped cream rising in snowy mounds over the cups, and the parks, and of course, the Prater ferris wheel. All these wonders might still exist but the omnipresent swastikas had a way of darkening the old, careless life of the Vienna she remembered. When she mentioned this to Count Andross, whose passport and papers seemed to open all doors, he reminded her,

"When there is a vacuum it will be filled. It is the way of life. And of history. There was a vacuum here."

She thought she understood him but she knew her college courses in World Government had been a mere primer of what she would meet here in Europe.

At this moment it was not so much frightening as ominous, reminding her that one day she might have to fill a "vacuum" in her own country, or let their neighbour and kindly mentor, the Fuhrer, fill it for her.

From the plane Count Andross walked with her to an old but gleaming black limousine whose Lichtenbourg plate carried the ostentatious HSH I.

"Your father's?" the Count asked as he saw her shake her head at the licence plate.

"No. That would be Mother. Father's cars simply say 'two'."

He said gravely, "Naturally," but when she looked at him he smiled. She couldn't hide her own cynical amusement. And something else, a feeling of warmth that surprised her on this cold December night.

"Good heavens! I believe I'm homesick. I actually want to get home, and as fast as possible."

"I'm glad. It could be a wonderful little country."

"Could be?" Whatever her private opinions she would accept no slurs from outsiders.

"I mean, if the war were settled."

"Do you think there really will be a negotiated peace?"

"Probably. Some of the king's, King Gustav's advisers think so."

He made a sign to the Lichtenbourg chauffeur who came across the dimly lighted area, bowing to Alexia while he took the bags from the Count.

Alexia had been so surprised by Andross's comment that she did not argue with him. But her few days in England had not given her any hope of a negotiated peace.

What about the whispers she heard in London, of mass deportees in Nazi occupied territory who were marched off to Work Camps? Dissidents, Jews, gypsies, Russian captives, Maquis forces, anti-Nazis of every European nation, were they all being deliberately worked to death?

She had heard snatches of remarks in the lobby at the Savoy, questions and discussions, an apparent lack of real knowledge that seemed terrifying in its ignorance. Was there something worse that lurked behind this horror? Something impossible to "negotiate" away? What was it?

The stocky chauffeur looked vaguely familiar, heavy cheeks and prominent eyes, a mouth with thick lips twisted a little in a kind of permanent sarcasm.

She thought: I know that mouth. Karl – Something. Mother's Nazi chauffeur when I was a child. He was thrilled because Adolf Hitler, leader of the National Socialist Party in Bavaria, was visiting Lichtenbourg City. Now, he's back. The Nazis must have forced him on Father.

Alexia did not expect an escort to cross the Austrian border to meet her. It would be especially awkward if either of her parents did so. The protocol was tricky since their station theoretically put them above the Gauleiter of the Austrian Reich, and that could not be countenanced in Berlin, except when the Kuragins made an official visit.

It was a shock when the car door opened and a lithe young man burst out to make a theatrical bow and greeted her in German. "Your Serene Highness! Johann Hofer, very much at Your Highness's service."

The young man's ingenuous behaviour amused Count Andross and in an effort to cover his laugh Alexia hurriedly acknowledged her escort's greeting.

"Thank you very much. Did my father send you to meet me, Herr Hofer?"

While Karl stowed away her suitcases, Johann Hofer bowed her into the limousine. Then he hopped in beside her. "Is it permitted, Highness?"

He had flashing teeth and bright eyes. In every way he was noticeably attractive. Unless he was a professional performer he seemed a little overdone, but not unpleasant.

The Count motioned Karl to his place behind the wheel and looked in at Alexia and Herr Hofer. "I take it you were given a message from the Royal Family to Her Highness?"

Johann Hofer was not in the least upset. He reached into the red slit pocket of his blue Lichtenbourg uniform and handed a sealed letter to Alexia. She recognized the creamy envelope with the flourishing gold initials on the flap: HSH. Yes. It was Princess Garnett's stationery and the note inside was scrawled on both sides in her well-known writing. It had been said of Princess Garnett Kuragin that her personal handwriting was so large it took her two pages to say Merry Christmas. She had written:

Darling, trust Hanni. He is the juvenile lead at the Theatre Royal. I've heard the glorious news about the will. If it weren't such a delicate matter at this time I would say "Let's celebrate". But Max is such a killjoy. See you soon, but not soon enough. All my love,
HSH G.

Alexia had been told by Tige Royle that when she was a child Garnett had been promised by Max that he would make her a reigning princess. It was apparent in everything around her that Garnett had not forgotten.

So her mother was already spending her inheritance, at least in spirit. Folding the letter Alexia nodded to the Count who had his hand on the door. "It's Mama. I'd know her writing anywhere. Makes me quite homesick." She was suddenly concerned. "But we aren't losing you, are we? I want my parents to meet and thank you."

"Sorry. Another time." He reached for her hand under the interested gaze of Johann Hofer. "This is goodbye, for now." He lifted her out of the seat, drawing her towards him.

She made no effort at resistance, putting her hands on his shoulders to make whatever he had in mind a trifle easier. As she hoped, he brought her face close and covered her lips with his. She was anxious to give as good as she got since she had been looking forward to this kiss with a quickened pulse, some erratic heartbeats, and now a violent charge of excitement that made her shiver in his arms. She felt the heat of his body as he took control of her mouth and she felt as if he drew her inside himself, an emotion no one had ever aroused in her before. Her mouth felt bruised but it didn't seem to matter. She wanted to be part of this hard-bodied, wonderful man and was frustrated by this bad timing, the place, and above all, the two witnesses.

The wretched chauffeur cleared his throat.

"Passport and visas, Highness."

Andross let her go, reluctantly she felt. He smiled as she looked into his eyes. It was an unusual smile for him. She thought there was excitement in his eyes. She hoped so.

Two men in uniform, the swastika prominently displayed, strode up to the limousine and saluted the Count, murmuring the litany, "Heil'itler."

"Osterreich Passport Control."

Andross handed them his Swedish passport which they both looked at briefly and returned. One of them agreed, "So. Expected," and slapped his passport back into his palm. "And the Princess Ava Alexandra of Lichtenbourg?"

She looked out, offering them her passport with its blue and red crossings of the national colours. This business always made her nervous, as if she were a spy. She had seen too many movies in California.

The Austrian studied her passport photo with interest. One said politely, "Not as pretty as Your Highness." He looked in, saw Johann Hofer who looked understandably nervous, and then stepped back, waving the chauffeur away. Hofer was sweating on this cold night.

114

"Passport already checked. Lichtenbourg Autobahn south."

Karl started the car with a roar that would have done credit to Dan Royle and Alexia could only lean out and wave to Count Andross. Tall as he was, his figure got smaller and smaller and she wondered if she would ever see him again. But surely life wouldn't be that cruel.

Alexia relaxed although they were still an hour or more from Lichtenbourg City. "Home," she sighed, trying to make casual conversation with her companion.

With the Passport Control left behind them Johann Hofer regained his lively good humour. "Wonderful little place. Really has everything. Like a haven in the midst of hell."

She stared at him. He realized he had gone too far and for some reason the idea troubled him. He blurted out, as if he feared her criticism, "That is to say, Highness, it is hell to be bombed by the enemy."

"It certainly is. I saw the bombing in London. In fact, I dashed into an Underground shelter when I heard Herr Hitler's boys overhead. No heroism for me. Have the Allies bombed Lichtenbourg yet?"

"Oh, no, Highness. I think they do not care to. Lichtenbourg is neutral. It might be of help to them if airmen are downed, you understand?"

She said, "I doubt if we could get anybody past the Axis borders. The Prime Minister of Hungary had some such idea and he ended up a suicide."

"Very true." He backtracked hurriedly with an ingratiating grin that lit his face so much she suspected it was part of his theatrical equipment. She didn't like him the less for that.

"My mother's note tells me you are with the operetta company here. I love operettas: *The Merry Widow*; *Showboat*; *The Desert Song* . . ."

He was delighted. She liked his enthusiasm. "Just so. *Die Lustige Witve*. I play Danilo. We play it very often, and the other Lehar too. And Kalman. All the Viennese operettas. We thought we would not be permitted to play the *Widow* but the princess gave us special permission."

"Why not play it, for heaven's sake? Don't tell me it's too sexy for the good burghers."

He seemed surprised that she did not know. "Oh, but you were not aware? Frau Lehar is a Jew."

That shook her. She was coming home to a world she had scarcely known. "Surely, the Nüremberg Laws do not apply in Lichtenbourg."

"Well, it is best not to be Jewish."

"My God!" She sank back against the cushion. Her instinctive movement made her feel that she was shrinking inside.

He seemed to blame himself for her condition. "Oh, but Highness, it is no threat to you, a pure Aryan. You must not concern yourself. It is what I keep telling the Princess Royal. Such a fragile lady, like rarest china. I have often been afraid she would break if used badly. A fancy of mine."

"What? Using my mother badly?" she asked him with an edge to her voice. "She isn't the sort who allows herself to be misused, in any way."

She was surprised to see that his face had reddened a little. He burst out, "No, no. Never. Who would misuse – I meant, when that delicate, pale skin is touched – not that I would know."

She smiled inwardly. He must be trying to conceal a crush on her mother. He wouldn't be the first who'd dreamed of holding Garnett Kuragin in his arms.

To make him feel easier she brought the subject around to his career which interested her. "Then you are a singer. I've always admired people with talent. In college all I

116

could think of to study was World Government. A lot of good that will do in a world at war."

He was obviously thrilled to be called an artist. "Actually, I'm a dancer. My singing is what they say – not so hot. I don't stretch for any high notes or any depth when I sing things like 'Silly Horseman' and 'Maxim's'. It's mostly a lot of charm and humour that's needed."

She loved both songs and guessed he would perform them well. "Nevertheless, I hope you will be performing soon. I'll make it a point to see you. I know my father has been awfully busy lately, working all hours, but I'll try to make it a family party and we'll all go. You'll have a rooting section. That's what we called it at Cal."

He looked delighted. "I would be honoured." He made a bow sitting down, not easily achieved without contortions. "You will all sit in the Royal Box, of course, and we will play directly to the Prince Royal and his beautiful ladies."

"Thank you, Herr Hofer. You are very gallant."

"Not Herr Hofer, please. And not Johann. He was my father. An old man. Everyone, even your esteemed mother, calls me Hanni Hofer."

"Very well, Hanni Hofer."

Karl, the chauffeur, had obviously been listening. His gaze caught hers with a kind of malicious amusement but he said without expression, "The border, Highness. They will check the papers for the entry stamps of the Osterreich."

Alexia sat up straight trying to cultivate the regal indifference of her mother, the attitude that all the world waited upon Garnett Kuragin. It might have been easier before Alexia went to the University of California. The campus had soon brought her down to size. She bit her lip nervously, but recovered when the uniformed officer appeared in the car lights, one hand up.

"*Langsam. Langsam!* Identification." Karl offered his papers but they were ignored. The guard walked to the car window, ordering, "Out!"

Karl explained Alexia's identity and the Austrian looked in at her. Then he saluted. "Highness, your papers."

With what she hoped was a supercilious smile she gave him her passport and that of her companion. He scarcely glanced at them before slapping them together and handing them back with another salute and the now familiar, "Heil 'itler!"

Did they say it so often that it had now become a subconscious rolling together of the two words? She saw Karl give the Nazi salute but somewhat to her surprise Herr Hofer also raised a hand in salute. It was a casual gesture, rather like Adolf Hitler's lame salute in the American newsreels produced by her godfather, Christopher Royle. What she wondered at was that the actor should salute at all.

She herself merely nodded, but again she was aware of the chauffeur watching Herr Hofer through the rearview mirror. No matter. They would soon be home in Lichtenbourg where no one she knew would have reasons to give the Nazi salute.

Even in the darkness the moonlight showed her the familiar landscape of the Lichtenbourg border beyond Austria. The skaters' pond, the fields now fallow, the little abandoned mill used by Lichtenbourg's smartly uniformed border guards, and above it all the blue and red Lichtenbourg flag snapping in the wind over their heads.

Two guards came out, bowing gracefully to Alexia. She reached out and, after a moment, each man shook her hand, bowing again and looking enormously proud. One of them called out to her in German: "Welcome home, Highness."

Yes. After all, it was good to be home.

Alexia sat forward as the lights of Lichtenbourg City

glowed before her, a far cry from the tension and eerie half-light of London and Vienna.

She looked eagerly down each remembered street as the limousine passed. She had never liked the baroque architecture of the newer buildings but some were so ancient they preceded the baroque by centuries, so old they leaned towards each other as they probably had done since the seventeenth century. The German style pervaded some of the dark, tunnel-like streets, especially behind the great cathedral.

The car drove past the big, glass-domed railway station at the west end of the spacious Boulevard Kuragin, known as the Boulevard von Elsbach before 1910, and headed for the New Palace at the far eastern end of the boulevard. Even at this distance Alexia's birthplace was not inviting. It seemed to her like a long, stolid face half hidden by the blackened metal "teeth" of the palace gates. This distant sight was almost enough to send Alexia back to the unique elegance of San Francisco. But as the limousine moved at a more sedate pace down the boulevard and then up towards the palace, she looked out anxiously to find nothing had happened to the slender, heroic statue of Prince Kuragin near the gothic facade of the cathedral. At this hour the moon cast a long shadow across the square.

"Exactly where he died," she whispered to the confusion of Herr Hofer who had pointed across the square in the opposite direction to the Opera House and was saying,

"You see? We cheer up the populace with light opera in winter. Let the heavy fellows shake the rafters in the spring." He added on an anxious note, "You will come to see us, won't you, Highness?"

She smiled and nodded but she hardly knew what to say. The gates of the palace had swung open. She saw what appeared to be hundreds of people, the entire household of the New Palace, covering every inch of the long palace steps. Exactly in their midst were the Prince and Princess Royal, waving to Alexia's car. They both looked dazzling at this distance, Prince Max in his white dress uniform with rows of complementary combat ribbons and medals, and Garnett, a very modern fairy tale princess in sleek lamé.

Alexia had the car door open before Karl got to it. She ignored his helpful hand and rushed to her family, wondering why she had waited so long to come home.

But just before she touched her mother a sinuous little man got between them, then apologized as if this were an accident, and called out a syrupy, "We welcome Your Serene Highness to Lichtenbourg." It was Janos Becque, wearing a red and black arm band with a swastika.

CHAPTER ELEVEN

Thank heaven Garnett Kuragin had no sense of the little Nazi's importance to her country. At least she revealed none, pushing him with the impatient remark, "Do step aside, Janos. You are in Her Highness's way. One would think she belonged to you."

"What a delightful thought, and so charmingly put."

Janos Becque chuckled. He didn't appear to be offended. His crowded teeth flashed in the series of old-fashioned golden globes that illuminated the west front of the palace.

Prince Maximilian reached for Alexia and she let him embrace her. His face also shone in the light but those famous features, delicate and handsome in an almost feminine way, looked worn, even haggard. When he was younger those perfect features, like those of a twenties movie star, had made him the idol of all the girls Alexia had known at her schools in France and Switzerland. The features remained but they were badly worn. His eyes twitched a little and a muscle in his cheek throbbed. He was consumed by worry and, perhaps, even fear.

He had been so eager to mount his soldier-father's throne, Alexia thought, and now that he had held that throne since 1918 he must have finally realized that the job was too big for him. Even before Hitler provoked the Second World War, Prince Maximilian had found that he lacked the strength, mental and physical, for the task.

Alexia had grown up despising him for one unforgotten weakness, avoiding him when she could. Now she tried not to be swayed by the hurt and humiliation in his eyes at his only child's rejection. But she knew tonight, surrounded as they were by enemies, or by friends too busy fighting to help them, that she must erase old memories and grudges.

Prince Kuragin would have understood. He remained Max's friend after his betrayal in 1918. He would have forgiven the way Max let the prince's assassins go free in 1929. A man of many weaknesses like Prince Maximilian could be forgiven much. Still, Alexia wondered if her father realized that sooner or later all these weaknesses would add up, and Maximilian Kuragin must pay.

"Poor Father," she caught herself, hoping he did not hear, but he was so pleased at her greeting that he merely smiled and kissed her forehead.

Her mother complained, "If you please, she is my daughter, too," which provoked much laughter from the household staff plus several distinguished, and some doddering, gentlemen of the Royal Council who also tried to get near her.

She found it embarrassing and pictured the mocking imitation of her college friends when her father turned her over to the bowing Council members and their wives who bobbed low curtsics. Feeling all too noticeable with what appeared to be half of Lichtenbourg watching and several news photographers from Berlin and Vienna grinding away news cameras, Alexia looked around for her mother.

Garnett, looking glorious, the night wind blowing through her soft auburn hair complete with a modest but shimmering diamond tiara, had just received young Johann Hofer. He bowed low before her on the steps, taking one of her hands in his two hands, touching his lips to her delicately curved fingers. Garnett tapped Hofer on the shoulder as if she were knighting him.

"Hanni, stop that. You are overdoing it. Turn and wave to your fans."

Alexia knew her mother's teasing ways but hoped everyone else knew them as well. Otherwise, without being aware of it, Garnett would be the subject of gossip in the European press, perhaps in America as well. She was probably so used to doing as she pleased that she did not realize the dangers.

Scandal, whether based on fact or mere gossip, could deeply hurt her country's efforts to remain free. And there was Max. His efforts at walking a tightrope between freedom and a Nazi takeover was already precarious.

The actor recovered himself quickly under the malignant eyes of Janos Becque. "May I report to Your Serene Highness the success of my little mission?"

To this Alexia added, "He was most efficient, Ma'am. Here I am, safe and sound." She had almost said "Mother", but remembered protocol in time. As Tige Royle had once told Alexia, no one is as fond of protocol as a tiny nation.

"And glad we are to see our wandering girl home," Prince Max reminded everyone as he put an arm around his daughter.

"Welcome indeed, Your Highness." Janos Becque was very close on Alexia's other side, smelling of a sickeningly strong perfume, possibly a shaving lotion. Without looking at the man whose breath itself was far too close to her left ear, Alexia felt a sickening revulsion and moved away towards her mother.

Seeing their princess kiss her mother's cheek, some of the crowd cheered Alexia again, mostly in German, a few in the more difficult Hungarian. Alexia smiled and waved while Garnett squeezed her daughter's waist, her eyes following Johann Hofer as the actor retreated through the crowd toward the great spiked boulevard gates.

Alexia heard and felt the sibilant whisper close to her ear. "Your mother is truly democratic. See how kind she is to the denizens of the theatre."

Alexia turned on him, with all her pent-up dislike. "You, with that swastika-thing, don't you love the people? Aren't you their saviour? So democratic, I always say."

The little Nazi's lips peeled back in his professional grin. "Entirely correct, Highness. I see you will need very little education."

Shivering with rage at the idea that he could teach her anything she murmured pleasantly in English, "My, Grandma, what big teeth you have!" She had caught him by surprise. He didn't seem entirely familiar with the allusion, or perhaps with English, but she was sorry to see that her father had heard her and frowned. She knew it was stupid to arouse the little Nazi bastard's enmity, though the chance had been irresistible.

Princess Garnett, too, had heard the English words. She stifled a laugh, then took Alexia's arm. "It is late, young lady, and you need your sleep after that horrid trip."

Alexia could only agree with her before she made another gaffe that might cause difficulty for her father. "I'd like that. Thank you." She gave the crowd a wave, turned her back on them and went up the steps to the long double doors, so like a lean, crabbed school mistress she had once known.

Alexia passed what appeared to be most of the household, all unknown to her, but she kept smiling and nodding. Most of them looked surprised. A few appeared grateful and smiled back. Everyone curtsied or bowed. She would have to get used to that reaction all over again.

She did know Frau Becque. She could not mistake that careful simpering smile, quite unlike the malicious grin

124

of her son. Frau Becque knew her place – none of the household was higher in the entire country – and she made certain that Alexia knew it as well.

Garnett left Alexia at the foot of the north staircase promising to come and "have a nice little gossip" when Alexia had bathed, been brought a late supper tray and was ready for bed.

"Meanwhile, Darling, I leave you in Frau Becque's capable hands. No one in this musty old palace knows more about the place than Little Beckie."

In Alexia's opinion "Little Beckie" did not like her nickname and was far from liking Her Serene Highness. She raised one pale eyebrow as she watched Garnett leave them. Like her son, she was short with a body whose bones were more than adequately covered by pale flesh. Alexia suspected she had some of Janos Becque's tensile strength. She was far from weak, despite her small size. She had one quality remarkably like her son's. Her smile never reached her pale, close-set blue little eyes.

"Your Highness will find an excellent view of the Boulevard Kuragin from your apartments. It was impossible to give you a garden suite for the moment. Those apartments are being renovated."

"I understand." It was late and Alexia was too tired to care.

There was a heaviness about everything as they reached the landing and passed a huge Renaissance statue of a female Kuragin ancestor holding scales, presumably weighing justice. Nowadays, she weighed two electric lamps. More practical but rather absurd.

Alexia remarked, "I doubt if they'll ever make a statue to me and hang scales or anything else on it."

"Who can know the future?" Frau Becque was no oracle but she seemed to have a second thought. "Unless Your Highness chooses her consort very carefully. A man who is thoroughly familiar with Lichtenbourg's history and its laws. Someone capable of ruling the Royal Council and making peace with our neighbours."

"Who on earth could that be?" Alexia asked, the soul of naive innocence. "Think of the difficulty of finding such a man."

The housekeeper tried once more. "Perhaps your good father could suggest one. The man may be closer than Your Highness imagines."

Alexia shrugged. "I just can't seem to think of anyone."

This left Frau Becque at a loss. She couldn't very well argue with such dense stupidity. She stopped before two impressive, if sombre, panelled doors. "Your apartments, Ma'am."

"Thank you." Alexia found two buxom blonde maids giving the parlour its finishing touches, scattering dust with their feather dusters. Frau Becque dismissed them. After a quick survey of Princess Alexia they hurried out, bobbing half-curtsies as they went. Alexia would have loved to know what they said. They already had their heads together when they closed the corridor doors.

Frau Becque showed Alexia around the parlour with its newly polished mahogany furniture, very ornate and built for long endurance, like the statue on the landing.

Alexia looked around, first at the huge desk; with a chair obviously built to accommodate a stout Prince Royal, then at the very masculine leather sofa, somewhat used, but good for another hundred years, and so many monstrosities belonging to past rulers who ate good, succulent German food, that she gave up and followed Frau Becque into the bedroom.

Thank God the huge four-poster bed was not canopied! And from somewhere a French dresser had been crowded in, a lovely delicate dresser of ivory stained wood with three mirrors. This and a beautiful matching highboy made up for some of the monstrosities. How these lovely pieces came to be here she couldn't imagine.

In California Alexia had become used to speaking her mind and she wasn't yet accustomed to Lichtenbourg ways. "Who was the last Heiress Presumptive?" she asked Frau Becque. "She must have weighed a ton."

The housekeeper's thin lips pursed in obvious disapproval before she explained, "That Heiress Presumptive was the niece of the last von Elsbach prince. She was Princess Ilsa, a beautiful creature. True Aryan blonde. Married a Hungarian. Very rich."

"And was he also a true Aryan blond?"

"Well, no. Very dark. But at his death she married an Aryan, you may be sure. Poor creature. She lives in the hope of the Lichtenbourg throne returning to the Elsbachs. It is a centuries-old battle. They would be here now but for the plebiscite promoted by the late Prince Kuragin. The people's rights, the vote of the man in the street, I believe they called it. And Prince Kuragin – well, very much a man of the people."

Clearly she didn't think much of all this democracy. Alexia bristled at the casual reference to Prince Kuragin but any explosion on her part would only cause more trouble for her parents so she merely said, "Fat or thin, Aryan or what-not, this furniture is ghastly."

"I see. Which pieces does Your Highness disapprove of?"

Alexia thought of London and the Blitz, the appalling food they lived on, the dogged courage. She decided not to make an issue of this furniture. "The things I like are the vanity dresser and the pretty highboy in the bedroom, but I don't suppose anything can be done, what with the problems of war around us." She could not help adding, "Though frankly, I feel as if I were in a coal mine."

"And is Your Highness acquainted with coal mines?"

Alexia was ready for her. "No. But I've been down in silver mines and some of them are just as dark. My great-grandfather, Tige Royle, took a group of us to see the Virginia City silver mines. That was how he started, you know."

"Really? How interesting!" Her eyebrows told Alexia nothing could be less interesting. "When the British and the Godless Russians make peace, which will be any day now, the matter can be brought to the attention of the Royal Council. My son, as you know, is the chancellor of Lichtenbourg." She started to the doors, then stopped. "I will send your maid to you. Her Serene Highness chose her. The girl will ring for your supper tray. You have only to tell her what you wish to order."

Alexia laughed to herself and muttered, "Naughty, naughty. Next, I'll be sent to bed without my supper."

"I beg your pardon."

Ignoring her Alexia turned away and went back into her dressing room. Due to the war and shipping problems she had sent over a carefully chosen but not plentiful wardrobe, taking to Miravel only the items she would need for a brief stay, which turned out to be even shorter than she had anticipated.

The wardrobe from California had been carefully arranged in the modern walk-in closet, probably one of Garnett's additions. Alexia looked through the knee-length dresses, two with pleated skirts and self belts, all with padded shoulders. The latter were played down as they did nothing for her. One very modern salmon outfit by a brilliant New York designer was a favourite along with two evening dresses, one of them a white crepe with a fringed skirt that swayed enticingly as she walked, or so Dan Royle said.

But aside from shame that she should admire herself in a fringed dress when millions were dying in battle and from

128

ill-treatment, Alexia was also tired. There had been forty hours without sleep, except those pleasant moments when she dozed off against Stefan Andross's shoulder. How unexpectedly tender he had been!

She had forgotten to ask her father if there were letters for her. If Dan had any time at all when he changed planes, or while he waited to take the Clipper across the biggest ocean in the world, he would write and tell her all the details; his adventures, as he liked to think of them.

She certainly would welcome a decent supper, light but warm, something to let her sleep and blur the nerve-wracking moments in different countries, waiting to see if all went well with their passports. When the maid sent by her mother came in and introduced herself, she was more than welcome to Alexia.

Brusque as she sounded, she was also tall and lean, with a bony figure that looked capable of taking on the world, including Frau Becque. She was not bad looking if she had cared to show herself to the best advantage which, obviously, she did not. She wore her dark hair in a blunt cut to the middle of her ears which called attention to her long, obtrusive nose.

"I hear you want my services, at least temporarily. Name's Polly Quint. You can call me Polly if you've a mind to. Or Quint." She wrinkled her nose at this, however.

Alexia was delighted. "You speak English, Polly."

Polly Quint stalked toward her. Alexia was not surprised by her long, forceful strides. "Well, Miss – I reckon I should call you Ma'am. I got stuck in this hell-hole after Mr Hitler's war started. I was what you might call a mother's help. American she was, like me, if you can believe it. She hot-footed it out of here the minute the Nazis marched into Poland. And we weren't even at war."

"And left you here? What a rotten thing!"

"That's what your ma said. She sure is one beautiful female. And a heart as big as all outdoors. I worked for one of her ladies-in-waiting who had kids. I made 'em shape up, believe you me."

Alexia laughed wholeheartedly, thrilled to hear this rough talk that sounded like a few people she had known back in California's hinterland. It was especially good to hear praise of her mother. "So you are here to make me shape up."

Polly Quint looked a little guilty but only for a moment. "Well, Ma'am, not exactly. I'm right handy as a ladies' helper, you might say. Here. Nobody's taken care of your coat. Let me."

She almost turned Alexia around bodily but got her coat off, one sleeve at a time, shaking out the wide folds of the coat skirt and picking up the belt she dropped. "Kind of Russian style," she remarked, examining it critically. "I'm no commie, mind you, but those Russians are having a rough time of it, I hear." Catching herself, she looked toward the hall doors. Her alarm was contagious.

"What is it?" Alexia asked. "I suppose being so near the Axis borders, we aren't expected to sympathize with the Russians."

Polly Quint rolled her eyes. "God, no! That old battle-axe hates them worse than the English, and she listens at keyholes. Or makes us do it. Then she tattles to her son. Believe it or not he's the Number One Boy in this two-bit country."

Alexia held out her hand. "You've got to be talking about Frau Becque. Shake."

Surprised, but pleased, Polly transferred the coat to her left hand and thrust out her right, squeezing Alexia's fingers until she winced but managed to keep smiling.

"Polly, I think we understand each other."

"OK. We've cleared that out of the way. Now, you want

130

me to turn on your bath – beg pardon, draw the bath – before I order up your dinner? Or supper? Whatever the heck it is?"

"Thank you. I'll wash and have something to eat. My mother will be here by then."

"Maybe she'll have a bite with you, Ma'am."

"I doubt it. Mother is strictly the champagne and caviar type. And I can't see myself ordering that tonight."

Alexia went into the dressing room where she was debating whether to change to a dinner dress or her last year's satin dressing robe when Polly threw her the robe with the explanation, "Read your mind."

"So you did." She was too tired tonight to start training Polly Quint who showed every sign of taking over her life. It didn't really matter tonight.

She was washing in the very modern bathroom when Polly called to her from the parlour. Alexia went to the window beside her where she could look out on the palace gates below. Beyond them a double string of lights marched along the Boulevard Kuragin, down to Cathedral Square with Prince Kuragin's statue and up towards the distant train station.

When Alexia was a little girl that station had been a magic carpet where the elegant Orient Express zoomed to a stop, having come from romantic Budapest and on its way to romantic Vienna. All gone now, thanks to the war. Trains still used the tracks but more often they were troop trains or cattle cars, tightly sealed, probably carrying war cargo that the citizens of Lichtenbourg were not allowed to see.

"What is it?" she asked Polly. "The lights in wartime? But, theoretically, we're not at war."

"Nope. Don't count on the princess coming to see you tonight."

"What do you mean? Why not?"

Polly was surprised. "Well, you know how religious the princess is."

"Mother? Religious?"

Polly pointed out a darkly clad woman with the hood of her opera cloak pulled forward, shadowing her face. The woman had just passed through the servants' entrance at the far north corner of the palace.

"That's her. She goes to Mass down at the cathedral several times a week, unless she's entertaining bigshots or something."

Alexia watched until the slim, graceful figure was half-way to her destination. When she turned away from the window she felt nauseated and avoided Polly's sharp eyes. The Garnett Miravel Kuragin that her daughter knew had to be almost dragged to church. Any church.

CHAPTER TWELVE

Some minutes later Alexia's late supper arrived. Polly Quint waved away the servant who had a slightly more bushy moustache than the Fuhrer and Alexia found herself being served a liqueur tasting of aniseed, which she hated. But this was followed by a succulent golden dish of Wiener Schnitzel with a really welcome German light wine.

Seeing Polly's hopeful expression, she managed a compliment: "Lovely. Delicious," wondering how she would ever get even part of it down after her long, nerve-wracking two days almost without sleep.

She usually had an excellent appetite and could only hope this was a specimen of the food to be expected, though she doubted it. The food served during her waits on the trip had never rivalled this. Maybe it paid to remain "neutral" like Lichtenbourg.

But there might be a reason. Small wonder. As Garnett had said in one of her summer letters: *We are forever entertaining the very top echelon of Nazis. We may thank our guests, no doubt, for the excellent table we keep.*

Leave it to Mother, she thought. My religious mother, who sneaks off several nights a week, close to midnight and without an escort, to attend Mass at the cathedral . . .? This was definitely not the woman Alexia had known for eighteen years.

As Polly Quint thought, the only logical answer for most forty-year-old-women in Garnett's high position might

133

have been love of God. The alternative could be an earthy lover, certainly not godlike. But Alexia had never heard serious scandal about her mother. There were jokes about her flirtations and hints at more serious assignations in the tabloids, but Alexia had always known that the one love in Garnett's life since her childhood was her husband, Max.

Once the dinner had been moderately disposed of, Polly Quint enquired when Alexia would like her bath run.

"Thanks but I won't be bathing for a little while. You run along to bed, Polly."

Polly shrugged. "Sure. You just ring that first bell by the bed post, Ma'am, and I'll come running. What time do you get up?"

"Usually at seven." Alexia wondered how long she would have to wait up for her mother's return. It was a matter that consumed her with curiosity and worry. It also occurred to her that if Polly knew about Garnett's midnight excursions, it was pretty certain that Frau Becque was in on the secret. Small wonder that the foreign tabloids had all the insinuations at the tips of their pens. Or, heaven forbid, in the lens of their cameras. No doubt someone very like Frau Becque fed the news to them.

Really! Ruler or not Garnett was incredibly foolhardy, sneaking around the city at this hour. Almost any citizen would recognize her. The double profile of Max and Garnett was on all the Lichtenbourg hundred schilling notes issued the year of their twentieth wedding anniversary.

Alexia muttered to herself, "I hope I'm never that stupid. If I was meeting a lover I'd hardly conduct the affair in front of half the city."

She wondered what Count Andross was doing at this hour. Probably in his Swedish castle and asleep if he had any sense. Wouldn't it be ghastly if he was married? She was positive that Nick Chance had discovered some

134

unpleasant secret about him and maybe that was it. Not that it should matter. Alexia would never get him, even if she used her mother's tactics.

Seeing how late it was she went to the bathroom to run her bath in the clean, polished porcelain tub and noticed that if she strained her neck a little she could see the north gate which her mother had used on leaving the palace.

Good. She bathed, using the scented French soap with which her mother was always provided, war or no war. Alexia looked up every few minutes to catch her first glimpse of Garnett when she returned from the direction of the cathedral. No luck. Few people were on the streets at this hour. Occasionally, three or four carefully behaved members of the Wehrmacht strolled along the boulevard on the south side of the square, coming out of the beerhalls or the popular German version of an English pub.

It seemed to Alexia that everything was not so "Aryan", in the old days. There had been the French cafés, more than one true English pub, an American hot dog and hamburger "joint". Endless nationalities that had fascinated the young Alexia. But now even the spaghetti trattoria was gone. So much for the Rome-Berlin Accord.

Tonight, as the limousine drove along the boulevard, she couldn't recall seeing anything that wasn't a photographer's second-rate Berlin. All but the bomb damage. When would Lichtenbourg begin to receive those wartime souvenirs?

It was one-thirty when she gave up, deciding she had missed her mother's return, and went to bed. The big, ugly four-poster, built for a real heavyweight or two, was surprisingly comfortable.

In San Francisco at Tige Royle's penthouse he had insisted she choose her own furniture for the bedroom she used. It had all been fashionable white-painted wicker that could be a sitting room for entertaining friends when the bed was turned into a couch with many pillows for backing. But the charming bed didn't have the solid, spacious comfort of this one. Maybe she could learn to like Lichtenbourg more than she had in her childhood. She might *have* to learn one day.

She was awakened by a noise at the distant parlour doors and forgot where she was for a minute. But something about that odd knock, more like a thump, reminded her of Polly Quint, and she got out of bed in a hurry, climbed down the three wooden steps, and grabbed her robe.

"I could've used a key," Polly said, "but I figured I'd be more formal, considering it's your first day."

How she managed to knock, or thump, baffled Alexia. Both her hands were filled with the big tray.

"How did you – " Alexia began.

"Used my knee."

Alexia grinned. She didn't make the mistake of trying to help Polly Quint who marched past her deciding, "Now you're rested, you won't want to be lying around in bed."

There seemed little for Alexia to say except, "Certainly not."

While she was eating the gingerbread served with her breakfast at the huge desk in the parlour, she asked very casually, "Did Mother get home safe from church last night?"

"Must've. She was still sound asleep when Gertrude went in with her tea and the morning paper. *Munchener Abend*, something or other."

Alexia was debating whether she should make an appointment to see her father some time when the phone rang. Having decided that her silent feud with the hardworking Prince Maximilian had lasted for too long she was delighted when Max himself was on the line. Himself, not even a secretary or a servant, she thought, touched by his gesture. She had humbling memories of her own indifference to him. The strange behaviour of her mother last night made her all the more anxious to make up for her own negligence.

"Yes? Father? Good morning."

She heard his voice with its perfect tone, warmer and more caring than she remembered. "I hope I haven't awakened you, Dear."

"No, Father . . . Sir. I've just finished breakfast."

"Splendid. I've been thinking of your long, tiring trip from California. And then, to have Lord Miravel die almost under your very eyes. It must have shocked you."

"Well, no, Sir. His condition was fatal. I'm glad he didn't suffer."

"Yes. We wouldn't like that. Of course, he and I never got on too well. He was always jealous of the time Garnett spent with me when I was visiting Miravel. But your mother felt his death. She hadn't expected anything in the estate you know. He made that quite clear last summer when he talked to Garnett."

One question had been puzzling her. "How did she find out that the estate and half the profits went to her?"

He laughed. "You know your mother. Last time she visited Miravel she made a friend of that physician. Not a surgeon, I believe, but she seemed to feel he and his daughter were adequate."

"Good God!" So the Tredegars had been Garnett's friends; yet they gave every indication of being loyal to Nick Chance.

"I beg your pardon."

"Nothing, Father. I know the doctor and his daughter. I wouldn't trust them any further than I could throw them."

He chuckled. "You musn't blame them too much. You know what charm Garnett has. Always did have. When I was a calf of a teenager she was able to wheedle anything she wanted from me. And she was a mere child at the time. But that is my Garnett."

"Yes. It certainly is. I know how busy you are, Father, but it would be terribly nice if I could see you for a few minutes this afternoon. Not anything important. Just a visit to make up for . . . all the time we've been apart."

He sounded pleased. "Of course. That was my idea, but I wasn't sure. You might have had more exciting things to do."

At the moment she didn't want anything exciting. She was still a little shaken by memories of several occasions when a passing plane might, or might not, be bent on blasting them out of the sky.

"I'd love to see you, Father, when you are free. Meanwhile, when Mother is awake and has a minute, I'll visit with her."

"Excellent. I'm a little worried about her lately. As you know, she is almost never sick. Strong as a horse, Tige calls her. He's promised to visit us soon. I don't know how, but if Tige says he is going to do something, he usually does it."

Alexia was enormously pleased. If anything was wrong in Lichtenbourg Tige Royle could probably fix it. She knew how much his visit meant to Prince Max because Tige seldom came to Lichtenbourg since his friend, Prince Kuragin, had been assassinated twelve years ago. Like Alexia, he had always blamed Max for not punishing the real killers. She wasn't sure how the Fuhrer and the Nazi Government would react, but it was probable that since America and Nazi Germany were not at war, they might be anxious to do business with him.

There was a matter almost as important, however. Alexia asked, "What is wrong with Mother? Why are you worried?"

"Well, lately I've been so pressed with conferences

about our part in the war, if any, that it seems to have had a bad effect on Garnett. She gets these headaches. Eyestrain from reading official papers, she says."

"I see." It didn't sound like Garnett at all. "Does she help you a great deal?"

He laughed gently. "I let her think so. She insists, you know. And then come these headaches late in the evening. But she is always thoughtful."

Maybe she really had matured. Alexia said, "I'm glad she helps you, Father, for your sake."

He assured her, "No question about it. She wants to. But she refuses to disturb me. She goes off by herself, poor lamb. A little fresh air in the gardens or on the east terrace always revives her, she says. But I don't like to think of her out there so late at night. Still, there isn't anything that can happen to her as long as she stays on the grounds. They are very well patrolled. You are coming to see me this afternoon then. Promise? You do remember my private study, sweetheart. Three o'clock?"

"I remember, Father. I'll be there."

Somebody interrupted him at that minute and the line went dead in the middle of his, "Glad to have you home, Alexandra."

The power was often interrupted these days due to air raids over the Reich. She strongly suspected they were also cut off through accident or design by their Nazi neighbours listening in and reporting to the Gestapo.

Alexia had been prepared for this and ignored it, but she couldn't ignore her father's innocent description of Garnett wandering along the east terrace at midnight.

Mother, what are you up to? She was almost afraid to know. Of one thing she was certain, Garnett did not wander along cold stone terraces at midnight any more than she hurried through dark streets disguised on her way to the cold stone Lichtenbourg Cathedral. Unless, of course, she was running to meet someone who adored her, a lover whose adoration she probably wanted more than his sexual attraction.

It had to be a man that was involved. But it was strange that for all her popularity in the tabloids they hadn't fixed on one man as the lover.

The idea itself was revolting to Alexia. Her own mother an adulteress? Did it run in families? She would never forget the passion she had heard whispered about between her grandmother, Lady Alix, and Prince Kuragin. But that had been different. She wanted very much to believe that wondrous love affair with its picture of Franz Kuragin hidden under Lady Alix's mirror, was different, special, the kind of passion Alexia herself might dream of. And there was an excuse for it, because Lady Alix must have found out about her husband's illegitimate son, Nick Chance.

But she could never believe that Max Kuragin had a secret son, or any other sexual secret. The one thing that was admirable about her father was his blind faith in his wife, and Alexia had a strong suspicion that this faith was misplaced.

She wondered if Tige Royle knew about his grand-daughter's night roaming. He had always been wonderful to Alexia, who was only his great-granddaughter, and his devotion to his own daughter had been legendary. All the same, his affection had skipped Garnett Miravel Kuragin.

Perhaps it was her easy, self-centred charm. Alexia rather liked that about her mother. She didn't trust her for a minute. Look at how Garnett had connived with the Tredegars to be sure she received Miravel. Had she paid them? Had she bribed them in some way, promising them an interest in the estate? And what could they have done to see that she was first in her father's will? There was no question of foul play. Luckily, the hospital at Miravel had certified Lord Miravel's cause of death. But a few words whispered in the dying man's ears might have done the trick. Especially as he had taken a fancy to Rose Tredegar. That was much more in Garnett's style. Alexia shuddered to think of the first flash of suspicion that had run through her head.

I've been away from home too long, she thought, getting ideas like this about my own mother.

She wanted to get along with her mother. She was not averse to Garnett's amusing charm. You could always see through it if you waited long enough. Just watching her connive was interesting, though Alexia doubted that Garnett's unacknowledged half-brother, Nick Chance, would share Alexia's amused interest in the selfish beauty.

Alexia let Polly Quint choose a suit for her and fasten the covered buttons down the back of the aquamarine wool jacket while she speculated aloud about her mother.

"What happens to people who are completely selfish? Do they ever have to pay the piper?"

"Couldn't imagine, Ma'am. Probably not their fault. Spoiled rotten, that's all. Stand up straight, I've got you fastened lop-sided."

Alexia did as she was told but wondered why she must be so carefully dressed and said so. "This is nothing. It's tonight you got to shine. His Nibs, I mean His Highness, said for me to pick out something you look terrific in. For the reception, you know."

"Who are we to impress? Hitler?"

"Lord, no. The Fuhrer has a war on. You know, Eastern Front and all. But they always come zooming into town here trying to borrow plant workers." She had lowered her voice suddenly which surprised Alexia. Polly Quint didn't look as if she would be afraid of anyone.

"Plant workers?"

"For munitions factories and all that. They've been combing the conquered countries, Belgium, Holland,

France. Their own buddies, too, like Hungarians and Romanians. Certain kinds of workers, you know. But His Nibs is trying to hold out. It ain't easy when – " She broke off.

Puzzled and uneasy, Alexia raised her head, catching Polly Quint's sharp-eyed gaze in the mirror. Reflected behind both of them across the room one of the corridor doors was opening gently.

Polly mouthed the word, "Becque."

Alexia did not turn around. "Frau Becque, you wished to speak to me?"

The door opened just wide enough to admit the little housekeeper. She had been caught at a disadvantage, something that didn't happen to her often. "Not to disturb Your Highness, but does Your Highness wish the breakfast tray removed?" It was as good an excuse as any. It might even be true.

"Thank you, yes. You may remove it."

Frau Becque recovered her usual authority. "Very well then. I'm afraid Quint has been remiss. You will remove it now if you please, Quint." Polly did not know which way to turn.

Alexia said, "Thank you, but I need Polly's services, as you see. Perhaps you will be so kind as to remove the tray."

Stiffbacked, Frau Becque did as she was ordered. Alexia half-expected she would leave the door ajar but apparently her pique was stronger than her curiosity. She slammed the door. Catching each other's eyes in the mirror, Alexia and Polly both grinned.

"That ought to shut her up for a little while, at least," Alexia muttered with satisfaction.

Polly reminded her, "She really is dangerous, though."

"Don't be silly. What can she do to me? And I'll certainly make it clear she's not to hound you."

Polly Quint looked back at the heavy double doors. "Sure, Ma'am. Whatever you say." But Alexia had an uncomfortable feeling that she wasn't convinced.

Now that Alexia was dressed and ready for the world she had no place to go. Everyone she cared about most was somewhere else. Dan had hived himself off over the Pacific somewhere into the December sunset, Tige Royle was on his way to Lichtenbourg, she hoped, and one other was missing; Count Andross.

She wondered if it was worth writing to him with the excuse of a "thank you" for all his help. And why not a casual invitation to the palace for a social weekend? Or, if he was that kind, a hunting session. In Lichtenbourg, distances were so small the prince's guests usually ended up in Austrian or Hungarian fields. Still, the Hungarian Prime Minister was a good friend of her father's and of Tige. She stopped Polly Quint as she was leaving. "Does the Prime Minister of Hungary still let Father's visitors hunt on his grounds?"

Polly's fingers slipped off the door knob. The big door closed with a loud rumble. After a moment she answered the question. "Oh, him? Poor guy. Not any more. Committed the good old hari-kiri a little while ago."

"Killed himself! But why?" She had heard this before but never known the truth of it.

"Things were closing in on him, I expect. Anyway, that's the way we heard it. They say he was making it easy for undesirables to escape. They had a lot of gypsies in Hungary you know, and Jewish merchants, bankers, people that figured they were safe from the SS as long as they had his backing. Guess they weren't. Your father felt real bad." She went out the door and closed it.

To Alexia the shock was the casual way such sinister hints were thrown out. It was almost worse than the United States where almost nothing was said of "things" happening within the reach of the SS. Except for a few radicals and the so-called "warmongers" spreading highly coloured tales of Nazi atrocities, most of the Americans remembered the lurid tales of the First World War and dismissed these as propaganda. Over here on the Continent the quickly silenced hints were suddenly more terrifying.

The shock of hearing that her father's friend had committed suicide because he could no longer help his desperate people brought it closer to Alexia. Surely her father wasn't involved in all this Scarlet Pimpernel stuff! He wasn't the type. He would be destroyed. And all the time he had been in such deep trouble Alexia had lived in luxury and ease far away from war and suffering in neutral America.

For a few cowardly minutes she wished she was back in nice, safe American territory. Of course, such thoughts hardly prepared her for her future when she was expected to succeed her father to the Kuragin throne.

She straightened up, reached for her handbag, and started out to refresh her memory of the city in which she was born. Maybe she would be able to borrow some of the bravery that seemed to have eluded her up to now.

There was less formality in the great, echoing palace than she had remembered, and many more uniforms, a good half of them German or Austrian, and peppered in among them the black SS uniforms with the silvery lightning stroke of the swastika. She did not want to make up a movie version of the faces she saw but there was no question about it that the Wehrmacht officers, who seemed aloof, were more obviously polite, inclining their heads or saluting whereas the Gestapo and others of the SS either studied her with cold deliberation or ignored her entirely.

Most of them seemed to recognize her. Because she was uncertain what was expected of her she smiled when smiled at and avoided the hard stares of the black-uniformed SS.

Out on the street the wrought-iron gates were guarded by two sentries in red piped French blue uniforms and shining silver helmets. To Alexia the handsome six-footers looked like actors in an A-plus movie. They were well trained statues and didn't blink when she went past them.

On the boulevard a newsboy was shouting his wares, selling papers briskly. The *Völkischer Beobachter*, Hitler's party organ, had a column about the need for more factory workers in Germany and the Osterreich. The pay was good, so the article promised, especially for munitions workers.

I'll bet! Alexia thought, remembering that the munitions works were the first targets of enemy bombs.

The newsboy had targeted a stocky man behind Alexia and a dispute followed. The man, in an ill-fitting civilian suit, pushed the paper aside and moved on just as Alexia turned around. For some reason the man stopped at once, turned back, and bought a paper. Alexia walked on and immediately heard the creak of her follower's new shoes. It seemed pretty obvious that he was protecting or spying on her but he was a little too obvious to be a spy. With a strong sense of depression she reminded herself, I'm back home again. Everything has returned to normal. She straightened her shoulders, set her mouth firmly, and went on.

She hadn't walked quite a block when a German staff car roared up the boulevard toward the gates of the New Palace and stopped. Alexia stared, partly because the morning sunlight glinted on the sleek golden hair of the stunning female in the car but chiefly because she thought she recognized Count Stefan Andross at the wheel with the blonde's arm casually draped just behind the neck of his jacket.

CHAPTER THIRTEEN

Alexia's first hope lasted about as long as it took her to study the Count's golden companion whose gloved hand so casually rested behind his collar. It had seemed, all too briefly, that he came sailing up the Boulevard Kuragin at full throttle just to call on Alexia. But it was pretty plain his companion regarded him as her property. This golden creature held herself, at least her head and shoulders, like a classic sculpture in marble, all hard, cool elegance. Her tiny straw hat was anchored so that wisps of her hair barely rippled in the winter air that edged Alexia's cheeks like ice.

Alexia disliked the woman on sight but stood watching with wild curiosity as one of the sentries challenged Count Andross then saluted and waved the car inside the opening gates. The car rattled past the west front of the palace grounds to the garages at the back of the north parade ground.

Alexia watched and wondered. Stefan Andross certainly knew his way around the royal residence of Lichtenbourg. What did that mean? If Count Andross was familiar with the palace, the palace must be familiar with him. Maybe the stocky guard trailing her would know. She looked back but he had stopped with more important matters on his mind. He had one of his shoes off and was rubbing his cramped toes. Poor man, he probably hated this job and would much rather be off marching in uniform somewhere with well-worn boots that fitted.

Alexia hesitated. She must impress Stefan with an entrance as dramatic as his, and even more important she must outshine this golden creature who was his companion. No easy job.

She decided to go on, let everyone wonder about her absence and maybe get a few ideas about proceeding against her golden rival. She turned at the second of the medieval side streets just off the boulevard. It made her feel less homesick for the good friends in California as she planned their Christmas presents.

The Gothic German script everywhere, in every window of Lichtenbourg, had always given her a little chill. She never understood why. But now, since Hitler was phasing out the Gothic and replacing it with Roman script of the Reich, she was again surprised to see how it changed the shops in her birthplace. They didn't look nearly so ominous now but there was a foreign quality about them.

No matter. The shop where they sold amusing birds and animals moulded out of lead was still going strong. Her mother had introduced her to it long ago. Garnett collected the various birds. For a woman with so few maternal instincts it was strange that her favourite lead treasure should be a mother bird feeding worms to her young whose beaks were wide open for the treat.

Alexia lowered the latch and went into the shop. Two men were busy talking at the other end of the counter. Just as in the old days the room was shadowed by the window displays of heavy tree limbs holding birds in various positions. The shop itself smelled pleasantly of fur boughs, balsam and other, less identifiable branches.

Alexia didn't recognize the middle-aged man behind the counter but his customer was her friend of last night, the actor, Johann Hofer. Both men stopped speaking a few seconds after she entered and she was puzzled by their language which seemed so close to German and yet was different.

She knew the Lichtenbourg patois. It mixed German with whatever other languages had left their vowels and consonants, mostly the latter, in this tiny country. But the language she heard today was not the mishmash code of her childhood which had been a mystery to most of the grownups.

There was something furtive about the shopkeeper and his customer as they turned around to greet her. The shopkeeper pushed his spectacles further up on his nose and asked in German, "The Fraulein wishes for my assistance? My little aviary, is to be enjoyed also, if you choose."

She wanted to say hello to Johann Hofer but he seemed tongue-tied at that moment, so she smiled at him, thanked the shopkeeper, and went over to examine the latest figures half concealed within a complicated balsam nest.

The actor whispered something to the shopkeeper then came over to Alexia. Before she knew what he was doing he bowed his head, with every wavy, dark hair in place, raised her hand to an area approximating his lips, and pretended to kiss her knuckles. Though taken aback she could hardly pull away as he greeted her. "Highness. How wonderful to see you again so soon!"

Embarrassed, Alexia babbled, "Christmas presents. I'm here to find some. I love these wonderful birds."

"Understood. And your gracious mother. A bird for her? She has a great fondness for them."

Emil the shopkeeper bowed and wiped his clean chapped hands on his rubber apron. "Her Serene Highness is an old and valued patroness. You recall, Hanni, how the princess had such a fondness for your birthday gift. She came personally to this very door to thank me. A great success, she said. Better even than your Christmas gift. You remember?"

The birds were very expensive and Alexia couldn't help wondering why young Hofer gave her mother such expensive gifts unless they were his way of repaying her patronage at the theatre.

She glanced at the actor and saw that he was just a shade uneasy. Surely he hadn't blushed? He changed the subject quickly and began to point out the charms of the lead-feathered figures while Alexia puzzled over his part in her mother's life.

If his interest in her mother was sexual it could be understood, considering her beauty and charm. But if Garnett had something sexual going with a young man almost twenty years her junior, she would not only be hurt but when the scandal got out, as it undoubtedly would, it might prove devastating to the Kuragin dynasty. Alexia wanted to get away from here as rapidly as possible.

"Well, I'll think about what I want. I haven't got my list with me. Perhaps Princess Garnett will be good enough to come with me some time soon and help me choose. Good day, gentlemen."

She turned to go and almost walked into her mother who was waiting for her chauffeur to unlatch the door for her. Since she was in the shadow of the ill-lit shop her mother did not identify her at once but she saw Johann Hofer and put out her hands in welcome.

"How very nice of you to – "

He leapt forward to point out Alexia. "Your Serene Highness, I have been honoured by the princess. She asked me to help her choose a few Christmas presents for her friends back in America. But I am sure your taste will be of great help to us. Isn't it so, Princess Alexia?"

"All of that," Alexia said.

Hofer went on eagerly. "By the merest chance I happened to arrive here at Emil Leopold's shop only minutes

149

before Princess Alexia. It was providential since the princess tells me she is not familiar with these lead pieces and was not quite certain which – "

Princess Garnett laughed, a familiar musical sound. "What a naughty girl you are, Alexia, lying to the nice young man. You know quite well I brought you here when you were barely three or four."

"Six," Alexia corrected her, also smiling.

"Heavens! Is it possible? Wolf, wait for us." With a flick of her forefinger Garnett motioned for her bodyguard-chauffeur to leave the shop. The big gaunt man in his blue Lichtenbourg uniform bowed and went out, carefully closing the door. He did not get into the German car but waited outside the shop, standing with legs apart, his right hand on the big Luger in a specially made sheath over his hipbone.

Alexia had once lifted a heavy German Luger and wondered if almost any weapon wouldn't be easier and quicker to handle, but she was busy now, wondering whether her mother had known she was here or had come to Emil Leopold's shop for quite a different meeting.

Hoping to cover her suspicions she changed the subject rapidly. "Herr Leopold, when I visited here years ago an elderly gentleman waited on me. He had white hair and wore a moustache. Your father?"

She intercepted a quick look between Johann Hofer and the shopkeeper before the latter cleared his throat and shook his head. "No, Highness. That was my ex-wife's father, Heim Lowenstein. He, I believe he . . ."

Garnett cut in unexpectedly. "Heim and his daughter, our Emil's ex-wife, have set up shop in Germany. The Lowensteins were born in Darmstadt, you know."

"Germany?" Alexia stared at the two men and her mother, all of whom avoided her eyes and behaved in a furtive way that was contagious. "Why Germany? I thought Jews were not wanted in the Reich."

What about the propaganda she had heard in the States? About hundreds of Jews and others called "undesirables" being pressed into heavy war work in the Reich and sometimes driven to their death. The more outspoken students and speakers at Cal's Sather Gate had hinted at even worse. And here was her mother sounding completely ignorant, talking about her old acquaintance, Heim Lowenstein, returning to the Reich. What about the dreadful things Alexia herself had seen in the newsreels, including the short subject her godfather, Chris Royle, had made about the bloody street crimes against the Jews called "Kristalnacht" in the German Reich? Was that only an isolated instance, something her mother and the Government of Lichtenbourg could conveniently ignore?

Garnett patted her shoulder. "Darling, there are good Jews and there are bad Jews, just as there are good and bad Englishmen. Or Lichtenbourgers when it comes to that. And some of these people commit crimes. They must be punished. But we've been assured on the highest authority that these labour camps are actually munitions works and more humane than just putting criminals in vile, lonely cells."

"But what are their crimes?"

Garnett looked over her head at the two men and smiled tolerantly at her daughter's naive question. "My dear Ava," that always made Alexia wince, but Garnett went serenely on. "For one thing, take gypsies. They steal. It's their way of life. We can't have people stealing from tourists and people like that now, can we?"

No need to remind her mother that tourists were the least of their worries now at the end of 1941. But Alexia asked, "Are they all Jewish gypsies?" The question was heavy with irony and the two men exchanged glances.

151

Garnett sighed. "Do come along. You are behaving in the most childish way. And before strangers. Come along."

On the way out of the shop Garnett reminded her, "It's very complicated. Just remember we are caught in a pincer here in Lichtenbourg. Never forget our danger . . . Hurry. Your father will want to see you."

"I have an appointment with His Serene Highness at three this afternoon," Alexia reminded her. Never let it be said that she failed to pay due homage to her father's title.

Is this what is in my future? she thought. Must we always compromise with evil? Better to be nobody, a young woman who could learn a profession, fall in love, marry and become "normal". How could she live with herself if she were forced to rule her country, the place of her birth, with all the vaguely sinister compromises her father and mother were making?

She still hadn't asked her mother what Count Andross was doing here in Lichtenbourg if he wasn't coming to see her. And with that beautiful blonde on his arm he didn't seem likely to be visiting Alexia Kuragin.

Garnett nudged Alexia. "Wave to Hanni Hofer and Emil."

Alexia looked back. Sure enough the two men bowed in answer to Garnett's wave. Their interest was confined to the reigning princess, not to her daughter.

By this time the big chauffeur-bodyguard had jumped to attention, bowing low to Garnett, a little less obsequiously to Alexia, before offering them each a hand up into the big German car.

"A gift from the Fuhrer," Garnett said, wrinkling her nose at the giver if not the gift.

Alexia examined the sleek polished black exterior and the even more luxurious cushioned grey interior, complete

152

with a little dry bar. Staring Alexia in the face was a miniature of Chancellor Adolf Hitler's head set into the back of the chauffeur's seat.

"I feel as if he's watching every move I make," Alexia observed. "How can you stand it?"

Frowning at Alexia's frankness Garnett tilted her head toward the chauffeur. So they couldn't even discuss something in their own car, in their own country. Alexia lowered her voice.

"Anyway, he looks exactly like a grocery clerk I know in San Francisco. He acts as if he's always trying to catch us shoplifting."

"Alexia, God in heaven! Have you no discretion?" having muttered this, Garnett raised her voice, her face lifting in her celebrated smile. "How generous the Fuhrer is!"

Ignoring this comment played for the chauffeur's benefit Alexia got to the point. "What is Count Andross doing here?"

"Who? Oh, that Swede who saw you back to the Austrian border. I've no idea. Is he here? I know we are expecting Tige. Max is terribly pleased, as you can imagine. It's been so long. Almost three years."

"Yes. Father told me."

Everything always looked a little better when Tige was around. Since his quarrel with Max years ago when Prince Kuragin was assassinated; everything in Lichtenbourg, especially the financial investments from foreign companies, had crumbled, leaving the government and various businesses headquartered in Lichtenbourg dependent to a great extent on Nazi investments. His infrequent visits since had been purely family affairs that had no effect on Lichtenbourg's financial status in the world markets.

"What will Hitler say about western investments returning?" Alexia wanted to know. "Will Tige be safe?"

Garnett looked at her. "You sound as if you care

more about Tige's welfare than that of your own country."

"As a matter of fact, I do." It was blurted out. Alexia was annoyed by her mother's ignorance on the subject of Count Andross.

"Well, my dear, for your information the Fuhrer is delighted that Tige is willing to make peace with us. When Britain collapses any day now the Axis will need someone who is acceptable to both sides for those settlements that take forever."

"What do they do then? All get together and turn on the Russians?"

"Hush."

Alexia thought of the nervous resolution she had seen in those British faces during the one air raid she had experienced. She couldn't resist reminding her mother, "What if the United States comes into the war? That would call for a new poker hand all around, wouldn't it?"

"Don't discuss things you can't begin to understand, dear. Just leave the war to older and wiser heads."

Like yours, Mother? Alexia thought, but was silent as they drove in past the sentries and under the long grey shadow of the New Palace.

Since there was clearly nothing to be learned from her mother about Stefan Andross, who seemed to be an unknown entity, Alexia excused herself and was ready to go to her depressingly heavy suite when Garnett stopped her. They were just being bowed through the Long Gallery side doors and Garnett cleared her throat and broached a touchy subject.

"Darling, it doesn't matter when we are alone but you really must curtsy and refer to me as 'Ma'am' when servants or important guests are around. It's invariably done. You ought to know that."

Alexia had been about to leave but stopped long enough

to bob self-consciously. Her mother was perfectly correct, of course. Etiquette was very strict and the smaller the country the more sensitive about it they seemed to be.

"Thank you, dear." Garnett waggled her fingers at Alexia and went along the gallery, elegant, graceful, nodding to various attendants in the way that had earned her their adoration. The only time she lost their adoration was when the subject of "raises" came up.

"I've been in the States too long, I can see that," Alexia told herself, quite forgetting to behave with similar regal splendour. If she hadn't been called, in a most unregal way, by Polly Quint she wouldn't even have been aware that they passed each other.

"Hi, Miss Alexia. Back so soon?"

"Back? I was hardly out of sight of this old barnacle."

Under the twenty-foot-high domed ceiling of the corridor her voice carried. Well, let it. Let the eager ears of men standing around in comic opera uniforms repeat her words to her parents. "Polly, come with me. I'd like to ask a favour of you. I'm trying to track down a visitor to the palace."

"Sure thing."

How good it was to talk with someone like herself, commonplace, real, not absorbed by a fairytale world which was ringed by evil; that might even be monstrous for all Alexia knew.

The double doors to her suite were wide open and a grinning, slightly obsequious, Janos Becque was just slipping out into the corridor. She wondered what he had found there while she was out.

"Ah, Your Highness. My little message was not necessary. I have caught you in the flesh, so to speak."

"Oh, my sainted aunt!" Polly muttered, thus saving Alexia the trouble of expressing her own feelings.

"Yes?" she said indifferently. "What message is this?"

155

A second later she thought, with sudden excitement, could the message be from Stefan Andross?

Janos Becque's eyelids, slanting over the green-olive eyes, repulsed her with their serpent-like look. Strange, when real snakes had never moved her to revulsion. But then she had never seen sharp teeth shining in the mouth of a King Snake or a graceful water snake.

"I'm asking for the honour of escorting Your Highness to the reception and state dinner tonight."

She recoiled, bumping into Polly. "Why you? Is the guest of honour Count Andross?"

His eyes opened wide in surprise. "Andross? Andross? But no, Ma'am. Royalty is to be entertained. Princess Elsbach. It's a peace mission. Very important to Lichtenbourg's future. Your Highness is aware of the Elsbachs' importance here, of course."

So far as Alexia knew the von Elsbachs had ruled the country, badly, before the death of old Prince von Elsbach in the early 1900s. It was said that the prince died of an apoplexy upon hearing the results of the People's Plebiscite, the first democratic vote in Lichtenbourg's history. They demanded that their hero, Prince Franz Kuragin, should succeed to the throne upon old Elsbach's death.

Alexia motioned for him to leave. He hesitated, clearly wanting her agreement to accept him as escort. She made it clearer. "I cannot see anything is to be gained from the Elsbachs. In the old days they tried repeatedly to murder Prince Kuragin. That will be all. You have our leave to go."

He bowed and slithered out between the open doors.

Polly Quint eyed her with uneasy amusement. "Just there for a minute, Miss Alexia, you put me in mind of Old Queen Vic. Not that I ever saw her in action."

"Queen Victoria never put up with creatures like Janos Becque. Did you see that damned swastika band on his arm?"

156

"Oh, that. You'll get used to them after a while here. Not to change the subject but you've got some mail, there on the desk next to Becque's note."

Seeing a San Francisco postmark Alexia tossed the other mail aside, including Becque's note, written with great precision in the now out-of-date German gothic type.

"The card. Look, Polly. My very dearest friend in all the world. Dan Royle."

Polly looked at the black and white view of the glamorous Golden Gate Bridge, only three years old.

"Boy, oh boy! That's something. Is he related to Mr Tige Royle?"

"Only by adoption. It's a long story, but he is my best friend."

Polly was sceptical. "You sure acted pretty interested in that Count you met in England."

"You don't understand. Dan is the brother I never had. There's nobody like Dan. He's got so much spirit. If you're in trouble he's the man to know. He'll make you laugh. I can't imagine anything he couldn't make a joke out of."

She turned the card over and read the message. How typical; Dan was not a long-winded writer.

How's my princess? No trouble getting there? Off on the Clipper in two hours. Wish me luck. Philippines, here I come. Love you, Dan.

Polly read it over her shoulder and shivered. "What a long way off! Two big fat oceans and all that land to cross back home in America. I hope for your sake, Ma'am, he knows what he's doing. Those Philippines are pretty close to Japan, or is my geography haywire?"

Alexia tapped the card thoughtfully against her teeth. "No, your geography isn't haywire, but I am beginning to think Dan is."

157

Meanwhile, Polly reminded her, there was her gown to be chosen for tonight's reception and state dinner. This was the first formal occasion where she would be seen by the representatives of the Axis and neutral countries as an adult.

She and Polly went through her wardrobe. Each gown was carefully wrapped in tissue paper in the long dressing room. Beneath the hanging garments were the matching shoes, petticoats, slips and some girdles that looked like medieval and deadly Iron Maidens.

Alexia felt more sickness than disgust. "Damn! I've never worn a corset in my life."

Worse than that, she and Polly were interrupted by a disturbance in the corridor followed by the arrival of Princess Garnett, also on a wardrobe inspection tour. The princess soon tossed out everything over which Alexia and Polly were debating.

"Only two floor-length gowns? My dear, what were you thinking of? You must be very special tonight to catch the eye of that awful Elsbach female. Princess, indeed! Gives herself such airs. But then, I've never trusted blondes."

Alexia grinned at Polly over the shoulder of her auburn-haired mother, though she said indifferently, "Well, Ma'am, that's all I've got. And why must I please Princess Ilsa, anyway? We're supposed to be having a blood feud, aren't we?"

"Never mind. Just take your father's word, it's important." She pursed her lips, considering the meagre wardrobe. "I wonder. You and I are almost of a size and I have my new ball gowns. Two of them I've never worn."

Considering that Count Andross was somewhere in this old rattletrap of a building, Alexia had no objection to looking her best. Besides, it occurred to her that, quite possibly, the blonde in Stefan's staff car was Princess Ilsa von Elsbach. Stefan, therefore, would be the von

158

Elsbach escort or bodyguard. A lovely solution to Alexia's jealousy.

Garnett shook her head once more at the poor selection of gowns to work from and, having summoned her personal maid as well as her mistress of the robes, Countess Gravelines, she went off to examine the possibilities in her own wardrobe.

Polly was amused. "That'll be the first time old Gravelines will have a chance to do what she's paid to do. She gets a thousand marks a year for the title."

Alexia figured rapidly. "Are you serious? Two hundred dollars a year?"

"It's the honour of the thing, that's all."

"I've got a lot to learn about running this country."

By the time her mother returned leading a troupe of ladies bearing ballgowns and their accoutrements, Alexia had received her first disappointment. Her father's private secretary, a shy and very serious young man, telephoned to express Prince Max's regrets. He would have to cancel her "interview" with him today. Official matters of state had intervened.

"His Serene Highness sends Your Highness his best affections. He is – " A little pause while the young secretary apparently was prompted by her father. "He would like me to express his disappointment and . . . he will look forward to the reception and the presence of Your Highness."

"Yes. I understand." She set the elegant ivory-coloured French phone back and turned to find herself surrounded by a glorious cloud of far too summery materials, most of them georgette, chiffon, lace and net. One by one her mother's ladies held Garnett's ballgowns up before Alexia.

Behind the ladies stood Polly, solemnly shaking her head or looking skyward in disapproval until the slender apricot satin was presented. The Countess Gravelines resurrected a bright little sprig of false flowers, the colour of a vivid sunset, and held it below the lowest point of the heart-shaped neckline. It would certainly call attention to Alexia's curves.

Everyone looked happy, ready to join in the chorus of praise, but watched Princess Garnett for their cue. Garnett groaned.

"Heavens! That was the very gown I had in mind for tonight." She looked around at the women whose faces fell in unison. Then she broke into one of her charming laughs and clapped her hands. "But how silly of me! I shall wear the green. It is just light enough to set off the emeralds His Highness gave me for my birthday. And for Alexia, the rubies?" She caught herself. "No. Not the rubies."

The Countess cleared her throat. "If Your Serene Highness agrees I would suggest the coral and pearl set. Such delicacy is suitable to the complexion of Her Highness."

Alexia took a deep breath. She couldn't quite see herself sweeping into the state hall with her mother's heavy ruby set weighing her down. Aside from everything else, it would add years to her age.

Her mother patted Alexia's cheek. "You musn't mind too much, Darling. You will have all the time in the world to wear rubies."

After the decision had been made, the measuring, ripping and pinning began. As the time rushed by Alexia whispered to Polly, "Will you see if you can find out what happened to Count Andross?"

While the ladies were fussing around, running in and out with the newly stitched slip and gown, Polly disappeared. But Alexia got little satisfaction out of Polly's efforts when she returned.

"Not here. Never heard of him."

Alexia had eaten nothing since breakfast and the first

thing she did when Garnett went off to supervise her own glittering transformation was to ask for a milkshake.

Polly laughed but the two wardrobe ladies Garnett had left behind to give her a long list of "dos" and "don'ts" were shocked. The elder of the two stately dames objected. "May I be permitted to remind Your Highness that your gown has been sewn upon you, so to speak?"

Alexia took several delicate breaths and felt the smooth satin lines over her still flat stomach – she felt that she would have room to eat at the formal dinner. However, there was no need to tempt fate. No milkshake. She wondered if they would know how to make one anyway.

By the time Garnett's hairdresser, Leopold, recommended by Magda Goebbels, had been called in, there was little time to do more than yield to Alexia's plea that her hair be simply done.

"No fake rolls of hair above my forehead and no hair-do that feels like cement."

The hairdresser, going against all his inclination, did what he could, creating a soft gentle coiffure, and went off shrugging hopelessly.

Alone at last, but for Polly, Alexia strolled across the floor, trying to kick the little demi-train behind her in a casual way. It was barely adequate but Polly applauded good-naturedly.

They were both a little shaken by a sharp knock on the door. Polly muttered, "It's that awful creepy little Becque, your escort."

Alexia straightened up, reached for the little gold ball and chain that formed her evening bag and hung the chain on her wrist, over her gloves. With what she considered admirable calmness she said, "Open the door, Polly. I am ready."

Polly whispered, "Marie Antoinette going to the guillotine."

She swung the door open just as Alexia said, only half-amused, "Oh, shut up!"

In the open doorway a dark, tall man in blue and gold uniform, the colours of Sweden, stood there with gloved hand held out to her. Say what they would, this was certainly Stefan Andross, and he had never looked more striking to her. "I believe I am your fortunate escort, Your Highness."

CHAPTER FOURTEEN

Her first reaction was delight but she managed to subdue this childish joy to a more sophisticated, "How nice to see you again, Count!" While she spoke she looked around the corridor, asking on a note of anxiety, "What have you done with my friend Chancellor Becque? He seems to be late."

"And will no doubt be later still." Not the least put out the Count took her hand, placed it on his sleeve, and asked, "Shall we give them all the pleasure they are waiting for?"

Since she couldn't think of any excuse not to, they walked along the corridor toward the massive staircase. He seemed in excellent spirits, not a care in the world. She wanted to kick him. Instead she blurted out what she had been aching to know: "Who is the beautiful blonde you brought to the palace?"

"Yes," he agreed as if he had given it a few seconds' earnest thought. "One might call her beautiful, I suppose. A good many have."

She said cattily, "The lady is well preserved, for her age."

"Older than you. Or even me, perhaps?"

"Well, isn't she?"

He laughed. It was a bright laugh, full of teasing and fun, reminding her how charming he could be. "I devoutly hope so."

"What?" She realized he was about to spring his surprise on her.

"My darling child, Her Serene Highness, the former Heiress Presumptive of Lichtenbourg, is my mother, Princess Ilsa von Elsbach."

She felt an instant's relief but then she understood the implications of his masquerade. She tried to remove her fingers from his sleeve but he closed his left hand over her fingers. "Don't be childish. I'm the same man you knew as Count Andross. It's my stepfather's name, an honest one."

"Then why the masquerade?"

He stopped at the top of the stairs and smiled ruefully. "You have me there. I knew you would think the whole thing was a dynastic plot. Your father warned me that you shared your family's hatred of the Elsbachs. They were not the best of rulers."

"Your grandfather tried every trick in the book to keep the Kuragins out of Lichtenbourg."

"No, my darling. That was my great-uncle. And a scoundrel he was. You won't hear me defending him. But your father needs help and it's our belief he will do better with the Elsbachs at his side. For one thing, Hitler has always gotten on well with my mother. Not everyone does."

"I can believe that."

She thought of all this loose talk about a union between the Kuragins and the Elsbachs. So that was all Stefan's pursuit of her added up to. A dynastic marriage.

She heard their names being trumpeted on the landing halfway down the staircase. "Her Highness, the Princess Presumptive, Ava Alexandra; His Highness, the Prince Stefan von Elsbach."

Stefan whispered, "A hundred kroner says my smile is wider than yours . . . Ready?"

She couldn't help laughing. "Make it Lichtenbourg marks and you're on."

The fact that they descended the wide staircase in such excellent spirits with each other obviously thrilled the crowded royal hall below where every face was raised to study them.

Prince Stefan whispered, "I wonder what would happen if you suddenly slapped me, just about now."

"Don't tempt me." She tried not to giggle but it was impossible to keep a straight face when she thought how absurd this toy kingdom playacting really was in the middle of a world at war. Her head was still spinning at the trick that had been played on her. How amused Nick Chance must have been, guessing that the attentions of "Count Andross" to Alexia were all meant to promote a dynastic marriage. Love had nothing to do with it.

What a childish fool I was! she thought. And yet, here she was, enjoying Stefan's company as she enjoyed no one else's. Even her feelings for Dan were quite different – not physical, not passionate. Why couldn't she enjoy a love affair with Stefan, lead him on, feel the wonder of real passion, and then bid him a pleasant goodbye? The truth was, she wouldn't want to give him up as a lover, only as a dynastic partner.

She heard applause and found herself and the prince surrounded by well-wishers talking about an end to the long, cruel feud between Kuragin and Elsbach. Little they knew!

An Austrian orchestra had been hired for the occasion and was giving the long, vaulted hall a lighter, more romantic touch with its Strauss and Lehar waltzes, but no one was dancing. The guests kept circling the foot of the staircase in the hope of seeing the evening's stars, the Prince and Princess of Lichtenbourg with the former Heiress Presumptive, Princess Ilsa von Elsbach.

When Alexia and Stefan had a moment to themselves she asked him, "Whose idea was it that the feud between our families should end?"

He offered her a wide, shallow champagne glass. As she took it in her hand he closed his fingers around hers. Surprised, she looked up. She liked his smile but her resolve to play fast and loose with him was a little shaken by the depth of feeling she thought she read in his dark eyes.

"My mother has been determined to win back Lichtenbourg since the Kuragins won it. I grew up hearing nothing but her insistence that it was ours. One method stirred in her clever little brain. I was to marry you."

She tried to but failed to slip her fingers out from under his warm hand. "So you followed me to Miravel and pretended to be someone else. You almost succeeded."

"Almost?" He lowed his head and kissed her, a light touch of the lips that was little more than teasing and might mean anything or nothing, especially since his action. attracted titters and applause from their audience.

She knew she had flushed at his touch but did not let herself take him too seriously or she would find herself an Elsbach and a tool of the ambitious Ilsa. Her light laugh was not as felt as it sounded.

"Are all the Elsbachs so persistent?"

"No," he confessed. "Only my late unlamented great-uncle."

"And your mother."

His response was not as light and joking as she expected. "By all means. How could I have forgotten the golden Ilsa?"

There was a sudden obvious clearing of throats and the sharp click of a staff on the wooden staircase. The pompous voice managed to silence all the chatter in the lengthy

166

hall. "His Serene Highness, Prince Maximilian of Lichtenbourg, the Princess Ilsa von Elsbach, Her Serene Highness, Princess Garnett of Lichtenbourg, Reichsmarschall Goering."

Like a good many others Alexia had to admit that the person who aroused her curiosity the most was not a member of any royal family but that huge, highly decorated airman responsible for most of the horrors of the London Blitz. She was prepared to hate him, but like a good many other dangerous people, he seemed to have a most pleasant public persona.

She began to think of a letter to Dan, all about this "monster" who was talking to Alexia's mother in the most amiable way. If, as she had been told, he was in a drug induced state it was hard to tell at the moment. He was much too busy being charming to Princess Garnett.

Prince Stefan looked down at Alexia. He appeared to sense her reaction. Perhaps he shared it but she couldn't tell. She knew that his government continued to do business with the Third Reich. Reichsmarschall Goering might well be a friend of his. Certainly her mother did not appear repulsed by the fat man who looked like one huge white ball, flashing in every conceivable area of his upper torso with ribbons and metal.

The orchestra struck up the Lichtenbourg National Anthem, led by an enthusiastic Johann Hofer and Alexia came to attention like everyone else. To her astonishment Stefan ruined her attempt at a straight face by whispering: "Whale oil."

He enjoyed her efforts to stifle a laugh. It was an effort that she finally managed to adapt to a sneeze. As the anthem swelled to its conclusion with Hanni Hofer's pleasant tenor ringing out: "God bless our Gracious Sovereign," Alexia pinched Stefan's arm. He did not jump or remove his arm from her waist, but he gave her an amused look. If only she could believe he loved her for herself and not his accursed dynasty!

While her parents were surrounded by palace hangers-on and well-wishers, Alexia wondered daringly, What if I married Stefan von Elsbach and then made him love me for myself? Why not? Other royal brides have gone through this, and still do. She had no time to debate the pros and cons. The partners had changed. Her parents sauntered over to her, Max with Garnett's arm in his. At some distance behind them Princess Ilsa von Elsbach and the German Reichsmarschall were pinned in the centre of a fawning crowd.

Alexia was unpleasantly surprised to note that the object of all this fawning attention was not the dazzling princess whose hair almost outshone her diamond coronet and gold lamé gown, but Hermann Goering. If it was possible for him to expand further in this glow of popularity he had done so. He seemed to know and enjoy everyone. There was nothing of the Fuhrer's bourgeois reserve about him.

She turned her thoughts to closer matters. Her mother looked as glorious as her rival, Princess Ilsa. Her auburn hair was worn in the Grecian fashion, held in place by a diamond tiara studded with emeralds, matching the earrings and the necklace whose emerald centre jewel lay just between her delicate breasts. Few men would look beyond her lovely bosom but her pale green chiffon gown clung to a still perfect figure.

"Well, Max, you've complained enough," Garnett reminded him as they reached Alexia and Stefan. "Here she is, in excellent hands."

Prince Stefan bowed at the same time that Alexia started to curtsy, but Max caught his daughter by the arms and stopped her. "Come now, child. Think of me only as your father." He hugged her to him much to the interest of those guests around them. Under this genuine display of affection Alexia felt a new warmth in her life. It was good to know she was more than a dynastic figurehead to him. She returned his hug, moved by his drawn and tired features.

As a youth and in his early manhood he had been called Prince Charming, with his much vaunted good looks and the princely way he wore his blue Lichtenbourg uniform with its full complement of medals and ribbons, one or two of which he had earned. His features were as perfect as ever, but they looked worn, like good glassware that had seen better days.

Part of Alexia's attention, however, remained on her mother behind her, who was talking to Prince Stefan with great animation. He remained his usual self, with just a suggestion of faint amusement. Thinking back Alexia realized that with herself he had sometimes been quite sincere, not always mocking. That ought to count for something, anyway.

Through the buzz of conversation which effectively covered the romantic melodies played by the orchestra, so many people were presented to Alexia that she could remember only a few particularly eccentric guests, not least of which was Reichsmarschall Hermann Goering.

He had all a fat man's jolly charm. Since her mother got on so well with him, Alexia was surprised when Garnett warned her, *sotto voce*, "Take care what you say. He is more intelligent than he looks." However, this didn't prevent Garnett from immediately signalling to the German again as he was exchanging some hilarious confidence with Princess Ilsa.

"You must assure my daughter that the Fuhrer endorses her engagement to an Elsbach."

Goering inclined his head to Princess Ilsa and with that lady's smiling assent he assured Alexia, "Nothing would please the Fuhrer more, Your Highness. He and

Princess Ilsa are longtime friends. I might say the Elsbachs have always been devoted to the Reich and a greater Germany."

"I could not have expressed it better," Princess Ilsa tapped his big shoulder with her ivory fan.

Alexia could imagine how her friends at the university in California would laugh at that Victorian gesture. She caught Stefan's eye and was happy to see that his eyebrows questioned her. She even read hope into his expression. She knew it was time she set everyone straight about her so-called engagement, but she found a dozen reasons why she should let nature, and these determined parents, take their course for the time being. Later, when she and Stefan were alone, she might make the break with him. Right now she wanted to enjoy his company for another hour or two. At the same time she certainly didn't want to marry into a family that boasted of its devotion to Old Adolf.

A young groom in the Lichtenbourg livery wove his way through the chattering, glittering crowd with a message for Prince Maximilian. "A gentleman has arrived, Highness. He does not speak very good German. He has no valet. He may be American."

Startled, Max looked at Alexia. "Good God! It may be Tige. Is he being made comfortable? Frau Becque has given him his old suite?"

"I'll go," Alexia volunteered. "Let me do it."

The groom interrupted. "Frau Becque insists that the German Reichsmarschall has the suite. Frau Becque does not recognize the American gentleman, so she says."

Alexia heard the inflection in the young groom's voice and had no doubt he disliked the housekeeper and was happy to repeat the scene verbatim.

Forgetting his well-known "quiet calm", Max said, "God damn the woman! If my wife weren't so insistent I'd be rid of that old hag tomorrow. Alexia, tell Her Highness I am

170

called away on an international matter. That, at least, is the truth."

"Let the groom or one of the footmen tell her, Sir. I'd like to go with you."

Max waved away her request and crossed the hall so rapidly that two Austrian photographers signalled each other and started to follow him.

Alexia swung around anxiously, wondering if she should stop them. She doubted if there was anything secret about her father's meeting with Tige, but gossiping photographers might make something out of it. If the SS which honeycombed Lichtenbourg thought Tige was pro-English and sneaking into Lichtenbourg there would be endless trouble.

Suddenly Prince Stefan was beside her. Would he make something suspicious out of Tige's unannounced arrival? He took her elbow. "Shall we put a little distance between your father and our nosy newsmen?"

"Oh, if we could!" Her real relief was in his understanding.

He led her out a side door into the south gallery and headed off the two Austrians beyond a sharp angle in the gallery. Prince Stefan was all amiability. "Gentlemen, we await you. Tell us which pose you prefer."

The bigger man tried to shake off Stefan's hand without offending him. All that registered with Alexia was the swastika armband on one muscular arm.

"Pardon, Highness. We have been called by the Prince Royal."

"Nonsense, old boy. You would not offend the son of the Princess von Elsbach. Your *gauleiter* in Vienna will have something to say."

The younger photographer nudged his companion and got his little Zeiss into position, ignoring the bigger camera dangling from cords under his own armband. "His

Highness is right. The Princess Ilsa is a friend of Seiss-Inquart."

The name of the *gauleiter* of the Austrian Reich was already known in America. Dan referred to him as one of Hitler's flunkies. But getting into the mood to fool these swastika boys, Alexia returned Stefan's breathtaking hug.

"Now," Stefan ordered as he kissed her. It may have been the champagne or his own skill but she found her entire body hot with desire as his mouth clung to hers.

It was the photographer who put down his camera with a "Whew!" and wiped his forehead. The older man looked around but his prey was gone. He shrugged and then grinned.

"Is pretty good, eh, Meinherr? This royal marriage?"

"This one is," Stefan said, taking the attention away from Alexia who was hot, flushed and embarrassed.

The two photographers gave Stefan the straight-armed Nazi salute and returned to the great hall. Stefan laughed and fanned Alexia with his hand. "I think our 'secret engagement' will be the talk of the town by tomorrow. No need to announce it formally."

She frowned. "I wonder how you jilt someone officially in Lichtenbourg."

"I don't believe it is permitted." He was more gentle now, giving her a feather-light kiss on the nose.

She was enjoying his nearness and the touch of his warm lips immensely when footsteps came to a halt just where the gallery turned in its sharp right angle. They could not see the men speaking but one voice sounded familiar. Alexia had heard that voice and that language this morning at Emil Leopold's shop.

It came to her then, the identity of the voice – Johann Hofer. The language was Yiddish.

She pulled at Stefan's sleeve, whispering, "Let's go."

He nodded. As they stepped out and started toward the

end of the gallery where her father had disappeared Stefan murmured, "I'd never have guessed. The Hofer lad who appears at the Theatre Royal."

"What about him? Do hurry. I want to meet Tige."

"Jewish. The boy is Jewish."

"Anybody can speak Yiddish," she told him snappishly. "Including me." Let him think that over.

"Now, perhaps you will tell me why we are playing this spy game," Stefan suggested. Though he said it lightly she had a feeling that he was more serious than he sounded. "I sincerely hope your father isn't running some underground railroad, rescuing the hunted and all that."

"No. It's nothing mysterious at all. But why couldn't my father play the Scarlet Pimpernel if he felt like it?"

"Because, my dear, he is no more equipped than you are. Where are we going?"

"To meet Tige Royle, if you must know. Tomorrow the German Ambassador to Lichtenbourg will probably meet Tige. Tige is very democratic. He'd even meet Hitler if Good Old Adolf asked to see him."

Stefan sighed. "I suppose there is no use in my asking you to show a little discretion. Good-old-you-know-who is currently the master of Central Europe if we except the Soviet Union."

"And Britain."

"Britain is not on the Continent. Why didn't your great-grandfather come in like any normal American, with the Stars and Stripes flying from his jeep? This way he makes your father look like a conspirator."

"He usually comes in quietly, settles into his suite and hold interviews with investors who use Lichtenbourg as a base. He doesn't care for fancy balls and state dinners and the rest."

"Very sensible," Stefan agreed. "What happened this time?"

Alexia explained that the housekeeper had given his apartments to Reichsmarschall Goering. "Becque," she added. "An awful woman. I don't know why Father puts up with her. He says it's because Mother insists."

"Becque. She is related to that little toad who was going to escort you tonight?"

"He is our chancellor, unfortunately, and a member of the Lichtenbourg Royal Council. How did you manage to take his place?"

"There are ways. We must find out where the shoe pinches. In his case I told him it was the Fuhrer's wish."

Revolting, she told herself. To think that if she did actually go through with the shotgun wedding, she would have Hitler to thank for it. But she laughed because she saw that he found it amusing. She couldn't imagine how the prince knew where the guest apartments were.

"My saintly mother prepared me for everything," he explained. "Even drew maps. Nothing missed her eagle eye."

He led her up a narrow staircase on the garden front of the palace and she immediately heard Tige Royle's voice from the open doorway of a small, panelled room that looked as comfortable as her father's private study. With the long vista of gardens and chalets belonging to the aristocracy and foreign interests of Lichtenbourg, and a fireplace glowing warmly, the room seemed far more comfortable than her own huge apartments. Tige would do well to keep this room.

He evidently thought so too. "For the last time, damn it, I'm perfectly satisfied here. It's not what I came for." Since he was speaking in English, Prince Max replied in the same language.

"I realize that, Tige. But it is only fitting. Besides, the Reichsmarschall will be gone by noon tomorrow."

"Still using drugs, I take it."

Stefan asked Alexia in a low voice, "Does he know everything?"

"Everything."

"Even so, I suggest we close the door."

He urged her into the room so quickly she looked back and then understood. Frau Becque was creeping quietly along the corridor in her usual fashion, walking close to the dusty, tapestried wall, like a crab edging its way along a beach.

The two men looked up, startled at Stefan's entrance. Tige had been taking his shaving kit and a striped nightshirt out of his old-fashioned, snap-top valise. Alexia, still looking behind her, sang out cheerfully,

"Are you looking for the Reichsmarschall, Becque? Poor man. Did you give him that dreary suite you used to force on Mr Royle?"

Even Stefan opened his eyes wider at that, exchanging a smile with Tige. Only Prince Max refused to be amused. "Frau Becque!"

Tige put out his hand. "You always were a stubborn kid. Leave it, Max."

It sounded odd but endearing for Alexia to hear her regal and handsome father referred to as a "kid", but to Tige, who had seen everything in his seventy-six years, most human beings must seem like children.

Frau Becque appeared in the doorway innocently. "Your Highness called me?"

Before Max could speak, Stefan put in, "Coffee and brandy for Mr Royle wasn't it, Your Highness?"

The woman was obviously offended at being given a kitchen order but after looking at each of the men, she said, "I will call the kitchen, Your Highness." She curtsied and went scuttling down the corridor under Alexia's watchful eyes.

"Close the door, Honey," Tige called to her, "and just come here where I can give you a big hug."

Tige held his arms out, still strong, still vital, as she always thought of him. She knew he would never change with that thick grey hair and all. A man of only middle height he still seemed like the California Redwoods – immortal.

He squeezed her until she cried out and laughed at the same time while Max slapped them both on the back, asking Prince Stefan, "Is this a family you wish to join?"

Alexia and Tige both looked around as Stefan said quietly, "I knew I did about ten minutes after I followed her into the Miravel railway carriage."

"Ten minutes!" Tige demanded indignantly. "What took you so long?" He grinned at Prince Max. "I may have made this trip for nothing. I only came to make sure you weren't selling her down the river for dynastic reasons."

Alexia forced a smile. If only he had ended his good wishes with a simple joke.

CHAPTER FIFTEEN

Alexia had originally supposed she was returning home to learn all there was about succeeding her father as the Princess Royal. To an extent this was still true, except that she must also learn Swedish and absorb much of that country's great history. She wasn't sure where her immediate future might take her. The only thing she had discovered about herself was a sexual passion for her future husband and a hope, not too forlorn, that he might one day love her purely for herself, dynasty or no dynasty.

The furore that overtook Lichtenbourg after the news of the Kuragin-Elsbach union proved to Alexia that there was no turning back. The Lichtenbourgers wanted to believe the union of these warring houses would give both peace and strength to their postage-stamp-sized country. It would also, if they were lucky, add a little strength to the country with the addition of the Reich's powerful northern neighbour, Sweden.

From beyond the borders of Lichtenbourg Adolf Hitler expressed his great pleasure at this rise in the status of the von Elsbachs who had always supported the National Socialist Party and he "was relieved to note there would be no necessity to land troops or SS to aid in the defence of this tiny but faithful friend." The hint of what lay in wait for Lichtenbourg without this dynastic marriage was all too clear.

The Fuhrer's expressed pleasure unloosed a hurricane of congratulations from the Axis Powers plus neutral Spain, Sweden, Switzerland and the United States.

When Alexia was away from Stefan she worried, still mistrusting the purpose of this contrived marriage, but the implied threat in Hitler's congratulations told her she could hardly back out now. Besides, the minute she saw Stefan again her excitement for him returned.

Tige and her family were overjoyed at her easy agreement to the marriage. Garnett's only negative comment was one that Alexia might have foreseen. "Darling, the whole thing is highly romantic, even though Max kept the matter so secret. Imagine his knowing about Prince Stefan's pursuit of you and never confiding in me. My only worry is that dreadful Elsbach woman. She's over fifty and really shows her age. Now, I suppose she will try to mother you in that dreary old chateau in Sweden."

Dreary did not sound very promising to Alexia but surely it wasn't any more dreary than the so-called New Palace in Lichtenbourg City. She had few facts to go on, remembering only the hours spent with Stefan waiting for the German plane and seeing nothing but the airfield and the little airport waiting room.

Would her mother's depressing idea of Alexia's future home in Sweden prove to be as accurate? Alexia knew she must expect very little. She kept reminding herself that much of the world was suffering far more than herself with her thoughts about dreary chateaux. A life with Stefan, now and after the war . . . Yes, concentrate on that. She found her future husband to be quite as companionable and kind and humorous as he had been the night of his arrival in Lichtenbourg. But eventually there must be more to the marriage than that.

Tige and Prince Max had apparently discussed Alexia's changing moods. They chose a time to rectify matters that

178

weekend when Princess Ilsa had been all smiles and humility to Garnett, suggesting, "I wonder if Your Highness would be gracious enough to give me your presence in my suite while my Berlin jewellers are present?" She lowered her voice discreetly, but not so discreetly that Alexia couldn't hear.

"You would know exactly what would please the lovely bride. Wedding presents, you know."

"Why not one of the old Elsbach heirlooms? The sentiment would be so touching," Garnett suggested while Alexia looked heavenward in dismay.

"Mother!" She knew this was Garnett's way of implying that the Elsbachs had gotten out of Lichtenbourg with half the Crown Jewels.

Nobody seemed to hear Alexia's cry. Princess Ilsa breezed over this awkward moment. "I believe Krieger-Wiek might have just the thing. You need have no fears. They are entirely an Aryan concern now."

"Ah! That does relieve me."

Alexia read a surprising sarcasm in that but fortunately Princess Ilsa did not appear to notice the inflection.

Although Alexia had no wish for Garnett to be branded as pro-Semitic by one of Hitler's notorious anti-Semites, she was relieved that, in spite of her mother's public utterances, she had not gone over entirely to the virulent Nazi policies. Still, considering Garnett's self-centred mind it was odd. Alexia wondered at her motive in this dangerous game. Was she concerned about the few professional Jewish physicians and bankers still under Lichtenbourg protection?

The two women had gone off to Princess Ilsa's suite volubly discussing the latest fashion hints from Nazi occupied Paris and questioning whether the famous "Coco" Chanel was or was not pro-Nazi.

Tige Royle must have been hovering around the corridor

179

waiting for their departure. He stuck his head into the living room only minutes later. "Honey, is the coast clear?"

Alexia looked around. "So it would seem. Do come in. You know I'd rather see you or Dan than anybody."

He came in but did not sit down. "I hope you are excluding that good fellow, your future husband."

She looked into his eyes with their glint of understanding and saw the devotion he felt for all his "adopted chicks" as he had once called her and Dan and her American godparents, Laura and Christopher Royle.

"Well now, Max and I have been discussing that very thing. Seems good old Stefan, just like a careful Swede, thinks he should be very careful with you, treat you like chinaware until the wedding. Does he think you are a virgin? Matter of fact, are you?"

She began to laugh and was barely able to stop when he put his hand over her mouth and looked around anxiously. "Your mother would kill me if she heard me blurt that out. But, well, these aren't Victorian days, Honey. And this may make that dumb Swede too careful with you. I don't mean, you know . . . I mean he ought to kiss you more. You should see how I kissed your great-grandmother, Honey."

"Stefan may be dumb, but he happens to be German and Hungarian."

"All right. That dumb Kraut."

Of course Tige could be correct. Stefan might be afraid she would resent too much of that marvellous exploratory kissing and caressing. Still, she didn't like Tige to think Stefan wasn't sexy.

"My darling old Tige, what do you want me to do? Seduce him?"

"No." He rubbed his jaw thoughtfully. "You musn't go that far. But he might think he has to be too careful of you or something. And he's dead wrong. I see a big misunderstanding here between you. Max does, too. Sort of. After all, eventually you are going to found a new dynasty and keep the peace for Lichtenbourg."

She gasped at this surprising view of her father. He might think such things but he didn't go around saying them aloud. "You mean, Father would like Stefan to deflower me, or whatever you'd call it?"

He was horrified. "Good God, no! Just what we might call a – a what they call the music that gets you in the mood for some damned symphony. More hand-holding and togetherness. More smooching."

What could he expect of a dynastic marriage? Her mood was not improved by this little family advice. Tige was always full of it. Once in a while he went a bit overboard.

"OK, Tige. Let's just let nature take its course. Meanwhile, I have two other college courses coming up – One in Crown Princess's manners and the other in Royal Constitutional Law."

She kissed his rough cheek, patted his arm, and shooed him out. He went, but stopped in the doorway to add in a stage whisper, "Kisses I said. Not any further, Honey."

"Sure, sure." A nauseating idea occurred to her suddenly. "Did you or Father have this kind of conversation with my fiancé by any chance?"

He stuck his head back in. "Well, not exactly. Maybe a hint."

She moistened her lips. "What did he say?"

"About what you said."

"You – !" She looked around for something to throw at him but couldn't find anything he deserved.

Meanwhile he reminded her. "The Royals and the Royles are all going up to the Royal Chalet for a Sunday night winter picnic, they call it. Kids stuff. But get yourself all gussied up. I'd like to see you outshine your Mama. Or better yet, both of them."

That made her laugh and she dropped the German paperweight she had been hefting.

"I'll go while the going's good," he promised her and ducked out.

Late that afternoon the line of palace cars started for the pavilion commonly called the Chalet on the near side of the Lichtenbourg range which Alexia remembered only from her childhood. At that time it had seemed very like a little fairytale castle with a long terrace overlooking the patch of Lichtenbourg countryside that spread out below as far as the New Palace and beyond.

Riding in Stefan's little Swedish car up the steep mountain road full of switchbacks and potholes, she explained, "I liked going up here. Prince Kuragin took me up the first time I can remember. He set me up before him on his mount. He was a superb rider. I wasn't afraid of anything when I was with him."

Stefan looked over at her. "That must be about the time we Elsbachs regarded him as our worst enemy. I am surprised you actually agreed to marry me."

"Well, I didn't, really. It was wished on me, you might say."

He gave her a side glance, "I'm glad it was you who said that, not me."

Wondering if Tige and her father had actually urged him to make winning remarks and resenting it she shrugged. "Oh, I don't mind. If I didn't marry an Elsbach I'd have to marry someone else on my dynastic level."

He laughed, not necessarily with any humour. "What is your dynastic level?"

"Well, it certainly isn't the Windsors. Or the Dutch or the Danes or your beloved King Gustav's family. Though I notice these Norsemen are quite good looking."

182

"Not the German Hohenzollerns or the Austrian Hapsburgs?"

She looked at him, her eyes sparkling. She would be sophisticated if it killed her.

"If I must, I must." He didn't seem to know what to make of her and considering all the talk of her immaturity and virginity, which she hated, she was relieved to keep him guessing. He had already admitted to taking his ambitious mother's advice when he first pursued her.

The limousine behind them threatened to pass them and Stefan, looking into the rear view mirror, asked, "Shall we let them pass?"

She looked around. "Who is it?"

"Tige and Her Highness."

"Which Highness?"

"My mother."

"Don't give an inch."

He smiled at that, keeping up his speed and blocking Tige who leaned on the horn, trying to beat them to the Chalet.

Alexia was relieved that her sophisticated act had to be laid aside. She wasn't at all sure it had any effect on him anyway. Surreptitiously she studied his profile. Not at all the delicate, princely good looks of a fairytale hero but hard-boned, with his dark skin that called attention to a straight, powerful nose and strong mouth. That mouth had taken possession of hers giving her an unforgettable excitement the night their engagement became known. Maybe he had been drunk that night?

Once in a while on the trip up to the Chalet he reached for her hand and covered it with his, as if to remind her that they belonged together. Or even that he loved her.

They reached the wide front terrace of the Chalet minutes before Tige who complained, "You left me in high dudgeon. Whatever that is. I'll have you know I could have won hands down if I hadn't been at the wheel of a damned hearse."

"Nonsense, my dear Tige," Princess Ilsa said, giving the American her flashing smile. "You were being gallant. You know I detest too much speed." She assured Alexia, "What a charmer our Tige is. He insists that I call him Tige. You understand, of course."

Alexia understood all too well. She saw no reason to explain that Tige demanded that of everyone. No matter. She noticed Stefan's cynical amusement at his mother's fawning on the tycoon, decided to let Princess Ilsa find out for herself that every time Tige flattered one of the ladies who fell for him there was another in the wings.

A number of liveried servants were lined up on the terrace in front of the two double-doored entrances, one of which had been created by the last Elsbach, as Stefan explained to Alexia.

"No one used those doors except his mistresses or a few special envoys. Secret agents, to us common mortals."

Alexia said, "He sounds delightful. I do hope you have inherited some of his little habits."

"No. Only the large ones." He hugged her to him in a way she found most satisfying.

Tige had been deserted by his fair companion who hurried up the marble steps to the group on the terrace which stayed in its own clump of German Army uniforms, mixed in with two SS men in black and several civilians, the latter also heavy with decorations including the swastika. Princess Ilsa gave one of the civilians the Nazi salute and addressed him by name.

"Herr Sternberg, how good to see you! Have you just come from the Fuhrer's eastern headquarters?"

The thin harassed-looking Nazi wore heavy-lensed spectacles and squinted hard at the Princess before he bowed, addressed her as "Princess", and then took the hand she offered.

"I am to offer my felicitations to Your Highness in your re-conquest of this remarkable little country."

Her Highness said pleasurably, "Wedding bells are always preferable to cannon."

"Though not always cheaper." Prince Max had come quietly forward. It was noticeable to Alexia, who bristled over Princess Ilsa's remark, that the entire entourage on the terrace bowed or curtsied to him as they had not done to the Princess Ilsa.

All the Lichtenbourgers present laughed at Prince Max's dry joke, repeating it to each other. Herr Sternberg also enjoyed the royal humour, but Alexia caught Tige Royle's eyes and saw that he had been watching Princess Ilsa thoughtfully. He made some remark to his granddaughter, Princess Garnett, who nodded.

She motioned to her maid and an equerry. They nudged everyone aside making a path for her to the terrace. Here she nodded to Herr Sternberg who bowed over her hand but did not shake it. Obviously he – or his master, the Fuhrer – was more circumspect with her than with the Elsbach princess.

Formalities dispensed with, Alexia understood Garnett's complaints that no one had invited the whole German Reich to the picnic. She wondered what she herself would do in such a spot, but the matter seemed to have been already dropped in the capable hands of Frau Becque.

An elderly male retainer in a faded uniform decorated with the letter 'E' showed Alexia and Stefan to their apartments which were separated by the suites of several other guests.

"Did you have anything to do with that?" she whispered to Stefan, pointing to the old man and then to the sleeve of his ermine-trimmed velvet coat. Stefan too had been

185

staring at the "E" and was puzzled by it. "Not even my mother would dare that. I'd hazard a thousand kroner the idea was Frau Becque's. What the devil is her hold over – " He hesitated, then went on. "Not over your father, obviously. We saw what he thought of her the night Tige Royle arrived." He left the only answer open.

Alexia puzzled about the little housekeeper's influence over her mother. She could think of one rather obvious secret and the idea terrified her. Did Frau Becque know about Garnett's occasional visits to "the cathedral" late at night? Alexia had seen her on another of those night excursions only once since the night of Alexia's arrival.

It would be even more shameful to her and the family, Alexia thought, if Stefan ever found out about it, and an absolute calamity if Princess Ilsa learned of it. Heaven knew what kind of a weapon it would be when Hitler's Government got hold of it.

Mother, how could you have been so stupid? It was the only thought she had on the subject, and it didn't help in any way.

She liked the little suite assigned to her. It was the same one she had known in her childhood, with a longer bed, unfortunately decorated with a tester and velvet curtains, but these would be handy tonight in the December cold, with the snowy heights all around them except to the west facing the city of Lichtenbourg far below.

Since it was Sunday evening, those who acknowledged the Sabbath at all had spread the word that although the little orchestra from the Theatre Royal would play through the long dinner, there would be no dancing. There would also be no outdoor winter picnic as the air was below freezing.

Princess Ilsa, trying hard to assert the old authority of the Elsbachs, argued that the new royal couple at least should be permitted to entertain everyone with some

186

waltzes while the well-liked Johann Hofer would sing to the orchestral accompaniment.

Stefan seemed willing. He looked to Alexia who was horrified about the dancing. "Anything I ever learned about the waltz I forgot ages ago. At my university in the States we stopped dancing the waltz ages ago."

"That puts us oldsters in our place," Tige joked. "Here I was, hoping to get a dance with the princess."

Princess Ilsa had no difficulty guessing which of the three princesses present he referred to. She rested a still-beautiful porcelain hand on his cuff.

"Herr Royle, permission will be granted, you may be sure."

"You don't like dancing?" Stefan asked Alexia with some surprise.

She concentrated on her dessert fork before she repeated the embarrassing truth, "I love waltzing when it's in the movies or on the stage in musical comedies. But I've never been very good at it. Not enough practice."

"We will have to remedy that." He looked into her face. "Do you really mind so much?"

She tried to be sophisticated about it. "I don't really mind." But truth got the best of her. "No. Honestly, I'd love to dance. Especially the waltz."

"I'm glad." He smiled, slapped her hand lightly, and went back to his Wiener torte.

An hour later any number of the curious and perhaps the amused casually glanced into the almost empty ball-room on their way to the dark, icy terrace to count the winter stars.

It was not nearly as embarrassing as Alexia had feared. "You see? I knew it at once," Stefan told her as they swung past the little orchestra. "You are a natural dancer, and feather-light."

Whirling around in his arms and held tightly against his

187

body in its dashing uniform, she felt almost as if they were making love. The only time she had ever sampled sex was in her Sophomore year, with a boy even less experienced. Tonight she felt that dancing with Prince Stefan was sexier than anything she might experience with anyone else.

Luckily, Stefan seemed to be enjoying himself as well. She felt his hand, warm against her thin silk dinner gown and she looked up, laughing.

"Half of the Chalet seems to be watching us."

She loved his smile but thought she read a slight anxiety in his dark eyes. "Are you sorry?"

"Not a bit. I think we are performing wonderfully."

That made him laugh and his eyes sparkled. "I do, too. They are all jealous of me, anyway." She wondered why she had ever been afraid of dancing with him.

Suddenly he stopped, still holding her, this time staring over her head at the open double doors with their golden hawk, the Elsbach emblem, on the cornice.

"What the devil?"

She looked round. The music had squeaked off into silence in the middle of a phrase. Two Germans in Wehrmacht uniforms rushed by, followed by Herr Sternberg, the man with the heavy spectacles. Then, the others came along, less excited but talking rapidly to each other.

"I suppose Hitler has just invaded another country," Alexia murmured.

"I wonder."

"Maybe it's Sweden."

His hand tightened on her bare arm. "Perish the thought."

The musicians, perplexed and nervous, were getting up.

Stefan transferred his arm to her waist and started the length of the ballroom with her. She said, "This reminds me of a book I read once in English Lit. *Vanity Fair*. The

Duchess of Richmond's Ball in Brussels. And Waterloo followed immediately after." She shivered.

By the time they reached the busy hall Tige Royle almost bumped into them. He stopped. Alexia couldn't miss the tension in his strong features.

"The Krauts just got the message from Tokyo. The Japs have attacked Hawaii and the American Fleet."

Alexia knew where the Hawaiian Territories were but her first concern she shared with Tige. "Dan got away from Honolulu, didn't he? He must be safe in the Philippines by now . . . Don't you think?"

She caught the look that passed between the two men. Tige sighed. "Honey, I wish they'd been as thorough on geography with you as they were with a lot of old, stale story books. The Philippines are only a hop, skip and jump from Japan."

Stefan explained more gently. "In a war with the United States their first priority would be the conquest of the Philippines."

It was impossible. Nothing ever happened to Dan. He was like Tige. If anybody got out, he would.

"How are the Germans taking it?" Stefan asked Tige.

Tige grinned in the way that had earned him his "Tiger" nickname. "Your mother tells me Hitler danced a jig when he heard it."

"Then the Reich is joining the Japanese?"

"Oh, sure. Leap on the fastest trolley car."

Alexia gritted her teeth and determined to take it all as the two men did. With an effort she said brightly, "Jolly little spot for you and me, Tige. We're in a trap. Just like Dan."

189

CHAPTER SIXTEEN

Stefan and Tige seemed to say so much to each other without speaking. Stefan answered Alexia. "No, Darling. The Fuhrer hasn't attacked Sweden yet. We're a cagey animal. But, Tige, you are another matter. God knows the free world can't afford to have you interned."

"Damn! I'm of that opinion, old man. What's your first advice? I can't just cut and run leaving my family to Hitler's tender mercies. But I've also got a kid over in the Philippines who is going to need all my help to get out of that hellhole."

Stefan started to speak but Alexia cut in with the logical reminder: "I'm going to be a member of Stefan's family. Hitler isn't going to anger the only major country between him and the Allies. He needs Stefan and Sweden."

Behind her, Stefan squeezed her shoulders and kissed the crown of her head. "You are absolutely right, my darling. As for young Dan Royle, this Hawaiian attack may be a mere token raid. We still don't know how extensive it is. It's unlikely they can stop America's huge Pacific Fleet from pursuing them and destroying the entire Japanese Fleet which they will need against Singapore's base and the others. I visited those areas. I also know how big the Pacific Fleet is. Unless, of course, the damage is greater than we suspect."

Tige swung around, cutting Stefan off. "That's our priority. Find out how bad the attack was. I'll make some calls. You two try and keep the more important Germans busy. Alexia, Honey, act as dumb as you can and keep them talking."

"I believe, Sir, I would have an easier time getting through," Stefan reminded him.

"But I've got a couple of code numbers here in this penny-ante town. And you and I can't both be gone at the same time."

Stefan did not argue. He hurried Alexia along the now deserted corridor, passing a door whose lock snapped suddenly as the door opened. Garnett came out looking dishevelled and panic stricken, her eyes wide with fear.

"Is it true, what the Austrians are saying on their stations?"

"I'm afraid so, Your Highness. We don't know yet how bad it is."

Alexia put in, "They may strike at the Philippines next, and Dan is there. Our Dan!"

Stefan looked at Alexia thoughtfully. She couldn't imagine what she had said that suddenly made him consider her rather than the present situation, now truly a world conflict.

Garnett, meanwhile, patted her face nervously with a fine linen handkerchief that had been spotless until now. It became stained immediately with makeup. She was perspiring. She carefully closed the door. Both Stefan and Alexia heard a bolt shoot into place on the other side of the door. Garnett had not been alone in that room.

Alexia gritted her teeth with anger and fear. Why did her incredibly foolish mother take such chances, and probably with Johann Hofer, a boy half her age? She saw Stefan glance at the door but Alexia thanked heaven he was discreet enough to look away quickly.

"I would like to get the truth about the damage, Your Highness. Do you think the prince might know?"

She shook her head, tears beginning to run through her mascara. "I've no idea. All Max ever does is talk peace. Peace with these Axis butchers. He did the same last year and then this spring when Hitler demanded workers for his munitions factories. They took mostly Jews and the few gypsies we have encamped among these hills. Most of them had escaped from Hungary and the Balkans."

Alexia turned to Stefan. "Don't you see how wrong it is to turn over refugees to the Reich munitions factories?"

But Stefan was not interested in individual rights and wrongs at the minute, with the rest of the world now engulfed in war. He said merely to Garnett, "You are perfectly safe, Madame. You are Aryan and of a royal house. Hitler can use you and the prince for his propaganda, and as a go-between with the West."

Garnett dabbed at her eyes. "But the others? The ones who aren't royal. Or – " She paused a moment. Alexia tried to warn her by a frown but she blurted on, "or the non-Aryans still in Lichtenbourg? You see how concerned my daughter is. Who is going to save them from deportation if even the United States is conquered?"

"Conquered, my foot!" Alexia warned her. "Mother, if you don't keep your mouth closed you're going to bring about exactly what you are most afraid of."

"Ah, here you are, dear Stefan," the Princess Ilsa sang out, unable to contain her joy. "Have you heard the news? The United States' Pacific Fleet was wiped out, totally destroyed by a few brave Japanese planes and miniature submarines." She smiled at the tearful, terrified Garnett. "What a triumph for the Axis, Your Highness! We will have peace before the first of the year, according to Oberstlieutenant Spiedel."

In a low voice Stefan told Alexia, "Keep your mother quiet. Interrupt her. Anything."

"And your mother?"

He ignored her sarcasm. "Let her talk her foolish head off. I've got to find out the truth. My own country will know."

Alexia found it surprisingly easy to keep the Elsbach princess chattering after her son left. It was almost as easy to keep the Kuragin princess quiet. She seemed stupified by fear and not entirely for herself. She must really care for young Hanni Hofer. If, of course, he was the man secreted in the room she had just left.

Alexia wondered if her father suspected anything. Poor man. He really had the weight of other countries and other people's troubles on his shoulders, plus a wife who was committing adultery in his own household.

Alexia worried a little about her father for whom she was building an affection based on pity. She felt a great comfort in what she saw as her future husband's strength. She had spent at least half of her eighteen years near men of strength, like Tige and Dan. It was good to feel that her future husband would be of their fibre.

Princess Ilsa had been the town crier for another Axis victory whose immensity she could only guess at. She gave Garnett and Alexia an absurd Nazi salute and went on her way to burden others, mostly Lichtenbourgers, with her glorious news.

Garnett tried to rid herself of Alexia's company as well. She wanted to wander up and down the hall outside the ballroom in the obvious hope of discussing the news with the person behind the bolted door. If he was Johann Hofer, whom Alexia suspected was Jewish, it was a nerve-wracking possibility.

The young entertainer was not nearly strong enough to survive what she supposed must be long hours and exceedingly hard work. What would become of him then, in a regime with such virulent anti-Semitic laws? It did not bear thinking of.

She had heard the scoffing and denials in the United States about Nazi crimes. Many Americans remembered all too well how they had been swayed by propaganda against the Germans in Belgium during 1915 – 1916. It had been a successful effort to bring America into the conflict. Ghastly stories were circulated about Germans who had speared infants on swords, raped whole villages of females, committed unspeakable atrocities everywhere. The stories had served their purpose. It would be difficult now to spread the truth.

She remembered the infamous "Kristalnacht" in 1938, crimes against Jews documented by the cameras of Alexia's godfather, Chris Royle, whose Jewish cameraman was murdered in the riots. Were the Nazis now committing similar crimes against refugees in "neutral" countries like Lichtenbourg?

It was horrible enough that the refugees in Lichtenbourg were endangered but would those Nazi talons reach out across the border for the protectors of the refugees?

When the Princess Ilsa left them and Alexia refused to leave her mother alone, Garnett said tiredly, "All right, then. Help me to my bedroom, dear. I feel as if I've been beaten with whips." It was understandable. Garnett was not made for heroism.

Alexia led her mother up to her suite which opened through double dressing rooms and baths to Prince Max's quarters. Alexia's father was in his dressing room standing in the dim light permitted them by the power connection of the Chalet to the city far below. He was examining his uniforms as if he had never seen them before. He dropped a uniform jacket and walked in to join the women. His Irish valet picked up the discarded jacket, put it over his arm, brushed it carefully and examined it again. Then he came after the prince to announce reproachfully, "Y'er Highness, it's going to be needing a press."

Max waved him away. "Yes, yes. Take it now. Do it immediately. I may need it tonight."

O'Leary bowed, went back into the prince's suite and closed the door firmly.

"Can you trust him?" Garnett asked.

"More than you can trust that Becque creature."

Alexia had no doubt of that. Turning away from her father to Princes Garnett Alexia saw her mother's pallor, accentuated by the streaks of mascara she had not yet been able to remove. Alexia could not help feeling that she had guessed rightly. The Becque woman was blackmailing Garnett, and the most obvious object of that blackmail was young Johann Hofer. Not only was Garnett exposed to disastrous gossip that might destroy her own position, but poor young Hofer was in even more critical danger from the spying Nazi housekeeper, especially if he *was* Jewish.

Hoping her father would not guess the reasons for Garnett's panic, Alexia said, "Have you heard any more, Sir? Is the American fleet pursuing the Japanese?" When he did not answer but continued to stare at his wife, Alexia went on hurriedly, "Tige or Prince Stefan will know any minute now."

Under that gaze which had seldom reproached the woman Max adored, Garnett pulled herself together, even letting an optimistic smile flicker across her stricken face. "This wedding is well-timed, don't you think, Max? We could use Stefan's influence."

He shook off what seemed like a trance. "Probably. If we are to surrender our last freedom to the Third Reich."

Alexia was so shocked she forgot the courtesies due to the Prince Royal of Lichtenbourg. "How can you say that? Stefan is no Nazi. He despises Chancellor Hitler."

"Does he? I wonder. Frankly, at this minute, I do not trust anyone outside the family." He looked around

195

Garnett's elaborate salmon and gold bedroom. "I see you've had that hideous gold chaise longue changed. You may have to make do for a time. I don't like to depend upon Vienna and Munich for all our trade, and if things go badly in the Pacific they may ultimately effect even Tige."

Garnett's eyes widened. "What has Tige to do with it?"

"He has backed several loans here. Without Tige's partners in the States and South America we may be completely bought out by the Reich banks."

Garnett looked down at her fingers, picking at the jewellery that Max and the Principality of Lichtenbourg had bestowed on her during their marriage. She sighed and held out her hands to Max. "Never let it be said that I am selfish. Take them, if they will help."

It was hard to say which one was the more surprised, her husband or her daughter. Alexia was ashamed of her own cynicism but couldn't help wondering how sincere the gesture was. Max, on the contrary, was genuinely touched. He leaned down and kissed her fingers.

"Not yet, Darling. Perhaps not ever. I have a conference coming up with Tige as soon as he finds out how things are really going in the Pacific. Maybe we will borrow one or two items, just for security. That ruby parure you never wear. You wouldn't miss that as much as those lovely emeralds you wore tonight."

Alexia, standing beside her mother, noticed an odd thing. Garnett stiffened and her fingers closed into her palms. "You could get more for the emeralds. The ruby set, I'm sorry to say, is being re-styled. God knows when we can get it back."

"Well, Darling, let's hope neither sacrifice is necessary." He kissed her cheek and then Alexia's and went back through the dressing rooms, closing the doors. Alexia

196

was surprised to hear him lock one of the doors. Did her mother and father never sleep together these nights?

Most of all, however, she was puzzled by Garnett's talk of re-setting the rubies. It wasn't like her. Garnett always left matters such as the re-setting of jewels to someone else. When such matters came up she almost invariably wound up with new jewels. She pursued the matter, knowing that if her mother was in great and secret difficulties, others would have to save her. She had never in her life been forced to face the consequences of her self-centred life.

"Mother, have you lost the rubies?"

Garnett raised her head. She appeared to be horrified. "Lost? My dear girl, how would I lose them? I never even wear them."

"They are being re-set?"

"I said so."

"Who has them? Let me go and recover them tomorrow. Then they can be put up as collateral for – " She stopped. Something startled and then evasive in her mother's eyes made her guess the truth. She lowered her voice. "Money. That's why you want them, isn't it, Mother?"

Garnett waved her away as if she were a fly. "What an imagination! If I wanted money for myself I would go to Max, as anyone would."

If I wanted money for myself . . .? For someone else then. Alexia swallowed hard. "Mother, please don't tell me you are running out on Father with that boy, just when Father needs you."

Garnett began to laugh. There was a note of hysteria in the sound that troubled Alexia almost as much as her suspicions.

"Do you actually believe I would leave Max? Ever? It's that poor boy I'm talking about. It began as a little flirtation, to pass the time, and I hoped to make Max

197

jealous enough to pay more attention to me than to his everlasting councils and meetings. Poor Hanni took our relationship seriously, but I straightened him out. Anyway, he's desperate to get out of here. He thinks they might take him in their next roundup of workers. He is Jewish."

"I thought Father had to give his permission on that."

"Yes. But suppose Max finds out. Could he, would he, allow it purely out of jealousy?"

There were an awful few seconds when Alexia suspected her mother would be pleased to think Max showed his jealousy so clearly. But Garnett asked with a very real tension, "You aren't surprised. How do you know about Hanni's background?"

"We heard him speaking Yiddish."

Garnett seized her wrist. "Who else knows?"

"Stefan heard him."

"God! And that mother of his?"

"I don't think so. Can't Hofer get out with less than a small fortune in rubies?"

Garnett removed her hand. "The money isn't for Hanni. I guess you'd call it blackmail."

Frau Becque. Alexia's head whirled. She understood for the first time how people in this world of terror and intrigue talked of killing. If Frau Becque were dead their problems might be more easily solved. While I'm at it, she thought, why not wish for the death of a few Nazis, beginning with the Chancellor of the Third Reich? But these were childish wishes. They solved nothing. She wondered if she could actually trust Stefan.

"How urgent is it, Mother? Is there some sort of deadline?"

"How do I know? If the Americans have answered the Japanese properly it will set the Fuhrer's armies back. The Russians will probably collapse. They can't hold out against Hitler's armies on the Eastern Front. But it's maddening, not knowing."

"Oh, Mother! All this and still you brought Hofer up here under Frau Becque's little pointed nose."

Garnett said querulously, "If you aren't going to be more sympathetic I wish you would go to bed. You will soon have all your time taken up by your wedding."

Depressing to realize, but during the last hour that had been very low on her agenda. She didn't even know if she could trust Stefan von Elsbach, who was actually German and Hungarian not Swedish at all.

She started to the door. Her mother watched her, looking dejected and forlorn. Alexia came back across the carpet, hugged Garnett and kissed her forehead. "It will all turn out well for you, Mother. It always does. Just keep remembering that." Then she curtsied and went out.

She walked up the unnaturally silent marble staircase and back to her own suite. Perhaps her little German radio would give her some news. She knew her parents had a radio connection that brought them BBC from London, but she doubted if she would get much honest news on her radio that would be favourable to the United States.

In spite of the snow-tipped peaks behind the Chalet there was only a trickle of warm water for her bath, the usual condition which had existed even in her childhood. Polly had done her best and apologized but both girls were much more interested in the events in the Pacific.

Polly had brought a book of maps from the Prince Kuragin Library on the gallery floor and the two girls tried to figure out where Dan Royle might be at the moment.

Polly was reassuring. "We Yankees have a huge fleet. You should see it. I lived in Long Beach, California, when I was a kid. A real sailor town. Nobody could lick those gobs. That's what we called them, gobs."

Alexia remembered seeing the ships sail in through the

Golden Gate when she was eating lunch or dinner on Fisherman's Wharf with Dan. They had looked invincible. Then she studied the various Philippine Islands, a United States Protectorate. They seemed to be mostly jungle, except for the Spanish look of busy Manila on the island of Luzon. An entire peninsula of jungle lay beyond.

"Bataan," she murmured. "It seems so exotic and far away. At least, they haven't been attacked yet. Nobody says so, anyway."

Polly was optimistic. "One thing about it. Your Dan would have a whole jungle to lose himself in. He sure wouldn't stay there at Clark Field getting bombed out."

A knock on the big doors made them both jump. It was Prince Stefan, asking to see Alexia.

Polly bobbed what would pass for a curtsy. "Surest thing you know, Sir. I'll be at hand if Miss – Her Highness needs me to help her with the bath. Hot water's awful. In fact, it's invisible. Just ring for me. The top button." She went out, closing the door.

Alexia wrapped her peignoir more closely around her body and tried to analyse the news from Stefan's expression. He looked his strong, sympathetic self, but his eyes did not reassure her.

She said abruptly, "Then the Germans are right. It's bad."

He nodded. Taking her hands and leaning over her he kissed her forehead. "It seems the fleet was caught entirely unawares, and they aren't the only ones. There are stories that Singapore will go next."

"Singapore?" That was beyond the Philippines.

"When I visited there after my mission for the Swedish planes the British called it the Gibraltar of the Pacific. No navy in the world could penetrate its seagoing defences." He pulled up a chair and sat down beside her at the desk. "There is a jungle at Singapore's back. I don't

think we need ask where the Japanese are infiltrating."
She looked into his face, pleading, yet aware that he could
offer nothing but sympathy.

"How can Dan get out? They're closing in all around the
Philippines. Surely America will put everything she's got
into rescuing their soldiers and administration people, and
citizens like Dan." He took a deep breath that made her
stare at him. "Won't they?"

"Unless their president decides the first priority is sending all its strength to Britain and Russia."

"It's not fair. Dan – I mean our people should come
first."

She felt his arm around her shoulders and realized how
childish she must sound. She tried to recover the calm with
which she had handled her mother's panic. "I'm sorry. We
have problems closer to us."

He took her face between his hands. "There will be time
tomorrow for us to solve the world's problems. I'm going
to see that you drink a stiff brandy and then I'm going to
take you to bed and see that you stay there until morning." At her expression which was half surprise and half
anticipation, he laughed lightly. "I assure you, there are
precedents. Besides, I intend to push for early weddings."

"Weddings?" She heard herself and realized she had still
made no objections to his plans for the night.

"Civil and religious. Here. Pull yourself together . . .
You don't have much on at that, do you? How fortunate
for me! You won't be so heavy."

"Don't be vulgar."

He laughed. "Drink this."

She hoped her fears for Dan and her mother would
recede into some vague nightmare that would be brushed
away tomorrow. Meanwhile, there was no man in all this
eerie and dangerous world that she would rather spend the
night with.

CHAPTER SEVENTEEN

"Shall we?" He reached for her and Alexia, remembering the excitement of his kisses and the close embrace of his body in their dancing, held out her arms.

Then she changed her mind. This was too childish, too unsophisticated. She turned to the brandy snifter. He had not overdone the "dosage" but she finished the brandy feeling less depressed, more free and uninhibited.

Too late she remembered that someone had told her this was how Garnett had been conceived between Sir David Miravel and Lady Alix. Still, Count Stefan was a lot more exciting than her grandfather must have been.

She set the snifter back. "Now, why did I say that?"

He had been watching her carefully and was puzzled by her question. "What did you say?"

She laughed. "I called you 'Count' in my thoughts."

She saw the small knitting of his brows, as if the answer had bothered him. To her relief he dismissed it lightly. "Oh, that fellow. Just so long as you don't confuse me with Dan Royle."

What on earth? Why should she do that? She had known Stefan less than a month. Dan was a part of her whole life. Where was he now, this minute? Running for his life through deadly tropical jungles? Lying blown to bits on Clark Field? Or suffering unbelievable cruelty as a captive? Please, God, no.

She forced herself back to the mood that the brandy had

brought on. "I thought you and I were going to warm up this old chalet." Her joyous mood sounded a little brusque even to her, but he pretended not to notice.

"If ever a place needed warming." He held out his arms, but she got to her feet, still reasonably steady.

"Take my hand. We are going to do this the way the Prince and Princess Kuragin should. Walking side by side."

"Prince and Princess Elsbach."

She said "ugh!" but took his hand and loved the warm, dark strength of his fingers with hers. He was still looking down as they walked into the bedroom together. She squeezed his hand and said enthusiastically, "I think I could love you."

"What?" he demanded, startled.

Was the brandy talking? "I mean, not just sexually, which I do – "

"Thank you."

"But dynastically, too. I'll bet we make a much happier marriage than most dynastic arrangements."

"I am happy to hear that. In other words, to quote your friend Dan: 'We may even make a go of it.'"

"I don't see why not. Have you been engaged very often?"

He pretended to think back into the dim past. "Once, when I was about twelve. My mother thought it would be ideal if I could marry England's Princess Elizabeth. She had just been born and, of course, she was not at that time the heiress to the throne, as she is now."

"Good heavens!"

"Astonishing to believe, I know, but the Windsors refused our offer. So did the Swedish Royal Family. So, you can see, you are my last hope."

She giggled before she remembered that Dan had told her that men hate females who giggle. It must have been the brandy. Whatever it was, it certainly took away all the inhibitions she had had in the old days with the boy at Cal. This was what she wanted, and from her future husband. His mere touch enflamed her.

As they reached the big bed she teased Stefan, "After all those rejections maybe you need a sip of brandy."

After a minute or so, during which he examined her hands locked with his he freed her fingers slowly. "You may be right."

Somewhat to her disappointment, he left her and retraced their steps to the desk in the outer room. When he returned after about five very long minutes she had decided to climb into bed and was in the process of removing her peignoir. She read the anticipation in his eyes, which increased her own excitement.

She shrugged out of the satin folds of her peignoir as he approached the bed. He had dropped his formal-fitting uniform jacket and was looking more sexually formidable in shirt sleeves, his shirt open over his chest. He was armed with his special smile.

"I would like to have undressed you."

She looked around for the satin heap she had kicked onto the floor but her view was obstructed by the pale globes of her breasts and the prominent aureoles of her nipples which seemed to fascinate him.

Almost subconsciously she raised her hands to cover her bosom. Her excitement increased when he took her hands away and bent to kiss the tip of each breast, his lips lingering on her flesh until the excitement she had dreamed of engulfed her and to her embarrassment she heard herself whisper, "Hurry."

He understood. She felt her body shivering as he carefully slipped into the huge bed beside her, his flesh never leaving hers, his body and his limbs imprisoning her. She knew there would be pain. It was always so at first. But his hands and the long, muscular strength of his legs held her so that when his hardness entered and thrust within her trembling, waiting body, she closed her own slender legs around him as if it were she who held him prisoner. She would remember forever that first burst of excitement she had been waiting for in their joining. It did not at once dissolve into mere trembling but rose until she cried out softly and out of half-closed eyes saw his own eyes like burning darkness staring at her body.

She could not imagine how many minutes passed before they parted and lay there looking at each other. She raised herself on one elbow, pretending to be insulted. "What? Am I so hopeless?"

"That is the first silly thing you have said."

She reached over, touching his face, moving him closer to her body. He made no resistance when she held him close so that his tongue licked the salt flesh between her breasts.

After that she was amazed when he demanded, as they made love once more with another burst of passion, "Do you still feel we are dynastic lovers?"

This time she knew he was having fun with her. She teased him, "Of course. A dynasty of twelve heirs, all Kuragin-Elsbachs."

He put his mouth to one of her breasts and, having left her weak with joy, he corrected her, "Elsbach-Kuragins."

Physically he was all she had ever dreamed of, but it seemed clear to her that the importance of his precious Elsbach dynasty would always come first.

Late in the night Stefan went back to his own apartments. "I suppose our conduct would shock your parents," he grumbled as he dressed. "But it shouldn't be long before we can forget these hypocrites."

"I doubt if it would shock Tige." She was thinking of that curious, embarrassed conversation he had with her before they left the New Palace this afternoon. Or was it yesterday already?

With Stefan leaving her she felt the grim war news engulfing her again. "Darling," she began.

"How nice that sounds!" He stopped pulling on one boot and kissed her bare shoulder. She caressed his hair.

"Is there any way the Allies can win the war now?"

He considered for several seconds. "Not now. It will take months, perhaps years, for the Americans to make up for this blow. The loss of life alone must be appalling – the capital ships, everything but the carriers. Thank God they were at sea. The others were sitting ducks. And the Japanese have the impetus. Even if they don't return to Hawaii there are invaluable Pacific bases: Wake Island; Guam, the Philippines. I touched down at those bases a couple of months ago. They will be essential to both sides."

She hesitated. "They have to take the Philippines?"

"With one of America's biggest bases there? Yes. It seems inevitable. Of course, I would set your Tige Royle against the entire Japanese Navy when it comes to that."

He reached over, kissed her cheek and got up, stamping into his tight boots. "Sweetheart, would you object to an early wedding? It seems necessary for the protection of Lichtenbourg, at any rate."

She thought, our night of love seems to be over. She reached down, pulled up her peignoir and threw it around her shoulders. She had forgotten how cold this damnable chalet was in midwinter.

In the bedroom doorway he stopped, had several second thoughts and came back to her. She knew perfectly well that at such a time their pre-marital sex was at the end of a long list of priorities. She had wanted to put off the problems and terrors that faced them both, at least until morning, but life was not for spoiled and complaining women. Even her mother had discovered that.

"I do understand," she assured him. "Let's just say, the sooner we get through with our weddings, both of them, the better I can help you." As he reached her she added, "By staying out of your hair."

He laughed at that but his eyes were tender. He kissed her again, then told her, "I certainly am glad I failed with the Windsors and the Bernadottes."

Through the nerve-wracking hours until daylight she remembered his lovely compliment. It made the events that followed more bearable.

Prince Max was closeted with his Royal Council most of the next day, thanks to the persistence of Chancellor Janos Becque.

Since Tige knew it was crucial to coordinate their plans, and above all Lichtenbourg's response to the expected pressures from the German Reich, he seated himself in the audience chamber to await his turn for an audience with the prince. He also had his own plans, a matter which might be of great concern to the Reich. Alexia reminded him of the danger from Chancellor Becque but was reassured by his humourous tweak of her nose.

"Yes, teacher. If Becque insists on remaining I'll say just what we want him to know. Your job is to look dumb – make that innocent – and agreeable, because I want to lay it out that America is going to worry if my great-granddaughter marries a friend of the Reich."

"What!" She was badly shaken.

"If I know that little weasel he's going to push for the marriage, on Hitler's orders."

She looked around the audience chamber with its fringed blue velvet portieres, the stiff, leather-padded chairs with curved Biedermeier backs and highly ornamented wall pilasters. Two waiters, directed by a footman, came out of the Royal Council chamber with trays of empty glasses and an assortment of half-empty bottles.

Keeping his voice low Tige pointed out, "Those tiny glasses are for Schnapps. A little glass goes a long way. A lot of Swedes drink it."

She was nervous but she grinned. "I'll remember that."

The longer they waited the more her nervousness grew, but she couldn't help thinking of the previous night with Stefan and hoped for a good opinion from Tige.

"You do like Stefan, don't you? You think I'm doing the right thing?"

He patted her hand. "Honey, you picked a right one. I sort of thought for a while that you and Danny would hit it off. Him not being of our blood and all, it would've been perfectly proper. He's awfully fond of you. As far as he's concerned, you're the tops."

The door of the Council Chamber had opened but Alexia paid no attention. She was shocked that Tige should misunderstand the two channels of her affections.

"Tige, I couldn't feel for anyone the way I feel for Dan. Even you." She could see that he was pleased but concerned.

"Then this fellow you're willing to marry, you feel something for him, I hope. He's actually a fine fellow, as I said. I've had him looked into."

She laughed. "I'm, crazy about him. In a different way. Very different."

Stefan's shadow fell across her face. "I shall take that as a hopeful sign, my love."

Uneasily she wished he hadn't heard. When he bowed to kiss her fingers and then raised his head, she tried to look into his eyes, but he avoided her, saying to Janos Becque who came along behind him, "We must take what we can get in this world and be grateful. At least the Fuhrer should approve."

"Even if the States don't," Tige put in gruffly.

Alexia knew they were playing some sort of game to throw their Reich neighbours off the track. All the same, this sly insincerity made her more anxious than ever. She couldn't help wondering if the lies expressed some hint of a real opinion. And what if Stefan wrongly interpreted her comment, which was perfectly true, about Dan?

"Well, of course," she said, falling in with their devious statements, "I want to marry just as the Fuhrer suggests. I suppose I must do as I'm told. You know Tige, that Nazi slogan for women: '*Kinder, Kuchen*' and whatever the other one is."

"How well you express yourself, my love," Stefan told her suavely. "You will be the very epitome of a true German hausfrau."

She frowned at him but he merely smiled and turned away. "Money, dowries and all that are such embarrassing subjects to everyone but my mother. I'll go and find her. She wouldn't want to be left out would she, Tige?"

"Don't ask me. I don't know the lady well enough."

Alexia wondered if Tige disliked the princess as much as she did. He had been friendly enough last night. Or was this more of the devious pretence going on around her? Were all these petty matters of a dynastic marriage more important than Japan's attack on the US Fleet and the explosion into another major war front? She reminded Tige, "You asked me about my feelings for Dan. What will happen to him? Or does anyone care?"

From the way Tige's square jaw set she knew she had hit a nerve, but she had to know someone was doing something. Before Tige could bring himself to answer her Stefan touched her hand, "Patience." The word meant nothing, but his touch reassured her in some unspoken way. It was an obvious message. She caught his eyes, nodded and to cover her own stupid protests she grumbled,

"I wonder how long it will be before this war is over and everyone goes home."

She was sure the two men relaxed. She must remember to control all these panic-stricken demands for action. If there should be some plan or hopes she would only make matters worse by calling attention to them.

As the last of the Royal Council left the audience chamber, several of them looking dejected Prince Max's one-armed equerry came out to summon Tige. He raised his voice for all the chamber to hear.

"His Serene Highness wishes to express to Herr Royle his regret that he must break diplomatic relations with the United States of America, due to the aggression of the United States in the Pacific."

Herr Sternberg had come into the chamber and heard the equerry's announcement. He tapped Tige's shoulder. "Herr Royle, the Fuhrer wishes me to inform you that your President Roosevelt is expected at any time to announce the existence of a state of war between your country and the empire of Japan. Your country is to be informed that at this time a state of war will exist between Japan's ally, the Third Reich, and your country."

"Thanks, old man." Tige saluted him, adding, "At least, this time we won't have to worry about a sneak attack."

Several men snickered. Alexia looked around, interested in this reaction from the Italian Consul of Lichtenbourg and a Portuguese liaison officer. Beneath the Axis surface of one and the neutral stance of the other, they had let their opinions be known.

The equerry motioned to Prince Stefan. "If you will be so kind, Sir, His Serene Highness wishes also to discuss with you the royal marriage when the Princess Ilsa and the Princess Garnett arrive."

"The sooner the better, eh, my love?" Prince Stefan

remarked, stopping to close his fingers on Alexia's wrist in a warning she understood. She looked at him without speaking and watched the men go into the Council chamber, all but Stefan who started off to find his mother.

Afraid to say anything, Alexia was terrified that she might betray her real feelings. How could she and Stefan make a life for themselves when every word they spoke, every action they took, would be a lie, often a lie hidden from each other?

Her mother passed without seeing her and went into the Council chamber. She had her auburn head high and was wearing a straw silk suit that looked stunning on her. If she was haunted by private problems she gave no indication except in the way the fingers of her right hand, laden with rings, kept opening and closing.

Princess Ilsa was escorted minutes later by Stefan and Herr Sternberg. She stopped at the door to the Council chamber and playfully teased him, "No further, my dear Hugo. Don't concern yourself. We have no secrets, you and I."

In fact, they have secrets from no one, Alexia told herself, except me. Considering how easily betrayal might result in international calamity, she was almost glad to be excluded.

Whatever went on in that room, it did not take long enough to arouse suspicious comment in the audience chamber. Someone inside that room lowered the old-fashioned latch of the door just as an Austrian civilian wearing a swastika armband hurried into the audience chamber. He was young, extremely thin, and looked more than a little harried. He raised his voice.

"It is war with them again. The United States. Like before. It comes again."

One of the older statesmen seized his arm. "Be silent.

211

It is the Fuhrer who speaks. Weaklings, these Americans."

The young man shook himself loose. "You don't understand. My mother told me how it was before. We won. Even the Russians gave up at Tannenburg. And then, like before, these Yankee Jew-lovers came. And they destroyed us. Even our emperor was driven out. Then we starved."

"In those days there was no Fuhrer," someone called from the back of the room. "You do not think he will be driven out by the Jew Roosevelt."

"It is the Jews and the other degenerates. They do this," another voice muttered.

Horrifyingly, to Alexia, the latest voice was calm, as if the hearers would accept this for truth.

Chancellor Janos Becque had come into the chamber and heard these complaints. He excited his hearers by his chuckle. "What? You think they defeat the Wehrmacht, the mightiest armies in history? Ask France. Ask Norway. Ask the British dogs who are hiding from our Blitz. Ask yourself who is greater? Our Reichsmarschall Goering and our General Rommel, or their pitiful American sailors, dying, not instantly but slowly, for many days, in the deep waters of Pearl Harbor?"

Alexia wanted to close her ears to these monstrous lies. She was shaking as she cried instead, "Liars! Liars! It's not true."

Little Janos Becque raised her hand which felt clammy and lifeless even to her. He chuckled again. "See what cowards you are? Even the bride of our Fuhrer's friend calls you liar. Now, answer our war declaration as you should, as good Germans. Heil Hitler!"

Although the room was filled with an assortment of nationalities, most of them Nazi sympathizers, only the Germans repeated the all too familiar shout, and to Alexia even they did not sound as they did at the Nuremberg rallies when it seemed to those who heard them that they might split the world in two.

She told herself what she wanted to believe and would not let herself believe otherwise. For all their "Heils" they were afraid. They still remembered another war in which they had been equally sure of their might. Or was she fooling herself as they fooled themselves?

The Council chamber door opened and Princess Garnett came out, summoning Alexia with one curved forefinger. "It is time, dear. Your signature is needed."

"Excellent," Chancellor Becque answered for Alexia. "The Fuhrer must be informed as soon as the signatures are witnessed. A union of great moment. It is a sign from on high that it should occur today of all triumphant days."

"A Godsend, you might say," Alexia put in sarcastically.

Becque corrected himself quickly. "Let us say our Aryan gods send this happy union on the very day the Americans begin their purgatory."

"Come, Ava," her mother reminded her in a business-like way that did not entirely conceal her fear of Janos Becque.

Remembering the new horrors the world, and particularly the country where she had lived so happily for several years with Tige and Dan and her college friends, faced she found it hard to meet all the welcoming smiles from those who claimed to be her friends inside her father's Council chamber.

She knew what to expect from Stefan's mother. The beautiful and ageless Princess Ilsa stood beside the Nazi Ambassador and Herr Sternberg whose heavy-lensed glasses seemed to read into Alexia's soul. Not that he would recognize a soul if he fell over it, she thought.

Behind the great desk under the light from two long windows, her father seemed to be relieved, and tried to let her know that business matters would soon be over. He seemed to have no thought for, or interest in, the tragedy that had occurred yesterday in another hemisphere.

She realized why he was relieved. If this wedding pleased Hitler, uniting little Lichtenbourg with a powerful and enigmatic neutral like Sweden, it was done through one of the few people he trusted, Ilsa von Elsbach. He was not likely to annex Lichtenbourg while the Elsbachs were involved.

She could expect nothing from her mother who had her own problems, but the greatest hurt came when she knew Tige and Stefan were going through with this charade. They both watched her, at least showing some concern, confidence and smiles at her approaching happiness from Tige and kindness from Stefan. She gave her fiancé the benefit of believing he was also concerned about her.

Why not? If she failed to go through with this they could probably expect Adolf Hitler and his armies to arrive on the steps of the New Palace tomorrow morning.

"My dear child," Princess Ilsa told her in a patronizing way that Alexia loathed. "Once you sign these papers you will have the delight of choosing your wedding robes for the cathedral ceremony. The Fuhrer warns me that we must not stint on coupons. The shops of Vienna and Berlin and Paris will be open to you."

She addressed the others then, all men except Garnett and Alexia. "What luck that Paris is now ours! We shall have the best of two worlds."

Stefan muttered, "Good God!" but everyone else ignored him.

"It must be done in a hurry," Garnett pointed out, "if the Cathedral service is to take place before Christmas." Her voice sounded flat, uninspired. No one except Alexia seemed to notice.

She was thinking of all the friends she had known

in college. Where would they be by Christmas? Where would Dan be? Had Tige lost interest in his adopted son? She hadn't thought it possible. Meanwhile, there was the mockery of grand robes and religious services that were meant to rival the coronation of a queen or a reigning princess. And with it all, Stefan von Elsbach, the man she loved, would have his foot on the next rung that would bring him to Lichtenbourg as the future Prince Royal, the title his ancestors had worn with the help of plots, counterplots and sometimes murder.

CHAPTER EIGHTEEN

"Why not wear my wedding gown?" Garnett suggested. "I wore it in the spring of 1919 and this is winter. But it was heavy. I remember how relieved everyone was that the war had ended. Maybe it will be a good omen."

"Oh, Mother!" Alexia protested, but left it at that. No need in pointing out that for the war to be over in the next two weeks it would mean that the Axis had won. That was a horror she would not admit.

The women went on chattering and fussing behind her. She stared out of the windows at the long, sweeping length of the Boulevard Kuragin. Just where it dipped down before rising toward the distant train station she could see the towers of the cathedral. The great church had been newly swept, washed and cleaned for the royal wedding.

How little this wedding gown talk mattered. Out in the Pacific, halfway across the globe, the Japanese were hammering at tiny Wake Island, defended by a handful of marines and civilian construction workers. Ten days ago, on 10 December, they had landed on Luzon, the Philippine island held by General MacArthur's shrinking forces, including the Philippine Army. Manila may have fallen by now. German rumour had it that Clark and Nichols Fields and Fort Stotsenburg were being blown to bits, and what remained of the defending US troops would keep fighting from the savage jungle reaches of

Bataan Peninsula. But this was only Axis propaganda. No one knew for sure. Tige said privately that the main body of the US forces under MacArthur would try to hold the little Manila Bay cave-like fortress of Corregidor until help came from the United States.

But Alexia had heard the low-voiced discussions between Tige, Max and Stefan. There would be no rescue. First priorities were in Europe. Last night Tige spelled it out.

He said nothing about Dan and she didn't bring it up. She knew by now that her own marriage was the price Lichtenbourg paid to keep its freedom. There was no pawn and no price left to forfeit in the Pacific.

The Americans and Filipinos, as Tige put it, were expendable. God knows what would happen to them in enemy hands.

"Alexia, dear," her mother called to her. "I am having my gown, the train and the hennin and veil removed from the Cathedral Museum. They will be cleaned and ready for alterations by tomorrow afternoon I should think."

"And quite ready for our little princess by 24 December," Stefan's mother reminded everyone happily. "I consider the honeymoon far too short, but it should be charming at the Andross Chateau. One of the loveliest in southern Sweden."

I'll bet, Alexia thought resentfully, determined to hate the place. Everyone seemed sure they would return so rapidly. As if her father couldn't handle the government of Lichtenbourg without the Elsbachs. She resented these hints because they made her deeply aware of the reasons for the marriage. She would like to believe Stefan had chosen her for something more personal. He loved her now, or gave every indication of doing so. But it hadn't been his first reason for pursuing her. She knew that.

Her violent reaction to a huge, formal wedding at this time was the only revenge possible. She found it hard to

217

carry over this anger to Stefan, however. He had suggested coming to her quietly on these nights which were full of sombre and terrifying thoughts. When she refused him as kindly as possible he shrugged, kissed her cheek, and agreed. He was surprisingly patient and understanding. But he watched her a good deal when he thought she wasn't aware of it.

Two days before the royal ceremony she tried on the heavy state wedding gown. It looked well now that it had been cleaned and shortened an inch in the hem and long, tight sleeves.

After the rehearsal of her vows she went to lunch with Stefan and Tige, still holding her head proudly. It came as a shock therefore when Tige said, "Honey, you are being awfully selfish. Do me a favour. Play some nicer role and make us all feel easier."

She was hurt and resentful. "I think, considering what is going on in the world, that I am behaving very well. There is such a thing as pride." She did not mention resentment and bitterness for those men given up as "expendable".

"Isn't that hitting a bit hard?" Stefan asked Tige. He gave Tige a curious little frown that Alexia caught.

But Tige persisted. "Pride has nothing to do with it. What I see is childish petulance. And it's not becoming, Honey."

He reached across the table, tapped her knuckles. "I'm telling you what I'd have told my very own Alix, long ago. In fact – " His expression softened as it always did when he spoke of his daughter who had died back in 1918. "I did tell Alix just about that, once or twice."

Alexia was more touched by the memory he conjured up of his beloved daughter than by his criticism, but she repeated his words, "Petulance. I hate that. It's so childish."

"Yes," Tige agreed. "It is."

Maybe her heroic effort to pay a tribute to Dan's suffering had backfired. She would have to re-think her disposition lately.

In spite of the unconcealed glee among the German-born citizens of Lichtenbourg at the continued Axis triumphs on all fronts, Alexia tried to learn from the conduct of Tige and a few others. Their passionate, if private, support of the Allies was certainly as strong as Alexia's.

Even Prince Max was unable to conceal his worry over the news, though he tried to dissemble around Chancellor Becque and the other pro-Nazis. As Alexia found out early on the morning of the wedding, even Garnett was brought to share Max's troubles. She had followed Polly with Alexia's breakfast tray into her daughter's suite with the cheerful news.

"Well, it's arrived. Today is your day. You mustn't be nervous, dear. Just remember how many Lichtenbourg brides before you have gone up to the chancel rail of that icy cold cathedral."

"There's something in that, Ma'am," Polly remarked, setting down the tray. As she was leaving she added to Garnett, "Anyway, I'll bet she's the prettiest bride they ever had."

"Ha!" Alexia jeered.

Garnett said impatiently, "Very likely." Then turned her back on Polly and strolled to the windows.

Alexia spoke abruptly, "How will Tige be able to get out of Lichtenbourg and save Dan when Hitler is liable to pounce on him as an enemy alien?"

Garnett seemed unworried. "The men will work it out. Trust them."

Alexia's worries were not so easily solved. "Tige hasn't tried to get out because he wants to see us through this wedding business. Isn't that it?"

Garnett was vague about it. "I tell you, it's being worked

out. Tige will be here until after the wedding. The Fuhrer wants this connection with Sweden and especially with that Von Elsbach woman. He won't do anything yet." Her thoughts turned to pleasanter memories. "I can see it now, my own wedding, as if it were yesterday. All the banners, and those shields at each lamp post with His Highness's initial and mine entwined. The chains of flowers draped across the boulevard." Her voice trailed off. Her fingers closed around a window latch as she stared down at the cobbled street in front of the palace.

Gradually aware of the silence, Alexia motioned for Polly to go. Then she got up and went to the window beside her mother. "What do you see? What is it?"

Garnett started nervously. "The bands on the sleeves. At least, that one."

Alexia was puzzled by her mother's tension. "You mean the swastikas? Probably German citizens, here for the excitement. I was told last night that half of the Third Reich and most of Austria were pouring in. Of course, if it snows, there won't be that much enthusiasm. See the dark, good-looking soldiers over there. Hungarians, do you suppose? One of them looks like my – like Stefan."

Garnett's fingers shifted. She began to drum on the glass. "No. The yellow bands."

For the first time Alexia studied one young man headed across the boulevard to an alley behind the shop that had once belonged to Heim Lowenstein. The man was gaunt in spite of his youth. He was holding the collar of his shabby raincoat close under his chin against the frosty December air.

"I guess that's a Star of David on the band," Alexia suggested. "He must be from Germany, come to see the festivities."

Garnett shook her head. "You know he couldn't get across the border. They don't let any of them out."

Suddenly it seemed to Alexia as if they were already in some Nazi concentration camp. As Garnett said they couldn't get out and God knew what was happening to them inside the Reich. They had no work or labour permits. They were not permitted bank accounts or pensions.

"How do they survive?" Alexia asked, shaken by the unanswerable problem.

Garnett shrugged. "There are a few. Hitler calls them his 'Honorary Aryans', according to Frau Becque."

"But if they don't let them out, what is that poor man doing here?" Another frightening idea occurred to her at the same time it came to her mother.

"It's Max's Council," Garnett said. "They've voted to make all the Jews in Lichtenbourg wear the yellow bands. There's an old woman with something pinned on her coat. My God! Would he stoop to that?"

"I don't think Father has much say about it."

Alexia strongly suspected that her mother would scarcely have noticed the sinister yellow band or the Star of David if she hadn't been personally involved with Johann Hofer. And Frau Becque knew he was Jewish.

But somebody had to make a stand. Lichtenbourg was still a free principality. Why else were they all rushing to marry Alexia off to a Swedish citizen?

"I'll go and talk to Father," she volunteered. "Those damned yellow things can be seen blocks away. If we aren't careful those Nazi thugs will be pouring through the borders and kidnapping our own citizens."

Garnett was so pale Alexia put an arm around her. "Mother, it was just a gruesome idea. I'll tell Herr Sternberg that I won't go through with this if Stefan and I are going to have our country invaded by foreign hoodlums."

"It won't do any good." Garnett pulled herself together. "But I'll do it. I'll say it's your ultimatum. I don't think

221

Max will ask why we're so interested. He has a very humane streak." She hesitated with her hand to her mouth. "Unless, of course, they are refugees from the Reich. Then they can demand their return as criminals, or something."

Alexia closed her eyes. "With all the horrors going on in the world I hate to remind you, but this is my wedding day. What do we do about that?"

Garnett hugged her. "I know, dear. I'll see what can be done. Meanwhile, when the women come to dress you and Sergei arrives to do your hair, just pretend you don't know why I've gone to see your father. I'll think of something."

The following hours seemed to flow into each other. Alexia felt like a department store mannequin. Expressionless, with her thoughts jumbled, she did all that was asked of her, turning, twisting, remaining rigid, wondering if all the efforts of breathless anxious women and one very confident male hairdresser would all come to nothing.

If the ceremony took place at all it would begin beside her father in the latest silver-grey limousine number one. This, presumably, was a tribute to Adolf Hitler, whose wedding gift it was.

Princess Ilsa, who came in to pass judgement on her future daughter-in-law, told her with considerable regret, "The Fuhrer is detained in headquarters on the Eastern Front. Those tiresome Russians will do anything to cause us trouble, even to pressing forward when the world knows they are defeated."

"The Kuragins were once Russian," Alexia pointed out but otherwise ignored her.

Garnett was still missing. What had happened? The procession was within minutes of starting in order to arrive at the cathedral doors sharply at noon for the radio hookup of organ fanfare, when Polly called Alexia to the phone. "Her Highness will take no calls," snapped Princess Ilsa who had taken over the duties properly assigned to the mother of the bride.

Polly displayed suitable humility and a pretence of surprise. "What, Ma'am? Not even from the bridegroom?"

The princess said nothing but waved elegantly towards the telephone beside the bed. At any other time Alexia would have been amused. Now she snatched up the phone with shaking hands.

Stefan's first words reassured her. "My love, I wanted to be the first to tell you that good Chancellor Becque, with His Serene Highness's permission, wants to rescind the law concerning yellow armbands for certain of Lichtenbourg's subjects."

"Stefan! Darling!"

"Please. I want to express it in the gallant chancellor's own language: 'The law seems to have been passed by a minority of the Royal Council during the absence of the chancellor and Prince Maximilian.' In that order."

"Does my mother know?"

"Know, my love? Of course. She and Tige Royle will even be sharing Chancellor Becque's limousine."

She didn't ask how it had all been contrived. Since Stefan was involved, the Swedish Crown might be behind the whole thing. "Oh, Stefan, I do love you."

He pretended indignation. "Well, I devoutly hope so. See you soon, Darling." He hung up.

Alexia turned to face the curious crowd, some of whom were her attendants. Six of their daughters would carry her train, and a heavy load it was, like dragging a twenty-five-feet carpet behind her. She prayed that no one would step on it, by accident or otherwise. If that happened she would be knocked back on her posterior, and possibly her head.

Luckily, the seamstresses, by working most of two nights, had removed the under layers of velvet and jewels, replacing them with delicate embroidery and seed pearls.

The gown itself, of a form-fitting silvery satin, when combined with the tall, medieval hennin and its long, flying satin ribbons, gave her an unexpected height. Her veil did not conceal her entire face, only her forehead and eyes. It flowed lightly down her back from the tip of the hennin.

Her nervous pallor was partly alleviated by makeup, but as she began to realize that the wedding really would take place, she regained some of her delicate but healthy colour.

She ignored the fact that her white satin shoes pinched across the toe of her left foot. You couldn't expect miracles.

Her father was obviously satisfied. He came to her suite on cue and said he had never seen a bride so lovely. "Except your mother, of course. Now, let me see. Place your hand on my cuff. Now, forward as we rehearsed."

She wondered if anyone, even her future husband, was as handsome and slender as Max Kuragin in his blue uniform with its red piping, all crowned by his highly polished silver helmet. She wished she had known the tired, frustrated prince better during those years when she had deliberately alienated herself from him.

They walked through the high-ceilinged hall and down the wide public staircase under a shower of "Ohs", "Ahs," and "God Save our Noble Prince!" along with an occasional "Heil Kronprinzessen!" which she could have done without.

Their regal march came to a halt in the public hall where the last of the wedding party was being herded into Chancellor Becque's limousine. The two princesses were seated in splendour, Garnett in green satin and velvet, her beautiful auburn hair set off by her favourite tiara with its Kuragin emerald surrounded by diamonds.

Princess Ilsa's golden splendour was, as usual, completed by a gold-cloth gown and surcoat, with an appropriately dazzling circlet of yellow diamonds in her hair.

Facing them, Chancellor Becque had decked himself out in a blue Lichtenbourg uniform to which he was not entitled, and two truly eye-catching diamond rings one on either hand. Still, he was eclipsed by his companion, Tige Royle, in a commonplace lounge suit and no jewels. His thick grey hair caught the breeze in the frosty sunlight.

"He always was impressive," Max said, noting where Alexia's attention was focused. She nodded. Max went on quietly, "Only one other man I ever knew had that quality. I never could equal my father. God knows I tried."

Was it out of his bitter envy that he had let Franz Kuragin's assasins go unpunished? She said, "I know." But wasn't it time to put away her own bitterness and his lifetime of envy? She curled her fingers around his gloved hand. "He would want us to forget."

She saw herself suddenly as she had been that day when she was five years old and they had all come out of the cathedral after celebrating the tenth anniversary of the royal wedding between Max and Garnett. She saw Franz Kuragin reach out his arms to lift Alexia into the motor car. Then the shot. And he was still reaching for her. Perhaps, in that instant, he hadn't known he was dying.

Was it an omen to see it so vividly now as they were on their way to the same cathedral? Please God, no. Banish the memory. As he would have done.

She said, "I'd feel a lot better if Tige had actually left Europe by this time. Anyway, let's only think of the future, good things, after this accursed war is over. Prince Franz would have wanted you to do that."

He looked at her. A smile broke through the sombre look she normally saw. "I believe you are right . . . Do you know, I feel better, so long as my daughter is in my corner."

She wished he looked less drained and worried, but she smiled encouragingly. "Of course I am. Now, Father, they're waiting. They can't have their show without you and me."

She felt the slight new spring in his step as they walked down together to the liveried chauffeur and the detective in his deceptive, blue musical comedy uniform. Behind Alexia, her attendants with their silk gowns fluttering, hurried to put her and her regalia into the limousine.

Alexia waved and smiled as her father did from his side of the limousine. It was not more than six blocks, but the car had to make its way gingerly through a surprisingly large crowd. For this day they seemed to have forgotten the troubles of a world at war.

Alexia was touched by the affection they showed the royal family. Her parents, especially her father, must have done something right in the twenty-three years of their rule.

Their arrival in the great cathedral square was greeted with cheers that almost drowned the booming chords of the two great cathedral organs.

She could never afterwards remember all the details of the service. When she read about them in the papers later she saw herself spoken of as "composed, proud, a true daughter of her parents", whatever that meant.

She recalled the chill grandeur of the cathedral but not the slow march to the chancel rail. She had one thought in mind: "Please don't step on my train." No one did. And "don't let me forget my lines."

Garnett looked confident and reassuring beside Max. Both of them smiled at her. That helped. The archbishop, a very old gentleman in robes that smelled of mothballs, made her want to giggle. Luckily, she didn't.

226

In spite of all her doubts and fears before she saw Stefan waiting for her near the altar at the far end of the nave, the sight of him banished doubts. Each step and each organ note brought her closer. Then he joined her, only a step or two, but his warm, vital strength was close. She could feel it even beneath the absurd masquerade in her mother's robes, fresh from the museum.

In making her vows, which sounded mechanical to her, she became newly aware of his own sincerity. She managed to remember her "lines" while staring at him, loving the tenderness in his eyes as he looked at her while he made his own vows to her. She refused to think how near she had come to losing him. That was the past.

The old archbishop didn't instruct the groom to kiss the bride, but when the short service was over and they had received his blessing, Stefan lowered his head over hers. She expected a mere touch, but his lips closed over hers and, without even thinking twice, she responded warmly, whispering afterwards, "I love you."

He put his arm around her, then tightened his grip. A few near them tittered at the romantic touch they had given to their vows.

Alexia flashed bright, heartfelt smiles to her family but missed Tige who had been concealed by the crowd around him. Garnett and Max returned her smile with genuine happiness.

They walked down the long aisle with an occasional nod and smile to the eager faces around them, none of whom they remembered afterward. When they were greeted with cheers in Cathedral Square Alexia realized she had put her arm around Stefan's waist. She started to remove it but stopped when Stefan taunted her, "Coward."

A black Swedish car pulled out of the lineup. The chauffeur saluted Stefan, bowed to Alexia, and stood at attention while the detective in a policeman's bucket helmet looked over the crowd from behind Alexia.

In a laughing panic Alexia objected. "Where is the limousine? I can't go off like this. Look at my train. And this stupid thing on my head. I can't even get into the car. The roof isn't high enough."

Stefan swept away this objection. "Your mother is a shrewd lady. Your father may have objected, but Princess Garnett made all arrangements. We are to have the use of an apartment behind the cathedral for an hour. Some actor loaned it to us. Your Polly has packed your cases. Then we head towards our honeymoon."

"In Sweden."

"Southern Sweden can be very nice. It won't be nearly long enough. We won't want to return to all the dull business of helping your father run a country, as we must some day. But get in, Sweetheart. Wait, Lundt. You'll have to throw this stuff in the front seat." It was a handful of her train.

Still laughing and shaking her head, she let Stefan remove her tall headpiece along with several hairpins. She climbed into the car while the Swedish chauffeur bundled up her train. Stefan went around the car, got in on the other side, threw the headpiece into the front seat, just missing the detective, and sat down with his arm around Alexia.

It was all very strange, this great hurry. Even love would hardly inspire this conspiratorial haste. By the time they pulled away from the square crowds were pouring out of the cathedral. Stefan opened the car window. Then he took Alexia's hand and waved it to her parents who were frantically waving handkerchiefs. But still, there was no Tige.

"I'm surprised your mother isn't lurking around," she said, trying to make it sound like a joke.

He didn't seem offended. "Don't worry. We will see her

sooner or later. She gets around. And of course, she's bound to report our big moment to her buddy."

"Her buddy?"

"Hitler."

I'll pretend I didn't hear that, she thought. In fact, I'll pretend she doesn't exist in our lives.

Still puzzled by all this conspiracy, she looked at the Swedish chauffeur and then at the back of the detective's neck. Thanks to the helmet she could see very little of it but there was something familiar. She leaned forward, resisting Stefan's clasp. Good God! Tige. She put her hand out, touching his shoulder. He looked around and winked.

"Getting out through Sweden," he explained. "Taking the Swedish ship to Tokyo, Honey. They're picking up American diplomats. Kind of a mutual courtesy, enemy-type. You can thank your Stefan for the idea as it affects me. Once I'm over there, we'll see."

"Oh, thank you. Thank you." She twisted around to her husband but he warned her.

"Don't touch Tige yet. Some of these street crowds may see us."

Feeling enormously relieved, she settled back. They drove out of the square and over to a narrow, medieval street behind the cathedral where the houses leaned so close over the street below that it was like driving through a tunnel. There was a scramble in the car as the two men in the front seat tried to bundle up the bride's regalia and Stefan helped her out of the car.

Due to a light snowfall the day before the gutter was still running with melted water and souvenirs of the royal wedding, mostly paper coronets, ribbons in the Lichtenbourg colours, and programmes of the Cathedral organ concert.

Alexia saw that the hem of her gown was mud-stained

despite Stefan's efforts but she laughed it off, too excited over Tige's rescue to care.

Tige said, "We'll wait for you here, like good little servants of the royal family. Don't take too long to change, Honey. We all know how women are."

Stefan played up to Tige's determinedly cheerful mood. "I assure you, I have my wife perfectly trained."

"If you have, you're a first, my friend."

The men laughed, but Alexia was already pushing open a street door that was ajar. Behind the door Johann Hofer stood, bowing, smiling, and calling her, "Your Serene Highness". His youthful eagerness was part of his good looks. Surely anyone so ingenuous, almost an innocent, in this corrupt and frightening world, could never be in danger.

"Thank you, Hanni. I am – how do you say it in Swedish? I am now Frau von Elsbach to you."

She started up the narrow staircase that smelled damp and mouldly. She looked back despite Stefan's hand on her arm. "Be very careful, Hanni." The young man beamed at hearing his familiar nickname and bowed.

Realizing that the longer she took, the more dangerous it was for Tige, she hurried on. Neither she nor Stefan made much of an effort to save Garnett's museum gown. She had been stitched into it and she yanked it off. Seed pearls flew in all directions. With Stefan's help she changed quickly into a blue wool travel dress and coat whose mink-trimmed hood was warmly welcome. By the time they reached the car again Tige congratulated them on breaking a new bride's speed record, but Alexia thought he looked alarmingly grim.

When the bride and groom were in the car Stefan leaned forward. "What happened?"

The "chauffeur" raised his little German radio.

"Berlin Radio says Wake Island, in the Pacific, will

230

be occupied either tonight or tomorrow. The American Marines are making what they call 'a last stand'. It is Christmas Day over there."

Tige did not look around. He said calmly, "After Wake and Guam come the others. They say the Philippines will be entirely in enemy hands soon. Means I've got to hustle."

The silence was so intense they could all hear the cheers for the royal family still going on in Cathedral Square.

Stefan spoke to the chauffeur. "Will this interfere with Jensen's work tonight?"

"No, Highness. He's covered. But they may have to set them up in your chateau until they can be flown out by Swedish planes. It will take time. And there are so many, always."

Stefan turned to her. "My love, it looks as though we may not spend our honeymoon at Andross after all. It will be occupied by those who need it more than we do."

Did he think she was so shallow and self-centred? She forced a laugh and kissed his cheek. "Who cares? I don't mind where spend my honeymoon as long as I spend it with my husband, silly."

Stefan drew her to him. "That's my girl. We'll see you off, Tige, and then sneak back into Lichtenbourg City."

Tige said, "I hear it's done by all the smartest couples. Get down to action faster."

Lundt, the chauffeur, flushed a little. Everyone else laughed. Alexia felt slightly hysterical but played up.

CHAPTER NINETEEN

A little after sunset on that particular wedding day the bride and groom surveyed the first home of their marriage. Stefan rubbed his chin and admitted, "As a honeymoon paradise, it does leave something to be desired."

There were little things about him that she was beginning to notice and love. One was his willingness to accept what came along and to adapt quickly.

She said, "Don't forget the view, Darling. Here on the third floor, what do you see? Look out of that south window." It was a high little window above the sink and beside a cupboard curtained with an old sheet to hide its kitchen contents. Johann Hofer must love lettuce, and at these winter prices. The tin bread box was full of it.

Stefan looked out the window and laughed. At a distance of about ten blocks the grey majesty of the New Palace loomed up. Its many barred windows facing west reflected the last red and gold rays of the sun.

One important item in the room was the double bed against the north wall. Alexia suspected that when her mother took her nightly strolls to the cathedral she simply walked four blocks north, behind the cathedral, to this bed, Hanni Hofer's bed.

Hofer had sacrifice his room and his bed to the newly weds. Stefan noted Alexia's interest in the bed and guessed her question.

"Where will Hofer sleep tonight? There is a service cottage in the gardens of the New Palace. He has obtained the housekeeper's permission, and the gardener's as well, to use the cottage while his apartment, our honeymoon nest, is repainted. Let's hope the good Frau Becque doesn't come here to supervise the so-called paint job."

She smiled but wondered if he knew how near to Garnett that would place Hofer.

She knew she had to talk to her mother, warn her that the knowledge of others might destroy Hofer and even the dynasty. But ironically enough she didn't know her own mother well enough to speak so frankly. She must learn to handle such matters. Mental bravery would be quite as important as physical bravery in her future.

Stefan examined the little gas stove with its two burners and a deep well for cooking spare-ribs, sauerkraut and potatoes together, or sauerbraten or other hearty dishes.

"I suppose this seems as foreign to you as the surface of the moon." He drew her to him with one hand. "No matter. That little restaurant on the street floor, we'll make it do. And remember, these are the 'good old days' we will remember some day."

She surprised him. "Much you know. When my godmother, Laura, wasn't at Tige's penthouse and he had company, Dan and I played cook and butler. Wait 'til you taste my Hangtown Fry."

"Sounds revolting, my love. I'll take your word for it." He was unpacking one of her cases now, which one contained a gown in salmon-coloured layers of chiffon, a pair of matching satin slippers, and a disgracefully practical towelling robe which struck his sense of humour.

"It's perfect. Maybe your Polly knew all the time."

She dropped it on the one chair the room afforded. "Perfect? I certainly never expected any man to see me in it. It's for getting out of showers and tubs and things."

233

"Well, my love, you'll need it here. The halls are freezing and the facilities, for want of a better word, are on the floor below."

She was revolted for a minute but determined not to let him think she couldn't take it, so she grinned and pulled the rejected robe back.

"What a smart girl Polly is! Probably thought all Swedish chateaux were clammy and cold."

He took hold of her shoulders, making her look up into his eyes. "Are you really happy, Sweetheart? Is there somebody you would rather be with tonight?"

How ridiculous! Where did he get these ideas? Unless he had them himself. "Who on earth would it be? Some imaginary Romeo?"

He held the salmon gown up against her playfully, with his attention exclusively upon the chiffon. "Dan Royle, for instance?"

She opened both her mouth and her eyes at such an idea. "But Dan is my brother! I mean, I've always thought of him like that. I know he's not, really. But to marry him would be like – well, incest."

He said drily, "Far be it from me to encourage incest in young ladies. Least of all, my own bride."

She dropped the robe and hugged him, feeling the vital beat of his heart against hers as it had been at the ceremony after their vows were made. She pretended to laugh but was terribly touched by the fact that he could be jealous of Dan. Even if he had married her to get control of Lichtenbourg eventually, he did love her. Didn't this just confirm it?

Having unpacked what might be considered common-place clothing for the next few days, Alexia felt a little nervous about making love immediately. The excitement and concern over Tige's departure by plane for Stockholm had caught up with her.

She was relieved when Stefan suggested they go down to the brasserie, an Alsatian restaurant in the basement that catered in part to Rhineland German tastes.

"The best of two worlds," Stefan pointed out as they descended the stone steps from the street level down to a warm, aromatic cavern lighted by smoking lanterns. This, combined with the pipe-smoking Lichtenbourg customers, made Alexia peer dimly through the smoky air. The waiter-chef in a heavy stained butcher's apron, led them to a distant table in an alcove near the kitchen.

"Very private, mein Herr. Our friend, Hanni, of the Theatre Royal, he made the arrangements."

It had been a happy thought. The food was as delicious as the odour from the busy kitchen, the mushrooms-rahmschnitzel superb, and the Mosel wine good enough for Alexia to drink an extra glass or two, "because she could scarcely feel it". Stefan stuck to beer.

When they made their way through the smokescreen and out into the nippy air of the street, they instinctively drew closer together. He watched her face as they made their way to the narrow staircase and took a deep breath before tackling the three steep flights.

"Happy?" he asked.

She tightened her grip around him. "Happy. This is the best honeymoon of all. Better than any old chateau."

He grinned but couldn't help the obvious question: "Just how many have you had?"

"Hundreds. In my mind. But I never thought of one like this."

"I'm glad. I think."

Climbing those endless steep stairs was not nearly as hard as it might have been. Nor was she tense and uneasy now about their lovemaking. She knew what she wanted. Above all, his skilled lovemaking was what she had dreamed of and been excited by in her years of sleeping alone. She had grown up with a sense that she would always be alone. She accepted that. Nothing tragic about it. What she had actually wanted in reality, as in her dreams, was passion. She had found it.

They undressed each other, Alexia thrilled to be imitating this masterful lover whose body, even his hands, aroused her so much. She did arouse him as she had hoped, by imitating his actions, his use of his fingers over erogenous spots on her body. She was not as skilled with her lips but his body kisses and the slow, feathery movements of his lips over her flanks brought her to an ecstasy that needed only his penetration to be complete. Could she ever learn to apply these special, erotic movements on him, making him wait for penetration until, like her, he wanted to scream?

Probably not, but she would give it a good try, and what fun practising in the days and years they would have ahead! At least, she had the satisfaction of exhausting him after their second orgasm. They both began to laugh, with her dishevelled head on his abdomen.

"Don't ask me to climb those stairs now," he complained.

She knew she was going to giggle and begged him, "Say something sensible. Dan says men hate gigglers."

That stopped his laughing. "The hell with Dan." He turned over upon her and forcibly took her, this time rough and unlike himself.

She understood, realizing she had triggered this response, and merely joined her own legs around his and held him to her. Surely, he must know that he was the man she loved.

When they broke apart she murmured, "I know something sensible. Right now, it must be tomorrow somewhere in the world, so, Merry Christmas, Darling."

"Merry Christmas, My love."

It snowed in the night, but they were warm together in

the deep, down pillows, the coverlet and blankets of Hanni Hofer's bed. On Christmas Day they borrowed much-used ski outfits from the brasserie's two elder sons. Disguised with goggles and parkas, they spent most of the day wandering incognito around the edges of the principality. They got as close to the Austrian and later the Hungarian borders as they thought expedient, and tried not to let the sights depress them.

Most of the Austrian border was fortified with barbed wire and sometimes, even in the open snow-covered fields, they saw bundled human beings peering out at them from behind the wire. Theoretically they were not in prison, the fields and the sky were open. But they were trapped. It was as if the ancient, singing beauty of Austria had become one huge prison.

The newlyweds were glad enough to wander back to the brasserie and the waiter-chef's hearty greeting.

"*Güten abend,*" and then, surprisingly, in English: "Merry Christmas, my friends. Come in, Come in. Special tonight. The good sauerbraten and my wife makes the torte mitt schlagg."

"We'll be as fat as Goering," Stefan protested.

His casual reference to the Reichsmarschall worried Alexia who wondered about the reaction this would bring, but the chef laughed uproariously.

"Impossible. A dozen tortes each meal it takes to be so fat. Have you heard the latest good one about Goebbels?" He excused himself to Alexia, lowered his voice and repeated for Stefan the latest scatological joke about the little Reichsmarschall.

Dinner came afterwards, delicious and memorable. There was a word so many used to describe the Austrians, if not the Germans, before the war. Although a Rhinelander, the brasserie's chef was *gemütlich*, a jolly, likeable, cosy fellow. There did not seem to be many like him left.

237

Maybe, if all went well, they would have several days more days of happiness here. Each day she awoke and thought, if we could have one more day . . .

It worked for six days.

Alexia stood on the toes of her boots looking out of the high window. She wondered if the sunlight glittering on the light cover of recent snow would expose them if they went out for a long walk up to, or near, the Royal Chalet and back. The snowy surface cast a bright glare and they might get away with wearing dark goggles.

Behind her, Stefan was reading the Viennese and Munich morning papers which screamed of victories everywhere, but especially in the Pacific. According to the *Abend Zeitung* the United States Navy had ceased to exist. After being wiped out at Pearl Harbor in Hawaii they would never rise again.

"Is it really that bad?" Alexia asked, looking back over her shoulder.

His matter-of-fact attitude reassured her. "It can't be. Even the Germans don't claim any flat-tops were hit. Thank God they were out at sea when the attack came. And frankly, I don't think the Fuhrer has any conception of the reserve power, the factories and organization over there. The manpower itself is staggering."

"I feel better." She turned back to the window. Then both of them heard what she thought must be thunder, but the sky was a clear and piercing blue.

"Thunder, on a day like this?"

He waved her to silence, got up and went to the window beside her. "Not thunder. I know that sound. I've heard it and seen it too often, in Berlin."

The goosestep.

She felt a thrill of terror. Had it come, the thing she and her father's government dreaded?

"Is Hitler taking over?"

"Not with that army. Sounds like a couple of dozen, maybe less. He's probably feeling us out. It will take more than that to capture tough little Lichtenbourg. They just want to throw a scare into the people. I'd better go down."

He reached for his parka and hesitated, looking for the Swedish uniform which was hung neatly on the old-fashioned coat-rack with two of Johann Hofer's highly decorated operetta uniforms.

Alexia said, "Shouldn't we show up in full regalia, let them know we stand with my father?"

"By all means, but a surprise might be more effective. I'll go down through the brasserie and up into the alley. An effective front should send the message back. Hitler has his hands full with the Russians at the Eastern Front. I doubt if he wants a full-scale bloodletting."

"That's true. If they attack you, Sweden will be angry and Hitler needs her neutrality," she pointed out.

He grinned, getting into his tunic. "You are such a comfort, my love." He gave her a quick kiss.

She made a desperate effort to be cheerful. "It was a wonderful honeymoon. Every minute."

"Just not enough minutes," he agreed. As she straightened the back of his tunic, she caressed his neck with her fingers and then felt his own lips warm against her hand.

Suddenly, she realized that they were doing this all wrong. "Darling, I'm the next Princess Royal. I should be beside you and Father." She added on a dry note, "And Mother, if she feels up to it."

"We can always borrow my own mother," he reminded her.

"God forbid! She's probably leading those storm-troopers."

He didn't seem offended, thank heaven. He looked at her as if he were sizing her up. "You may be right. We will present a united front, both families; so they can't play one against the other. But promise me to stay behind the main doors. Along with a few guards looking appropriately dignified, Maximilian and I will meet them."

She took the hand he offered as they went down the gloomy little back staircase which was marked at every landing by the refuse and garbage of that floor. It might have been revolting but Alexia felt the exhilaration of doing something brave for her country and she had enormous confidence in Stefan.

From Frau Maria Keller, wife of the brasserie chef, Stefan borrowed an ancient but serviceable little French coupé in order to be at the palace for the arrival of the noisy goosesteppers. They were all waving flags with black swastikas sewn in the centre. They could be seen now on West Cathedral Street just one block west of Stefan and Alexia.

Followed by Frau Keller's good wishes, Stefan started the little car with a spurt that threw Alexia back against the worn seat. He reached over with one hand to steady her but she was indifferent to small matters.

"Never mind. We must reach home first."

With a side glance Stefan repeated, "Home? Sweetheart, I do believe you are beginning to accept the cards fate has dealt you."

She laughed harshly. "Why not? It looks like this is where we pay for all that bowing and scraping we get."

"Exactly so."

Without looking at her he took up her fist, brought it to his lips and then let it go. The pressure of his fingers on her hand had been like a vice, but the pain was nothing.

They beat the marching men and a few women to the New Palace, entering behind the North Gate, through the gateway to the royal gardens where, long ago, Lord David Miravel had dug up ancient Roman remains and written a massive book about it. One of the wrought-iron gates was opened for them as soon as the sentry recognized Stefan's face on the diplomatic passport and saluted.

"The princess gave orders, Your Highness. We were to expect you immediately after her messenger reached you."

"We anticipated the messenger," Stefan said. "You are to be commended on your diligence."

They drove into the grounds and Stefan parked Frau Keller's car behind the old and rarely used royal stables. They could hear the marching feet and the rhythmic yells of "Heil Hitler!" and "Reich Lichtenbourg!" which filled Alexia with fury.

"Filthy traitors! After all my family has done for them!"

She was brought to a realization of her dangerous overreaction when Stefan warned her, "Remember, no heroics."

"Sorry." She restrained herself with difficulty feeling murderous.

She and Stefan entered the great hall by the north doors, pushing their way through panic-stricken palace attendants and servants, led by the eighty-year-old Lord Chamberlain. He was trembling with anger and gripping a sword that must have seen service during the Napoleonic Wars.

Halfway down the great hall the barred glass entrance doors were open, guarded only by two uniformed sentries. Prince Maximilian was on the top step in one of the dress uniforms that became him so well. He had raised his arms and was trying to speak over the teeth-rattling rhythm of the Nazi shouts.

Alexia was astonished that only a little over twenty people could bring the entire principality to a halt, but half of Lichtenbourg must be crowded around and behind them, watching to see which side was going to win, she thought with cold cynicism.

The centre of attention was the flagpole in the forecourt below the palace steps, where limousines at royal functions made the semicircle that brought their passengers to the palace steps.

Some enterprising traitor had brought down the Lichtenbourg flag and sent up the obscene travesty with its swastika in the centre.

Prince Maximilian broke off, realizing he could not be heard, and looked around for a minute. He appeared grey with fatigue and nervousness. Stefan elbowed his way through the crowd of terrified palace retainers and started out of the open door several yards behind Max. Alexia got as near as she could to the open door but was caught by Garnett's hand.

"Oh, Alexia, he'll be killed," she cried frantically. "He's not well. His heart is bad. He shouldn't be there."

"Mother, be quiet!"

As she spoke, Alexia saw another figure out of the corner of her eye. Princess Ilsa had come out at the far end of the steps. The sun made her look like a fire goddess. Alexia wondered if she had chosen this moment to proclaim a new regime under the Elsbachs. Her son ignored her. He moved quietly down the steps behind Max who stepped foward, picking up the discarded royal flag.

Puzzled by what they hoped would be a conflict between the two royal families, including Princess Ilsa who was a well-known pro-Nazi, the ambitious young would-be stormtroopers slowly quieted down. The square at the palace end of the Boulevard Kuragin, now jammed with people, became so silent a sealed train passing through at the far end of the boulevard could be heard. Its eerie whistle sounded like a woman screaming as it hurtled its way across the city and on to the Austrian border without stopping.

Alexia moved past her mother, terrified for her father and Stefan, yet she had never been more proud of them.

Stefan moved down step by step behind Max until Max reached the flagpole. No one in the great crowd had moved. Stefan stopped. Obviously, he realized Max would never live down the humiliation if anyone tried to help him perform this small but symbolic act of heroism.

Max worked with the cords, his fingers shaking a little. Then the Lichtenbourg flag went up the pole. As if the heavens were with him, an icy breeze swept across the square, catching the flag at the top of the pole. It whipped noisily over the crowd. No swastika there.

Stefan removed his uniform cap by the bill and waved it, shouting, "Heil Lichtenbourg! Kronprinz Maximilian, Heil!"

It was enough. The crowd took up the cry. The goosesteppers, confused, looked around, muttered to each other and two or three joined the cheers. Princess Ilsa swept down the steps, smiling, addressing a few remarks to the marchers, mentioning "The Fuhrer". It was contagious. They joined the cheers.

Pale and shaken, Prince Max turned from the flagpole and started up the steps toward Stefan. Alexia and Garnett rushed out to meet him.

Suddenly, the cheers became uncertain, fading into groans and cries. A woman screamed. There were more screams amid a loud hum of voices. Garnett ran down the steps with Alexia at her heels. But already, Prince Max was swaying, both arms clutching his breast. Halfway up the steps he stumbled. Stefan and one of his equerries were the first to ease him down to the steps.

Garnett pushed her way to the fallen figure, huddled in a foetal position, still clutching his breast. She raised his head, cradling it in her lap. Alexia felt her father's neck beneath the stiff collar of his tunic. His pulsebeat seemed horribly irregular. But at least his heart was still beating.

Having examined him, Stefan raised his head and signalled the equerry. "Very likely his heart. Where is his physician? You and you. Something for a stretcher. Hurry, damn you!"

"Dr Valdemar is coming," Princess Ilsa told her son. "I've ordered them to have a room made ready. At once!"

Alexia tried to talk to her father, ignoring her tears that blurred his face to her, but with all the excitement around him she knew she could be more useful with her mother. She helped the terrified Garnett to her feet and, seeing Janos Becque close by watching these events with interest, she summoned him.

"We must make the princess as comfortable as possible in a room adjoining my father. Go and see to it."

His attention seemed to dart about until he saw Princess Ilsa who said icily, "Do as you are told. Fuhrer's orders."

"He'd be better off in Vienna," Becque muttered.

In Vienna, completely surrounded by the enemy? Alexia had never hated this swine so much, and she resented almost as bitterly Princess Ilsa's invoking of the name of their bitterest enemy. But she was dumbfounded when Chancellor Becque looked from the princess to Alexia and grinned.

"The old guard changes, eh? We take our orders from the Elsbachs. Prince Stefan, his wife here, and above all," he looked over at Princess Ilsa, "above all, the Fuhrer's good friend." He grinned.

"Just so," snapped the princess. "Until Prince Maximilian is on his feet again."

"Wait!" Alexia cried, but they ignored her.

Becque's bow included both Alexia and the Elsbach princess. "There is more than one way for the Fuhrer to take power in Lichtenbourg. Nein? You are to be congratulated, Madam Ilsa."

PART THREE

The New Reign

CHAPTER TWENTY

During the illness of the Lichtenbourg Prince Royal, under the Constitution, the royal heir was appointed to temporarily occupy his position in the Royal Council. There was a proviso that the president of the Council, in this case Janos Becque, must co-sign all documents in the name of the absent Prince Royal.

Though Alexia feared and detested Janos Becque she found herself with other, secret problems. She had always thought love and trust went hand in hand. But that was before her father's exhaustion and the angina pectoris attack left the way open for her to share with Stefan the high position for which she had been trained.

She loved Stefan passionately, if love meant sexual attraction. She had no quarrel with those unforgettable nights they still shared. She did think, once in a while, that he must have had extensive experience in the past, but when she rather gingerly hinted at this once to her only confidante, her maid, Polly, the latter grinned at what she obviously considered naivete.

"Excusing the liberty, Ma'am, but you haven't done a lot of experiencing, being so young and all. He's not the type that carries on with every Tom, Dick and Harry. That is – " as Alexia laughed, "every twit that throws herself at him. And I can tell you this. In my place, you hear all the gossip. There's no gossip about His Highness. Now, until your good pa got sick we did hear a little about Princess

Garnett. But that's a whole different story."

"You don't hear it now?" Alexia asked nervously.

"No. Poor young man, he's so besotted with your mother he just hangs about here when he ain't on the stage. Tries to be of help."

"My husband and I owe him our wonderful honeymoon, even if it was cut short."

"Yeah, he's a good boy. We all wish him well, though I'm not so sure about the old devil, Frau Becque."

She brushed Alexia off as the latter passed her going out into the hall of their new suite. This, at least, had been an improvement on her old rooms. "Good luck, Ma'am."

"Thank you, Polly."

In spite of Polly's reassuring talk, Alexia found it hard to shake off the suspicion that she had been right in the first place. Even before Stefan followed her to Miravel he had determined to marry the heiress to the throne of Lichtenbourg.

She gave him the benefit of believing his childhood teachings were at fault and the ambition of his mother to get back the power her family had so ill-used. But every waking day when she entered her father's Council chamber, she seethed with a secret anger.

She couldn't forget that Stefan had obtained his power through marriage. It was not something he had been born to. Despite this, she was clear-minded enough to admit that Prince Stefan von Elsbach was a stronger ruler than her father had been. It was painful to visit Max in the elegant little palace that had once belonged to the Hapsburgs in Vienna, and to see how anxiously he asked for all particulars about the Council meetings, all the bills that had been passed, the decisions made, and then how he carefully gave orders about their passage or repeal, as if he would still be obeyed.

Garnett could not handle it. She hated Princess Ilsa,

hated the government business, and resented anything that upset Max. But she was indiscreet and spoke too loudly in the company of doctors and nurses at the little palace. Alexia and Stefan had an unspoken agreement never to discuss a serious matter in her presence, particularly one that might give the German Government information they didn't want it to have.

During the first months after Prince Max's attack and their own rise to "temporary" power, Stefan had seen to it that he and Alexia entered the Council chamber together. But in March Alexia made a series of excuses to linger behind her husband, coming in a quarter of an hour later. Her excuses were always trivial: her hairdresser had not finished; she had interviews with the housekeeper; or she must solve some palace retainer's problem.

By April it must have occurred to Stefan that she invariably arrived only minutes after the other council members were seated. Including Stefan, they all arose respectfully to greet her. It became a tradition.

She was obviously the Princess Royal, ruler of Lichtenbourg. There was no Prince Royal until Prince Max came back. She had made sure her husband kept to the role of Prince Consort. Fortunately, he did not seem to be humiliated. He managed very well by ignoring it.

She admired him more than ever, but did not change her habit. She wanted him to know that though he had originally intended to marry her for the post of Prince Royal and joint ruler, he had not succeeded.

The occasional and scattered news from Tige came to Lichtenbourg only by Swiss Red Cross to Swedish neutral envoys, and from Sweden to Lichtenbourg by diplomatic pouch addressed to Stefan.

When Alexia came to the Council chamber on a bright, sunny morning in late April of 1942 everyone stood up for her. But she saw at once that there was something here much more important than mere protocol.

During the last few weeks the news from the Pacific had been devastating. Over Radio Berlin, with few contradictions from the BBC broadcasts heard in Prince Max's presently unoccupied study, there had been nothing but gloating, boasting, and the Horst Wessel song repeated *ad nauseam*. The mighty Singapore naval base of the British Empire had fallen; Luzon and Mindanao in the Philippines had gone; now Batain had fallen and still no word of Tige or Dan Royle. Alexia expected nothing better today.

Everyone welcomed her as usual. Stefan, who had kissed her warmly upon leaving their bedroom an hour ago, now saluted her hand with another kiss. She could see that his dark eyes were full of excitement. If he had smiled she would have put his excitement down to happiness, or at least good news.

At the far end of the chamber on the dais where the semicircular conference table curved around toward the seats in the pit of this miniature theatre, Alexia saw Princess Ilsa. The princess sat with her still-slender legs crossed and one of her high-heeled pumps swinging back and forth. She was apparently one of those women who never looked anything but their best. She called to Alexia across the semicircle of men.

"Good morning, Alexandra. A little news from the battle-front." She yawned. "And for God's sake, no boring cheers, please."

This explained the light in Stefan's eyes, though he took care to remain outwardly neutral.

Today, for once, Janos Becque had an agenda of greater importance.

"I will not bore Her Serene Highness and others by mentioning the bits of cornice that showered the boulevard last night from the Kreditanstalt-Lichtenbourg Bank, because of late news developments."

250

For weeks now Janos Becque had managed to bring in a personal matter, pointing out the business advantages to the country if taxes were set aside to repair the crumbling cornice of the old Wien Kreditanstalt bank building in Cathedral Square, near the Theatre Royal. Everyone suspected Chancellor Becque had invested heavily in the bank which would be re-opened under charter with Lichtenbourg connections. Since this was so obviously a ploy that would ultimately fill only Becque's pockets his weekly, and sometimes daily, complaints about the physical deterioration of the old building were swept under the rug.

Everyone sat up with renewed interest. He went on: "Your Serene Highness may not have heard about the latest Allied disasters in the Pacific."

"I have heard." Alexia took the chair left vacant for her beside Stefan.

Becque continued. "And Corregidor, the United States Garrison under General MacArthur is expected to surrender any day. It is said that they are starving to death and the ammunition seems to be depleted."

Stefan put in drily, "I wouldn't count on the capture of General MacArthur. The American president would be a fool to lose him. I have met the man and, believe me, he will be needed for the re-conquest."

"Herr Becque," Princess Ilsa said in her bored way, "You take forever to get to the point. It seems that Japan was raided on 18 April by heavy bombers of the United States. We are told there was, shall we say, a bit of damage?"

Stefan caught Alexia's eye. Though her heart beat rapidly, she shrugged. "How nice for the Allies! Though not, I suppose, for the Axis. Still, when we play with sharp toys we are all liable to be hurt." Stefan took her hand and squeezed it as she sat down.

251

After that, no more was said about the bombing of Japan, or even about Janos Becque's pet project. He and one other reported on the unexpected difficulties "our friends of the Reich's armies" were having on the Russian Front and a large contribution from Lichtenbourg would be of great service to the Reich. "Either men or money. Possibly both." He added that there had been some incredibly high casualty figures among the enemy.

Alexia let them argue other matters until Chancellor Becque brought up a new subject and addressed Alexia directly.

"Your Highness will be distressed to learn that two of the attendants caring for Prince Maximilian in Vienna have been found to be Jews. They may be responsible for the seizure His Highness suffered in the night."

"What!" Alexia's cry was echoed by other councillors. Stefan raised his head sharply. Only Princess Ilsa seemed little impressed.

"Was it a drugs overdose?" one of the councillors asked in a furtive, breathy voice.

Chancellor Becque nodded. "Incredibly. Yes. But the wife of one of them was removed from the Reich recently for seditious utterances against the Fuhrer. Last night was probably the man's revenge. He got the female attendant to assist him. Both have been replaced."

Stefan demanded, "What of His Highness now?"

Becque examined his fingernails with great interest. "I am happy to say plans are being made to remove His Highness to Berlin where he will receive the best of care. Obviously, better than he has been receiving from these decadents in Vienna."

"No! Not for any reason!" Alexia cried. "I won't stand for it."

"Nonsense," Princess Ilsa chided her. "So long as Chancellor Becque represents His Highness's interests on this

252

Council poor Prince Max can recuperate better in Berlin. You must be sensible, my dear. The Fuhrer's own physicians may attend him."

The argument that followed was furious. Of the six councillors, four thought Berlin would be safer for their ruler. Two were less vehement but lacked enthusiasm for placing their legal ruler in the hands of Adolf Hitler.

Alexia sat numbly through the rest of the meeting, her thoughts in turmoil. There must be some way to get her parents back to Lichtenbourg. She knew that force would be worse than useless. Most of Lichtenbourg's land forces had joined the Axis Armies, some in the Waffen-SS and others making up part of the Hungarian and Czech forces now on the Eastern Front. The Wehrmacht's reputation and the world-shaking success of National Socialism's leader had been enough for the Lichtenbourgers of German descent.

If Max and Garnett were to be rescued it must be by trickery, and this would be a temporary business at best. It would simply bring the Gestapo over the border more quickly.

She longed to discuss it with Stefan but had no faith that he wouldn't betray something to his mother. She started to mention it when the meeting broke up but saw Princess Ilsa nonchalantly wave to Stefan, reminding him, "We entertain Chancellor Becque tonight, remember. Tomorrow is the dear fellow's birthday."

I'd like to strangle him, Alexia thought. She couldn't say it aloud, but she also found it impossible to return Princess Ilsa's malicious smile.

Stefan walked back up to their apartments with Alexia. He said nothing during the walk. He was thoughtful which encouraged her a little, and several times he looked around, frowning. She would have given much to know that he was planning the rescue of her parents. On the other hand, she was fearful for his safety if he tried a rescue and was caught at it. It was also extremely important that the rescue take place without leading to the occupation of Lichtenbourg by the German Reich. But Stefan, of all people, would recognize that.

She had another great fear, that he would confide to his mother any plans he might have.

In their apartments he latched and bolted the two doors. The reassuring scent of brown earth and young plants came up to Alexia from the famed Royal gardens. Two storeys below the Elsbach apartments the east balcony ran the length of the building and the stone balustrade was bordered by tubs of homely but bright red geraniums that lent their pleasantly acrid scent. Beneath the balcony rhododendron bushes bordered the wide expanse of gardens. The apartments were one of the many advantages the new rulers received. Alexia, fearing for her family if they were packed off to Berlin in the shadow of the Fuhrer, would be delighted to return to her original Victorian suite if they could have Max and Garnett safe.

Stefan walked to the windows, opened them to the cool sunlight and northern blue skies. He seemed satisfied that no one far beneath the windows could hear them but he lowered his voice all the same as he came back to her.

He took her by the shoulders. It was meant to be a gentle grip, she knew, but she felt the hard-boned strength beneath the gentleness.

"Alexia, you are the daughter of princess. Sometimes, it is necessary to remember that."

"Sounds pompous," she remarked, resenting that he felt he must tell her this. "What is this leading up to?"

"Simply that we must walk with care. Try not to show our violent feelings."

"If you mean cheer the idea of my father being

attended by Hitler's doctors, or being a helpless prisoner in Berlin . . ."

He sighed at his failure to make her understand. "No, my love. No cheers. But don't give away your real feelings. Theoretically, Hitler's offer is a generous one. Even an honour. We are not supposed to suspect his real motives. Whatever is done must not be connected to us, you understand?"

She did. The disgusting thing was that he had been right. She could seriously impede any efforts against the Reich by showing them her real feelings. She said finally, "I know. I understand." It was the best she could do. Under no circumstance could she say she was sorry for what she had believed. "Then something will be done? Do you have a plan in mind that won't throw this country into Hitler's lap?"

He removed his hands from her shoulders. Her flesh felt chilled where he had warmed and given her strength.

"A dozen plans. I wish I was sure one of them might work." He smiled at her disappointment. "Sweetheart, now comes your part."

She saluted. "Ready, Your Highness."

"You must make all the plans for magnificent birthday festivities. Presents, too. Everything. An elaborate dinner with only the best served; every envoy, every consul, including the Ambassador from the Third Reich."

She frowned. "What about his mother? Frau Becque will want to get into the act."

"Let her. But the elegant and expensive suggestions must be yours."

"I see. I think."

He must have some sort of plan. Meanwhile, the idea of a birthday ball for the loathesome Janos Becque at least gave her something with which to blur the terrors in her mind.

He studied her and seemed satisfied. "Just pretend it's for someone you love."

She tried to make a joke of it. "My husband, of course?"

He pursed his lips and frowned as if deep in thought. "Or maybe Dan Royle."

She smiled but her voice was flat and businesslike. This was no time for his sensitivity about someone who might be suffering tortures this minute.

"I'll do that. Dan Royle it is."

Still, her worries had not left her when he went away.

She began work at once on her tasks for the birthday ball, secretly appalled by the idea of wooing Janos Becque's friendship. She still asked herself, "Why?" a score of times during her busy day.

Frau Becque was not too surprised and went instantly to work. She was not nearly as surprised as Polly Quint who demanded of Alexia, "You mean to celebrate that snake, Ma'am? He's behind all the political shenanigans in Lichtenbourg."

Alexia put one finger over Polly's mouth and said sweetly, "That's perfectly true. Chancellor Becque is responsible for everything that happens here. We must never forget that. We owe him so much."

Polly was as puzzled as Alexia had been, but she accepted it as her mistress had. "OK, Ma'am. I'll go along with it. Do I have to give him a present, too?"

"I think it would be diplomatic."

Grunting, Polly went off to find something suitable and cheap.

Alexia had a bright idea and sent one of the footmen off to Lichtenbourg's best appliance store behind the Theatre Royal in Cathedral Square. Among other gifts she explained to him, "A very special item he has hinted at a number of times. He wants a little radio that picks up far-off places. His own is broken and he says he enjoys those foreign news broadcasts so very much."

Alexia breathed more normally again, said "Whew!" and went to Frau Becque, asking what her son particularly wanted.

"I am afraid, Your Serene Highness, Prince Stefan has already deprived my son of the one great gift he had prayed for," she reminded Alexia coyly. Seeing only a blank question in Alexia's eyes she went on, "Records would be welcome, Highness. What a pity the performers at the Theatre Royal haven't records for sale! Unless, of course, it should be discovered that there are non-Aryans among them."

Alexia wanted to say "So what if there are?" but she refrained with an effort and said instead, "According to our police there was a rumour about one or two of the leads but it was spread by a jealous tenor who has since escaped to Switzerland."

"Escaped?" Frau Becque repeated.

Alexia bit her tongue. "Sneaked across the border, I believe. But it turned out that his accusations were false. He himself was wanted by our police for listening nightly to the British radio. As you know, that has been made a crime, except in cases like my husband's when he is reporting his views to his good friend, Josef Goebbels, in Berlin. How kind Herr Goebbels has been! But I would certainly be suspicious of anyone else who listens, especially in secret."

"How true!" Frau Becque said going back to supervise the chef and the sous-chef.

"What a happy night," Alexia murmured after her. "Birthdays are the most wonderful times, I always say."

By sunset Alexia found herself actually pleased by the festive look of the New Palace, with its ribbons and decorations and elaborate preparations for the birthday banquet.

In the Council chamber Prince Stefan jokingly relinquished the only high-backed armchair at the long table. "Just for the meeting, bitte, Councillor Becque; since you are the man of the hour."

The Council had met all afternoon with several subjects high on the agenda. How much of a "loan" Lichtenbourg's small treasury should offer to the Reich was a matter that took precedence. Everyone knew the news that things had not been happily concluded against the Russians meant that more men and materials would be required from the Reich's "faithful neighbours".

Councillor Becque mentioned, as a plaintive joke, that the repairs to the cornice on the Kreditanstalt building might make a handsome birthday present to him, and they could borrow labour from the next batch of Reich prisoners who were sent in the cattle cars through Lichtenbourg from Hungary and Romania.

"We could even write off this Reich loan in exchange," he added brightly. He looked for confirmation to Princess Ilsa, an invited guest at the meeting, as he always did when matters concerning the Fuhrer were discussed.

Princess Ilsa had been buffing her long, beautifully manicured fingernails. Hearing her name spoken by Councillor Becque, she looked up and considered his question.

Most of the Council heaved a sigh of relief. The princess held each of her hands to the light while reminding everyone, "The Fuhrer never forgets those to whom he owes a debt."

It was such a casual remark, Alexia couldn't understand why she herself was the only one who shivered a little.

This time, luck and his birthday were with Councillor Becque. It was decided to examine the heavy Germanic stone building and make a decision as to the amount necessary to restore its splendid old cornice.

"Tomorrow. First on our agenda," Prince Stefan agreed

to Alexia's surprise. "Unless anyone suggests we should cancel our celebration and go tonight."

"I don't like it," Janos Becque objected. "By tomorrow no one will be sober, birthdays being what they are."

Everyone denied this vigorously and Becque was forced to shrug off his persistent effort. "Well, then, unless something crucial is to be done, we celebrate tonight. I daresay we must all dress ridiculously, as for a coronation."

It was a hint that he would like to see everyone dressed to the hilt, so Prince Stefan announced, "We believe it only fitting to our most distinguished citizen. Meanwhile, we will all go and make ourselves elegant for our Janos."

He rose and offered his hand to Alexia while Councillor Becque, his little lean body stuffed with pride, went around the end of the table and gave his own hand to Princess Ilsa.

Alexia waited until she and Stefan were back in the reasonable privacy of their apartments before she mentioned her own frantic concern.

"I've done my duty. I've seen to the birthday banquet for our worst enemy. Now, can you please give me some assurance that my father and mother won't be carted off to Berlin and placed at Hitler's tender mercy?"

He looked at her, his eyes serious enough to make her fear the worst, but he seemed confident and she took new courage. "Sweetheart, there are plans. Two, in fact. One is a backup in case the other goes wrong. I can't tell you what will happen. I don't know myself except that it will be tomorrow. All Germans, and all Austrians, are not National Socialists. They do what they can, if possible covered by the law so that neither they nor those they help are compromised."

"I understand."

"Good. When the last days of this war come these people will be of great help to the Allies. Meanwhile, they must not be compromised. But rulers like your father, weak or strong, are needed, too. I have only a few contacts myself. Contrary to your hopes, my darling, I am not a dashing secret agent. I represent Sweden, a strictly neutral power. Our king believes neutrality is the only way to save his people. It may not be brave but it is a matter of survival. So please hope, or pray, or whatever gives you comfort, but say nothing about your real feelings."

She supposed it was the best he could offer her and she should expect no more.

Stefan's valet knocked on the adjoining door. Stefan kissed her and left.

The royal housekeeper, Frau Becque, in her best flowered georgette gown would be among the equerries and sentries at the head of the higher servants.

As dusk faded into starlit blue darkness, with all the golden bowls of light outlining the west face of the New Palace, the limousines were first seen touring up the Boulevard Kuragin.

It must be too early. Councillor Becque hadn't joined the champagne-happy guests yet. But the cars moved upward inexorably.

Stefan and Alexia exchanged looks. Princess Ilsa was busy flirting with the distinguished old Austrian Consul who had arrived earlier than expected. Alexia excused herself and crossed the long great hall which was bordered at both ends by marble staircases where the upper servants and attendants stood.

With huge hydrangeas decorating her gown, Frau Becque stood very straight, looking so regal she seemed to have borrowed height. She barely curtsied to Alexia, obviously remembering that this was her son's night. Alexia congratulated her on her son's birthday and asked, "Shall we send someone to Councillor Becque to announce the first arrivals?"

Frau Becque's pale eyebrows went up. "I am certain he will arrive at the correct moment, Highness. This is not the first such banquet for my son."

"No. Of course not." It was difficult to get through to the woman.

Frau Becque persisted, "He is always being acclaimed."

"I am sure that he is. Still – "

A slight commotion at the double doors caused Alexia to turn abruptly. The Swedish Envoy was already being welcomed by his friend, Stefan, and the German Ambassador had arrived in proper black and white evening dress with decorations and the inevitable swastika.

Alexia said tartly to Frau Becque, "I don't think your son wishes to snub any of the Fuhrer's appointees. Perhaps he should be sent for." With that she walked back to join her husband in welcoming the suave, handsome, cold-eyed man who appeared quite capable of reading all their minds.

While her hand was being kissed by the German Ambassador, Alexia glanced over at Frau Becque. A servant had pushed his way through the crowd on the staircase behind her and now bent his head to give her a quiet message. To Alexia's surprise Frau Becque, who seldom gave any indication of surprise, swung around and went up the staircase, making her way between a dozen or more of her fellow employees.

The Austrian Consul had just enquired where Herr Becque was. Stefan glanced around. "Probably supervising the banquet seating, if I know my councillor."

Alexia excused herself to the German Ambassador and was about to leave the group when they began to discuss re-structuring Berlin. The Ambassador mentioned that the war would soon be over, what with the great successes in the Ukraine. He stressed this as if he waited for a denial. High on the agenda, he said, after the imminent fall of Britain, were the plans between Hitler and his munitions minister, Herr Speer, to make a new world capital out of Berlin.

"Albert Speer is an architectural genius," the Ambassador informed Stefan and the Princess Ilsa. "It will mean almost the complete re-designing of our old nineteenth-century Berlin."

Alexia remembered that her father and Herr Speer were friends who, oddly enough, did not talk politics, and she heard as she left the Ambassador, "What a glory in the place of the dear old Berlin! I have heard discussions of an arch of triumph three times the size of that decadent affair in Paris."

Glad to be rid of this talk for a few minutes, Alexia went on across the crowded hall following the housekeeper up the stairs.

Frau Becque went directly to her son's elaborate study which he often used to entertain chambermaids or other young females when he didn't care to be driven up to his massive hotel suite facing the royal gardens.

The valet unlocked the door and stood aside for the two women to enter.

"What is it?" Alexia asked. "Is he ill?"

Frau Becque snapped, "Certainly not. He has been delayed. More chunks of stone have cracked off the Kreditanstalt building and he went down to inspect it."

She took up the telephone and gave the operator a number. After more than a full minute's wait the caretaker came on the line. Frau Becque moistened her lips and gave her name. She listened but did not speak again. With trembling fingers she turned over the receiver to Alexia, shaking her head.

In Alexia's ear the caretaker repeated in panic, "Councillor Becque. A chunk of cornice fell at the southwest corner of the building. The street police found His Excellency beneath it."

Whatever Alexia's feelings toward Becque, this was appalling, especially as it raised certain suspicions in her mind.

"Is there any hope?"

Behind Alexia, Frau Becque's voice was blurred and vague. "He is gone? My little Janos is gone?" She reached out into the empty air and finding no support, swayed and crumpled to the floor in a faint.

Though pitying a mother's grief, Alexia was still relieved. She had not been born to intrigue and the chancellor's death would not be the result of her lies about him and his "interest in foreign radio broadcasts".

CHAPTER TWENTY-ONE

It was the most majestic funeral since the death of the last Prince Royal, Franz Kuragin, thirteen years before. Few local citizens loved the late Chancellor Janos Becque as they had loved Prince Kuragin, but with the German Ambassador and Princess Ilsa von Elsbach insisting, together with Heinrich Himmler's Gestapo just across the border, it was generally agreed that Janos Becque deserved the full treatment.

In fact it was Princess Ilsa's suggestion that a memorial of some kind be subscribed "by all good citizens". She would open the subscription with five thousand marks. She also insisted that Prince Max and Princess Garnett be brought back for the funeral, whether Max was recovering or not.

"They must learn to pay their respects, like all good friends of the Reich." This highly publicized interview which appeared in the Austrian and German press earned her and Lichtenbourg the commendation of the Fuhrer himself.

Whatever the princess's reason for bringing the royal couple back to Lichtenbourg, Alexia felt she could now hint to Stefan something of her original suspicions about Becque's death as they drove to meet her parents at the train station. It had been a great relief to hear the report of the street police and two building inspectors from Munich that the broken bits of the old building's cornice had been cracked and on the verge of separating for some time.

Stefan was driving an old, confiscated American Chevrolet and obviously enjoyed the lack of pomp and circumstance in this form of travel. He had one arm around Alexia. Perhaps he didn't guess the suspicions she had harboured the night Janos Becque died. She ran her finger over his jawline and he grinned.

"You may have one hour – make that two – to keep torturing me."

She laughed, loving the renewed trust between them, free of suspicion. "Darling, did you wonder about it at all, the night Janos Becque died?"

He glanced at her and then considered his answer. "Well, at first I wondered who had called Becque to the building at that hour. It must have been past sunset. But it seems to have been legitimate. The caretaker had almost been hit by flying bits of masonry."

One reason for her suspicion about Stefan's involvement had been the knowledge that he used his Swedish chateau as a half-way-station for people escaping the Reich protectorates. He denied to her that he was a leader of an "underground" escape route, but what did he call his efforts to save proscribed people from the Reich? No matter. If she had once thought him capable of murdering Janos Becque she no longer believed it. There had been a certain horror in knowing someone she loved was capable of such a secret and sinister act.

She settled back, fully satisfied, reminding him suddenly, "And we knew in the Council chamber that he was dying to inspect the place that night."

He drove up the slope toward the big, glass-roofed railway station and Alexia felt another surge of relief at the thought that, for the time being, at least, her parents were not to be sent off to Berlin and the tender mercies of Hitler's doctors.

"I don't care what your mother's motives were in getting my parents back, it worked out marvellously."

"She's a clever one and no mistake." He pulled up at the end of a row of parked cars and bicycles and scores of people crowding into the station. Stefan got out, came around and took her arm. "Well, Sweetheart, your parents seem to be popular with their people."

She hugged his arm to show her pleasure but pinched him quickly. "He's here."

Puzzled for a few seconds, Stefan then saw the eager excited figure of Johann Hofer, waving a bouquet of long-stemmed mountain flowers carelessly wrapped in the *Munchener Abend Zeitung*. The entertainer was trying to make his way into the station ahead of the crowd.

Stefan agreed with Alexia's concern. "The poor young fool is going to attract attention to himself. Of all people." He looked around, then said quietly. "He can least afford to be noticed by our Nazi fellow citizens. Three-quarters of those we've been getting out through our Danish groups are Jews. We can't afford to have them attract attention. It just makes it harder. Denmark is in Nazi hands and our Danes are at risk every night."

Meanwhile Hanni Hofer had pushed his way ahead of the crowd and would be one of the first to greet the prince and princess as they stepped down off the train.

The cheers went up, echoing against the high-domed ceiling, as someone caught sight of Prince Maximilian's handsome, pallid features in the vestibule where he stood waiting for the train attendant to stand to attention on the station platform beside the train steps.

Taking their cue from Johann Hofer who led them using his bouquet as a baton, the crowd began to sing the Lichtenbourg royal anthem. Alexia joined in with tears

266

of pride and nudged Stefan to add his deep baritone. He obliged.

Someone recognized them in the crowd and pushed them forward. They found themselves just behind Johann Hofer. They could hardly get closer without walking over him.

Prince Max smiled at the crowd. He raised his arm and waved one hand which pleased the crowd, who called out his name as he descended to the platform where he turned and raised his hand to Princess Garnett. She appeared then, glorious in a sapphire wool suit and heavy sable coat. Alexia murmured.

"I never know how she does it, but in spite of everything, she always looks beautiful."

Stefan struck a stance and pretended to consider. Garnett waved to everyone and received Hanni Hofer's flowers as a suitable tribute, thanking him prettily as she passed him with her husband.

"No," Stefan decided. "I prefer the daughter."

Well pleased, Alexia laughed and took his arm again. They followed her parents out of the station, finding themselves joined by Johann Hofer. He was still looking ahead at Princess Garnett but his step was less jaunty. Alexia apologized for her mother.

"I'm afraid she didn't see you. All this crowd."

He shrugged but thanked her. "Very good of Your Highness."

Stefan said, "I've wanted to thank you for our honeymoon. Do you know, with your talent you would be exceedingly popular in Sweden. It might make you an international success. We would be happy to sponsor you."

"We owe you so much," Alexia put in, hoping he might realize that he would be safer elsewhere.

Hofer was shocked. "Oh, but I couldn't do that." He

seemed at a loss for words, then added, "My contract is with the Theatre Royal here in Lichtenbourg."

"But you must." Stefan cleared his throat and she shut up. Obviously, this sort of thing was not her game.

They heard their names called and several of the crowd pointed them out to Max and Garnett. Surrounded by well-wishers, they were looking perplexed. Everyone had offered them transportation but Alexia whispered to Stefan, "They're looking for a limousine." She sighed. "They really are naive."

He was amused, waved to the royal couple, and pointed to the blue Chevrolet behind them. They looked back and jumped as if it had been a rattlesnake.

Alexia hurried to her parents, wondering that she had held her childhood grudge against them so long. They were delighted to see her, Garnett elbowing Max aside to hug her little girl, then flying into Stefan's arms while Max embraced his daughter. As he held Alexia's cheek against his briefly, he whispered, "She has come back to me."

Alexia was deeply touched, even when, after a little twinge of disappointment, she realized he was talking about his wife. He added, "In my mind she was always my little princess, you know. I can still see her at Miravel when she was three or four. I made her a gold paper crown and she announced to us all, 'I'm, going to be real live princess. Max will make it so with my very own crown. Max is the only one in all the world who can do that.' How enchanting she was, and here she is, not changed an iota."

"How right you are, Father!" He was too absorbed in his dream to hear any irony in her agreement.

Alexia hoped her mother wouldn't insist on sitting in the front seat of the Chevrolet with Stefan but luckily Garnett was determined not to leave her husband for a minute. Maybe his near death had reawakened her love for him.

Her maid and a palace equerry tried to wheedle the royal

pair into an elegant German car that had just driven up but Garnett was being obstinate today. She got nimbly into the back seat of the Chevrolet before Max or the equerry could help her.

Alexia looked at Stefan, made a little face, and gave up trying to compete with her mother.

All the way along the Boulevard Kuragin, with its light standards and buildings shrouded in black, clumps of people cheered as the very obstinate car passed and both Garnett and Max waved. Already, crowds were gathering around the cathedral, ready to watch the entrance of mourners from all the Reich countries.

Since the funeral itself would be private and take place in Becque's Bavarian home town, all the resources of Lichtenbourg were thrown into the solemn memorial service in the little country where he had been so active, acquiring citizenship and ultimately, the highest civilian office.

Alexia would have liked to avoid the memorial services at Lichtenbourg's historic cathedral but her presence was one of the penalties she paid for her position.

On that sunny spring afternoon she did her duty but could not go so far as Garnett and Princess Ilsa who dabbed their eyes now and then with lacy bits of handkerchief. The old archbishop, obviously enjoying his opportunity to stand in the limelight, expounded on Janos Becque's superb leadership, his Aryan ideals, and his effort to make Lichtenbourg a true and faithful neighbour to the Third Reich.

Alexia did not dare to look at anyone else. She knew the rumours about the ill-treatment of other religious leaders by the National Socialist Government, and could only hope the archbishop was either senile or covering secret activities by a loud vocal support of the Reich.

With the memorial services completed, Janos Becque's

coffin was sent off the following day accompanied by his black-clad and veiled mother, to his native village in Bavaria, outside Munich. As a special mark of princely favour she was accompanied by two palace footmen, a royal police agent, and the secretary of the local Nazi Party, to make her journey easier.

"Back to Munich," Alexia remarked to Stefan, "where it all started."

"Unless it all started in Braunau where, I believe, Hitler was born," Stefan said, giving it some thought. "Or Vienna where they might have encouraged his painting. Then he could have been a third-rate artist instead of a first-rate disaster. They certainly made a mistake there."

But with Prince Max back in his proper place, Stefan, Alexia and several of the Council were concerned over how to keep him in Lichtenbourg. At the first Council meeting since the chancellor's death the matter took priority.

Prince Ilsa reminded them of the charter signed at the time the Kuragins were returned to power in 1908.

"We had hoped His Highness, Prince Maximilian, might receive the proper care for his ailment in Berlin as the Fuhrer graciously suggested."

Alexia looked furiously at Ilsa and then turned to see Stefan's reaction to these word but he was busy sharpening a pencil with his penknife. She could have kicked him but her father was seated between them in his proper chair as presiding officer. The death of Janos Becque had, at least, given her father a delay before there might be pressure exerted to get him back into the Reich.

He added to the princess's remark a thought that might spell something positive. "However, my services are needed here, Your Highness. Our charter clearly states that the chancellor presides only when the Prince Royal is incapacitated."

Stefan threw down his penknife. It made a little metallic noise that caused several councillors to jump nervously. He picked up his father-in-law's thought.

"Since our chancellor, unhappily, has expired, and the Prince Royal is very much present, we cannot afford to let our prince leave the country. I hope Your Highness understands how much you are needed here."

To Alexia's fascinated gaze Prince Max almost, but not quite, smiled. "I regard my presence in Lichtenbourg as a matter of Kuragin honour. I cannot let my own personal welfare take precedent. It would be dishonourable. I must remain here."

He offered his hand to Stefan who got up and bowed over it, followed by everyone else at the table including Alexia who curtsied, and last of all Princess Ilsa, with a certain sardonic amusement.

Stefan than announced, "Although our hearts go out to our brave neighbours fighting in Russia and across the globe, it is my duty to announce that certain Pacific news has just been confirmed. A battle has taken place in an area called the Coral Sea or Seas, I'm not certain, in which the Reich's Japanese allies have suffered heavy losses."

There were murmurs around the table. Alexia could have sworn most of the faces looked pleased. But Princess Ilsa, looking bored, added: "I believe there was more to the report. The United States lost an aircraft carrier. What was the name? Yes. The *Lexington*." She began to collect her handbag and her copy of today's agenda.

Taking the hint, others likewise prepared to leave until Emil Muhler, a painfully thin, tubercular leader of the local Nazi Party, reminded everyone, "We have not yet discussed the Fuhrer's suggestion that we recruit another company of volunteers to join our triumphant brothers on the Eastern Front."

This was received with a notable lack of enthusiasm

which Herr Muhler stemmed further by the reminder, "As you are all aware, the Fuhrer is nothing if not fair. He does not wish to answer in kind the constant intrusion of Lichtenbourgers shooting game along the Reich borders. In his well-known consideration for human life, especially the young people, he points out that at any day the poaching from Lichtenbourg will try his patience and he must cross the Lichtenbourg borders to seek out these reckless people who have no consideration for children and animals." He waved a letter before them.

Whether it came from Hitler or one of the many who acted for him did not matter. The warning was a clear one. He had his ready-made excuse and would use it at any time. No one could miss the Reich emblem at the top, surmounted by the ubiquitous swastika.

"Herr Muhler has been good enough to show the letter to me," Prince Max said getting up from the table. "It will, of course, be discussed in private council in my study. I have placed it on the agenda."

Several of the Council breathed a sigh of relief and got up with the prince. Only Stefan and Alexia exchanged glances. Matters like this were certainly not of help to a man recovering from an attack of angina.

One other had taken the matter seriously. To Alexia's surprise Princess Ilsa went around the end of the table to Prince Max and said something to him. He nodded, touched her hand and thanked her.

Curious, Alexia thought. Whatever the woman had said it appeared to give Prince Max a little relief. He did not look so haggard and careworn. And, of course, Alexia could not forget that it was Princess Ilsa who, for reasons of her own, had found a way for Max and Garnett to be saved from whatever fate awaited them in Berlin.

In the end, after many assurances to Berlin about Berlin's latest demand, Lichtenbourg managed to round up a company of pro-Nazi sympathizers. To these were added the malcontents and bullies who had begun to imitate the Jew-baiting and murders of the infamous German Kristalnacht. For the time it quieted the complaints of Lichtenbourg's terrifying neighbour. Few people in the little principality thought of anything else.

Only Alexia was more concerned with the Pacific war news. Surely the American naval victory over the Japanese at some unknown islands called Midway must bring Dan Royle's rescue nearer.

The Axis radios blared out the triumphs of their own hero, Field Marshal Erwin Rommel, in North Africa, only to have him stopped, first by the breaking of his over-extended supply line and then by the British and Anzac armies. But Alexia's own great victory was a v-mail letter-envelope sent to Stefan from Stockholm in the diplomatic pouch. The writing, very like Tige's but much less flamboyant, ran over the envelope side of the letter.

Stefan gave the flimsy little blue paper to Alexia and watched her open it. She read the first lines and clutched her husband's wrist. "He's got him. Dan is back in the States, temporarily at Tripler Hospital in Honolulu. I can't believe it."

"Knowing Tige, I can," he remarked, pleased by the news if not as ecstatic as she was. "Has MacArthur captured the Philippines?"

"No. But he will. Listen:

Dear little girl, and old Stefan too. Got him back, thanks to a P-T Boat, some fast work, the Air Force, and the fact that Dan had escaped from that hell-hole with two buddies while being shipped to another prison camp. Picked them up on Mindanao. All together the

273

kids weighed less than three hundred pounds when we got 'em. One poor devil died in the plane before we reached Oahu.

Physically our boy is getting better every minute. Gradually getting the old spirits back. But he's got a little hangup. Just as well you won't be seeing him for a while. All he talks of is his girl, Lexy. Says the thought of you and that picture of you he took at Ocean Beach in SF was all that kept him going. His buddies on Bataan used to offer bits of food to him to get the picture. Kind of pitiful.

I don't guess anybody will ever know the hell they all went through. But you can take comfort that your picture gave them a little feeling of home.

Like a dummy, I told Dan how I got out of Lichtenbourg to Sweden and now Dan wants to dash over and rescue you, not from Stefan but from Hitler. Kind of scarey. Have to watch the kid like a hawk. Tell Stefan we're doing our part, wherever it takes me. Love from the Royles.

"I never doubted that," Stefan said. "I only wish he had kept quiet about the 'escape' business here in Lichtenbourg."

Of course, Stefan was right. But Alexia couldn't let that interfere with her relief that Dan, her almost-brother, was safe.

After that she was about the only person not surprised when the Allies continued their first tentative sweep on all fronts.

In late November there were Allied landings at Casablanca and other North African cities which sent a nervous spasm through the Axis sympathizers in Lichtenbourg. Everyone asked everyone else, usually in whispers, "If they are just across the Mediterranean, what is to prevent them from going up the boot of Italy, or hopping to Sicily and on up to France?"

It was commonly discussed that the Fuhrer's greatest strength might now be mired down in the mud and snow before Stalingrad on the Eastern Front. No one wanted to think of a typical Christmas with a tree and St Nicholas while the powerful Wehrmacht tried to dig in for the grim Russian winter.

Princess Ilsa organized aid for the soldiers on the Eastern Front and was joined at once by Frau Becque who ran errands for her and the committee during her spare hours. Stefan and Alexia congratulated the princess on gaining the confidence of the palace housekeeper and were surprised by her lack of enthusiasm.

"She sees too much, that one. Always prowling, looking. If I didn't know better I would suspect the woman is trying to sabotage our humanitarian work."

Helping the German Army to enjoy Christmas was not high on Alexia's list of priorities but she thought Frau Becque's interest was a kind of memorial to her dead son. It was rather touching, she confessed to Stefan.

Stefan seemed more puzzled than touched. However, there were so many more world-shaking events as the Allies advanced, along with 1943, that they soon lost interest in Frau Becque, except in her palace capacity.

Dan had written to Alexia and Stefan care of the address given to Tige and told them very little about his experiences. But he kept harping on how much help he could be in Stockholm if he were allowed to join the Danish group in getting refugees to Sweden. He concluded two letters with the promise: "I am practising rowing. I'll bet those Danes and Swedes could use me. Tell you the truth, I'd sacrifice anything to put a crimp in Hitler's plans."

Alexia said doubtfully, "He always was too brave for his own good."

"That we don't need," Stefan remarked. "He wouldn't be risking just his life but those of many who aren't so foolhardy."

She knew that was true, but it was so like dear old foolish Dan, she felt as worried as if he really had been her foolhardy brother.

CHAPTER TWENTY-TWO

During one of their private luncheons that Alexia and Stefan had all too seldom, a representative of the Swedish Consulate brought diplomatic pouches to Stefan. Stefan had issued orders that any news from Stockholm be delivered at once.

"Anything from Tige?" Alexia asked, although this eternal question was beginning to sound less hopeful in recent months. All she knew or suspected was that he remained in North Africa in Oran, trying to do official business with members of the Vichy Government who would not see eye to eye with the Free French under General de Gaulle in London. As Stefan said, that could take forever.

A lean tanned young male secretary to the Swedish Consulate covered his smile at Stefan's remark, and having received his thanks, hurried off to a meeting at the Consulate.

"Now, there's a boy in a hurry," Alexia remarked. "And can they really get a suntan in Scandinavia?"

"All the comforts of home," Stefan said. "The Consulate has problems about the Kattegat Waters. They flow down between Denmark and Sweden and the German Government suspects we are using them to get certain people out of Nazi hands. It's touch and go. I certainly hope that if any of them know the truth they have sense enough to keep it to themselves. We need all the help we can get right now, since they got the word from Hitler."

"What word? Not threatening the Swedes, surely?"

"God, no. But the ones we've questioned mention a final solution."

"To the war?" How bad could it get, she wondered, when Hitler and his minions began to realize the Allies were closing in.

She knew Stefan well enough now to suspect there was more to his remark than the casual way he agreed with her. "The war?" And then, vaguely, "Oh, yes. The war."

What else? She couldn't imagine anything more horrible than for Hitler's gang to go on fighting long after they had lost. But, what else?

She closed her eyes for a minute, seeing the dream that must keep the world from complete collapse. One day, perhaps not too long from now, there would be peace and rebuilding, a new world with no Nazis, no one to upset the balance of power. A beautiful dream. Unless a danger came from some other direction. No. She wouldn't think of that.

"I'm glad we don't have any children," she said abruptly.

That shook him out of his thoughts, whatever they were. He reached across the table, squeezing her hand. "Darling, I'd hate to think there would never be another you. We need our children. Otherwise, what is the future? Think. What would be left?"

He went back to his papers from Sweden. "Ah! A letter from Miravel. Probably censored. I can see the black marks through this tissue paper. It is for your mother."

"Maybe the rents and profits from the last six months at Miravel," she said hopefully.

"Not very likely. I don't imagine the British Government will let Nick Chance send money out of the country at a time like this." He reached for the telephone and called Garnett's suite. Elated, Garnett came hurrying to their small dining room.

"I can use the money, believe me," she remarked, opening the tissue letter with Stefan's butter knife.

Alexia and Stefan exchanged half-smiles. They both understood Garnett's chief attraction. She was so ornamental, her auburn hair bright as ever, with help from whatever rinses she and her maid had worked out, and it set off beautifully her new rust-gold suit sent from occupied Paris. She certainly kept herself up recently in better shape than Stefan's mother who had started to show her age.

Her happy expression faded as she read between the many black streaks made by the British Censors.

"No cheque," she announced, shaking the envelope-letter to be sure. "My so-called brother has probably stolen my few pennies, not to mention my pounds sterling."

Stefan mentioned the currency laws adding, "They are at war, you know. Does he say what the profits were?"

Garnett looked over the letter on both sides. "It isn't Nick's writing. Well, well. It seems to be Rose Tredegar, the daughter of Father's physician? Dear soul, he may have had something to do with Father's remembering his poor, stranded daughter in his will."

Alexia rolled her eyes heavenward and even Stefan only just resisted a smile. "You need not have worried. I was told by young Dan Royle that Lord Miravel never loved anyone but Your Highness."

She tacitly admitted this but added, "One can't be too careful, especially with bastard sons floating around everywhere."

"Not everywhere, I hope." Alexia laughed, which annoyed her mother. She asked, "What is this Rose Tredegar up to?"

"A tentative secretary to Mr Chance, so she says." Garnett read the letter again, all the sense she could make of it between the censorship marks. "I suppose we may soon expect more bastard children hanging about my estate."

Stefan grinned but Garnett ignored that. She was irked again by Alexia's, "Mother! For heaven's sake. Stefan will think you were raised in a barn."

"Don't quote your idiotic Americanisms to me, Ava Alexandra. You may find Nick has cheated you out of your own inheritance. Have you seen a penny of Father's money? Do you know what Nick is up to? This girl says he's on his way to sainthood, figuratively speaking, I hope. And saints are liable to use anyone's money, if the cause is good."

This caught Stefan by surprise. "How did he manage that?"

She waved the letter. "Any profits from the estate are put to excellent use in the service of the villagers, especially the Elder Home, their transportation, medical matters in the nursing home area – some of them veterans. Well, need I go on?"

"An admirable gesture," Stefan said after a moment's pause.

Garnett said, "Here. What do you think of this? *The villagers are saying no one at Miravel Hall, even the late Lady Alix Miravel, ever did so much for them as Mr Chance. Even the vicar says so. One or two are calling his actions saintly.*"

Alexia looked at Stefan to see what his reaction was. If he had planned to marry her before he even knew her, the possible loss of Miravel might have some effect upon him.

He merely reminded Garnett quietly, "No one but the munitions makers profit now, but after the war you will find Lichtenbourg's profits in furniture-making and stamps and tourism, not to mention winter sports, will

280

more than make up for the losses to a village still living in the eighteenth century."

Garnett sniffed. "I do detest goody-goodies." She threw the letter on the table where it landed on Stefan's cup of ersatz coffee, that grainy drink extolled as "healthy and patriotic" by the Axis governments. The letter's black censorship streaks soon mingled with the black coffee.

Garnett looked from Stefan to Alexia, saw that they were not quite as shocked by Nick's activities as she had expected, and stalked out of the room.

Alexia looked after her mother, marvelling that she still wore such high spiked heels in times when every step taken could turn a woman's ankle between the cracked and broken cobblestones, in disrepair since long before the war.

Alexia couldn't help feeling that another enemy lay in wait when Frau Becque, having finished her Reich army charities, was spending all her time in her usual profession at the palace. As if they felt guilty and were trying to make it up to the mother of the dead man, almost everyone but Alexia and Garnett was especially kind to Frau Becque. Alexia and her mother felt nothing but contempt. Alexia asked her mother, "How did you pay off the woman? I see Johann Hofer is still playing at the Theatre Royal. The party from the palace will be going to see the operetta and it would hardly be a performance without the city's famous 'Prince Danilo'. But is it safe?"

Garnett shrugged. "Simple, really, for the moment. The good Frau may deck herself out with rubies until she gets tired of them or sells them. I suppose she's going to want my sapphires next. But I'll see the old hag dead before I give her my emeralds."

"Wouldn't it be easier to get Hofer out of Lichtenbourg?"

Garnett looked at her impatiently. "He says he can't

leave me. He seems to think my own Max might do me harm. Jealous, that's all. Young men overreact. Poor boy. They get so boring after a while."

Alexia went away telling herself that her own mother was just about as cold-blooded as Stefan's pro-Nazi mother.

With the fall of the Mussolini Fascist Government in Italy, Berlin war news burst out of every Lichtenbourg radio loud-speaker assuring the people that tales of Allied successes in Italy were greatly exaggerated. The Wehrmacht would send them all back into the Straits of Messina.

Princess Ilsa, for some reason, had little interest in the Axis stories. She was definitely acting older lately. She moved more slowly, complained of "cricks" in her back and was slower in getting out of her chair in the Council chamber. She even surprised Alexia at a private dinner one day by asking, "When am I to have grandchildren? Any time soon?"

Stefan looked oddly hopeful as he waited for Alexia to answer, but she had to disappoint them both. "I'm sorry. Not so far. Maybe next year."

"Next year," the princess murmured. "Such a long time." She refused the champagne poured for her. "Bad for my stomach. It's that stupid ulcer I got years ago when both Prince Kuragin and Prince Max turned down my marriage proposals."

"Mother, you are a born liar," Stefan told her, but she did not take offence.

"No. It's quite true. We all know where Prince Kuragin's heart was and I suppose your mother, my dear, had Max at her feet. Never mind. But I am ashamed of you on another score, Stefan. I want to see an heir to the Elsbachs on the throne. I'm getting older. Hurry up."

Stefan laughed. "You will never get old, Mother."

The princess dismissed the matter in her cool, amused

282

way. "Probably not." Then she debated as to what gown and certainly what jewels she should wear to impress the locals tonight at the Theatre Royal where a performance of *The Merry Widow* was being staged for the benefit of Lichtenbourg's "own heroes freezing and dying on the Eastern Front".

"I have every confidence you will find something," Stefan told her when he kissed her hand and went off to the afternoon meeting of the Council.

Leaving the princess's apartments, and having seen Stefan off in the opposite direction down the long corridor, Alexia was surprised to pass a scruffy looking young man whose truculence and surly manner made her think of the "Heil Hitler, goosestepping" young men she had seen several times on the streets.

She could hardly doubt that Princess Ilsa was closely involved with the people who supported the Fuhrer. What a terrible and frightening woman! She carried on her nasty business even during her illness, whatever that was.

The number of pro-Nazis had been shrinking with the Axis fortunes, especially with the new danger on two fronts, the East and probable invasion from the West. But those who remained loyal to Hitler were more violent than ever.

Late that afternoon a group came marching up Kuragin Boulevard towards the palace where they milled around waving Nazi banners and calling out the usual anti-Jewish slogans, interspersed with yells against the Americans and the Russians.

Alexia went across the corridor to see if they were doing any physical harm but luckily, by this time, having aroused no one except a few bored pedestrians, they were breaking up. Alexia latched the window again and returned to her apartment. The lights were already glowing in the long corridor and she was surprised to find that no one had lighted her sitting room. It looked full of shadows, barely illuminated from the east by the tiny globe lights of the royal gardens.

Alexia blinked in the darkness. "Polly, where are you?"

Suddenly, two cold callused hands slipped over her eyes from behind her. Her momentary fear, that this was a terrorist attack by pro-Nazis, subsided as cool lips touched her neck and she pulled away indignantly. No one but Stefan was allowed that familiarity. Sounding like someone in an old melodrama, she swung around, stared at him in the twilight and cried, "How dare you!"

The intruder was young and lean, almost too lean, his flesh curiously dark, leathery and old. In spite of his grin, his eyes looked enormous in a face that seemed drained of the youthful light-heartedness she remembered so well. Only his grin was the same and it faded with her unthinking words.

Her failure to recognize him had reminded him of what he looked like, the terrible changes. She tried to make amends. "Oh, Dan, it's you!" She hugged him as hard as she could. "It's so dark in here. How could you scare me like that?"

He did not respond for a few seconds but as she stammered her excuses, his grin came back. "I thought it would be kind of funny. Guess I had another thought coming, wouldn't you say?"

By this time she had come to her senses. "No. Of course not. Only Polly always loves to raise the palace light bill, just to annoy Frau Becque, our housekeeper. I hope Becque doesn't know you are here. I've a feeling she can be very dangerous."

Polly's voice came from the dressing room next door. She had the door open and came in, rather gingerly, as if unsure she was wanted. "I'm the only one that knows. They called from the North Gate. I told 'em I was expecting my brother. So here he is. I figured, from what you've said about him, this had to be it."

"He's it all right, Polly, would you mind – ?" She motioned to the corridor door but Polly was already locking it.

Dan insisted, "These old Krauts don't scare me. I've been scared by experts."

Alexia scolded Dan, knowing it was useless. Even Tige couldn't handle him when he made up his mind. "Don't you know what can happen to you, Dan? You are American. If any of our local Nazis start talking you could be interned, or shot as a spy."

He had flinched when she said "interned". She couldn't imagine what memories that brought back, but he was less impressed by the idea of being shot. "Honey, I came across the way Tige said he got to Sweden. Only in reverse. Some terrific Danes were a godsend, them and the Swedes. I have a Swedish passport from a fellow who knows Stefan. Phoney passport, but these days a lot of them are. None of these Krauts you have here would remember me. I was only a kid last time I was here. And bashful as all get-out."

Devoted as she was to him it made her even more appalled to think of how much trouble he would cause Stefan and his friends. He should never have used Stefan's name to get the fake passport. It was foolhardy. And worst of all he had risked Stefan's life, because Stefan would probably have to get him out.

"Why did you come? I mean now, when it's so dangerous for everyone who– " She amended this. Those haunted eyes were beginning to look hurt. "For you and everyone."

"Because I knew you needed me. How else are you going to get out of Hitler's clutches? You don't have a single American in this hell-hole right now."

"Dan . . . " She made him sit down. His parka was still damp. Evidently he had been out getting soaked in last night's shower. She put her hands on both arms of the chair, imprisoning him. "Dan, I may look American. And God knows I talk American. But I'm not American. Actually, I am a Lichtenbourger. Dan, I love you for being so noble, but I am a married woman who loves her husband. Do you see?"

Polly had heard all this and stirred but Dan went on staring at Alexia.

"All that marriage business was something they talked you into. That's what I came down to after we reasoned it all out."

She exhaled sharply. "Who are *we*?"

"My buddies and me. Who else? That's about all the Jap sons-of-bitches didn't take away. Your picture." His thin fingers groped for hers. "I remember one day on the march. A guy ahead of me, he was one of my buddies, he fell in the road. We hadn't had a drop of water in days and it must have been 110 degrees. I don't know. Anyway, this guy from Cairo, Illinois. He used to get sore when we didn't call it right. Kay-ro."

"Dan, I can guess, a little, a very little, what you went through."

"No. You can't. Nobody can that wasn't there." He pulled his hand away. "That poor bastard from Kay-ro, well, their trucks ran over him. Every goddamned one of 'em. He looked like one of those face cards in a poker hand. Right into the asphalt."

She felt choked and shaken. How could she expect him to understand when she explained how things were? *She* couldn't understand.

He said in a dull monotone, "They told me in Honolulu that the press called those weeks the Death March. Sure as hell wasn't a Life March. I'll tell you that."

He saw her face and shrugged deeper into his jacket, pulling himself together. It must have been a terrible effort but he gave her a flickering smile.

"OK, kid. You don't want to be rescued. I thought maybe we could use your Lichtenbourg passport. I'd be your servant or something. But I can get back. No problem. Long as I don't meet anybody I know. Like that little bastard, Goebbels. Interviewed him and his buddies in '41, you know. Before I went up to Miravel."

"I remember."

"Miravel. Seems like a thousand years ago." He laughed. "Boy! were we ever that young?"

"You've come a long way," Stefan said quietly as he came in from his dressing room, locking the door behind him.

Dan jumped nervously. It hurt Alexia to see him. He had always laughed away "nerves". He got up to shake hands with Stefan.

"Your escape was magnificent," Stefan said. "But I guess that's old hat to you."

Dan grinned. "Yeah. I kind of pictured myself doing the noble thing for Lexy here. Looks like that American slogan just about fits: was this trip necessary? I've got a feeling I'm going to have to swim back." He pulled his parka closer. "You guys really are rugged. That Baltic Sea and the other waters, Kattegat? Cold, I'm telling you."

"Well, we'll see if we can get you a warmer wardrobe going back." Stefan and Alexia exchanged quick looks. "Is there anyone here who might recognize you?"

"No. At least, I'm not that dumb. I only met the bunch in Berlin and around that neck of the woods. Interviews, back in '41."

Stefan was relieved. "That's good. Berlin's heavy brass are concentrating on the Stalingrad Front and the French coast these days. You can trust Polly here, by the way. But don't let anyone else see you."

Polly nodded. "I'll see to it, Sir. God willing."

Stefan kissed Alexia lightly on the forehead. "I'll be off to talk over a few things with a friend or two. I'm afraid you'll have to stay here until we return from the theatre tonight. Then we'll have it worked out."

Alexia reached for his hand. He looked down as if puzzled, and then smiled. She murmured softly, "I love you. Take care."

He said, "Of course. I always do."

She remembered something that had troubled her. "And don't say a word to your mother about this, will you?"

"My mother," he repeated. She was surprised that he did not agree with her at once. Then he said, "Right. Polly, we won't forget your help. Will you see that Alexia is ready in time? We'll have a brief supper before we go. Darling, order enough for one more. Tell them it's for me. We'll work it out." Then he was gone.

Shaken with nerves but determined not to let Stefan be ashamed of her, Alexia suggested to Polly that she order up a pre-theatre supper for two while Alexia dressed. "In all my regalia," she added.

"You'll need me for that," Polly reminded her. "But never mind. By the way, we don't want any servants walking in on us. I'll bring up the tray myself."

"Good thinking. Dan, I'm afraid you'll have to take what you can get."

"I don't care. I could eat a live tiger if it strolled by. No rice, though, thanks. Not even the rancid stuff I got used to." He sat down again, huddling in the big chair, as if he didn't want any of his body outside the safety of the chair.

A full supper tray came, balanced superbly by Polly. She

288

and Alexia had the satisfaction of seeing Dan pitch in. He always did have a healthy appetite but his eagerness now was a painful reminder of what he had suffered in captivity. Alexia laughed at the succulent Wiener Schnitzel which Dan started to devour. She asked Polly, "How did you do it? Wiener Schnitzel as a little pre-theatre snack?"

Polly looked embarassed but explained: "I said you and His Highness had made love a while ago and it had whetted his appetite."

Alexia was amused but flushed a little when Dan looked up from his plate. Then he went on eating.

Alexia returned to her dressing room. Polly slipped the chalk-white crepe gown over Alexia's head, careful not to let a curl of her hair fall out of place. They had just finished this ticklish operation when Dan opened the door. He still had his napkin in his hand.

"Lexy, somebody just knocked on the door."

In a panic Alexia and Polly looked at each other. Alexia whispered, "They know I'm here. You brought the tray up." She took a breath, stiffened her back, and walked into the sitting room with as much composure as she could muster up.

"Who is it?"

"Ilsa von Elsbach, my dear. Come to lend you my necklace. You are wearing the Elsbach earrings, aren't you? Diamonds with white are so Aryan, you know. Let me in."

Polly shook her head frantically as she pushed Dan toward the dressing room. But Princess Ilsa was already trying the latch. "Alexia, don't tell me you are hiding a lover. Do let me in. Or must I call that dreadful Becque woman?"

CHAPTER TWENTY-THREE

Alexia glanced over her shoulder. Polly and Dan must have vanished into the dressing room. She reached for the corridor door latch, opened it and said crossly, "What on earth is all this disturbance about? I beg Your Highness's pardon but I don't need any more jewels. If you were looking for my husband he will return at any time, but I don't think he's in the market for jewels either. And to answer Your Highness's other question, I do not have a lover in my sitting room."

After this harangue she stared at her mother-in-law. Ilsa looked striking as usual in a magnificent two-layered champagne gown, her painfully thin body ablaze with topaz jewels. She smiled that curiously bored smile as Alexia gaped at her.

"My dear child, you find I have lost a little weight? But you may too if you follow the régime an old acquaintance of mine prescribed."

"Not at all," Alexia stammered. "I mean, are you feeling perfectly well?"

"At the moment I would like to remove myself from this draughty hall."

Alexia opened the door wide, let her in and then bolted the door behind her. Princess Ilsa did not seem to notice. She sat down, crossing her legs gracefully, in the chair Dan had used. She pursed her mouth and flicked her tongue over her lips. "I wonder, dear, may I have a little water? I seem to be dreadfully thirsty. Probably something I ate."

"Of course." For some reason Alexia felt guilty for not offering her water before. It was absurd. How did she know the woman would be thirsty? She poured water into one of the crystal glasses on the tray but before Alexia could hand her the water Ilsa seized the glass which Dan had half-emptied and drank it until there wasn't a drop left.

Alexia asked, "Is that why Your Highness wanted to see me? You were thirsty?"

Ignoring this, Ilsa looked her up and down as if studying her. "My child, you are hopeless. You act as if you were planning to blow up the palace. I've never seen anyone more nervous."

Alexia drew herself up haughtily. "I'm not the one who is gulping up water like a nervous conspirator." That was stupid. No need to make the enemy aware that you know.

The princess said, "Ah! Just what I needed. Water. I have a dreadful craving for it lately. One would think I had been poisoned." She got up while Alexia stared at her, stupefied, and walked to the dressing room door.

It was difficult to open but she put her knee against it, champagne chiffon and all, and pushed it open. Alexia rushed in after her. Polly stood there looking enraged but doing nothing. Beneath that rage was undoubtedly a good, healthy fear.

Her Highness did not look around. She went to the big mirror opposite the long closet half-filled with Alexia's clothes. Ilsa stood before the mirror, rearranging the exquisite dusty-gold coiffure that she had probably created herself. What a strange, glamorous creature! When she shook her head she showered the makeup table with gold dust. But nothing could outglow the diamond and topaz tiara that was dainty but elegant and managed to give her majesty without taking from her beauty. It was smaller than anything Alexia's mother wore, but the result was more regal.

Alexia looked into the glass and was shocked. Ilsa's eyes were fixed on Dan's eyes, staring back at her. For some reason Dan blinked, stopped looking tense and grinned at her. Then he shifted a few inches out of sight, behind the door.

Ilsa opened her mouth at the mirror, examining her white teeth. "Old, old, old," she said. "Even my teeth. That prescription certainly didn't do me any good." She bent over suddenly, then straightened. "Damn that ulcer!"

Alexia reached out to help her but Ilsa brushed her away and, picking up her heavy, gold-studded evening bag, she opened the door and went out into the sitting room. At the corridor door she stopped. "Has Frau Becque seen – ?" She tilted her head towards the dressing room.

Alexia didn't argue or explain Dan. It would be pointless. "No."

Polly put in, "No, Ma'am. He is my brother. Come to see me."

"Keep that thought." Ilsa looked older. In German her voice frightened Alexia more than plain English might have done.

"Do you know why Becque asked the chamberlain for a seat in the orchestra tonight?"

Puzzled, Polly said, "That's silly, Ma'am. She doesn't even like operettas. She likes heavy stuff. Wagner and all."

"She is what you call, up to something."

Leaving the two younger women in a bad state of nerves, Princess Ilsa went out into the corridor, then rattled the hall latch and ordered through the door, "Bolt it!"

292

Dan peeked out of the dressing room. "Maybe she's on our side."

Alexia and Polly silenced such naiveté immediately. Then Alexia went into her dressing room, ordered Dan out, and with Polly's help, gave herself the final touches that would turn American-educated Alexia Kuragin into the Princess Royal, Ava Alexandra.

Even when she met her father and mother at the foot of the great staircase she was momentarily expecting a catastrophe. There was one comfort. Her father looked as if he might be expecting a splendid evening, free for once of his usual worries. He was in evening clothes made heavy about the breast by decorations from other tiny nations and several very large neighbours, including a silver swastika, a birthday present from "Lichtenbourg's friend and protector, the Third Reich".

Garnett held his arm firmly, looking her usual flirtatious and gorgeous self in her favourite jade green with her famous emeralds.

She complained to Alexia, "That tiresome husband of yours had business with the Swedish Consulate or Embassy or something. We are to go without him. I can see it now, his late arrival with that feline mother of his amid the cheers of the multitude. Always trying to show up your dear father."

Alexia was sure Stefan must be working to get Dan to safety. This left a residual fear that was even stronger. Was Stefan in equal danger? A life without Stefan was inconceivable but a small flicker of hope for Dan began to burn.

Princess Ilsa was missing, too. Surely she wouldn't endanger her own son. And why would she warn Alexia against Frau Becque if she was the ardent Nazi-sympathizer she was supposed to be?

While Max waved to his admirers Garnett lowered her

voice to tell Alexia with some pride, "I've finally made my stand with Becque, the old devil."

Alexia felt something ominous in her mother's proud boast. "Why? What happened?"

"This morning. Marta, my maid, was just returning with my jewellery. Polished, you know. And Becque began to admire my emerald set. Held one of these earrings up to her fat neck. Thought it made a handsome decoration. I told her no in no uncertain terms. 'Do your worst,' I said. 'No emeralds, or anything else, for that matter.'" Garnett nodded emphatically. "You should have seen me. She won't dare try anything."

Alexia felt the sweat start on her forehead. "I can imagine." Now, of all times! It was one more twist of the chord.

Waving and calling to the royal family, crowds milled around the newly refurbished theatre whose stage door was separated from the Wien Kreditanstaller by the alley where Janos Becque suffered his accident. Alexia looked down the alley as the limousine passed. The rubble had long since been cleaned up but the building was a shell, considered unlucky by Lichtenbourgers.

Alexia looked away quickly. She got out of the car with the police agent's help and crossed the cobblestones to the elaborate baroque entrance of the Theatre Royal. Most of the cheers were for her parents, but she cared little about popularity at that moment.

It was as well she didn't care. Several young Nazi thugs yelled anti-royalist slogans at her and her family, interspersing them with a number of "Heils!" and even the old-fashioned "God Strike England!"

She murmured to her police escort, "I thought they had abolished God."

He gave them a fast, cynical glance. In his job he didn't find anything funny.

The group were led up a red-carpeted staircase, past the other boxes to the entrance hall of the royal box above the stage. The Lichtenbourg colours in velvet and the Kuragin crest in gilt were everywhere. The chairs at the front of the box which would be seen were stiff, straight and likewise heavily gilded. Behind them were the blue velvet, overstuffed chairs, chiefly to be occupied by elderly and bored males.

In the narrow hall behind the box the royals waited. The theatre manager, resplendent in his tailcoat and two small medals from the First World War, came out, bowed to the three royal personages and led the way through the elegantly lit box to the front rail where he bowed deeply. The audience in the packed house arose, applauding the newcomers, and the orchestra struck up the royal anthem. Many of the audience sang and the invigorating sounds covered the entrance of Princess Ilsa behind the Kuragins.

When the royal family were seated Prince Max moved back, giving his place to the von Elsbach princess. After a smile and a nod, Garnett turned and began to exchange gossip in a loud voice with the Hungarian Consul's wife in the next box.

Alexia was too anxious to wait. She kept looking at the princess who seemed to have friends all over the theatre; the pit, the auditorium, the boxes, and the tiers above them. While she gave them her casual smile she pointed out to Alexia the important guests, especially the rows of Wehrmacht soldiers currently guests of Lichtenbourg during their recuperation from battle fatigue and other wounds. As she pointed to the various members of the audience she murmured, still smiling languidly for the benefit of those watching the royal box, "Your friend will soon be a Swedish diplomatic courier. Now, stop looking so worried."

Alexia forced a toothy smile. "And my husband?"

"Safe, as long as that creature is here. Do you see her?"

Alexia, who had looked for Frau Becque the minute she entered the royal box said, "Third row, opposite the first violin."

"Of course. What a charming creature, to be sure."

Alexia laughed without feeling in the least humorous. She wondered if she was a little hysterical.

The Merry Widow overture began, filling the theatre with the sounds of the old Austro-Hungarian Empire, the beauty and excitement, the melancholy, the hussars and gypsies and waltzing gallants. All gone, Alexia thought. Even the gypsies were now being hunted down in the Reich and its satellites.

There was vociferous applause when Johann Hofer entered, looking stunning in his white uniform wildly decorated with red and gold. Alexia and Garnett joined in the applause and the young actor looked up at their box, bowed low and threw the royal family a kiss. It was daring, but he was obviously thrilled by his reception.

Then came a male voice from somewhere deep in the darkened theatre auditorium. "Juden! Juden!"

To Alexia's surprise and delight these cries were answered by cries of "Quiet! Silence!" and booing. A small scuffle occurred in one dark corner near the alley exit. She assumed that the troublemakers had been ushered or thrown out and the show went on.

But although Alexia had never seen Hanni Hofer perform before, it was obvious even to her that he was frightened to death. His voice quavered on his solos and duets, even the immortal "Women" and "Maxim's" whose great charm was their light-heartedness.

Alexia grew more and more nervous. She could occasionally hear chants and shouts outside the walls of the theatre. There was unrest in the audience. A few began to gather up evening capes, fur coats and handbags, and some left at once. There was a larger exodus between the acts.

Alexia looked to see how her family had taken this. Garnett was urging Max to do something, leave, probably. But Princess Ilsa sat like a carefully carved statue, showing no emotion whatever. Was she enjoying it? In spite of her reassuring news about her son and Dan Royle was she actually what she had always been, the notorious "friend of the Fuhrer"? Alexia felt sickened.

Twice Ilsa signalled behind her to an usher in royal livery. Once she received a crystal glass of water. She drank rapidly as if consumed by thirst while she watched *The Merry Widow Waltz*. The waltz got its usual thunderous applause. Hanni Hofer and his beloved Widow Sonja were at their graceful best when Ilsa signalled the usher again. Alexia heard her whisper a curious order. "Locked. Until we arrive." The usher bowed and left the box.

During the excitement of the dance Frau Becque was still in her seat, stiff and motionless, except for the fingers of her two hands which were laced together tightly. Alexia could almost fancy she saw the knuckles whiten with the woman's tension.

Remembering what Princess Ilsa had said, she was relieved that the woman remained in the theatre. But why the tension? If the housekeeper intended to cause trouble in the palace about Dan and Stefan, and she might not even know about them yet, why did she wait so long here? The show was nearly over and everyone would be leaving. Why wait until the entire royal family was present to stop her by one means or another? At least she had the comfort of seeing her here and knowing she had been here since before the operetta started.

Meanwhile, Max and Garnett obviously agreed to

remain for the finale, the curtains calls and the announcement of the profits going to "our brave men on the Eastern Front". But just before the curtain came down on the colourful last act at Maxim's, an usher came in silently, bowed to Princess Ilsa, and gave her a slip of paper.

Max and Garnett had their attention occupied by the wild, tuneful doings onstage. Ilsa muttered an apology to Prince Max and left the box with her handkerchief to her forehead. Alexia looked down at the audience, saw that Frau Becque had left, and hurriedly followed her mother-in-law.

In the hall Princess Ilsa ordered one of the two Royal Guards, "Come with me." To the other, she said, "Send more guards to the box at once," adding, "there will be detectives in the Elsbach livery in the lobby. Bring both of them."

She went rapidly down the stairs with Alexia, through a narrow passage smelling of stale, perfumed powder, old cigarette stubs and dry timber. In the lobby Alexia could hear the audience crying, "Hofer! Hanni Hofer!"

"What's happening onstage?" Alexia asked as the two tough, Germanic-looking Elsbach guards pushed ahead of her to join Princess Ilsa.

One of them looked back. "The actor does not appear for his curtain call, Highness."

They raced after Ilsa and the guard she had borrowed from the royal box. Their goal was backstage. Alexia followed breathlessly, trying not to trip over her evening skirts. Johann Hofer's dressing room was wide open but the young actor had gone. Princess Ilsa stopped and leaned against the open door, fighting for breath.

"Too late," she told Alexia. "I sent him a warning through the usher. I had vague hints this morning that there might be a riot. Instead, like a fool, he ran right into their waiting arms, and either Garnett or I was meant to run after him to an appalling death."

She motioned toward the stage door into the alley and two of the police hurried out with guns drawn. They left the door swinging open. Alexia tried to help the princess who pushed her away, dropping the note that had sent them into this deadly business. Alexia read the note by the stage doorman's light: *I am desperate. I will try to avoid them by the alley. Save me. Come alone. Quickly.* It was signed *H*. Obviously, Hanni Hofer. But was it his writing? Would anyone ever know?

Alexia ran toward the stage door. Out in the alley an animal must have been run over. She could hear the hideous, inhuman shrieks and yelps of pain. Through the nightmare sounds came the greater nightmare, "Juden! Juden!"

In the doorway she saw two of the guards the princess had sent. Almost simultaneously they raised the heavy, murderous guns and fired. She thought for an instant they had struck the suffering creature but their targets were a dozen youths with knives. She saw the steel glisten in the light from the Boulevard Kuragin beyond as two of the creatures, whimpering and yelling for mercy, dropped their weapons and surrendered.

Under the boulevard lights Alexia made out the once-white uniform of Hanni Hofer, a mass of blood and torn flesh. Behind her Alexia heard Princess Ilsa's voice, first to the police, "Send Claus to me. He is at the boulevard exit." Then to Alexia, "I suspected when I heard the woman had especially asked for a seat. She's been seen wandering through the ruins here where her son died. She wants all the royal family to suffer, one by one. And this poor devil was only a pawn. I suppose it was her idea of a blood sacrifice on the ground where her son died."

There was another reason, as Alexia knew very well.

Her mother had neglected to pay the latest ransom, her emeralds.

"If my mother had gone into that alley alone," Alexia reminded her, "she would have died, too. Or you would have died."

But Princess Ilsa was too busy watching the police to pay any attention. One of the lobby police guards who had been running after the hoodlums knelt to examine the boy, then got up. He came back to the princess. "Dead. Emasculated and cut to pieces. Several got away. I hope we can find the damned little monsters."

"But we will find one of them in particular, I give you my word," the princess said in her usual voice, light as windbells.

CHAPTER TWENTY-FOUR

Princess Ilsa turned to Alexia. "Go and join your parents, my dear."

"If you need me, Stefan would want me to stay with you."

"I need you for this, listen carefully. Go to your apartment and ask Becque to come. You may have to wait a few minutes, until her escort reaches the palace."

"Escort?"

"Never mind. Do as I tell you. Tell her something terrible has happened."

The princess signalled to the officer. "Karl, escort Princess Alexia to her family and see that they get to the palace safely. Where is Claus? Ah, Deming, I want Claus at once. Tell him *at once*."

"But you?" Alexia asked. "What about you?"

The princess smiled. "I will be there presently. Promise me you will do exactly as I say. You see, I have a small debt of my own to pay. Karl, be off with her to Prince Maximilian's car."

People did not ignore her commands. Alexia gave up and went along, wondering if she was going to betray her own weakness and be violently ill in front of the guard.

The death of her son must have sent Frau Becque over the edge. Obviously Johann Hofer had been murdered in part as a warning to Garnett who refused to give her the emerald earrings. Even if she had given them to the woman, other jewels would have had to follow. There would have been no end.

But there was the possibility that the monstrous little woman would return to the palace and find Dan still there. Even worse, if she was out to destroy the family for some perverted revenge she would be a deadly threat to Stefan it she knew his part in tonight's dangerous activities. And what was Princess Ilsa's part in Frau Becque's vendetta?

Alexia found Garnett waiting in the limousine in front of the theatre. She was weeping silently, her careful makeup smudged by the sodden handkerchief in her fingers. Alexia hoped desperately that no one had told her the details of young Hofer's horrible death.

She remembered the delightful young man she had met the night she returned to Lichtenbourg. Even then poor Hanni was frightened of his background. And yet his youthful fixation upon the Princess Garnett had been so great he refused to leave while the danger gathered around him. Alexia clenched her fingers until they ached.

Max came out almost on the run, when he saw Alexia. "Get in quickly. There may be a riot. They say the young star was well liked and they are going after the killers."

He almost lifted Alexia in before he climbed in himself. He was pale and nervous but angry, too. He tapped on the glass partition and his chauffeur, looking understandably relieved, drove off up the Boulevard Kuragin to thc New Palace.

Garnett managed to speak as Max was escorting her up the palace steps. "I know that witch had something to do with it. She wanted my jewellery. Or maybe just to torture me. She never wore the rubies."

Max did not seem surprised. He put his arm around her. "My dearest, that poor boy mistook your kindness for something deeper. I myself offered to send him out to safety. He refused." He hesitated at the top of the steps and looked back. "By the way, I think we must dispense with Becque's services in spite of the Fuhrer's temper tantrums. One of my guards saw her go out into the alley. If you can believe the incredible, she actually looked at the body."

Alexia stared back over the city, the only one between Hamburg and Budapest still lit. Its small, dim, golden lamps made it look like a fairyland. Down in the Cathedral Square there was still a pool of blue-white light where the murder had occurred. Cars of the state police and several horses with their military mounts remained at odd angles in and out of the point where the alley met the boulevard.

Followed by a footman, Alexia and her family went up to the second floor and the apartments of Garnett and Max. Frantic to get to her own rooms, Alexia closed her eyes to the things she had seen, but it was no use. They remained embedded in her consciousness.

"I could strangle her myself," she muttered.

But her father said in a puzzled way, "I beg your pardon, my dear."

She was brusque to the point of hoarseness. She had things to do. For the first time she trusted Princess Ilsa. "Nothing. Good night."

Her father kissed her on the forehead, then urged her, "Try not to think about it, there's my girl." Then he went into their suite to comfort his wife.

Alexia started rapidly along the corridor and ended by running up another flight of stairs to the rooms she shared with Stefan. Alexia seldom carried keys in this huge old place and nervously tried the door of her sitting room, calling Polly's name in a low voice. There was no answer but the door was unlocked.

The rooms were deserted. Polly had left a note on the little round mahogany table under the garden windows. Horrified by what might be Polly's enormous indiscretion,

Alexia read it: Gone to see my brother off to his factory job at Hamburg."

Not so indiscreet, after all, unless the word Hamburg betrayed the train as the method of travel instead of the Swedish plane.

She took the receiver off the telephone on the desk and said, "Send Frau Becque to me at once."

The operator apologized, "Frau Becque has not rung in yet from her theatre trip tonight, Your Highness. I will ask her to see you the minute she rings in. Ah! One moment, Highness. She is ringing now, undoubtedly for her calls."

In a few seconds Frau Becque's voice came on. She sounded just a trifle shaken. Not without reason. "Yes, Highness. At once. Pardon my nervousness but I was present at the command performance tonight and the horror was more than I could take. I had to be escorted back to the palace by one of the Royal Guards. I believe he is a Royal Guard. Ulbrecht?"

Something was said on the phone in a low voice. Alexia wondered if Princess Ilsa had allowed for this problem. She didn't want the little housekeeper to arrive with her very own guard. She wasn't sure what Princess Ilsa had in mind.

Minutes later they arrived, Frau Becque in her black cloth coat and black felt hat with a turned-down brim, and behind her a frightening apparition: a big blond young man with a blue uniform jacket that was too small for him and huge, powerful hands that were not in the least too small for him. He had a curious innocent look that did not match his general physique.

Frau Becque introduced him. "Ulbrecht. He works at the palace in an extra capacity at royal functions. He did me a great service tonight, Highness. I must have taken the wrong turn out of the theatre and almost fell in with those rioters. But Ulbrecht came along just in

304

time. What is it that you wished to see me about, Your Highness?"

What indeed? Here was the good Frau, but where was the enigmatic princess? Alexia finally came up with the foolish order, not at all suited to a person of the royal housekeeper's stature: "My husband and I would appreciate it if you would send up a bottle of good German wine. From the Rhine, I think. And some cakes. Tortes. That kind of thing."

Frau Becque frowned and looked affronted. "Am I to understand that Your Highness could not obtain these things from your maid? She looked around and, leaving Ulbrecht, walked through the room, opening the bedchamber door and looking in. "But where can she be, this elusive maid of yours, Highness? It appears that I will be interviewing new domestics."

Treading very carefully, Alexia realized that Frau Becque's spies had probably reported the contents of Polly's note already. No use in denying that Polly was gone or that she had a "brother".

"My maid went to see her brother off to Hamburg. I only hope he isn't caught in one of those dreadful saturation raids."

"Ah, yes. Of course." She was busy looking around the bedchamber, opening the big, old-fashioned armoire. "Curious. I had the impression that she was an only child."

"Your impression was clearly wrong." Alexia got up and went to the bedchamber doorway, watching as the old harridan raised the bedclothes and looked under the mattress.

Furious at the sheer audacity, Alexia snapped, "That will do, Frau Becque. You may go now and carry out my order."

"As Your Highness wishes." The woman raised the end

of the mattress and Alexia caught her breath. A blue
parka had been shoved hurriedly under the mattress. Frau
Becque took it out, shook it, and held it up. "Very useful.
Especially, I am told, in the American ski resorts."

"Or the Austrian resorts?"

Frau Becque held the parka up by the neck. "Quite
true. But it is against the Reich laws to buy and parade the
produce of the enemy, more especially if one is the enemy.
Amerikaner. 'Made in America.' " She shook her head. "I
am very much afraid this was worn by an enemy. And now
he is off to pollute the Reich's very heart. Hamburg."

Alexia called her bluff. "Call the station. Do you think a
Lichtenbourger at the station would obey you against the
orders of His Serene Highness, Prince Stefan?"

The woman laughed. "That train will stop at the border
which is less than an hour from here. The SS will be
waiting."

The big, blond Ulbrecht came to the doorway and
Alexia backed away from him. She didn't want to leave
herself in this obvious trap. Frau Becque threw the parka at
him. "Evidence, my friend. We will take this. But first – "

She reached for the telephone on the stand at Stefan's
side of the bed. Ulbrecht made no movement except to
drop the parka on the bed. Alexia rushed for the woman
at the telephone. Frau Becque was sure to call Vienna
and the SS, probably Gestapo would take Dan off as the
woman said.

Frau Becque had already lifted the phone from its
rack. There was a momentary tussle. Alexia knocked
the receiver out of her hand, every second expecting to
be attacked from the rear by Becque's huge aide.

Frau Becque, though short and somewhat stout, had a
kick like a mule and Alexia winced as that big peasant
shoe hit hard at her shinbone. She found herself slapping the fat face with a furious sound that made the

woman's head twist half around but did not seem to stop her.

Alexia pulled the telephone cord out of the wall while Frau Becque shrieked with rage. Then both women got the same idea at the same time: the telephone in the sitting room. Alexia ran through the doorway and reached across the small table. The receiver fell off the phone in her excitement and she saw Frau Becque's pudgy hand reach for it.

A cool amused voice behind them stopped both women. "What an eager housekeeper you are, Frau Becque! One would almost be tempted to write you a reference."

Aghast, both antagonists swung around, staring at the corridor door which Princess Ilsa closed and bolted behind her. Frau Becque's little blue eyes opened to an impressive size. She smiled, but it was more of a grimace Alexia thought as she pulled herself together, wondering why the big guard did nothing to the princess.

The housekeeper recovered enough to ask in a choked voice, "Will nothing kill you, She-Devil! Why aren't you dead in that alley with young Hofer? You are like a spider I try to stamp out but still you will not die." She swung around to her big guard. "She told them to drop the cornice pieces that murdered my son, a loyal follower of the Fuhrer."

Princess Ilsa shrugged. "Your son would have sent Prince Maximilian to his death in Berlin."

"My son would have been the ruler we need. A simple plebiscite, backed by the Fuhrer's army. Ulbrecht, think! This stupid Princess Alexia, she cannot realize. This is her husband's mother, this monster, liar and hypocrite. She was never with the Fuhrer. You must see, now, tonight."

The big guard said nothing. He simply watched and listened, but his eyes were on Princess Ilsa even when Frau Becque spoke to him.

Frau Becque repeated, "She is an enemy of the Fuhrer, this monster. She must be destroyed!"

Claus Ulbrecht spoke quietly for the first time at a nod from Princess Ilsa. "You, Frau Becque, you poisoned my good friend, the princess. You poisoned this country. Tonight, you caused a boy to die. Hideous business. Always you work in the dark. Never out front, except to watch. You are the spider, Frau Becque."

"It is a lie. All she says is a lie," the housekeeper insisted.

"A lie? I do not talk lies." Alexia felt nervously that the big man was losing control in reciting his grievances. "You caused my father to be sent to a camp. What camp? How do I find him? The princess tried to find him. When she did, it was too late. Do you know about these camps, Frau Becque?"

"Claus," Princess Ilsa cut in, seeing that he had grown more excited. "It is over. She admits what she has done. Alexia, pour a glass of water for me, there's a dear."

Frau Becque chuckled. "It is too late, Highness. They say the doses were enough, even before you stopped taking them."

Alexia shuddered but she poured the water with hands that shook. "What is to be done, Your Highness? At her trial, I mean."

Frau Becque looked her disgust at such naiveté. "How am I to go, Highness? A drop on the head? A knock down a staircase? I should have known better than to trust a half-witted creature like this Ulbrecht, but he arrived so handily when I was trying to get away from the theatre. Too handily. I might have known . . . The Fuhrer is right to have his kind destroyed. Like the Jews and the rest of the inferiors."

Princess Ilsa was leaning back against the wall of the dressing room. She looked like a death's head and the sight of her banished any pity Alexia might have had for the poisoner.

Ilsa said, "I will confess that for a time I was almost as naive as our Alexia. Thought it must be nerves. Or an old ulcer returned." This seemed to strike her as amusing. "As though I would have nerves, after these recent years of fighting that little Austrian painter in my own way."

"Devil!"

"Possibly. You and I would understand that, dear Becque."

Frau Becque was grimly pleased. "You could never prove it against me. It was purchased in Vienna at my son's orders, to use upon – never mind."

"My father, in the hospital!" Alexia realized suddenly. She felt as if she herself had taken arsenic.

The housekeeper, looking around, saw no help for her and added contemptuously, "He was useless, your father. He would have betrayed the Fuhrer besides all else."

Alexia closed her eyes. She heard Ilsa say in that light but oddly sinister voice, "Why do you not sleep well, Frau Becque? Why must you take morphine to sleep? You would do better to count sheep."

"A lie. I never took morphine in my life."

The princess shook her head sadly. "I have heard it said all over the palace. It is much gentler than arsenic. But I suppose you and your son thought of that when the arsenic was purchased. I've no idea who started the rumour of your taking morphine here in the palace. To relieve you of memories about your son, I imagine. Such painful memories."

Frau Becque swung around and bumped into Claus Ulbrecht. He took her, not ungently, but with one hand around her waist and the other across her twitching mouth.

Ilsa said, "Alexia, my dear, go down and wait for my son. I have called him. The other matter is safe."

"But someone may have seen the note Polly left," Alexia protested.

"What? You mean Polly is not permitted to have a visit from her brother? He has a perfectly honest passport and works in Hamburg." The princess sipped more water. "If there was another young man, I assure you he is a diplomatic courier on his way to send King Gustav our warm regards. I believe it is a birthday affair. Something of that sort."

Weakly, Alexia made her way to the door, looking back only once to ask, just before she left the room. "Does Stefan know?"

"About his poor, grey-haired mama?" The princess shook her head. "Men need not know everything we ladies are up to, I always say."

There was a peculiar, gurgling sound from Frau Becque. Alexia recognized it as a laugh. It was the last sound Alexia heard from that room as she closed the door and went along the corridor to the staircase.

CHAPTER TWENTY-FIVE

The great hall was empty and the golden lights that illuminated the long front of the New Palace were out. They must have had word of an Allied air raid in Bavaria or Austria.

Alexia waited in the shadows of the flagpole's cement base where her father had once been a hero. Before her she could see several guards parading on duty inside the wrought-iron gates.

More than half an hour went by before a small pre-war Swedish car came up the boulevard toward the palace. The car lights blinked some kind of code and two guards opened the gates.

Alexia could see Polly sticking her head out the open window, her straight hair flying in the chill wind as she bellowed to the driver, "It's us. Safe and sound!"

Stefan brought the car to an abrupt halt and leapt out, waving to one of the guards to remove the car. Polly didn't wait for anyone to help her out. She climbed out and headed, like Stefan, for the half-frozen Alexia, still in her evening gown and jewelled, high-heeled pumps.

Stefan's arms warmed and comforted Alexia as nothing else could. He kept murmuring in her ear, "All's well, Sweetheart. He's on his way to Sweden. Only one stop. A safe one in Denmark."

"Then you didn't send him by train?"

"Do we look daffy?" Polly asked. "If we were going to use the train, I wouldn't have left that note."

Alexia returned Stefan's kisses with a passion she had never known before. He was all she wanted in the world.

"I don't really care, Darling. I just have you safe. Oh, Stefan! I never want us to be separated again."

Stefan walked with her to the steps. He kissed the top of her head and promised, "Never again. And now, it's bedtime for us. You look tired out. You shouldn't have worried about me so much. I was perfectly safe."

"Thank God for that."

"Sweetheart," he scolded. "You know you shouldn't have waited out here in this icy cold. You ought to have remained in our rooms where it's safe and warm."

She began to laugh. She was still laughing when Stefan hugged her to him, saying worriedly over her head, "She shouldn't have become so cold, my poor darling. She is hysterical."

"Yeah, poor kid," Polly agreed, much concerned. "It's hysteria, I think. We'd better get her back to her rooms, fast."